Tommy frowned, but before he could reply, something lunged out of the dark and wrapped pallid arms around him. Teeth scissored into his neck, and he gave a yelping scream. The sound of it jerked Westlake back to full awareness. The dead woman rose on unsteady feet and took a step towards him. He stared at her in stupefaction for long moments. Long enough for her to gather herself and lunge towards him.

The pistol kicked in his hand. It was instinct, and he didn't question it. Regret wasn't for the moment; it was best saved for later. His aim was perfect – center of mass, straight to the heart, do not pass Go. The dead woman staggered, but didn't fall. His eyes narrowed, and he fired again, aiming at her head this time. It took two more shots before she went down. By then there were others, and no time to think about anything but escape.

ALSO AVAILABLE

ARKHAM HORROR
Wrath of N'kai by Josh Reynolds
The Last Ritual by S A Sidor
Mask of Silver by Rosemary Jones
Litany of Dreams by Ari Marmell
The Devourer Below edited by Charlotte Llewelyn-Wells
Dark Origins – The Collected Novellas Volume 1

DESCENT: JOURNEYS IN THE DARK
The Doom of Fallowhearth by Robbie MacNiven
The Shield of Daqan by David Guymer
The Gates of Thelgrim by Robbie MacNiven

KEYFORGE
Tales from the Crucible edited by Charlotte Llewelyn-Wells
The Qubit Zirconium by M Darusha Wehm

LEGEND OF THE FIVE RINGS
Curse of Honor by David Annandale
Poison River by Josh Reynolds
The Night Parade of 100 Demons by Marie Brennan
Death's Kiss by Josh Reynolds

PANDEMIC
Patient Zero by Amanda Bridgeman

TWILIGHT IMPERIUM
The Fractured Void by Tim Pratt
The Necropolis Empire by Tim Pratt

LAST RESORT

Josh Reynolds

ACONYTE

First published by Aconyte Books in 2021

ISBN 978 1 83908 104 0

Ebook ISBN 978 1 83908 105 7

Cover art by Riccardo Crosa & Paolo Francescutto

Distributed in North America by Simon & Schuster Inc, New York, USA

Printed in the United States of America

9 8 7 6 5 4 3 2 1

ACONYTE BOOKS

An imprint of Asmodee Entertainment Ltd

Mercury House, Shipstones Business Centre

North Gate, Nottingham NG7 7FN, UK

aconytebooks.com // twitter.com/aconytebooks

For my editor Gwendolyn, without whom this story would be dead – and not the fun kind of dead.

PROLOGUE
Westlake

Westlake found the ride out to the Pine Barrens bumpy and uncomfortable. Largely, this was due to the fact he was stuck in the trunk, his wrists duct-taped together, and his body aching from the beatdown they'd given him beforehand. As beatdowns went, he'd had worse, but he'd chosen not to volunteer that fact. Guys like that might have taken it as a challenge.

There were two of them. He knew one – Tommy Waingro. A thick-necked little know-nothing from Staten Island. Tommy had more muscle than brains, and he'd gotten the first punch in, not to mention the second and the third. The other guy had only joined in after Westlake was safely kissing the dirt.

If he'd seen them coming, he might've done better. Then again, maybe not. Tommy was tough, and he'd been itching to use that gun he'd flashed if Westlake gave him the chance. So Westlake took the beating, as well as the indignity of being shoved into the trunk, and having to listen to muffled arguments about the best place to bury him. Better than getting shot out of hand.

He used the time to try and figure out how they'd found him. He quickly concluded that someone had talked. The Feds had promised him he'd be safe, but, well – they were the Feds. They'd have said anything to get him to agree to a deal. They were desperate to take down Bonaro. Come to that, so was he.

But he'd stalled. Because he didn't just want Bonaro. He wanted the money Bonaro owed him. Not so much because he needed it – though he did – but because of the principle of the thing. Bonaro owed him, and Westlake always collected on his debts.

Of course, there was something to be said for letting the past go and moving on with one's life. If he hadn't stalled, he wouldn't currently be in the trunk of a car, heading for what he suspected was the Jersey Pine Barrens. Because of course a nitwit like Tommy would think burying someone in the Barrens was a good idea. In Westlake's humble opinion, pop culture had a lot to answer for.

They'd taken his phone, so he fumbled around in the dark of the trunk, looking for something – anything – that might be of use. He found a screwdriver rolling around and fumbled to grab it. He had a vision of himself popping the lock on the trunk from the inside and then – what? Climbing out? Good way to get a fatal case of road rash.

So, instead, he slid the screwdriver into his sleeve. And waited. Westlake was good at waiting. He was, by nature, a patient man. A man not given to rash action or foolish vices. His only real flaw, as society might judge things, was a decided lack of scruples when it came to other people's possessions. Money, mostly. Jewelry, on occasion. Cars, when necessary.

But he'd never stolen a life. He'd never had to. If you planned it correctly, had the right crew, you never needed to fire a shot. Guys like Tommy, they didn't understand. They thought shooting someone was the height of entertainment.

The car bumped suddenly, axle creaking, and he bounced off the interior of the trunk. He could hear cursing from the front, and something rolled under the wheels. The idiots had hit something – a deer maybe. Were there deer in the Barrens? He wasn't certain. Trees made him nervous. He liked concrete and glass and steel.

The car kept bumping. Metal clattered. Then, a sudden brake. They'd arrived, or the car had broken down. Either way, he figured he didn't have much time. The trunk opened. Tommy looked down at him, his grin positively satanic in the crimson glow of the car's rear lights. "Enjoy the ride?"

"Not as such." Westlake peered past him. The sky was as black as pitch and full of stars – not a hint of pollution. They were definitely out in the boonies. "What'd you hit?" he asked, glancing towards the smeared streak of roadkill that extended out behind the car and into the dark. It stank like the East River at the height of summer. Whatever it had been, it had lost chunks of itself.

"Nothing," Tommy said. "A deer, I think. Doesn't matter." He looked at his friend. Tommy was short and built like someone who spent too much time at the gym. In contrast, his pal was long and lean and dressed like he wished he were in Atlantic City. "Help me get him out of there. Quicker we do this, the better."

"There's no call for this," Westlake said, as they hauled him out of the trunk. They weren't gentle about it, and he banged his head against something metal. They let him fall to the ground in an inglorious heap, then kicked him a bit when he didn't immediately pop up like a jack-in-the-box.

"No call for it, he says," Tommy barked. "You hearing this, Frankie?"

"I heard it."

"You believe the stones on this guy?"

"Maybe he's just stupid."

Tommy squatted down, plucking at the pleat of his slacks as he did so. "That it, Westlake? You just stupid?"

Westlake rolled over onto his back. "Let me take an IQ test and get back to you." He looked around. They were in a clearing, surrounded by veritable walls of oak, Atlantic white cedar, and pitch pine. Or, as Westlake thought of them, trees. A good spot to hide a body.

Tommy grinned. "Funny."

"Funny enough to let me go?"

"Ha! Sal would have my balls if I let you go."

Westlake hauled himself into a sitting position; no easy feat with the tape wrapped around his wrists. "At least take the tape off, Tommy. You owe me that much."

Tommy slapped him. "Keep my name out of your mouth. I don't owe you nothing, except a shallow hole in the Barrens." He stood and looked at Frankie. "Get the shovel."

Frankie frowned. "You get the shovel."

"I'm not digging. I got to watch him." Eyes narrowed in

mounting annoyance, Tommy gestured to Westlake. "Get the shovel."

"I can't dig, Tommy. My back – I got that thing with it, you know?" Frankie gestured helplessly. "It locks up."

"Then we'll get you a massage. After you dig."

Frankie grunted and bent to retrieve the shovel from the trunk, muttering obscenities under his breath. Westlake felt a moment's sympathy for Frankie, but it didn't stop him from stabbing the screwdriver into Frankie's leg with all the strength he could muster. The screwdriver bit, cartilage popped, and Frankie gave a high-pitched scream. Frankie dropped, clinging to the rim of the trunk to stay on his feet.

Tommy froze, but only for a second. It was long enough for Westlake to propel himself forward and drive his head into Tommy's well-padded midsection. Tommy staggered, and Westlake stumbled past, running into the tall timber. He heard Tommy shout something and then heard the telltale whine of a bullet creasing the air somewhere to his left.

Thankfully, it was dark, and there were plenty of trees. Westlake pressed his back to one and waited, working at the tape on his wrists with his teeth. Tommy would be along shortly. He had a bad temper and not much in the way of smarts. It was why he was still doing this sort of thing, rather than running something important. The mob had two sorts of guys – wiseguys and smart guys. Smart guys ran things, handled money, and never went to prison. Wiseguys did everything the smart guys were too smart to do. That included disposing of inconvenient contractors like Westlake.

He heard the soft hiss of grass against Tommy's slacks.

"You better come out, you lousy piece of crap," Tommy said. "Don't make me walk into the woods after you."

Westlake waited in silence, counting the steps. He'd only get one chance. Tommy wouldn't give him two. "You really screwed Frankie's knee up, man," Tommy continued. "He's going to complain about that the whole ride back. So thanks for that."

Twigs snapped under Tommy's feet. The tape finally tore. Westlake flexed his newly freed hands – he had big hands, knotted and sinewy. The hands of a violent man. Westlake didn't think of himself that way – didn't like to think of himself that way – but he knew it was in him. A seed of red that could flower at any time. Tommy was about to find that out the hard way.

"You know, you really pissed Sal off, Westlake," Tommy continued. "I ain't never seen him that mad, and I've seen him angry, plenty. But you… you really got under his skin. Even Vinnie couldn't calm him down. And he did try."

"Remind me to thank Vinnie next time I see him," Westlake muttered under his breath. Vincent Spinoza was Sal's consigliere – his number two. It was Vinnie who'd set up the job, been the point of contact. Vinnie was a smart guy, not a wiseguy – or that was what he liked to think, at least. But Sal was the money man.

Tommy was still going. "Weasel like you, I bet you told the Feds plenty."

Westlake frowned. In fact, he'd told the Feds nothing. Tommy and Frankie had scooped him up before he'd had the chance. Sal – Salvatore Bonaro – had obviously gotten word that Westlake was about to turn state's evidence. In retrospect, he'd been foolish to think the man wouldn't have eyes and ears in every federal and state agency.

Another twig snap. He smelled Tommy's cologne. The black barrel of a Glock eased into view, and Westlake tensed. One chance. That was all he needed.

Somewhere, Frankie screamed. Tommy cursed and turned – the barrel of the Glock vanished. Westlake stepped out from behind the tree and brought both fists down on the back of Tommy's neck. Tommy grunted and swayed, but didn't fall. So Westlake hit him again. Tommy dropped, and the pistol dropped with him. Westlake caught Tommy with a knee to the jaw and sent him ass over teakettle.

Westlake started looking for the pistol. "You know, all of this could have been avoided if Sal had just paid me what he owed me," he said, mostly to himself. He knew Tommy wouldn't care. "All I wanted was my cut – instead, he throws me to the wolves. How's that fair, I ask you?"

Frankie screamed again – a long, drawn-out wail that spiraled up into something shrill. Then, all at once, he fell silent. Westlake paused, his hand on the grip of the Glock. Frankie had every right to scream, but this was something else – a cry of terror. A prickle of unease crept up his spine.

"F-Frankie?" Tommy called, shaking his head. He rolled over and tried to sit up. He was recovering faster than Westlake had expected. "Frankie, where are you?"

"Shut up," Westlake said. He picked up the pistol and waited. The car's lights only provided a thin watery illumination, but it was enough. He could see something moving. But it wasn't Frankie. He heard Tommy get to his feet.

"You son of a bitch, I'm going to–" Tommy began. Westlake turned and pointed the pistol at Tommy. That shut Tommy up, but only for a minute. "You ain't going to shoot me," he said, somewhat hesitantly. "Everybody knows you ain't got the stones to shoot nobody."

"Yeah? Want to test that theory?"

Tommy frowned, but before he could reply, something lunged out of the dark and wrapped pallid arms around him. Teeth scissored into his neck, and he gave a yelping scream. Tommy's attacker was a woman, Westlake thought. Or she had been. What she was now, he couldn't say. Her skin was raw, and her skull looked like a cracked egg, slick with yolk. Her remaining eye rolled in its socket as she chewed on Tommy, who gurgled curses as he pounded ineffectually at her with his fists.

Westlake was still staring in bewilderment as the dead woman tore out Tommy's throat. The sound of it jerked him back to full awareness. The dead woman rose on unsteady feet and took a step towards him. He stared at her in stupefaction for long moments. Long enough for her to gather herself and lunge towards him.

The pistol kicked in his hand. It was instinct, and he didn't question it. Regret wasn't for the moment; it was best saved for later. His aim was perfect – center of mass, straight to the heart, do not pass Go. The dead woman staggered, but didn't fall. His eyes narrowed, and he fired again, aiming at her head this time. It took two more shots before she went down. By then there were others, and no time to think about anything but escape. Westlake's breath caught in his throat.

They ghosted out of the trees on broken feet and deadweight legs, closing in on him. They looked like they'd been through hell – bloody wounds abounded. He didn't bother to worry about what was going on, or what had happened – he just bolted for the car. A primal panic lent him speed. Whatever was going on, it wasn't natural. It was utterly outside his realm of experience, and his mind refused to deal with it.

He'd always been good at compartmentalization. At boxing off his fear, his worry – the things that could get you caught or killed. Now? He shut off his brain and ran, and the dead followed, slowly but surely.

When he reached the car, he saw what had happened to Frankie. They'd made a mess of him – three of them, one of them looking like roadkill, with mangled legs and a torso that was mostly a spill of intestine. He wondered, in the part of his brain that was still capable of analyzing such things, whether that was what they'd hit with the car earlier. Even as the thought occurred to him, he fired, and they went down quicker than the woman. But, like her, these shambling creatures tried to get back up. He realized suddenly that he was praying under his breath – half-remembered catechisms from an ill-spent youth. If God was listening, he gave no sign.

He kicked the mangled *thing* aside, ignoring the hands that groped at his shins. The keys were still in the car. He slammed the trunk and made his way to the driver's side. He paused and watched the dead stagger towards him.

Tommy was now among them. Head tilted at an awkward angle thanks to his missing neck muscles, he groped blindly towards Westlake. Westlake levelled the pistol, paused, and then lowered it.

"Thanks for the car, Tommy."

He got in, put the car in gear and headed for the road, leaving the dead stumbling in his rear lights.

"I'll let Sal know you tried your best, when I see him."

CHAPTER ONE
Car Trouble

Four months after that night in the Pine Barrens, Westlake was driving through north-eastern New York in a car that wasn't his, with a golf bag full of guns and a gym bag full of food, swiped from the local Stop-n-Go. It wasn't much, but Westlake hadn't had much appetite since the night the dead had risen, and the world had effectively ended.

He was feeling fairly serene, despite it all. The end of the world had had a remarkably calming effect on him. Before things had collapsed, he'd been worried about the Feds, the Outfit, where he was going to go, what he was going to do.

None of that mattered now. The world was … simpler. He had only a single outstanding marker to collect on. Then – what? He didn't know. Maybe Atlantic City. He'd always liked Atlantic City. It was like Vegas, but not in a desert.

Westlake hadn't had many attachments, before the apocalypse. He couldn't afford them, in his line. He had few friends, all of whom were in the life or retired from it. He had his money and his freedom and that was all he needed. Four months in, though, he was starting to miss other people – not to talk to, but just to see. To hear. Ones that didn't want to gnaw his face off.

To distract himself from such thoughts, he took in his surroundings. The town was called Saranac Lake, which was a strange name given that the lake in question was called Lake Flower. It was small, as such places went. Squeezed between Lake Flower and Lake Colby, with the mountains looming over it all.

Not the mountains he was interested in, though. He was heading east, towards what he'd heard was called the High Peaks area. Not that he could tell the difference. All mountains looked pretty much the same to him. That was why he'd brought maps.

Downtown resembled the background of a Rockwell painting – all red brick and white fences. Someone had spent a lot of money to make it look appealing to a certain sort of middle class American. Westlake had always hated these sorts of places – the streets were too narrow, too many faces walking on said streets, and too many cops. No cops now, though. Not much of anyone. Not alive, anyway. Thankfully, he was just passing through. He had a long-delayed appointment in those mountains.

The streets were empty, but the sound of the car brought the undead out of hiding. They stumbled through broken doors and out of alleyways, drawn in his wake by the growl of the motor. He didn't pay much attention to them, but kept the car at a steady twenty miles per hour. No sense burning more gasoline than he had to. It was getting harder to come by. So long as they stayed behind him, he was content to leave them be. He only had so much ammunition, after all. Let someone else handle them.

And there *was* someone else; maybe not close, but definitely in town, or in the woods. He could see the telltale signs of looting – scavenging, rather. The busted windows, the wide-open doors; the spray-paint on the latter, to mark which ones had already been searched. He'd seen enough in the past few months to recognize it for what it was. He wished them luck, whoever they were.

He guided the car around a stalled-out tow truck. A zombie lurched into his path, and he clipped it, sending it spinning out of sight. It appeared that a horde was spilling out of what might have been a diner, in pursuit of a dog. The dog had something in its mouth and scampered out of sight. These towns were always lousy with strays – not that he minded. He'd always had a soft spot for animals. He tried not to think about farms and pet stores as he left the dog and its pursuers in his rearview.

A gauntlet of stalled and parked cars made it slow going. He kept moving, kept his eyes on the road, but his hands tightened on the wheel. Getting boxed in would be a bad idea. He glanced up at the rearview mirror, checking on his pursuers.

They were still coming. Of course they were. They didn't stop. They never stopped. But they were slow and stupid and that meant if you were smart, you could stay one step ahead of them. He'd never had difficulty with that. Done it enough times before the apocalypse.

But he wouldn't relax until he was clear of the village and

closer to his destination. Saranac Lake was one of several villages scattered around Lake Flower. The lake was split between three towns, and its shoreline was – or had been – almost entirely in private hands. But he didn't care about any of that. He was aiming for the Adirondacks.

The mountains stretched across the horizon, just above the tree line. A black swoop of peaks and slopes that grew taller and more imposing the closer he got. He wondered whether there were roads up into the mountains. He knew there had to be maintenance trails and such. The real question was whether the car could make it.

It was a good car, with a sunroof and a GPS that no longer worked, but it wasn't made for off-roading. He'd picked it up at a dealer's lot south of Fishkill when his last one gave up the ghost. He'd run over too many zombies and busted the transmission all to hell.

Westlake preferred using a car to using a gun. Both were loud, but one had the advantage of being in motion. He had learned early on in the apocalypse that moving was good. Zombies were slow, but they didn't stop. Shoot one, there'd be three converging on you a few seconds later. Shoot those three, there'd be six more on your ass before the bodies hit the ground. They just kept coming, like the tide.

But a car – or even better, a truck – and you could paste four or five at a time, and keep rolling. The only problem was, that sort of thing took a toll on a vehicle. Luckily, there were still plenty of cars around – in lots, dealers' showrooms, on the street. Getting gas was always an adventure, but what was life without a bit of risk?

A flash of brown cut across his eyeline and he tapped the

brakes in time to keep from running over the dog. The same dog he'd seen earlier. Somehow the mutt had lapped him. And it wasn't alone – it had brought all its friends along, plus a few it had picked up along the way. Too many. More than a dozen. "Shit," Westlake muttered.

Startled by the near miss, the dog took off up the street, running flat out. One of the zombies broke away from the herd and sprinted after the animal. A runner. Westlake recalled the first time he'd seen one with a queasy sensation. But as bad as the fast ones were, the big ones were worse. He pumped the accelerator as the zombie churned after the animal. The runner was alternating between two legs and four in a disturbing fashion. The dog was doing its best, but the zombie was closing the gap.

Westlake swerved and gave the undead a tap with the bumper, knocking it sprawling. His wheels ground its head and torso to mulch as he continued on. He didn't see where the dog went, and he didn't waste time looking. One good deed was enough for the day.

He caught sight of something in his rearview mirror and grunted. Another runner. Only this one was chasing him. It was dressed like a jogger, sweatband and all. Even had what was left of a pair of earbuds flapping behind it – hard to wear earbuds with no ears, he supposed. He considered another swerve, decided against it. No way it could catch him.

He was so busy keeping an eye on the jogger that he didn't see the new one up ahead, until it hit the hood and had its rotten face pressed to the windshield. Instinct prompted Westlake to hit the brakes. Experience told him that was a stupid idea. Instead, he hit the accelerator, hoping to dislodge it. It snarled and hammered at the glass with broken, mangled fists. Eyes like poached eggs glared at him through a spiderweb of cracks. It had been a woman once; dressed for a hike, maybe, going by the backpack.

Without taking his eyes off it, he groped beside him until his hands found the Glock – Tommy's Glock. It had come in handy since that night, though he'd always preferred revolvers. They didn't jam, easier to load. But when the world provided, only an idiot complained. He swung the pistol up and pressed the barrel to the glass, aiming for a spot between the zombie's eyes. He hated to bust the windshield, but sticking your arm out the window around zombies was a bad idea.

He turned his head and fired. The windshield buckled, and the zombie pitched back and was pulled under his wheels. He heard something clunk in the undercarriage and cursed. In a fight between a car and a zombie, the car always won – but sometimes it was a pyrrhic victory. Using the pistol, he busted out as much of the windshield as he could, his ears still ringing from the gunshot. At this point, he needed to see more than he needed the protection.

Unfortunately, what he saw wasn't good. He'd slowed down, and the tide had caught up with him. They were everywhere – clogging the street, leaving him no room to swerve. That left only one option: plow through and hope the car didn't stall. He gunned the engine and slammed into them. Bodies flew, thumped, and rolled.

For the first minute, he thought he was going to make it. Then, in the second, the car stalled, fishtailed, and crunched into a lamppost hard enough to make him bite his tongue.

The ache of the crash radiated through his back and neck, but he ignored it and fumbled at his seatbelt. They were already closing in – the ones that were still standing, at any rate.

By the time he got himself loose, they'd already swamped the car. Fists battered at the windows, and the car creaked as the weight of the dead pressed against the frame. Some scrambled at the cracked windshield, ripping their fingers on the jagged edges, trying to get in. They clawed at the glass and the metal with dull, animal need. Westlake ignored them. He'd gotten good at ignoring them in the months since the world had gone down the tubes. Unless one was close enough to put its teeth in you, it wasn't important.

The car rocked suddenly. The airbags deployed, punching him back into his seat. Something big had arrived. Or maybe bloated was a better word; the zombie's skin had swollen to shiny tautness, and he could see intestines and muscle tissue straining within.

The big zombie gave a guttural groan and brought both heavy fists down on the hood of the car again, further denting the metal. Steam whistled out as the radiator split. As the giant groped towards the busted windshield, it used its other hand to slap aside those zombies who got too close. From behind the airbag, Westlake emptied the clip into it with next to no effect, save to make it madder and draw new zombies closer.

He needed to get out. He squirmed out from behind the airbag and hastily reloaded the Glock. No way to get to the other weapons or his supplies – the windows were already buckling. A good thief knew when to cut his losses.

He lashed out at the control panel with his foot, hitting the button for the sunroof. They weren't on top of the car yet.

He didn't panic as he hauled himself out, zombies clutching at his ankles. Nor did he panic when the first of them clambered up the trunk of the car, arms stretched out. He pivoted, fired, and moved on to a new target. Plenty of those – they were all around him. The car buckled, shocks popping like thunder. The big one had bellyflopped onto the hood.

Westlake turned, teeth bared, like an animal at bay. A hundred thoughts ran through his head as the bloated face heaved itself into view – plans that would never be enacted, unfulfilled dreams. Atlantic City.

Suddenly angry, he fired, and the creature reared, causing the car to bob like a ship at sea. Westlake fell to the street – the Glock skidded from his hand. A walker toppled onto him. The big one reached down and hauled it off, flinging it aside as easily as a man might toss a bag of garbage. Then it reached for Westlake.

Westlake let it grab hold of him – better than being torn apart by the others. As it dragged him upwards, his hand went to his belt and the black Velcro sheath there, containing a Schrade folding knife. He whipped the knife free and snapped the three-inch blade into a fixed position. Then he jammed it into one of the zombie's bulging eyes until he felt the tip scrape something solid. It staggered back, still holding him. One ponderous step. Two. Three. Then it was clear of the rest.

Westlake twisted the blade. Fluid spurted and he ducked to avoid it. No telling what it might do if it got on him. The zombie spun in a slow gavotte, carrying him along for the dance. Westlake tore the blade loose and stabbed at its pulpy skull, again and again. Its grip tightened, and he increased the pace of his stabbing, trying to find some weak point. Finally, it sagged. He jerked his knife free, and it released him. He fell to the street, panting, a scream held back in his mind. Saw the Glock and scrambled for it as the rest shambled towards him.

Westlake snatched it up – and felt a vise-like grip fasten on his ankle. The big one was still in the game. Ignoring the spurt of terror that seized him, he emptied the weapon into the fat zombie a second time, turning its head to mulch. It released him, and he backed away as the rest closed in. He heard a bark and turned. The dog stood on the other side of the street, watching him. It barked again, as if in invitation, turned, and ran.

Westlake ran after it.

CHAPTER TWO
Ramirez

Estela Ramirez leaned forward, binoculars fixed on the street. She could hear the herd, or horde, or whatever you wanted to call it, but so far none of them had so much as poked a rotting head into sight. She didn't know whether to feel relief or annoyance.

"I told you it would work," came a soft whisper from beside her. Ramirez glanced at the young woman crouched near her on the rooftop. "Attila knows what to do."

"Kahwihta, no offense, but your dog has a brain the size of a peach pit," Ramirez said, bluntly, her hand resting on her sidearm. The presence of her service weapon had always been something of a comfort to her, even before the dead had risen. Now it felt like a totem – a connection to better times. A time when things made sense.

The world had gone crazy, and for a time, Ramirez had thought she might go crazy with it. Those days were thankfully past now. She'd found something to keep her busy. A reason to keep breathing – to keep fighting.

That was why she was crouched atop the tarpaper roof of what had once been a hardware store, along with half a dozen other survivors, all of whom were experienced enough to keep their eyes on the street, rather than each other. As far as Ramirez was concerned, this was enemy territory, and she expected her people to treat it that way. "I once saw him get into a staring contest with a garden gnome," she added.

"Yeah, he's got it in for that gnome," Kahwihta Trapper said, cheerfully. The two women were a study in contrasts. Ramirez was tall and built like an athlete – even now, when a decent protein shake was hard to come by, she had muscle to spare beneath her battered leather jacket. She had been an FBI agent, before things went sideways. She wasn't sure what she was now, other than alive – a state she intended to maintain.

Kahwihta was smaller and rounder, and while Ramirez was as American as apple pie, Kahwihta was Canadian – or Cree, rather. Mushkego, to be exact. From Moose Factory, Ontario. She was a long way from home. She'd been studying at Empire State University on an environmental sciences scholarship when things went bad. She'd adapted remarkably well, all things considered. She seemed to regard the apocalypse as an extended field study.

"Ten to one that dog is zombie-chow," Hutch murmured, from her other side. Ramirez glanced at him. Hutch wasn't particularly tall, but he was as wide as two men put together. He wasn't fat, per se, just big – the sort of big that came from lots of manual labor and big meals and not enough focused exercise. Curly, stringy hair hung down around a wide, unshaven face, and he still wore his colors, though the outlaw motorcycle club he'd ridden with was a thing of the past.

Like the others, he was armed. A coiled bullwhip hung from his studded belt, and he cradled a short-barreled Stoner 63 with a box magazine in his arms, occasionally giving the weapon a fond pat. Like most of their gear, it had been commandeered from the local National Guard armory. The whip, though… that was all Hutch.

"Maybe, maybe not. Either way, keep it to yourself," Ramirez said.

"I'm just saying, they eat dogs, too."

"I'm aware, thank you."

"Though I don't think that mutt would be much of a meal."

Ramirez looked at him. "Why are you still talking?"

Hutch made a placatory gesture and turned away. Ramirez sighed and turned back to the street. He wasn't wrong; one day, that damn dog wasn't going to come back. If it had any sense, it'd have already upped stakes for the woods like the rest of the strays. But as dogs went, Attila was pretty dumb – or maybe just loyal. Either way, she said a silent prayer on the mutt's behalf and kept her eyes on the street.

They'd emptied out around seventy percent of the village over the last three weeks. It was easier to do, now that there were more people. But it also meant that what they found didn't stretch as far. Soon, they'd have to expand the search radius even farther from the camp, and that was dangerous. They were already too far out for her liking. As it was, if the trucks broke down or ran out of gas, they were a five-hour hike from home.

She glanced down at the street below, where the vehicles were parked. Two pickups, Hutch's motorcycle and what had been a delivery van for a catering service. A number of sheet metal plates had been welded onto the three larger vehicles, theoretically giving the occupants some protection. The only real problem with it was the added weight – none of the vehicles were what you'd call fuel efficient, and now they were even less so. They kept them rolling on siphoned fuel, but even that was either going bad or running out.

But that was one of many cans she was currently kicking down the road. They were running low on everything, and there were more zombies every day. Long-term planning had never been her forte. She'd always been the day-by-day sort, but that wasn't good enough anymore. Not when she had people depending on her.

Ramirez pushed the thought aside as she heard a dog bark and saw a dark streak bounding across the street towards the hardware store. Attila was back. The dog leapt through the broken display window and was scrabbling up the iron access-ladder a moment later. She wasn't sure who'd taught the animal to climb ladders, but it came in handy. Probably the same person who'd named him Attila, given the tags and collar he'd been wearing since Kahwihta had found him.

Attila was a brown and black dog of indeterminate parentage. He was big, but not heavy, and had the lean look of a hound. His dark eyes were either soulful or utterly empty of anything approaching self-awareness, depending on who you asked.

She glanced back at the street. She could hear the sound of walkers doing what they did best. Their groaning cries hung heavy on the air. She hated that sound. Something about it reminded her of the droning of insects, and her stomach did a little flip-flop.

"Good boy," Kahwihta murmured, giving the dog a quick scruff. She looked up at Ramirez. "Sounds like he got them all going in the right direction – just like I said."

"Yeah, yeah," Ramirez said, smiling. The young woman's plan had sounded crazy the first time she'd suggested it. Then, all her plans sounded crazy. But they worked, often as not. "Now we just need to hope they keep going that way and don't wander off – or worse, stop dead."

Kahwihta smiled. "Pun intended?"

Ramirez grunted. "Get up. While they're distracted, we've got scrounging to do." She turned. "That goes for all of you. On your feet and remember the drill. No one goes anywhere alone, in and out, and the trucks loaded up as quick as possible. We miss anything, we'll get it next time. Hahm, you're on medicine duty."

Hahm, a stout Asian woman dressed in coveralls, her hair hidden beneath a kerchief, nodded and tapped her pocket. "Got the list. Antihistamines, anti-inflammatories and baby aspirin." She hefted a sledgehammer onto one broad shoulder and headed for the ladder.

"Tampons too," Kahwihta interjected.

"Relax, they're on the list." Ramirez paused and fixed Hutch with a steady glare. "Essentials only, Hutch. No booze, no pills – not this time. No screw ups. You read me?"

Hutch gave a lazy salute. "Loud and clear, boss."

"Call me boss again and I'll feed you to the next batch of walkers we come across." She looked at Kahwihta and motioned to Attila. "Think he can do another circuit? I want to make sure we don't have any surprises waiting for us." Attila wasn't smart, but he made for good zombie bait. A few barks and the walkers would pour out of whatever hidey-hole they'd wandered aimlessly into and follow the doggie. The only problem was the runners. Most weren't fast enough to catch a dog, but every so often one managed to get too close for comfort.

Kahwihta frowned but nodded. "Probably, but he's getting tired."

"We're all tired."

Kahwihta took two handfuls of Attila's jowls. "You heard her. Go play." The dog barked and headed for the ladder. Ramirez heard Hutch curse as the dog clambered past him down the ladder. A few moments later, Hutch and the others were spreading out, hitting the closest storefronts. They didn't worry about noise – strictly smash and grab. Early on, they'd tried to do things quiet, but that took too long. Better to be quick and loud, despite the attention it drew from the locals.

Attila was already out of sight, racing around somewhere behind the buildings on the opposite side of the street. She could hear him barking – then, a screech of tires. The unexpected sound had her on her feet. She swung the binoculars around. "Did you hear that?" she asked. "That was a damn car, wasn't it?"

"Sounded like one to me," Kahwihta said, joining her at the edge of the roof. "Who'd be crazy enough to drive through town?"

"Somebody who doesn't know any better." Ramirez

spotted a flash between the buildings and heard the screech of compacting metal. The tenor of the zombies' groaning changed, becoming something eager and desperate. They had new prey. Attila was off the menu; lucky dog.

Hutch came puffing up the ladder. "You hear that?" he panted, looking winded. "Sounds like somebody's got trouble. Should we...?"

"Should we what?" Ramirez asked, not looking at him. "Help them? And how do we do that, exactly?" She paused, peered for a better look. "There. Just at the intersection. Looks like the car wrapped itself around a lamppost." She glanced at Hutch. "The others...?"

"Down by the trucks, loading what we got. We didn't get far. The walkers haven't noticed us yet, but it's only a matter of time."

"No. I don't suppose you did." She tensed as a gunshot punched the air. Instinctively, her hand fell to her own weapon. The car was swamped, with walkers all over it. She could see a few runners jittering around the edges of the crowd, and a hulking shape lurching towards the front end of the car. "Shit. We got a brute."

"Really? Let me see." Kahwihta snatched the binoculars from her grip and peered towards the confrontation. "That's the first one of those we've seen this close to the camp in a month. They don't usually wander too far from home." She glanced at Ramirez. "This isn't good. That means those aren't just locals down there."

"Probably followed the car," Hutch said, half-heartedly.

Ramirez shook her head. Zombie numbers had been on the increase for a few weeks now. Just a few stragglers at first, then more. Too many. They hadn't figured out where they were coming from yet. Down out of the mountains, maybe.

"Doesn't matter. They're here now, and there'll be more of them before too long. We need to let the other camps know tourist season has begun." She took the binoculars back from Kahwihta and saw that the new arrival had managed to make it to the top of his car. He wasn't screaming, which was a point in his favor.

When the brute heaved itself after him, she figured he was done for. He put a shot into its head, and the car bobbed like a cork on the ocean. The guy, whoever he was, went down, but was back up again a moment later. When the brute went for him again, she caught the glint of the knife and whistled appreciatively. "Well, damn."

Hutch leaned forward, squinting. "He stabbed the shit out of that bloat-bag. Whoever he is, he's pretty badass. Think we should help him?"

"Might not have time. They're on his tail and more are coming. I think he used up his luck." Ramirez focused the binoculars, trying to get a better look at the man's face as he scrambled away from the fallen zombie. Something about him seemed familiar, but she couldn't say what precisely. Just a feeling. Like she'd met him somewhere before.

Maybe he was a Fed – or had been. A cop, maybe? She'd known a lot of cops. Then his face jumped into focus and she knew. "Sonnuva…"

"What?" Hutch asked. "You know him?"

"I know him. What is he doing out here?" Ramirez was already pushing past Hutch as he made to reply, heading for the ladder. As she hit the doors of the hardware store, she realized she wasn't afraid of the zombies getting him. She was afraid of him getting away.

The others were quickly loading up the trucks as Attila skidded around the corner and bounded towards them, barking to beat the band. The man was just behind him, running flat out. When he saw her, he slid to a stop, a confused look on his face. She drew her service weapon and aimed at him. "Down," she shouted.

He went flat and she fired. The runner that had been about to tackle him went down in a heap just behind him. He clambered to his feet just as the rest rounded the corner. No more runners, thankfully. Just garden variety walkers. Still deadly, though.

Westlake – and it was definitely Westlake – trotted towards her. He smiled.

"Special Agent Ramirez. Long time no see."

CHAPTER THREE
Extraction

Ramirez kept the pistol levelled. Westlake seemed at ease, despite the situation. He'd always been a confident asshole. "Stow the Glock, and put your hands on your head," she said, the familiar authority rolling off her tongue. "Have you been bitten?"

"No." Westlake did as she asked. "That your dog?"

"No."

"You should really have him on a leash. There are laws."

"Shut up and walk towards me – slowly." She backed towards the trucks and called out to the others over her shoulder. "Everyone into the trucks – we're done here! You too, Westlake. Come on."

He came, if somewhat reluctantly. She could practically read his mind. "If you try to run, I'll put one in your leg, and you'll be lunch."

Westlake glanced back at the approaching zombies. "That'd be unfortunate."

"Keep walking, and keep your mouth shut."

Hutch and one of the others had already begun picking

off the faster walkers – the staccato boom of Hutch's Stoner 63 rattling what little glass was left in the windows and drawing in more of them from the other end of the street. They'd woken up the whole town. They were about to be surrounded. She thought quickly, then called out, "Hutch, we need a distraction."

He glanced at her. "So? Send the dog!"

"I'm sending you. Go play cowboy."

"Isn't that more Labrand's thing?"

"Go, Hutch!"

Hutch cursed, slung the Stoner, and reached for his bullwhip. He stretched the whip between his meaty fists as he started towards his motorcycle. Westlake watched him go, then turned back to Ramirez. "What now?"

"Get in the van."

He looked around. The walkers were getting close enough to smell, stumbling out of doorways and broken windows. "If I say no?"

She reached into her jacket and pulled out a collapsible baton. She extended it with a snap of her wrist and caught a too-close walker wearing the remnants of a highway patrolman's uniform across the head, flattening it and sending the Smoky the Bear hat flying. Her pistol bucked in her hand as she put another – this one dressed for a day at the lake – down. "Into the van now!"

"Don't have to tell me twice," Westlake said, hustling past her. Kahwihta was waiting at the van, with Attila. Unlike the rest of them, she didn't bother with a firearm. Instead, she carried a cattle-prod. She activated it as Westlake approached.

"Want me to give him a zap?" she asked, cheerfully.

"Hey now…" he began, hands raised. He actually sounded worried, for a wonder. Ramirez considered letting Kahwihta do it, just to watch him squirm. But, in the end, she shook her head. They had more important things to do.

"Not unless he tries to run." Ramirez holstered her pistol and caught the eye of another survivor, Labrand. The big, gawky looking man in the sweat-stained Stetson may have dressed like a refugee from a honky-tonk, but he was good with a gun. "Labrand, you're driving." She tossed him the keys. Behind them, the zombies were still approaching.

"You got it, boss." He touched the brim of his hat and hurried towards the driver's side.

"Don't call me boss, damn it," Ramirez called after him.

Westlake turned. "Hey, look, you got guns – let's go back to my car. I got stuff in there I need. Stuff you need too, from the look of it."

Ramirez knocked another walker sprawling. The others were falling back. She heard Hutch's motorcycle growl to life. "Forget it. Load up! We're out of here in three."

"But my car–"

Ramirez turned. "Get in the goddamn van!"

Westlake got in the van. She turned back to the street. The walkers were too close now, and too many. But Hutch would handle that.

She paused, one hand on the door, watching as the biker peeled out, filling the air with fumes and drawing every dead eye in the vicinity. As the motorcycle swung in a tight circle, leaving black marks on the street, he uncoiled his bullwhip and gave it an almost lazy crack. It caught a walker around the neck and Hutch dragged the zombie off its feet.

Hutch whooped and sent the motorcycle roaring up the street, dragging the walker in his wake. The rest stumbled after him, attracted by the noise and motion. At the last second, Hutch let the walker roll loose, bowling over several of its fellows. The rest kept after him.

Ramirez knew from experience that the distraction wouldn't last long. She and Kahwihta slammed the loading doors shut. Ramirez banged on the metal partition that separated the cab from the back of the van. "Labrand, get us rolling!"

The van started up, and a moment later the convoy was rolling east, heading back to camp. A moment later, she heard the grumble of Hutch's bike, and felt a flicker of relief. The van squeaked its way up the road, and she grimaced as she banged her head against the wall. The shocks were shot, and the whole vehicle felt as if it might collapse into pieces at any moment. But it was better than walking.

Westlake sat across from her and Kahwihta, looking annoyed and eyeing the supplies scattered on the floor. She settled back and looked him over for the first time. He looked about like she remembered. He was one of those guys who wore his history on his face. Every kick, every punch – it was all there. The first time she'd met him, she'd thought he was a boxer, if a bit skinny.

Instead, he was a thief, and a good one. He'd pulled off a dozen jobs on the East Coast solo, and God alone knew how many out west without so much as a sniff of being caught. Then, one day, the FBI had lucked out, caught his crew, and before you knew it, Westlake was in custody and turning state's evidence.

She'd been assigned to protect him. It turned out he hadn't been interested in protection. He'd slipped his detail one night, a few weeks before the world fell apart, and vanished. Her superiors hadn't been happy. Come to that, she hadn't been happy either. Seeing him here was something of a surprise. Then, if anyone could make it through the zombie apocalypse in one piece, it was Westlake. The question was, why was he here?

"My name's Kahwihta. Kahwihta Trapper," Kahwihta said, startling Ramirez from her reverie. "What's yours?"

"Don't talk to him," Ramirez said.

"I'm Westlake," Westlake said, offering the young woman his hand. Ramirez knew he was only doing it to annoy her. He was good at it.

"First name or last name?" Kahwihta asked.

"Just a name." He glanced at Ramirez. "So where are you taking me?"

Ramirez looked at him. "The lodge."

"And what's the lodge?"

"Welcome to the Van Hoevenberg Lodge, situated on the pristine shoreline of Heart Lake," Kahwihta said, as if reciting from memory. The accompanying gestures were somewhat over the top, in Ramirez' opinion. "To the south, you'll see Mount Marcy and Algonquin Peak – two of the highest points in the state. To the north, Mount Jo. We hope you'll enjoy your stay."

Westlake stared at her for a moment before turning his attention to Ramirez. She sighed. "It's a big place. Lots of room. Lots of resources. Or it was. Less now."

"I bet."

"You could say thank you," Kahwihta said, studying him curiously.

"Thank you," Westlake said, after a moment. He seemed bemused by the young woman. Ramirez knew how he felt.

"Not us. Attila." She knocked a knuckle against the dog's skull. "He led you right to us, like a good boy. Aren't you a good boy? Yes, you are. Yes, you are."

Attila panted his appreciation.

"We'll call it even," Westlake said, smiling.

Ramirez thought about hitting him. Instead, she asked, "What are you doing here?"

"Passing through."

She frowned. "No, you're not."

"What makes you an expert on what I'm doing?"

"Because I know you, Westlake. You don't like the woods. You're a city boy."

"Things change."

"Not that." Ramirez reached over and took the Glock from him. It was empty, but that was easy enough to solve. Westlake was the sort of guy to have an extra clip somewhere.

"That's mine," he said.

"I don't think so." She checked the chamber and slid it into her waistband. "You don't usually carry a gun."

"It seemed prudent in the current climate. Am I under arrest?"

"That depends," she said, knowing he was needling her.

"On?" he asked.

"Whether you answer my questions."

"I am nothing if not forthcoming. Ask away, Special Agent Ramirez."

"I'm not a special anything, anymore."

He smiled, and she knew he was trying to get under her skin. Guys like him liked to get on top of you, verbally. They'd get you pissed and suddenly you were answering their questions instead of the other way around. "Once an agent, always an agent. I think John Wayne said that," he added.

"John Wayne said a lot of stupid shit," Ramirez said. Kahwihta snorted in laughter.

Westlake shrugged. "Never was a fan, myself. More of an Alan Ladd guy."

"Color me surprised," Ramirez said. He could be charming, when he wanted. She remembered that. But it was all an act. A way to get you to lower your guard.

Kahwihta looked at them. "So do you two, like, know each other?"

"You might say that." Westlake sat back, and found himself eye-to-eye with the dog. Attila ruffed softly and laid his wide head on Westlake's knee. He looked at Kahwihta. "Does he have to do that?"

Kahwihta smiled. "He likes you."

"I thought dogs were supposed to be good judges of character," Ramirez said.

Westlake grunted and absently stroked the dog's head. "I'm not a bad guy when you get to know me."

"Says the thief."

"Really?" Kahwihta asked, a touch too eagerly for Ramirez' liking. "What'd you steal? Were you like a bank robber?"

"What didn't he steal?" Ramirez said. "Bearer bonds,

diamonds – you even knocked over a casino in Atlantic City once, didn't you, Westlake?"

"Allegedly."

"I wonder what it's like for you now, nothing left to steal."

He gave a thin smile. "You'd be surprised."

"Then illuminate me. You only go where there's something to steal. But there's nothing out here but trees and… what?"

Westlake said nothing. Out of habit, she suspected. She drew her sidearm and set it on her knee, thumb on the hammer. "Why are you out here, Westlake?"

Kahwihta shifted nervously, but said nothing, for which Ramirez was grateful. She was bluffing, but Westlake didn't need to know that.

"Like you said, you're not a Fed anymore," he said. "I don't have to say anything."

"I might not have a badge, but I do have a gun, and my patience is running out." She didn't lift the pistol, but her finger tapped the trigger in a meaningful sort of way. Once, it might have been an empty threat. These days, she wasn't so sure.

"You never did have much patience."

She lifted the pistol. "Less, now."

Westlake lifted his hands. "You can't shoot me."

"Not a Fed anymore, remember?"

"What'll your friend here think?"

"I'll ask her later." Ramirez spoke harshly, but quietly. "Start talking, Westlake – or I'll commence to shooting."

Westlake sighed and scrubbed his scalp. "If you'd intended to shoot me, you'd have done it in the street. Or you'd have left me to the locals."

Ramirez lowered the pistol. "You're right." She studied him. Same old Westlake. He was so certain of himself it hurt. Like he was the one in control. He'd been the same the day she'd met him. Smug. Like the whole world was his for the taking. She banged on the partition. "Stop the van."

Kahwihta looked at her. "What's up?"

Ramirez ignored her. "Stop the van!"

The van stopped. She opened the doors and gestured. "Out."

"Me?" Westlake asked, all innocent.

She tapped her sidearm. "What do you think?"

Westlake got out of the van. The convoy had pulled off the road. Trees stretched like cathedral walls to either side of the road. Labrand was already half out of the van's cab, one hand on the old-fashioned Colt holstered low on his hip. "Something wrong?" he drawled, eyes flicking to Westlake.

"No. Keep an eye out. And tell the others to stay in the trucks. I want to have a chat with Westlake." She turned as Kahwihta made to follow. "You stay here too."

Kahwihta frowned. "Are you sure?"

"Positive." Ramirez tried to smile, but wasn't sure the young woman bought it. She motioned with her weapon. "Over there. Off the road."

Westlake didn't argue. She followed him into the trees. It was quiet here. Everywhere was quiet now, mostly. Not even any insects this time of year. Barely any animals. Westlake looked around as he walked. She wondered if he was thinking of running.

"Stop," she said, softly.

He stopped. "What now?"

Zombicide

"Now we talk."

"So talk." Westlake crossed his arms and leaned against a tree. At ease, even in the wilderness. She hated him even more.

"I want the truth, or I'll put one in your leg and leave you for the walkers."

"You won't do that."

Ramirez took aim at his right leg. "Try me."

Westlake licked his lips. "I don't remember you being this hostile last we met. Did I do something to piss you off?"

"You might say that, yeah. When you pulled your disappearing act, it didn't really do my career a lot of good."

He shrugged. "My apologies."

She waved it aside. "So what happened?"

"Sal Bonaro happened."

Ramirez blinked. "That explains that." Guys like Bonaro had eyes and ears everywhere. Once he heard that Westlake was planning to talk, he'd have moved to silence him.

"Yeah. Fat lot of good your bunch were, by the way. I thought the FBI were supposed to be good at protecting witnesses."

"Only if the witness wants to be protected," Ramirez said, annoyed by the jab. "What were you doing out here?"

He said nothing. She fired. Not into his leg, but into the ground near his feet. He yelped and jumped. "Jesus! Fine. I'm looking for someone."

"Who?" Ramirez demanded.

Westlake looked away. "Sal Bonaro."

Ramirez blinked. "The same Sal Bonaro you just said tried to kill you?"

"I didn't say he tried to kill me."

"You implied it. Besides, what is Sal Bonaro doing in the Adirondacks? He's even more of a city boy than you."

Westlake shrugged. "What do you think he's doing? He's holed up, waiting for all this to blow over like everybody else." He gestured in the general direction of the mountains. "Up there. Somewhere," he finished darkly.

Ramirez stared at him. Then she lowered the pistol. Bits and pieces of old briefings came back to her – half-heard gossip and tall tales. Watercooler talk. That was what she'd thought at the time, at least. "When you say holed up, you mean…?"

He smiled and leaned forward. "What do you think I mean?"

"It's here?" she asked, softly. "The Villa?"

Westlake nodded.

She ran a hand through her hair and laughed. "Holy shit. I'm glad I didn't shoot you, Westlake. Because you might just be the answer to our goddamn prayers."

CHAPTER FOUR
Accord

A whistle sounded from the road.

"That was a signal," Ramirez said, as she turned towards the sound. Westlake wasn't listening. He dove for her weapon. She jerked around as he caught her wrist, and her fist punched into his belly. He staggered and gasped, but didn't let go. She hit harder than he'd expected. He was still wheezing when she kicked his legs out from under him, and he fell on his ass.

"OK, I admit," he panted, hands raised. "That didn't work out as I'd hoped. Let's pretend it never happened."

"I take it back, you are an idiot," she said, backing away from him. "Get up."

"I'm OK here, thanks." Westlake wondered if he could get to his knife before she pulled the trigger. He doubted it, and honestly, he didn't particularly want to.

He had the outline of a plan in mind – not a good one, but it might be the only one that got him where he needed to go.

He was starting to realize that his original plan to head into the mountains alone had been somewhat flawed.

He'd known from the outset that his odds of success were infinitesimal without a crew, but putting one together these days was impossible. He'd decided to do it alone anyway, more out of stubbornness than any real hope of success. But Ramirez might hold the answer to that particular problem.

"Get up, Westlake. They've spotted hostiles. So get up and let's get back to the van."

"I don't think so. See, I don't think you have my best interests at heart. In fact, I think maybe I ought to chance it on my own."

"Oh no, you're not getting out of my sight, Westlake." Ramirez lifted her weapon, and he tensed. The Ramirez he'd known, however briefly, wouldn't have pulled a stunt like popping one off next to his feet. She'd changed – there was something in her eyes. A hardness that hadn't been there before. The plan started to crystalize. If Ramirez was as desperate as she looked, then he had the advantage. He decided to push it, and eased to his feet.

"What are you going to do, Ramirez? Shoot me?"

"If I have to."

"I'm willing to roll the bones on that." Westlake stepped back – and darted into the trees. The same way he'd done with Tommy, that night in the Barrens. Ramirez wasn't Tommy, but there were other similarities. Like dead people in the trees.

The walker seemed to stumble out of nowhere, hands grasping. Westlake ducked and rammed his shoulder into the zombie's midsection, knocking it over. It clawed at his legs as he stumbled over it. He lashed out, pulping its skull with the steel toe of his boot.

"Westlake!" Ramirez shouted. He paused, saw her raising the pistol. Fear filled him as he heard the shot. A walker in a waitress uniform toppled, its fingers snagging in his coat. He shoved it aside and turned, looking for a safe direction. There wasn't one. No matter. He wasn't really trying to escape. Just like he hadn't been trying to escape the night the cops came for him.

Not really. Not when the threat of turning state's evidence was the only real leverage he had over Sal. Sure, he could have gone to war – could have hit every Bonaro joint on the East Coast, bled the Outfit of every dollar he was owed. But that had never been his way.

He preferred to keep things simple. Efficient. You could adapt on the fly with a simple plan. A simple plan was a hard plan to ruin. Not impossible, though. He'd found that out the minute Tommy had thrown him into the trunk of a rental car. But Ramirez wasn't Tommy. She'd see sense. Or so he hoped.

He stumbled as a new walker grabbed the back of his coat. This one wore a padded jacket and a cap with ear flaps – a hunter, maybe, who'd never made it home. Westlake pivoted, snatching his knife from its sheath and snapping it open in one motion. He slammed the knife into the dead thing's skull, dislodging the cap in the process. He kicked the twitching zombie back and turned. More of them lumbered closer – how many dead people were in these woods?

Westlake spotted Ramirez out of the corner of his eye

and went flat as her pistol barked twice. Two zombies, both in varsity jackets, collapsed like puppets with their strings cut. Ramirez reloaded smoothly as she strode towards him. "That was stupid."

Westlake leaned into it. After all, he now knew she valued him alive, despite her threats. "Hey, you're the one who stopped your little convoy so you could threaten me in private."

He knew he'd scored a point when Ramirez looked away. He paused and decided to be charitable. "Thank you."

"For what?"

"Saving my life. Just now."

"Yeah. Don't make me regret it. Come on, and don't run again." He followed her through the trees, back towards the vehicles. Just before they reached the others, he came to a decision. He stopped. She turned and looked at him.

"I've got a proposition for you," he said.

"Now isn't the time."

"Now's the perfect time. You're desperate, otherwise you wouldn't have pulled this stunt." He narrowed his eyes. "I'm guessing you're running low on everything, aren't you? Guns, medicine, food. Every camp I've passed on the way here has had the same problems. Too many zombies and not enough of anything else."

Ramirez flinched slightly. If he hadn't been watching her face, he'd have missed it. He pressed on, speaking quickly. Knowing every minute they wasted was another walker heading right for them. "You said I was the answer to your prayers – well, maybe you're right. You want the Villa? You can have it, and everything in it, if you help me."

"Help you how?"

"If the stories aren't bullshit – if it is a fortress – well, I might need some help getting inside." He smiled and held out his hand. "So what do you say? Deal?"

Ramirez made to answer, when another whistle sounded. Then, brusquely, she said, "I'll think about it – come on! Back to the van!" She turned and ran. Westlake followed. He spotted a few more walkers lurching through the trees, but not many. Even so, one was too many for his liking.

When they reached the others, he saw that they'd had trouble as well, but had dealt with it quietly. Baseball bats, shovels, hammers and the like had done the job as well as a bullet. Labrand trotted towards them, his Colt in his hand. "Everything OK, boss?" he called out.

"We're fine," Ramirez said. "Status?"

Labrand tipped his hat back, a look of relief on his hangdog face. "A-OK. But we got more walkers incoming. We need to skedaddle." As if to emphasize his point, he swung the Colt up and snapped off a shot – dropping a walker that had just ambled onto the road. The dead man's toupee went flying off as he fell. "Like now," he added, as more walkers came out of the trees.

Ramirez and Westlake hustled back into the van, where Kahwihta was waiting with Attila. As Ramirez closed the doors, the young woman said, "So what was that about?"

"We needed to have a chat," Ramirez said.

Kahwihta looked at Westlake. "About what?"

Westlake shrugged. "Ask your boss. If you don't mind, I'm going to take a little nap. It's been a tiring day." He cleaned his knife on his trouser leg and slipped it back into its sheath.

He glanced at Ramirez. "I don't suppose I can have my gun back now?"

"Not yet," she said, refusing to look at him.

Westlake nodded amiably. "No hurry." He closed his eyes.

"Did you see any walkers in the trees?" Kahwihta asked.

Westlake cracked an eye. "What?"

"Can you describe them for me?" He saw that she had a small Moleskine notebook out, and a pencil. "What were they wearing?"

"Clothes?" he said, bemused.

"What type? Winter wear? Hiking gear?"

He opened both eyes and stared at her. "I don't know, sorry. Wasn't really paying attention to their sartorial choices, if you get me."

"No need to apologize," she said. "Just try and pay attention next time, huh?"

Westlake looked at Ramirez. She smiled thinly. "She's a zombologist."

"Environmental biologist," Kahwihta corrected. "Possibly thanatologist. Like it or not, the walking dead are now an environmental factor, and one in need of study." She held up her notebook. "For instance, I've been trying to map migration patterns."

"Which means?"

"Zombies move – mostly very slowly, but they do move. I've been trying to figure out if there's a pattern to those movements."

"They follow us," Westlake said. He'd seen enough over the past months to know that much, at least. Zombies went where the food went.

"Yeah, but how do they know where we are? How do they know anything, given that they're, well, dead? How does one walker spotting someone turn into thirty walkers, or worse? Do they have some way of communicating that we're not aware of? Are they even capable of something so basic?" She leaned back and tapped her notebook. "I've got reams of data, but no answers."

Curious despite himself, Westlake asked, "So why do it?"

Kahwihta smiled. "I figure someone's got to. Might as well be me."

Westlake found it hard to argue with that. He sat back and tried to rest. It wasn't easy. The van wasn't the most comfortable conveyance. Better than a prison van, but not by much. He glanced at Ramirez. "Tell me about the lodge."

She frowned. "What do you want to know?"

"Are you in charge?"

She laughed. "Hell, no."

"Everyone calls you 'boss.'"

"Because she is," Kahwihta said, not looking up from her notebook. "Even Attila knows that." The dog looked up at the sound of his name. Ramirez grunted.

"They do it because it annoys me."

"Good reason," Westlake said. "Is it the only one in the area?" Most of the camps he'd passed by or through were small things, isolated and isolationist – people were wary of strangers these days, especially when everyone was scrounging for basic necessities. There weren't many of them, either. Staying in one spot was dangerous, unless you had walls and plenty of weapons.

Ramirez frowned. "There are two other camps nearby.

One near North Elba and another close to Averyville. We're the largest; sort of a hub. We stay in contact with the others by radio and help them with supply runs when we can – and vice-versa. We trade what we don't need for what we do, and give any extra."

"How charitable."

"It's not charity; it's common sense. If we didn't help each other, we'd be isolated and picked off in no time. Instead, we've managed to survive."

"How many people?"

"Somewhere between not enough and too many," Ramirez said, bluntly.

Westlake sat back. "So what you need is a bigger space, and one more easily defended. Sounds like the Villa to me." He resisted the urge to smile. It was always nice when things went according to plan – even a half-baked plan like this one.

"I told you I'd think about it," Ramirez said.

"What's there to think about? You said yourself – I'm the answer to your prayers. The Villa is the answer to your prayers. And I can help you get it."

"What's the Villa?" Kahwihta interjected.

Westlake looked at Ramirez. "You want to tell her, or should I?"

Ramirez glared at him, but only for a moment. She sighed and ran her hands through her hair as the van bumped along. "It's an urban legend. At least I thought it was. Westlake here says otherwise."

Kahwihta leaned forward eagerly, notebook forgotten on her lap. "What sort of urban legend? I'm guessing it has something to do with the mob?"

Westlake blinked. "How'd you guess that?"

"There used to be speakeasies all through these mountains."

Westlake laughed. "It used to be one, certainly. It's more like a hotel, these days."

"A hotel?"

"A big one." Westlake gestured for emphasis. "Hidden in the mountains. Safe from the prying eyes of the Federal government, local law enforcement – maybe even God himself. And I know where it is."

CHAPTER FIVE
The Lodge

They reached the lodge just before dusk. Labrand honked the horn as the van slowed. Westlake heard gravel popping beneath the wheels as they came to a rolling stop.

Ramirez flung the doors open and jumped down out of the van. Kahwihta and the dog followed. Westlake hesitated, looking around. The van and the trucks had pulled into a gravel parking lot through a maze of concrete barricades. As Westlake watched, men and women hauled rolls of barbed wire back into place between the barricades.

"Keep an eye on him for a minute," Ramirez said.

Kahwihta saluted lazily. "Will do."

"I'm not going anywhere," Westlake said, as he sat on the bumper of the van.

Ramirez looked at him. "Damn right you're not. If you try, you'll get a tap from her cattle-prod."

"Might even turn it on first," Kahwihta added, gesturing with the prod.

Westlake shrugged. "I'll sit tight." He turned his attention back to his surroundings. The lodge was a large two-story split-frame, made from stone and timber, crouched on the shore of the lake. It was a long structure, and something about it put Westlake in mind of a fort. Towering spruce and pine stood thick and tall all around, with what looked like only a single road through them.

Smoking chimneys topped the high, peaked roof, and he could just make out the edge of a deck overlooking the water. A long dock jutted from beneath the deck, and extended out into the lake proper. It was lined with chain-link fencing, topped by what he thought was barbed wire. Spotlights had been set up at its end. More lights sat atop the roof, and along the makeshift walls that enclosed the lodge.

The walls that he could see were mostly a hodgepodge of sheet metal, timber, and chain-link, with construction scaffolding running along their length. A secondary defensive line of sandbags and more concrete barricades had been erected just behind them. It all had a temporary look to it – like it was in the process of being taken down, or put back up.

Inside the walls, it looked even more like a construction site. There were stacks of wood and cement sacks everywhere. A makeshift fuel dump of plastic jerry cans had been erected under a lean-to of tarps a somewhat safe distance from the lodge. Most of the fuel would be going bad about now, he knew. He wondered how they were planning to run their vehicles after the last of it was gone.

Jury-rigged systems for rainwater collection had been set up all over the place, and someone had torn up the ornamental flower beds to make room for more useful crops – though what they could grow in this sort of soil, Westlake wasn't sure.

He could smell smoke and food: cooking. Chili, he thought. His stomach rumbled. He hadn't had cooked food in a long time. Not since before Tommy had taken him for a ride, in fact. There were people everywhere – not many, but more than he'd expected. Most camps he'd passed through held only a dozen individuals, if that. This place was practically hopping in comparison.

"Impressed?" Kahwihta asked, sitting beside him on the bumper. She had her cattle-prod across her knees and was gently stroking Attila's head.

"You could say that." He looked at her. "How long did this take to set up?"

"I wouldn't know. We're not finished." She smiled. "It's sort of a work in progress." Her smile faded. "Materials are hard to come by these days. I think we've raided every construction site between here and Albany."

Westlake grunted. His eyes strayed to Ramirez. She was talking to the fat biker. She'd taken his Glock. She didn't trust him – which was smart of her, he had to admit. But she knew she needed him. That meant she wasn't planning to shoot him. Not yet, at least.

"She doesn't like you very much," Kahwihta said, as if reading his thoughts. "You seem alright to me," she added. "Attila likes you, anyway."

Westlake looked down at the dog, who was drooling on his shoes. He shook his head. "Well, that's something. How long you been out here?" he asked, watching Ramirez.

"A few months. I was up here when everything… y'know."

Zombicide

Westlake was silent for a minute. Then, "I was in Jersey."

"Long way to come."

"Yeah," he murmured. Ramirez turned his way, a smile on her face. The smile faded the moment she saw him looking. He'd been as surprised to see her as she'd been to see him. He hadn't given her much thought since he'd slipped his security detail in New York, with plans to go meet Sal. In retrospect, he should have known better. Ramirez started towards them. "Well?" he asked. "What now? Going to slap me in the pokey?"

"Not if you watch your mouth." Ramirez looked at Kahwihta. "Take over the unloading for me. Make sure Hutch doesn't swipe too much."

"Sure thing, boss."

"And don't… no, forget it. Never mind." She sighed and gestured to Westlake. "You, come on. Inside." She started towards the lodge.

"Where are we going?" Westlake trudged after her. The adrenaline had long since worn off, and he was feeling frayed at the edges. He wanted something to eat, and to sleep, in that order. He had a feeling he wasn't going to get either until Ramirez was satisfied.

"I'm going to introduce you to some people, and then we're going to go talk about how you might be able to help us."

Westlake paused. "So you decided to trust me after all, huh?" He let none of the elation he felt show on his face. He'd been certain she'd see the sense of it. That, and desperate people tended not to look gift horses in the mouth.

Ramirez stopped halfway up the wooden steps of the

lodge, but didn't turn around. He could read the tension in her shoulders, the way she held her head. "I wouldn't go that far," she said. "But you're right. We need each other. And we might be able to help each other." She turned and looked down at him. "Especially if your pal Bonaro is alive."

Before he could reply, an African-American woman with gray-flecked locs came down the steps towards them. "Estela," she said. "Welcome back."

"Frieda," Ramirez said, as she threw her arms around the other woman. Westlake paused, startled. Hugs weren't something he associated with Ramirez. He studied the newcomer. Frieda was tall, and dressed in black BDUs and a flowing, colorful scarf, with a machete sheathed on one hip. She held Ramirez for a moment, then stepped back. "You're still in one piece," she said, laughing. "I think Saoirse owes me a beer." She looked at Westlake. "Who's this? Another stray?"

"Something like that," Ramirez said. "Dunnigan in?"

"Where else would he be?" Frieda indicated the lodge with a nod of her head. "We were going over the supply lists when I heard you were back." She paused and asked hopefully, "Insulin?"

"I think so. You'd have to ask the others. I was a bit distracted." Ramirez gestured to Westlake. Frieda gave him a longer, more considering look.

"Westlake," he said, extending his hand.

"Frieda. Frieda Calmet." She looked at his hand, and then at Ramirez. "I assume you checked him for bites. Just because some folks don't turn, it doesn't mean we need to get sloppy about it."

"If a zombie bit Westlake, it would die of blood poisoning." Ramirez gestured to them both. "Come on. We're going to go have a chat with some people."

"What's up?" Frieda asked, falling into step with her.

"Let's wait until we get inside."

"That doesn't sound good," Frieda said, tossing a suspicious look at Westlake as she held the door for them.

"Hey, this is some place you got here," Westlake said, changing the subject. The interior of the lodge was warm, and there were people inside. Not many. Mostly kids. He wondered how many of them had been on camping trips when it had all gone south. "Big. High walls, lots of trees. Nice lake for fishing."

Ramirez grunted. "The walls are shit, the trees make it hard to see what's coming, and the lake is full of zombies."

"And it's not that big," Frieda added. "Twelve rooms, including communal bunking areas and a dining hall. It used to be a place where the upper crust came to rough it, but it got turned into a public facility about thirty years ago."

"Lucky for you, huh?" Westlake said.

Frieda snorted. "You might say that. You might also say we had precious little choice." Westlake grimaced. He was trying to be friendly, but Frieda was taking her cues from Ramirez. She glanced at him. "You look tired."

"I've been on the road."

"New in town, then?"

"You might say that."

"Where are you heading?" she asked.

"What is this, twenty questions?"

"It's rare we get visitors." Frieda paused. "Other than... you know."

"Yeah. You seem to be safe enough, though."

"Not really. The locals are all over the mountains. And in the lake. On the road."

Westlake frowned. "Didn't see any."

Frieda gave him a mirthless smile. "Doesn't mean they're not there."

Ramirez stopped in front of a door and swung it open without bothering to knock. "Inside, Westlake. Try not to embarrass me."

"Wouldn't dream of it," Westlake murmured, stepping past her. The room was large, with a set of windows overlooking the lake. A big stone fireplace occupied one wall, with an impressive rack of antlers above it. There was a long couch and a few upholstered chairs, grouped around a low coffee table.

Westlake could imagine sitting in this room, sipping coffee, watching the sun rise over the lake. The image was marred somewhat by the heavy boards someone had nailed across the width of the windows. He didn't wonder why. "They ever get past the walls?"

"On occasion," Ramirez said. "Runners – the fast ones. They can climb when they're in the mood, though not easily. And the big ones – the brutes – they can knock over most anything, if they get up a good head of steam. Even the concrete only does so much."

"They common around here?" Westlake asked.

"I hadn't seen any in a while. First time I saw one, I passed through a camp near Utica." Ramirez' gaze went vague for a second, and her voice trailed off. "Guess we're lucky." She swallowed and shook her head. "*Were* lucky, at least."

Frieda looked at her with a raised eyebrow. Ramirez grimaced and explained, "Runners and a brute. In town."

"But where there's one, there's more," a new woman's voice interjected. Westlake turned as a woman in a wheelchair rolled towards them. She brought herself to a halt just in front of him and looked up at him. "Saoirse Breen at your service. I'm what you might call the mayor of this little township, though I assure you the election was thoroughly rigged in my favor." Her voice had a soft lilt to it – Irish, maybe. She was middle-aged and pretty, her red hair streaked with white. Her arms were bare and muscular, her hands clad in fingerless weight-lifter's gloves.

"You're in a wheelchair," Westlake said, without thinking.

Saoirse looked at Ramirez. "Oh, he's a quick fella, then."

Westlake grimaced and gestured apologetically. "Sorry – just… didn't expect it, is all." He put on a smile. "Must make it easy to outrun the dead, huh?"

"I got the advantage on the straightaway, but the curves are murder." Saoirse rolled herself backwards. "Dunny! Ramirez is back, and she brought us a stray."

"Who's Dunny?" Westlake asked.

"Jerome Dunnigan," a big man near one of the windows said, offering his hand. Westlake took it. "Only Saoirse gets to call me Dunny, on account of she ignores me when I ask her not to." He was dressed in flannel and a puffer vest with a faded company logo on it. He wore a battered ballcap and a pair of hatchets hung from his belt. "So who are you?"

"Westlake."

"Glad to meet you." Dunnigan went to a tiny fridge set back against the wall. He pulled out a quartet of beers and passed them out. "Have a brew."

Westlake stared at his. "It's cold." He hadn't had a cold beer in months.

Dunnigan smiled. "Lodge has a generator system. Long as we keep it fueled up, we've got power. Makes a lot of noise though. Tends to draw unwelcome visitors."

Saoirse popped the cap on her beer with the table edge and the flat of her hand. "And I keep saying, if we could find some solar panels, we wouldn't need the generator."

"You're free to go look," Ramirez said.

Saoirse laughed. "I thought that's why we had you."

They all chuckled at that, but underneath Westlake could hear the strain. "So, he another Fed?" Saoirse asked, a moment later.

"Even better," Westlake said. He took a sip of the beer. It tasted stale, but he drank it anyway. It'd have been rude not to, and after four months without company, he wouldn't commit another social faux pas. "I'm a thief."

CHAPTER SIX
Unloading

Kahwihta prowled along the fence-line, mind elsewhere. Attila trotted at her heels, receiving his just due from anyone they passed – mostly scritches and head-rubs, but a few treats as well. Fewer of those every day, though. Fewer of everything.

She knew she was supposed to be overseeing the unloading, but the others knew what to do. And despite Ramirez' comments, Hutch hadn't stolen anything in months. Even then, he mostly stole junk – empty bottles, sugar packets and the like. Nothing serious.

She glanced towards the lodge. Ramirez and Frieda had escorted Westlake inside, probably to talk to Dunnigan and Saoirse. She could guess what it was about. The lodge wasn't safe. Not really. They'd only survived as long as they had because of the unique circumstances. Plenty of vacationers, with the gear needed to rough it and a broad range of skills. Fishermen, hunters, hikers. Also three IT specialists, a marketing consultant, and one yoga instructor. But while her core had never been stronger, yoga was no substitute for food and building materials.

Attila gave a soft whuff, and she paused. Beyond the makeshift fencing, the trees stood tall and brooding. She studied them for long moments, then looked down. "They're getting closer, huh?" Attila thumped his tail in reply. She patted him and moved on.

The dog was better than any early warning system she'd yet seen. Animals and zombies didn't mix. The zombies didn't care whether it walked, crawled or flew, they'd eat it if they could catch it. She'd seen walkers dogpile a bear, once. It hadn't been a pleasant sight.

Attila whuffed again, scenting the air. He had somehow survived on his own for what must have been weeks before she'd run across him. He'd come sniffing around her camp for food. She'd been able to count his ribs, and he'd seemed deliriously happy with the half-eaten gas station sandwich she'd fed him, despite it being several weeks past the expiration date. Since then, he hadn't left her side.

Sometimes, she wondered who he'd belonged to, before the dead had risen and the world went topsy-turvy. Whether he'd been a part of some family vacation that had ended all too abruptly. Had he gotten separated – lost? Or had they chased him away? What must he have thought, to see the ones who'd fed him, who'd loved him, turn on him and try to eat him? She tried not to think those thoughts, though. Too maudlin by far, and they served no purpose save to lead her into thinking about her own family, far to the north.

She shied away from the past and tried to focus on the

present. The dead were on the move and had been for weeks. They were leaving the towns, heading into the woods. They were drawing closer to the camps. Not quite looking for them, but on the way to finding them all the same. Things would get even more difficult when they did.

The defenses were good enough to keep out lone walkers, even the occasional runner. But the greater the number of zombies, the less secure those defenses looked. Sometimes, she wondered if maybe she would have been better off staying on the mountain. Like Sayers.

The thought of the former park ranger made her frown. Sayers had been living– or hiding, rather – in the lodge when Dunnigan arrived. She'd upped stakes for the wilderness not long after, complaining about the number of people. To her, more people meant more zombies. Sayers was a weird one. They rarely saw her these days. She hunted and fished and prowled the mountains and kept to herself.

The sound of laughter made Kahwihta turn. Hutch, Labrand, and a few others were unloading the trucks. The haul wasn't great this time around. Mostly canned goods, some vitamin multipacks, a shrink-wrapped box of bottled water… all of it useful, but very little of it interesting. No guns, no ammo. The sort of stuff other scavengers left behind. She wandered over, trying not to look like she was eavesdropping.

"I'm telling you, town's tapped out," Labrand was saying. "We either got to head up the road apiece, or start hitting houses around the lake." She didn't know much about Labrand, other than that he'd been on vacation when zombies started putting the bite on everyone, and he looked like a cowboy who'd gone to seed. That image was only enhanced by the old-fashioned Colt revolver he carried low on one hip.

Hutch dropped a crate of empty milk bottles onto the ground. "What we need is some proper accounting." In comparison to Labrand, she knew everything about Hutch – more than she wanted to, in fact. Hutch had showed up with Ramirez, and had quickly made himself very useful. He was one of those people who seemed to have been in training for the apocalypse all his life.

Hahm hefted a garbage bag full of pill bottles and tossed it to one of the others. The stout Korean woman shook her head. "I thought you were an outlaw biker, not an accountant." Hahm, like Labrand, was something of a closed book. All Kahwihta knew about her was that she'd worked at an elementary school and had arrived with a gaggle of grade schoolers, after making contact with the camp by radio. Hahm didn't like to talk about it, and Kahwihta liked to think that she wasn't the sort to pry.

Hutch made a rude gesture. "I'll have you know I was club treasurer. And as treasurer I grew adept at spotting chicanery."

"Adept?" Labrand said.

"Chicanery?" Hahm added.

"Screw both of you," Hutch grumbled. He picked up a milk bottle, sniffed it, and said, "How much booze we got left?"

"Enough to have a party," Hahm said, tossing another bag out of the truck. "Why?"

"I was thinking Molotov cocktails." Hutch bounced the

bottle on his palm. "I bet one of the other camps has some booze. We could make a few dozen cocktails, draw all the zombies into a contained area – *fwoosh*! No more zombies."

Labrand grunted, took off his Stetson, and ran a hand through his thinning hair. "How you going to get them all in one place?"

"Hell, I bet our zombologist has some ideas," Hahm said, looking at Kahwihta. "What about it, college girl?"

Trying to hide her embarrassment at being spotted, Kahwihta ambled over. "Depends. The walkers – sure. But the runners? The brutes? That might require some creative thinking."

"We got that in spades," Hutch said, confidently. "I bet the mutt could draw them in."

"Not if you're the one throwing the bottles," Kahwihta said. Hutch looked insulted. Before he could reply, she went on, "Have you ever heard of a place called the Villa?"

Hutch grunted. "Why do you ask?"

"The guy we picked up in town mentioned it."

"Yeah, who is he, by the way?" Hahm asked. "Ramirez knows him, doesn't she?"

"If she does, she don't like him much," Labrand added.

"He says his name is Westlake." Kahwihta shrugged. "I think he's a criminal – or he was. We didn't really get a chance to chat."

Hutch put down the bottle and looked at her. "Wait – Westlake? He said his name was Westlake? You sure about that?"

"I'm not deaf, so yes."

Hutch laughed. "Well shit. That's interesting."

"Why? Who is he?" Hahm punched him in the shoulder. "Share the gossip."

"He's a thief. Like, a really good thief. Like a guy who robs casinos, professionally. That type of thief." Hutch scratched his chin. "What's a guy like that doing out here?"

"What are any of us doing out here?" Labrand said.

"He said he's going to the Villa," Kahwihta said. "That's why I was asking if you'd heard about it. You're the only other criminal I know."

Hutch gave her a look, and she smiled sweetly. He snorted. "Yeah, but I'm a petty criminal. Like, I sold some weed and maybe some guns once or twice. Westlake is like one of those guys they make movies about, you know?" He shook his head. "A real asshole, in the best sense of the word."

"There's a best sense of that word?" Hahm asked.

"You know what I mean."

"Clearly we do not," Labrand drawled.

"You were telling me about the Villa," Kahwihta reminded him.

"I wasn't." Hutch laughed again. "I thought that place was in Vegas."

"You've heard of it, though?"

Hutch gave her a lazy grin. "Of course. Anyone who ever spent more than a week in the joint has heard about it. Nobody ever believed it was real. It was like the Dutchman's treasure, you know? It's a story cons tell each other." He scratched his chin. "At least that was what I thought."

"He seems to believe it's here. In the mountains."

Hutch sat down on the tailgate of the truck. "Well strip me naked and tattoo my rear."

"Not even on a bet," Hahm said. "So what is it?"

"It's a hideout – but, like, the ultimate hideout, you know? A place wiseguys could go and last out a damn siege, if they were of a mind. It's supposed to have everything you could want or need, so long as you had the cash to pay for it." Hutch looked at Kahwihta. "You sure he said he was looking for the Villa?"

"Definitely," she said.

He whistled. "If that's the case, we might be looking at the big one." He slapped the bed of the truck with his hand. "No more need to make supply runs, no need to risk getting chewed on for half a bottle of baby aspirin." He glanced towards the lodge. "Westlake – shit. If it is him, that's a stroke of luck there, I'll say that."

"It's about time," Hahm said, softly. "We've been needing some."

A growl from Attila interrupted them. Kahwihta turned as one of the guards walking the fence shouted out a warning. Lights clicked on and swung, searching until they hit several shapes shambling down the road towards the lodge.

"Tourists," Labrand said. His hand fell to his Colt.

Hutch waved him back. "Only a handful. Let whoever's on duty handle it." Even as he spoke, however, Attila started barking. More lights came on to the east. No shouts. Everyone knew what the lights meant. More tourists, coming down the trails. There were plenty of walkers in the mountains, and sometimes they wandered down for a visit.

"More than a handful," Hahm said. "Think they followed us?" She reached down for her sledgehammer.

"Of course not," Hutch said. He sat up.

"They did," Kahwihta said. Hutch looked at her.

"You can't be serious."

She ignored him and started towards the fence, notebook in hand. It was camp policy to let walkers get close to the fence, and then put them down as quietly as possible. Zombies liked noise, and the less of it there was, the better.

Men and women walked the fence, sharpened lengths of wood or rebar in their hands. Whenever a zombie got close enough, they'd shove their makeshift spears into its head. Walkers were dumb, and they'd stumble right onto something lethal if you gave them enough encouragement. It was the others you had to watch out for. Runners were smarter, though only marginally. They'd still go after the closest target, but they'd do it a lot faster. Brutes weren't smarter, but they were harder to put down.

But worst of all were the older zombies. The ones who'd been dead since the opening days of the outbreak and had gone lean and skinny from lack of food. They knew how to hide. There were other types as well. She'd observed some walkers that twitched and growled like hyperactive animals. They'd burst out of a horde like champion sprinters – faster even than runners – if they got a look at a potential meal.

She jotted down notes, accompanied by the soft squelch of rebar punching through rotted brains. The walkers fell, and would have to be cleared away and burned in the morning. Zombies were more active at night, for some reason. She wasn't sure why, yet, but she had several theories percolating in the back of her head.

A crawler gripped the bottom of the fence and bit at the metal with broken teeth. She glanced at Attila. "Sit." The dog sat. He whined as she approached the crawler, but didn't move. He knew better.

Kahwihta crouched down in front of the zombie, sketching it with quick, steady lines. The zombie was wearing a fishing vest and a tattered flannel shirt. The remains of a fishing cap hung askew on its ruined head. She wondered who he'd been. A local, maybe. No way to tell, really. The crawler glared at her with empty hunger. She felt no fear of it, only a sort of muted sadness. It was a broken thing, a stranger to the natural order. "It must be a sad thing, not to be a part of the world anymore," she said. She believed in the interconnectivity of all things. But zombies didn't seem connected to anything. At least, that she understood yet.

As if sensing her pity, it redoubled its efforts to gnaw through the fence, even as it tried to force itself through the gap in the links. She watched it, taking notes on how it moved, and, more importantly, how it dealt with the obstacle. Most zombies didn't deal with obstacles at all – they just kept going until they hit something they couldn't knock over or squeeze through, and then they stopped. But some were more persistent, and they were becoming more common as time passed.

She finished her notes, set her notebook aside, and drew an icepick from her coat. She reached for its scalp, deftly avoiding its snapping jaws. She'd been bitten before and survived, but she wasn't planning to repeat the experience. Holding its head still with her free hand, she punctured the zombie's brain via its ear canal with one quick thrust of the icepick. The crawler slumped with a disgruntled exhalation.

She cleaned the icepick on her trousers and stood. Behind

her, Attila was growling steadily. Out beyond the edge of the light, more shapes stumbled. Not many, but more than usual. She felt a flicker of unease as she rejoined the others.

"Do you have to do that every damn time?" Labrand asked, his expression one of disgust. He was more squeamish than the others, at least when it came to doing things that didn't involve putting a bullet in something.

"Do what?"

"The thing with the icepick."

"I don't like guns," she said. "There's more of them coming down the road. Someone ought to let Ramirez and the others know."

"I'll do it," Hutch said, dropping off the tailgate. "I want to see what they're talking about anyway." He started towards the lodge. "If it is the Villa – could be just the thing to save our sorry asses."

Kahwihta turned back to the fence. There were almost a dozen bodies piled up along its length. But Attila was still growling. Absently, she stroked the dog's head.

"Let's hope."

CHAPTER SEVEN
Real Estate

"I don't recall us sending you to get us a thief," Dunnigan said. He was looking at Westlake now. Ramirez silently encouraged the latter to stand up straight and look like a professional. As if reading her thoughts, Westlake straightened slightly. Westlake was the sort of guy who always tried to make himself look smaller and less noticeable than he really was.

"We can always use another scrounger," Saoirse said. She pulled a pack of cigarettes out of her wheelchair and selected one. She glanced at Ramirez. "Want one?"

"No thanks," Ramirez said, though she did. Badly. She'd quit just before the apocalypse. Her third attempt. So far, she hadn't surrendered to temptation. The fact that cigarettes were hard to find made it easier.

Saoirse shrugged and lit up. She'd been on holiday when things had gone bad, or so she claimed. She'd never mentioned family, or any sort of significant other. Then, a lot of people didn't like talking about what went on those first few days after the dead had risen – Ramirez included. Regardless, Saoirse had a way about her. And she had a head for organization. That came in handy these days, when they had almost forty people, including kids, to take care of.

"I had another use for him in mind," Ramirez said.

"Oh?" Dunnigan turned his gaze on her. "And what might that be?"

Saoirse might be the mayor of their little community, but Dunnigan was the sheriff. He had been one of the first to see the potential in the lodge. He'd been a trucker and had been asleep in the campground when the first walkers had stumbled down the road. He'd turned his rig into a shelter, and set about organizing foraging parties over the course of the following days.

By the time Ramirez had shown up, Dunnigan had already overseen the clearing of the lodge and the first few fortifications they'd made. Even better, he'd been carrying a load of chain link fencing, concrete mix and the like to a construction site somewhere north of them. It was a lucky thing for everyone he'd stopped when he had. Without the materials he'd been hauling, they'd never have been able to make a go of it.

Frieda stepped close to her, one hand on the small of her back. Ramirez turned and smiled. Then she cleared her throat and said, "We need to move."

The words tasted unpleasant in her mouth. For better or worse, this place had become home. More, it was a place of safety – of familiarity – in a strange new world. But if the experiences of the past few months had taught her anything, it was that you couldn't count on the familiar. The others traded looks. They'd discussed it before, but come up with no workable options.

"Tell us something we don't know," Saoirse said, finally.

"I might have found us a place to go." She felt Frieda's hand tighten on her shoulder and she reached up and clasped it. Frieda had been in Saranac Lake on a corporate retreat when the dead rose. They'd met in those early weeks, gotten to know one another. The old cliché – one thing led to another. She pulled Frieda's hand around and kissed her knuckles. Westlake saw the gesture but said nothing, for which she was thankful.

Saoirse gestured to Westlake. "And what does he have to do with it?"

"I know where it is," Westlake said, sipping his beer.

Ramirez looked at Dunnigan. "Ever heard of the Bonaro crime family?"

"Who hasn't?" Dunnigan said. "I was a long-haul trucker before all this shit hit. The Bonaro had a grip on a whole bunch of the local teamster unions for years."

"Yeah, well, the Bonaro are smart. That's why they outlasted almost all of their rivals. The FBI took bites out of their organization – small fry. No one important." Ramirez looked at Westlake. "Until our friend here."

"He doesn't look like a mobster," Saoirse said.

"I'm not," Westlake said. "What I am is the guy who can get you to the Villa."

"Which is?" Frieda asked.

"It's a mob hideout," Ramirez said. "Off the grid, somewhere remote, best of everything that money could buy. Or so the stories say."

"Stories?" Saoirse said. "You don't know?" She looked at Dunnigan, who frowned, but said nothing. Ramirez could read the doubt on their faces. She pressed on.

"We thought it was an urban legend. A few agents were convinced it was a floating operation – a hotel one year, a yacht the next. One guy in the Las Vegas field office insisted it was actually at the top of one of the casinos." She looked at Westlake. "But our friend Westlake claims that it's been here in our backyard the whole time."

"How does he know?" Dunnigan asked. He sounded suspicious. Ramirez didn't blame him. Everything she knew about Westlake told her he was running an angle. He wanted to get inside the Villa, but why? It had to be important to him, whatever the reason.

"I knew the guy who put in the toilets," Westlake said. Ramirez frowned, but Westlake went on before she could interject. "They had a whole new water system installed and got new toilets to go with it. The guy who put them in, he used to… well, give me a head's up on occasion. You know what I mean."

Ramirez stared at him. Of course he'd had people on the inside. It should have occurred to her sooner. That was how guys like Westlake operated. "You had a plumber casing places for you?"

He shrugged. "Doesn't matter now. No more plumbers."

Dunnigan grunted. "Plenty of plumbers. Just no running water." He grabbed a chair and sat down. "Maybe you should start from the beginning."

Westlake took another sip of beer. "OK. So. Back about a hundred years ago, there was a mine up here in the Adirondacks. When the mine shut down, a bunch of bootleggers took it over and hid their booze in it. Somewhere along the way one of them got the idea to turn the place into a speakeasy. Which they did when the mine got turned into a lake. It was so profitable that they decided to expand the business…"

Frieda cleared her throat. "Not that I've got a thing against the occasional history lesson, but what's the point of all this?"

Westlake looked at her. "I'm getting to it. So anyway, these bootleggers – the Bonaro – expanded the business. Made their speakeasy into a hotel of sorts. Neutral territory for those with the right connections. Dutch Schultz stayed there. Capone. It was supposedly a place where deals got made – it's where Lansky and Luciano had their talks with the Department of the Navy, during World War II. At least according to a guy I knew."

Frieda opened her mouth, but Westlake didn't pause. "Anyway, the Bonaro expanded the joint multiple times over the years. It got bigger and bigger, until it was less a hotel than a fortress. Everything you'd need to hole up and wait out a Federal siege or, say, a zombie apocalypse. They called it the Villa."

Dunnigan leaned forward. "And it's here? In the Adirondacks?"

"Hand to God." Westlake raised one hand and put the other over his heart.

"Where, exactly?" Saoirse interjected.

Westlake smiled and shook a chiding finger in her direction. "I'll tell you that when you agree."

"Agree to what?"

"A deal," Ramirez said. The others looked at her. "Westlake knows where this place is. He wants help getting in."

"Help from us," Frieda said, frowning at Westlake.

"In return, you can have the place," Westlake said. He looked around. "It's easily twice the size of the lodge, and probably better protected. Think of what you could do with that. Think of how many lives you could save."

"Westlake, enough," Ramirez said. "You don't need to make the hard sell here."

"Does he not?" Saoirse asked. "Because this sounds too good to be true."

Frieda nodded. "Saoirse is right. What's the catch?" She looked at Ramirez as she asked it, and Ramirez felt a flash of guilt, quickly banished.

"It might not be unoccupied," she said. She glanced at Westlake, daring him to argue. "He seems to think Salvatore Bonaro was headed up here when the dead rose."

"I'm guessing that's bad?" Saoirse asked.

"He's the current head of the Bonaro," Ramirez said. " Which means, if Westlake is right, he won't have come alone."

Dunnigan was silent for a moment. Ramirez knew him well enough to know that he was weighing the pros and the cons. "We haven't seen anyone go up the Adirondacks – or come across any sign of such a place. If they've been up there since all this started, why haven't we seen hide nor hair of them?"

"Like I said, it's a fallout shelter." Westlake finished his beer. "Bonaro was probably planning to come up here anyway, before everything went to hell."

"Why?" Frieda asked.

"Because Westlake here turned state's evidence – or was planning to," Ramirez said. "He was going to tell the Feds who he was working for when he and his pals hit that armored car in Milwaukee."

"Bonaro?" Dunnigan guessed.

Westlake shrugged. "Someone connected to him, anyway. Sal doesn't like attention, so chances are he was already up here. The Villa ain't some cabin in the woods. It's the center of a very big, very illegal web. Sal probably locked the joint down when the first news broadcasts hit the airwaves."

Saoirse frowned. "It's been months. That's a long time, these days. If they had supplies, they might have run out."

"My guy said they had enough food to last for years. And not just food. They got a greenhouse, they got generators, they got solar panels, they got their own water, they got comfy sheets, and they got enough guns and ammo to gear up a small army. All of which Ramirez says you need."

"I still don't understand how they could hide such a thing," Frieda said.

"Best place to hide something is in plain sight," Westlake said. "They had it on the books as a resort for a time – everything legal and above board, but that didn't last long. Then it just sort of vanished."

"Vanished?" Frieda asked, doubtfully.

"Yeah, you know, records got torn up and maps got changed."

"They changed the maps?" Saoirse asked, in astonishment.

Ramirez ran a hand through her hair. "Easy enough to do

when you have that sort of money and influence."

"Except the old ones." Westlake cracked his knuckles. "I'm talking real old, pre-war maps. The sort you can only get in antique stores and flea markets."

"And you had one?" Ramirez said.

"Did. Unfortunately, it was in my car. Which you did not want to go back for." Westlake smiled thinly. "So much for that, huh?"

Ramirez rounded on him. "Why didn't you say so?"

"You never asked," he shot back.

Ramirez was about to respond, but felt Frieda's hand on her arm. She swallowed what she'd been planning to say, her mind whirring to piece together Westlake's plans. "It doesn't matter," she said slowly. "You wouldn't rely on a map. You must know where it is."

Westlake hesitated. Then nodded. "Yeah. I do."

"Good enough." She looked at Dunnigan. "We've got people here who know the area. Labrand, for one."

"Sayers," Saoirse added. "She knows the mountains better than anyone, even Labrand."

Ramirez frowned, but didn't argue. She didn't care for Sayers much. The former park ranger was a textbook misanthrope. Her idea of helping people was putting a bullet in them before the zombies got to them. But Saoirse was right. Sayers knew the High Peaks better than anyone in any of the camps.

"If he's right, the Villa could solve all our problems in one go," Ramirez went on. "We'd have room for everyone, food, and ammunition. We could move up there, then strip the camps at our leisure and start fresh."

"The camps… you mean bring everyone in on this?" Dunnigan asked.

"Why not?" Ramirez gestured. "We could use the help, after all."

Dunnigan took his cap off and scrubbed the back of his head with a rough palm. "We need to do something. I just don't know whether this is it. Going up into the mountains, with the way things have been – that's not like riding down the road in a truck." He glanced up as someone knocked on the door.

Ramirez turned to see Hutch poking his head through. He looked worried. That was never a good sign. "What is it?" she asked.

"Some tourists came to visit," Hutch said.

"Tourists?" Westlake asked.

"Walkers," Saoirse supplied. "Most of the zombies we get these days aren't local. They wander in from out of the area. Or so our resident zombologist swears."

"She knows what she's talking about. I wish she didn't, but she does." Ramirez looked at the others. She could tell that they still weren't convinced, not wholly. Westlake was an unknown, a self-professed criminal, and she was asking them to take a bigger risk than just strip-mining an abandoned town. She looked at Hutch. "Hutch, show Westlake the sights while we talk in private."

"What about the tourists?" Hutch began.

"Labrand and the others can deal with them," Ramirez said.

"Whatever you say, boss." Hutch gestured to Westlake. "Let's take a walk."

Westlake looked like he wanted to protest. Ramirez cut him off with a glance. "You've made your pitch, Westlake. Now give us a minute."

Westlake met her eyes and nodded, reluctantly. "Fine." He let Hutch lead him out of the room.

Ramirez waited until they'd gone before she spoke. "I know it's a long shot, but we're down to the wire here."

Dunnigan sighed. "Yeah, yeah, I know."

"Remember when we hit that big-box store over near Lake Placid?" Ramirez went on, pressing her case. "We got volunteers from all three camps. That way, no one got left out and no one took on too much risk. Why not do the same for this? It'll benefit us all, right?"

Frieda nodded. "I agree with Estela."

"Quelle surprise," Saoirse said, but with a smile. "I do too, as it happens. What about you, Dunny?"

Dunnigan scratched his head again, adjusted his cap, and nodded. "May as well share the risk, if we're sharing the wealth. I'll put the call out. We'll see who bites." He fixed Ramirez with a stern look. "You certain he's on the level?"

"About this? Yeah. Yeah, I think so."

"You think or you know?"

Ramirez was silent for a moment, wondering how best to answer. Then she shrugged. "Heck if I know, Dunnigan. Either way, we have to hope he's right. We don't have much of a choice."

CHAPTER EIGHT
Decisions

"Come on, man, this way." Hutch crooked a finger, and Westlake dutifully followed. He knew why Ramirez had sent him out, but that didn't mean he had to like it. He could tell that neither Dunnigan nor Saoirse knew quite what to make of him or the story he'd told. If Ramirez hadn't been desperate, she might have been equally doubtful. He briefly wondered what he would do if they all decided not to help him find the Villa.

They went out through the kitchen. Hutch stopped long enough to retrieve a cooler and led Westlake outside, onto the back deck. It looked out over the lake. The rails had been raised and extended, the thick wooden slats covered in sheet metal and barbed wire. The deck was covered, and the roof had been built up into something resembling a watchtower, with makeshift ladders nailed to the support beams.

Westlake could hear people walking across the roof above

them, and the soft murmur of conversation. Hutch led him to the edge of the deck, and a pair of brightly colored plastic chairs. A bullhorn sat on the deck beside them. Hutch gestured to the other chair as he sat, and set his gun down. "So you're *the* Westlake, huh?"

"Yeah. What about it?"

"Heard stories about you while I was in county lockup."

"Shouldn't listen to those kinds of stories." Westlake sat. "Pretty out here." The moon was up, the sky was full of stars. The surface of the lake was like a mirror.

"Yeah. View to die for." Hutch laughed – a guttural growl of noise that seemed to emerge from somewhere near his belt-buckle. "So, it true you were the guy behind that armored car job in Milwaukee?"

"Got to be more specific than that."

"The one where the money got set on fire."

Westlake smiled. "Money was small potatoes. We were after bearer bonds."

"Why'd you burn the money, though?"

Westlake was silent a moment. Then, "Matter of principle."

Hutch grunted and flipped open the Styrofoam cooler. It was full of grainy ice, and several bottles, capped with cork. "Ramirez doesn't seem to think you got any – principles, I mean. Never seen her that sore at nobody."

"She's entitled to her opinion." Westlake looked at the other man. "So, how'd you two meet?"

Hutch grinned. "I was living up in Malone, running an… extralegal Canadian pharmaceutical importation business, you might say. Insulin, mostly. Anyway, somebody somewhere got wind, spilled the beans. Ramirez was part

Zombicide

of the task force they set up to catch little old me. She was just serving the warrant when the dead rose and started chowing down on folks – including the rest of the task force. So we, ah, put aside our differences, you might say. Got out of town on my bike."

"Really? Can't imagine that."

"I mean, she made me ride behind her, but it's still my bike, y'know?"

Westlake laughed. "That sounds more like Ramirez."

Hutch nodded. "She's tough."

"That's one word for her."

"How'd you know her from before, I mean? She bust you too?"

"Not quite." Westlake scratched his jaw and looked out over the water. "Protection detail. She was supposed to keep me safe."

"Did she?"

"Didn't give her the chance."

"I'm guessing that was a mistake."

"One of many I have made in my life."

Hutch laughed and reached down into the cooler. He fished out a bottle and offered it to Westlake. Westlake took it, popped the cork, and drank a sip. He grimaced. "Grape soda?"

"No booze, no pills. Boss' orders." Hutch had the good grace to look embarrassed. "I sort of had my problems with both, if you get me."

"I get you." Westlake took another sip. It was worse than the first, if that was possible. "Jesus. It tastes like flat battery acid."

Hutch took a long pull from his own bottle and smacked his lips. "Yeah. My bad. I make it myself." He sniffed. "Bit of a, y'know, connoisseur when it comes to pop."

Westlake shook his head and looked at the water again. It was almost pretty in the moonlight. "How long you think it'll take them to talk things over?"

Hutch shrugged. "Depends." He cut his eyes at Westlake, a sly smile on his face. "You really know where the Villa is?"

"You know about it?" Somehow, Westlake wasn't surprised.

"I've heard some stuff."

"Only about half of it is true."

"Hope it's the good half." Hutch took a long swallow of soda. "Because let me tell you, we ain't got shit going on here."

"That bad, huh?"

"Way I see it, we ain't got much choice. It's either find the place – or we die. Not immediately, but eventually. We've got maybe another month's worth of ammunition and food, if we're careful. If not... barely a week."

"You could leave. Hop on your bike and shoot off over the horizon."

Hutch snorted. "And go where?" He ran his fingers across the faded club patch on his vest. "Nobody to ride with, nothing to do except not get eaten. Not much of a life."

"Not much is better than none."

"That's a matter of opinion." Hutch emptied his bottle and set it carefully back into the cooler before selecting another. "Save the bottle."

"Recycling?"

"Manner of speaking. Sometimes I reuse them – refill them, re-cork them. Sometimes I make them into Molotov cocktails. Depends on my mood."

Westlake chuckled, but the sound died in his throat as he caught sight of something moving out in the water. He tapped Hutch, and the big man leaned forward, then stood with a curse. "Should have goddamn known." He reached for the bullhorn and activated it. Then he reared back and shouted, "Floaters!"

Spotlights flared on above them, striking the water. Zombies waded through the shallows, covered in reeking weeds, their bodies swollen from prolonged submersion. Maybe twenty in all. Staring down at them, Westlake wondered how long they'd been walking under water. They didn't need to breathe, after all. They could walk forever, if they wanted.

"Does this happen a lot?" he asked, the grape soda taste still lingering in his mouth.

"Not so much at first, but recently, yeah. Too often. Usually, they just sit in the lake. It's why we stopped fishing out there."

They watched as the floaters rattled the fencing, trying to find a clear path to shore. Westlake glanced at the Stoner sitting beside Hutch's foot. "Shouldn't you shoot them or something?"

Hutch grinned. "I wish. Gun is too loud. More of them I shoot, more of them show up. We got to do it the old-fashioned way – Muriel!" He turned in his chair and shouted behind him. "Hey, Muriel!"

"What?" a creaky voice called out. Westlake followed

Hutch's gaze and saw a grandmotherly woman, clad in military-issue BDUs that were too big for her, and a bow cradled in one sticklike arm. She hobbled towards them.

"Floaters, Muriel. Thought you might like to get some practice in."

"Did you now?" Muriel sucked on her false teeth and made her way to the rail. She peered over the side, selected an arrow from the quiver on her hip and nocked it. Hutch leaned towards Westlake.

"Watch this."

Muriel let the arrow fly. A floater fell back into the water. Hutch applauded. "Fine work, Muriel." He looked at Westlake. "She makes a mean banana bread, too. When we've got bananas… and flour."

Muriel selected another arrow and loosed it. Another floater sank down into the shallows, the arrow stuck clean through one of its eyes. Her third arrow wedged in a breast-bone. The floater staggered, but didn't fall. "Shoot," Muriel said, in exasperation. She turned to Hutch. "Make yourself useful and go get my arrows back. Ain't got many left."

Hutch snorted. "Maybe you shouldn't miss."

Muriel flipped him the bird and Hutch gave a bark of laughter. She turned back to the rail and selected another arrow. Westlake watched her, impressed. "Tough old lady," he murmured as she let it fly.

Hutch nodded. "You got to be, to survive this long."

"What's her story?"

"From what I heard, it involved a cigarette and a gas station and a ka-boom heard across the county." Hutch looked at him. "What's your story, Westlake?"

"Thought you'd heard all about me," Westlake said.

Hutch grunted. "That was pre-zombies Westlake. I want to know about post-zombies Westlake, you dig?" He drained his bottle and set it aside. "Can't imagine running around out there alone. Drive me crazy."

"I like being alone," Westlake said. He sat back, watching Muriel send another arrow humming home. "I liked it, anyway."

"No man is an island," Hutch said.

"No, I suppose not." Westlake closed his eyes. "You get used to it. The quiet, I mean. Nothing but your thoughts to keep you company."

"My head's mostly full of theme songs. Remember *Have Gun, Will Travel*? That was a great theme song."

Westlake grinned. "Duane Eddy. 'Ballad of Paladin.' Classic."

"Television was great," Hutch said, dolefully. He looked so sad in that moment that Westlake wondered if he might cry. Hutch shook himself. "Ah well."

"I'll take over, Hutch."

They both looked up, startled. Ramirez held two more beers in her hands. She handed one to Westlake. "Go do something useful," she continued, indicating the door. Hutch nodded and gave Westlake a commiserating look. Then they were alone, save, of course, for Muriel and the others on guard.

Westlake listened to the hum-snap of Muriel's bow and said, "What's the verdict?"

Ramirez tapped her bottle against his. "Congratulations. We're going to steal a Villa."

"You don't sound happy about it."

Ramirez dropped into Hutch's seat and leaned back with her eyes half-closed. "I'm not. Not really."

"How is it any different than looting a town?"

"Why don't you tell me, Westlake."

"What do you mean?"

"You had four months," she said, tipping back the beer. "Why did it take you four months to get around to this?" she elaborated.

"I had other, more immediate concerns. As we all did." He paused. "Took me a few days to get my shit together." He tapped his head. "Up here, you know?"

Ramirez nodded. "I know. But why now?"

"Why not now?" Westlake set his beer down on the deck and tapped his fingers on the armrests of the chair. He watched the moonlight on the water. It was pretty – except it was full of zombies. So maybe not that pretty. "The truth is, it took that long to get here. I went for help first – remember Handy McClellan?"

Ramirez frowned. "He's a fence, isn't he? Worked out of a storefront in Trenton?"

"Was. Was a fence. And a friend." Westlake fell silent, his mind on that night. Handy had holed up in his store, locking himself in. It had taken Westlake most of the afternoon to get in, and when he did … Handy hadn't been in the mood for much save dinner. He still remembered the kick of the pistol, as he put what was left of Handy down.

"You went looking for help," Ramirez said, softly. "A crew."

Westlake nodded, looking at his hands. His knuckles

were white in the moonlight, and he forced himself to loosen his grip on the chair. "But nobody was around. Or if they were, they weren't in any condition to be of use."

Ramirez took another sip of beer. "I'm sorry. About Handy, I mean."

Westlake looked at her. "That's why I want to make a deal. That's why you can trust me. I'm starting to think I might need a crew. Especially if the mountains are this infested with zombies."

Ramirez looked at him. "You still haven't said what you're after."

"That's my business."

She turned and poked him in the chest, hard enough to hurt. "And I'm making it mine. You're going after Sal, aren't you?"

"What if I am?"

Ramirez fell silent. Westlake gave her a few moments, then said, "If Sal is up there, he's going to cause trouble for you eventually. Trouble for everyone. Better it be handled now than when you're not ready for it."

"Maybe."

"No maybes about it."

She finished off her beer and sat up. "Dunnigan is contacting the other camps now. If they want in on this, they'll send volunteers to help. If they don't, we'll go with who we can get. One way or another, you'll have your crew." She looked down at him. "Until then, you should get some sleep."

"Where, exactly?"

Ramirez looked around. "Here's good. I'm told it's nice to

sleep under the stars. I'll send someone out with a blanket."

Westlake watched her go back inside and shook his head. But he was smiling when he did.

CHAPTER NINE
El Calavera Santo

Westlake was awoken by a kick to the back of his chair. He sat up with a curse, fumbled for a gun that wasn't there, and nearly fell out. He blinked up at Ramirez and realized he'd slept far longer than anticipated, even if it had been a restless slumber. "What? What is it?"

"Breakfast." She tossed something onto his chest. A cellophane wrapped sandwich, like something from a gas station. He squinted at the expiration date. "This is a month old."

"Expiration dates are suggestions, not the law," Ramirez said. "I should know, right? Eat quick. We're about to have guests."

"Guests?"

"The other camps. They're sending people. I don't know who yet, but they should be here soon." She went to the edge of the deck and cursed quietly. Westlake joined her, chewing on the stale sandwich. There were a dozen bodies on the lake shore, looking like pincushions. Muriel had been busy. But there were more floaters, grasping at the fences and moaning softly.

"More than there were last night," he said, quietly.

"Yeah," Ramirez said. "They're on the road as well. Must be forty or fifty of them. Kahwihta thinks they followed us from town."

"Long way to come."

"Not for them." Ramirez studied him. "You look terrible. Did you sleep?"

"As well as I ever do." Which wasn't well at all, but he didn't see any reason to tell her that. The dreams had started after that night in the Barrens. Bad ones, mostly. Dreams of being surrounded by dead hands, the feeling of teeth in his flesh – of dying, like Tommy. Only not really. He took a bite of sandwich to hide his sudden shiver. "If there's zombies out front, how are these guests of ours getting in?"

"Through the front gate, how else? Come on." She led him back inside and to the front doors. Labrand was waiting for them on the steps. He tipped his hat to Westlake.

"Howdy, Sleeping Beauty," he drawled. "Have a good rest?"

"Good enough," Westlake said. Past the cowboy, he could see the road and the fences. He nearly choked on his sandwich. There were zombies all over the fences. Anyone who could, had a piece of rebar, a stick, or, in one case, a sharpened oar, and was thrusting them through the chain link at the walkers. It wasn't as easy as it looked, and more than one person lost their implement, either to a walker's awkward collapse, or because it had been yanked out of their hands.

The people at the fences were a motley lot – truckers, campers, a few yuppie types in puffy coats and begrimed slacks. Older kids carried extra spears and handed them out to anyone who needed them. A narrow, stoop-shouldered man with a battered straw boater on his head scuttled along the line, taking pictures with a disposable camera.

The walkers were equally distinct, now that he wasn't being swarmed. Among the broken wrecks were nurses' uniforms, suits and ties, and far too much denim. No class divisions on either side. Not anymore. Westlake took another bite of his sandwich. "I passed by maybe half a dozen groups this size on my way up I-87."

Ramirez didn't look at him. "Yeah? What about it?"

"Just making conversation."

"Do me a favor and don't. How are the fences holding up?" This last was directed at Labrand.

Labrand glanced towards the front gate. "Be better in a minute, when Hahm gets the jumper cables on." The air shivered with a sudden fat crackle and the accompanying wasp-hum of electricity. Labrand pushed his hat back with an appreciative whistle. "There we go now. That's what I'm talking about."

All along the fence line, walkers were jittering and thrashing. Oily smoke rose from those who'd pressed themselves to the fence. A moment later, the hum faded, leaving only the hiss-pop of burning meat. Walkers slumped or fell, still twitching – not all of them by any means, but a good portion. "What the hell was that?" Westlake demanded.

"Electric fence," Labrand said. "Sort of. Can't keep it on more than a few seconds or it'll blow out the generator, but it does the trick when they crowd us like that." He took off his hat and flapped it as the smell of cooked zombie rolled over them. "It smells awful, though."

"I'll take the smell over being eaten any day," Ramirez said. "Right. I'm going to the gates. Labrand, grab some of the others and start pulling the trucks around behind the lodge, just in case. I want to be able to get everyone out quick if we have to."

Labrand nodded and trotted off.

"I'm surprised the trick with the fence worked," Westlake said, holding his sleeve over his nose as the wind turned, carrying the stink of burning meat with it.

"Sometimes it doesn't," Frieda said, walking up from behind them. "Sometimes it just sets them on fire, which is a whole different set of problems." Her arms wrapped around her chest as she surveyed the fence. "More of them every day."

"I did warn you," a new voice interjected. Westlake turned to see a woman in a gray-green uniform sitting on the porch nearby, watching the fence. She was lean and sharp featured, her hair shaggy and short, as if she'd cut it without the aid of scissors. As Westlake watched, she drew a hunting knife from a sheath on her belt and flung it down, where it stuck point first in the dirt. She reached down, pulled it free, and threw it again.

"Sayers," Ramirez said. Westlake detected an under-current of hostility in her voice.

"Ramirez," Sayers replied, without looking at them. There

was even more hostility there, if that was possible. "I told you this would happen. Letting all these people stay here is just going to get them, and you, killed."

"I don't imagine you'll be too broken up about that."

Sayers smiled. "At least it'll be quiet afterwards."

Westlake glanced at Frieda. "She got here before dawn," she murmured. "Still not sure how she got past the fences." She studied the other woman with a cool eye. Westlake leaned towards her.

"Something I should know?" he whispered.

"Depends on how much you like gossip."

Westlake smiled ingratiatingly. "People in my profession practically live off it."

"Sayers used to live here, before we arrived. To say she was not happy about the sudden appearance of other survivors would be an understatement."

"Not community-minded, then?"

"Not so as you would notice. She got pissed off with all of us breathing her air and headed for the tall timber. Took a chunk of supplies with her. She doesn't like Ramirez much. Before you ask, the feeling is mutual."

"So why's she here?"

"Because Ptolemy is coming."

Westlake frowned. "Ptolemy?"

"From the camp near North Elba. They used to have a thing, I think. Before the apocalypse."

"And now?"

"They do not. She blames Ramirez."

"She got reason to?" Westlake asked.

Frieda shrugged. "You'd have to ask her. Or Ramirez."

Westlake glanced at Ramirez, and took in the anger in her eyes, the set of her mouth. "I think I'll pass," he said.

Ramirez turned on him. "What are the two of you saying?"

"Nothing. What are we going to do about the zombies?"

Sayers sat up suddenly. "Listen," she said.

Westlake frowned. A moment later, he heard it – an engine mixed with a high-pitched jingle. The engine's growl grew loud, overshadowing the monotonous groan of the dead. The vehicle burst into view, racing down the main road. It was covered in so much wood, sheet metal, and barbed wire that he couldn't tell either make or model, though he thought it might once have been an ice-cream truck.

It hit the rearmost zombies with a wet thump, and he saw bodies flip and fly as the truck barreled deeper into the horde clustered near the gates. As it did so, the edges of the horde turned away from the lodge and started to fold in as the armored truck forced its way forward. "They're just going to get swamped," Westlake said, watching in disbelief.

Frieda laughed. "You're going to want to watch this, man – it's going to be good."

"Right, time to get to work," Ramirez said. She started towards the gates at a jog. Westlake followed, wondering what she was planning. Ramirez snatched up a piece of rebar from the rack as she approached the gate. "OK, folks," she shouted. "We all know how this goes. Give them a minute to get ready, then we go in and mop up. No lollygagging!"

She punctuated this last statement by pointing her rebar at a young woman wearing a black hoodie and a hockey mask. "Yeah, yeah," Olivia said, pulling the mask down. She hefted a trident made from rebar and gave it a jaunty spin. "Let's do this."

Westlake watched as Ramirez signaled the survivors on gate duty – a stocky man in a prison jumpsuit, and a woman dressed like a model for an outdoor magazine – to be ready to open the gate. On the other side, the ice cream truck had slewed sideways before coming to a halt, its engine growling and the music blaring shrilly.

Westlake grabbed her arm. "You're going to open the gates?"

Ramirez turned, grabbed a length of rebar, and shoved it into his hands. "How else are they supposed to get in?"

"That's crazy!"

"Feel free to stay behind." Ramirez gestured. "Get ready!"

Abruptly, the music ceased. As the walkers reeled in confusion, the driver's side door of the truck burst open, clocking a zombie in the skull. A man swung out and dropped lightly to the ground. He was big and dressed in jeans and a black western shirt with white and red floral designs – and a mask, as well. A black and white wrestling mask, resembling a stylized skull. He paused for a moment, posing for a crowd that existed only in his mind.

"Who is that?" Westlake asked, staring at the apparition.

Ramirez laughed. "El Calavera Santo. The Holy goddamn Skull. I was hoping he'd come." She signaled the gate crew. "Open them up!"

As the gates were hauled open, the newcomer rolled up his sleeves, exposing brawny forearms. Then, with a wordless shout, the masked man bounded towards the closest zombie and knocked its rotten head clean off its shoulders with one meaty fist. Another blow lifted a second zombie off its feet and sent it crashing to the ground in a broken heap.

Behind Westlake, Olivia and some of the others started cheering. Calavera paused, but only for an instant. He plowed into the walkers, moving more gracefully than a man his size ought to. He caught a walker and tossed it up, then caught it by the legs as it fell.

Calavera spun lightly, swinging the discombobulated walker by its ankles. He smashed his improvised bludgeon into its fellows with a joyous shout, before letting what was left of the walker splatter against the side of his vehicle.

The walkers were unimpressed by this show of martial improvisation, and closed in. Calavera deftly avoided them and scrambled up onto the top of the truck. He shouted something, keeping the creatures' attentions on him as Ramirez led her people out.

As they stepped out of the gate, Ramirez punched her length of rebar through a walker's skull, twisting it as she wrenched it loose. Westlake followed her example, using his rebar like a club. The walkers were distracted – caught between two hostile forces, or maybe two meals – and uncertain which to go for first. Westlake clubbed a walker to the ground. This one wore what was left of a yellow hi-vis vest and a hard hat. He cracked it in the head, but the hard hat kept him from pulping its skull.

It clutched at his ankle, but Olivia hurried over and drove her trident through the zombie, pinning it down. Westlake nodded in thanks, flicked off its hard hat with the tip of his rebar, then impaled its head.

A hand on his shoulder caused him to whirl, the rebar

coming up. It slapped against Calavera's palm, and he nodded in greeting. He was six nine, if he was an inch. "Hello. I do not believe we've met." His voice was like a tiger's purr, with only the slightest trace of an accent.

"Westlake," Westlake said, staring up at the masked man.

"You may call me Calavera." The big man turned and waved the truck forward, and it started to roll, crunching fallen walkers beneath its wheels. Olivia and the others made way for it, cleaning up any walkers still too close to the fence. The rest of the zombies stumbled in the truck's wake as Ramirez and her people retreated inside. Westlake and Calavera were the last to enter. The gates closed with a rattle, and the padlocks hurriedly snapped shut.

On the other side, the dead began to gather anew.

CHAPTER TEN
The Plan

"Two. Two guys," Westlake muttered, "That's what they sent."

"Two more than we had before," Ramirez said, as she shut the door behind them, wondering how the day had slipped by into evening so quickly. Westlake was clearly disappointed. She wondered what he'd expected. It wasn't like there was an army around here going spare or a set of specialized criminals at his service. "And you've got to admit that Calavera counts for at least three by himself."

"At least," Westlake said, looking over at the masked man. Ramirez followed his gaze. Calavera had gotten a towel somewhere and was cleaning his hands of the gore that stained them. "Where did you find him?"

"He found us. Came wandering into the camp over near North Elba one day, escorting a group of survivors, claiming a saint had told him they needed help."

Westlake glanced at her. "And you – they – bought that?"

"He kills zombies with his bare hands," Ramirez pointed

out. "What are they going to say? 'No thank you, please move along?'"

Westlake frowned. "Got a point, I guess. What about the other one? What's his name – Ptolemy?" He indicated the second of the newcomers. Calvin Ptolemy was a narrow, dark-skinned man of indeterminate age. He stood away from the others, looking ill at ease.

His hair was chopped square and buzzed tight, and a set of cheap black-framed glasses rested on his nose, making his eyes look bigger than they were. He wore secondhand tactical fatigues beneath a heavy barn coat, and carried a variety of weapons, both obvious and otherwise. "He's a quiet guy," Westlake went on. "Hasn't said two words to anyone."

Ramirez snorted. "You don't know the half of it. He had his own podcast, back before all this. Real Art Bell type. He went on these two-hour screeds about secret Masonic conspiracies and nanites in fluoride."

"And someone thought it was a good idea to send him?"

Ramirez had been wondering about that herself. She recalled that Ptolemy didn't like to leave his bunker without good reason. Even then, he did so only for as long as necessary. That he'd volunteered was something of a surprise – or a sign of how bad things were getting. Before she could reply, Ptolemy wandered over.

"Agent Ramirez," he said, nodding politely to Ramirez. He didn't offer to shake hands. He never did. Something about germs. "We thought it best to come together. Safety in numbers." He nudged his glasses back up onto his face as he looked at Westlake. "And you would be Mr Westlake, was it?"

"It was and is," Westlake said. He held out his hand. Ptolemy inclined his head but ignored the outstretched hand. Westlake lowered it awkwardly.

"Dunnigan implied you are the bearer of glad tidings."

"That depends."

"On?"

"How you feel about climbing a mountain."

Ptolemy blinked, and a look of mild surprise crossed his face. "Ah." He paused. "Is that why Elizabeth – Sayers, I mean – is here?"

Ramirez turned. Sayers leaned against the wall near the windows, ignoring everyone as was her wont. "Yeah." She'd been surprised when Sayers had answered the radio. She had been even more surprised when the former park ranger actually showed up.

"A warning would have been appreciated," Ptolemy said, watching the former park ranger with an inscrutable expression. His gaze flicked back to Ramirez. "Area 51."

"What about it?"

"I have come to the conclusion that it is where all this started. We should investigate."

Ramirez blinked, thrown. "And how would we do that?"

"The airport has planes available. I suggest–"

"Maybe after we handle this?" Ramirez said, quickly. Ptolemy peered at her for a moment, as if trying to determine whether she was serious, or merely humoring him. Apparently satisfied that it was the former, he nodded.

"Very well. The airport, Agent Ramirez."

"Afterwards," Ramirez said, with a brief smile. Ptolemy nodded again, turned and, after a moment of hesitation, made his way towards the window and Sayers. Westlake watched him go, a frown on his face.

"He seems… intense."

Ramirez glanced at him. "You're right, he is intense. But also smart. And a good shot. Two things we need."

Westlake grunted, but didn't reply. He and Ramirez joined Frieda and the others. Dunnigan had already broken out the beer. Helpfully, a table had been set up, covered in all the maps they'd been able to scrounge from the visitors' center.

Hahm sat at the table, along with Labrand and Hutch. Kahwihta sat nearby on a stool, scratching Attila's head. Ramirez had spoken with all four of them individually on what they were looking for over the course of the day, and all four had quickly volunteered. They all had something to contribute, or could be counted on to keep their heads. With the addition of Calavera and Ptolemy, that gave them a team of eight. Sayers would make nine, if she agreed.

Ramirez cleared her throat. All eyes turned towards her. "We all know why we're here, I trust?" she said, for the benefit of the others.

"We do, and it's bullshit," Sayers said, bluntly. "Utter bullshit. Places like the one you're describing don't exist."

"I assure you, it does," Westlake jumped in.

Sayers glanced at him with obvious suspicion. "And who are you, exactly? I've never seen you before."

"I'm the guy who's telling you that this place exists."

"And it's here? You're certain?" Sayers shook her head. "Can't be."

"It is. Mount Marcy, to be exact."

"Impossible." Sayers glared at him. "There's nothing there. I know these mountains."

"I'm sure you do, but hear me out," Westlake said. He went to the table and paged through an old guidebook for the area. "See, here's the issue – the guidebook says it should take about eleven hours to walk the trail to the southwest slope from here. But the guidebook assumes there's an infrastructure in place to keep said trails clear." Westlake looked back at her. "Have you still been keeping the brush cut, this whole time?"

Sayers frowned. "I don't use the trails."

Westlake nodded. "Which means everything is likely to be overgrown, washed out or otherwise untraversable." He smiled. "Hey, at least it's not snowing, right?"

Ramirez waved him to silence and hoped Sayers understood what Westlake was driving at. "What he's saying is that we need a guide, and that's you." She paused, coming to terms with attempting to make peace. "I know we've had our issues, but you could help a whole lot of people here, Sayers. We need this place. We need it bad. The lodge won't last another month. Not at this rate. You might not have realized it, hiding out up in the tall timber, but things are getting bad. Lots more walkers, a lot less to salvage. This place could be the answer to our prayers."

"I'm not hiding," Sayers growled. She matched Ramirez' glare with one of her own. "I'm just not a fan of making things easy for the zombies."

"Then why are you here?"

Sayers' eyes flicked towards Ptolemy. It was so quick that Ramirez almost missed it. "You called, I came. You want me to go, I'll go." But she didn't sound as if she meant it. She took a deep breath and stepped back. "For the sake of argument, what's your plan?"

"Simple," Ramirez said. "I take a crew up into the mountains, find this place and check it out. Ensure that its safe for us. Then we can make plans from there."

"What sort of crew?" Sayers asked.

"Volunteers." Ramirez looked around the room. "The people in this room are the only ones who know about this, and I'd like to keep it that way until we know what's what, so–"

"There are zombies in the mountains," Sayers interrupted. "Lots of them. Any group going into the mountains runs the risk of encountering significant opposition. Worse, they might draw zombies down on the lodge, and the other camps as well." She looked around. "I've been warning you all about this for months. The minute you set up shop here, you might as well have started ringing a dinner bell."

"There was nowhere else to go," Frieda said.

"You could have gone anywhere else," Sayers said, rounding on the other woman. "You could still go. Dunnigan's rig alone–"

Dunnigan spoke up. "My rig's got enough fuel to get as far as Plattsburgh, but I can only carry twenty, maybe thirty people. Less if I got to haul supplies."

Ramirez jumped in. "Anywhere we go – supposing we can move everyone – is likely to be swarming with zombies and picked clean to boot. No, we need a place to make a stand. To plant crops, to build walls, to live."

Frieda looked at Westlake. "And how about it, Westlake? Is it that sort of place?" Her eyes narrowed. "What exactly are you expecting to find up there?"

"A glorified hotel. Sal would have brought a few dozen guys with him, maybe some friends. Maybe family. There'll be employees too. Cooks, custodians, that sort of thing."

"A few dozen guys, he says," Frieda said. She looked at Ramirez. "That sounds like you need more than a few volunteers. How were you planning to get in?"

Westlake paused. "It depends on how the place is set up. I was going to scout it out first, get the lay of the land. See what the viable points of entry were."

"If there were any, you mean," Frieda said.

"There are always points of entry. You just have to identify them. The real problem is how to get close to the place without being spotted."

"You are assuming someone is on the other end of any security system that might be active," Ptolemy said.

Westlake nodded. "A good rule of thumb is to assume that someone is always watching."

"Of course, there's no guarantee that anyone is even alive up there," Ramirez said. "Otherwise, I think we'd have seen some sign of them by now."

"The other reason you might not have seen any sign of them is because the place doesn't exist," Sayers interjected.

"But if it does… if the Villa is real, and I think that it is, then it'll be the answer to our problems. We just need to find it." Ramirez looked at Sayers. "Which is where you come in."

"And what if I say no?"

"Then we continue without you," Ptolemy said. Ramirez

thought she saw Sayers flinch, though Ptolemy's voice had been nothing but mild.

Sayers ran her hand through her shaggy hair and looked around. "You're all agreed on this?" she asked, in evident resignation.

Calavera slapped his big hands down on the table. "Indeed! This is a noble quest, and I would not miss it for the world."

Sayers looked at Ptolemy. "Calvin…" she began.

Ptolemy wouldn't meet her eyes. "If there is a chance, we must take it," he said, simply. Sayers sighed and turned to Ramirez.

"Fine. Where am I taking you?"

"We told you," Westlake said. "Mount Marcy."

Sayers rolled her eyes. "Yes, but Mount Marcy is one of the highest peaks in the Adirondacks, and heavily forested to boot. I need a bit more to go on." She paused. "You said the southwest slope." She pushed Westlake aside and leaned over the maps on the table. "The problem with most maps is that they're based on older cartographic records. So if something is removed, due to lack of importance or – well…"

"Because someone didn't want it on the map," Westlake supplied. "It's not even on any satellite imagery and that takes lots of money or influence or both."

"But some things cannot be entirely hidden, no matter how many bribes you pay. It would need to be a sizeable area for the type of facility you are talking about." Ptolemy bent over the map as well, running his finger along the grid lines. "Southwest slope, you said?"

Westlake nodded. "Yeah, near an old iron mine."

Ptolemy looked at Sayers. "Ring any bells?"

Labrand coughed politely. "Lake Cutter," he said. Ramirez and the others looked at him. He leaned back in his chair. "Quarry lake on the southwestern slope. Nothing else there but trees, as far as I know."

Ramirez looked at Sayers. "What about it?"

Sayers licked her lips. "Maybe."

Something in her voice made Ramirez pause. She studied the other woman, but Sayers' face gave nothing away. Maybe it was just Sayers' obvious reluctance she was hearing. She resolved to talk to the other woman about it at the first convenient opportunity. She clapped her hands together, drawing the eyes of the others. "The important thing is, can we get there from here?"

Sayers shrugged. "We can take the Van Hoevenberg Trail, towards the peak. It used to be that you could hike the trail in a few hours, but given how many zombies are wandering around up there, we should at least double that time." She hesitated. "Of course, there are worse things than walkers in these mountains."

"Like what?" Westlake asked.

"Bears for one. Coyotes. Cougars. All of which have gotten very used to eating human beings in the last few months, thanks to the walkers. Plus, trail collapses – flooding… There are a hundred ways to die up here, if you're not prepared."

"Which is why we need you," Ptolemy said, softly. He reached out and took Sayers' hand. She looked at it for a moment, and then pulled away.

"Yeah. So you said." Sayers stepped back from the table. "We'll leave at first light."

"So you'll do it?" Ramirez asked, surprised despite herself.

Sayers didn't look at her. "I'll do it." She took a deep breath. "I need some air." She headed for the door.

Westlake sat down. "Well, glad that's settled."

"Yeah. Me too." Ramirez looked down at the map. There was no telling what they'd find up there. Maybe salvation.

Maybe something else.

CHAPTER ELEVEN
Blindside

Calvin Ptolemy did not sleep, in the conventional sense. Instead, he relied on a set number of calculated micro-sleeps to refresh his mind and body. Anywhere from five to fifteen minutes, at staggered intervals throughout the day. He had trained himself to conduct a number of repetitive tasks while engaged in these micro-sleeps, including disassembling and cleaning weapons.

Unfortunately, he found it difficult to enter the necessary state of relaxation in an unfamiliar place.

The lodge was quiet. As he walked out onto the deck, he heard nothing save the chirp of insects and the quiet murmur of those on guard duty. Sayers was sitting on the deck rail, her legs kicking idly as she stared out over the water. She was engaged in demolishing a can of beans that she'd gotten from somewhere.

He stood behind her, saying nothing. He started to speak several times, but the words wouldn't come. His hands clenched. Then he reached into the pocket of his coat and pulled out a stick of jerky. He held it out to her.

She looked at it. "Yours?"

"Latest batch, yes."

She took it and sniffed it. "Smells better than the last." She took a bite. "Tastes better, too." She gave him a smile, and he felt a familiar flutter in his chest. "Why are you here, Calvin?"

"Ramirez and Westlake explained…" Ptolemy began. Sayers shook her head and offered him the can of beans.

"I didn't ask why they're here. I asked why you're here."

Ptolemy took the beans, automatically scanning the expiration date stamped on the bottom of the can. Sayers raised an eyebrow. "I'm not trying to poison you."

"Just making sure."

"The expiration date is only a suggestion."

"Often a good one," Ptolemy said. He took a bite of the beans to be polite and handed the can back. Sayers took it and continued eating.

"You haven't answered my question," she said, mouth full.

"Fitness is only another name for survival," he quoted. "Darwinism: that survivors survive. Charles Fort." He adjusted his glasses. "Things are less than optimal. Resources are dwindling. Something must change." He studied the water below, and the forms bobbing in the shallows. The floaters clutched at the fence-line like drowning men, their mouths moving noiselessly. "We are running out of time. We are losing the war before we even have a chance to fight back."

Sayers snorted. "Still thinking of it as a war?"

"What would you call it?"

"The end of the world." She finished the can and set it down beside her. "We're done, Calvin. Why get stressed about something you can't change?"

"Who says it cannot be changed?" He paused and looked at her. "We have had this conversation before, I think."

"We have."

"Right before you left," he said, his tone accusing. Sayers tilted her head back and looked up at the roof.

"I had to get out of there, Calvin. I needed space."

"So you went to hide in the forest."

"Not well enough."

"You did not have to answer the radio." He paused. "Why did you?"

She was silent for a moment. Then, "I wanted to see you again."

"You could not have known I would be here."

"If anything could drag you out of your bunker, it would be something like this," she said, smiling thinly. "You don't believe there's really a mafia hideout in the mountains, do you?"

Ptolemy scratched his chin. "No. I think this Westlake is a former government agent, and we are heading to a secret Federal installation. Or maybe not. The fate of all explanation is to close one door only to have another fly wide open."

"Fort, again?"

Ptolemy nodded. "There is truly a quote for every occasion."

Sayers stared at him. "I've missed you," she said.

Ptolemy blinked. "I have missed you as well. Is that why you agreed to help?"

She turned back to the water. "Don't let it go to your head."

"Whatever the reason, I am glad you are back. I am glad you are helping us."

"I'm not doing it for you, Calvin, as hard as that might be for you to believe." She turned, slid off the deck railing to stand, and looked up at the lodge. "This is going to be a waste of resources these people don't have. You'd be better off moving into one of the ski resorts over near Lake Placid."

"Those places are no safer than here."

"Then go away. Head towards Lake Champlain, or better yet the Canadian border." She looked at him. "They'd listen to you, Calvin. Maybe not Ramirez, but the others would."

"If this place is real, is it not worth seeing if it could be made viable? A true redoubt, where some seed of humanity might yet find soil fit to grow?" He made to reach for her but stopped himself. "I believe the risk is worth the reward."

"And you trust this Westlake?"

"No. But I trust Ramirez."

"Even though she's a government agent?"

"So were you, once upon a time," he said.

"I was a government employee, Calvin. There's a difference." She glared at him. "You shouldn't put so much faith in Ramirez. She's always been trouble."

"Why? Because she wishes to help people?"

"No. Because she talks other, more impressionable people into acting against their best interests. Like you."

Ptolemy paused. It was an old argument. The same

argument that had driven them first together and then apart in the months after the apocalypse. Sayers had seen the rising of the dead as an opportunity to abandon a world that had never treated her well. Ptolemy had seen it as a catastrophe – a natural disaster of epic proportions, but in the end no different than a flood or a wildfire. Sayers had argued that they were under no obligation to help anyone; Ptolemy had known better.

Now, more than ever, people needed to stick together. Disagreements needed to be put aside in the face of a common enemy. An enemy that threatened to overwhelm them all, regardless of how cleverly they might hide themselves away. Ramirez understood that. That was why he'd volunteered to come. If she said there was hope, then there was hope.

But he said none of that. Sayers understood his position, and he understood hers. There was nothing more to be said on the matter. They stood awkwardly in silence for a time. Then, when he could no longer stand it, Ptolemy asked, "What were you doing up there? After you left, I mean."

"Nothing."

"Nothing?" He raised an eyebrow.

Sayers sighed. "I wanted to enjoy myself, Calvin. To read books and grow beans and not have to worry about anything."

"Unfortunately, the world is never that simple, Elizabeth." He reached for her hand, but she avoided his touch. He frowned, puzzled, but continued. "Even so, I respected your decision. I did not agree with it. But I respected it."

"You mean you were too busy to come after me." She

looked him dead in the eye. "The camp came first. I knew that, even before I left."

"Sustainable isolationism is a fantasy concocted by fringe libertarians and religious fanatics. Humans are social animals and work best in groups." He took off his glasses and began to clean them. "I calculated the odds and made my decision."

"So did I." Sayers paused. "Germ warfare."

"What?"

"Germ warfare. That's what caused all this."

Ptolemy laughed.

Sayers frowned. "You give me a better explanation," she demanded.

"A conspiracy within the government, obviously."

Sayers laughed. "It's always the government with you."

"Not the government. A conspiracy within the government."

"What's the difference?"

"The more moving parts a conspiracy requires, the less likely it is to be effective." Ptolemy adjusted his glasses. "A conspiracy by the government would necessitate the participation of hundreds of individuals, any one of whom might give the game away."

Sayers shook her head. "Got it. No conspiracies."

"I didn't say that." He shook his head, warming to his topic now. "Many conspiracy theorists prefer the idea of a large conspiracy because it lends a sheen of organization to an otherwise chaotic world. I, however, am more inclined to a less tidy theory – that of the gambit pileup. Not one conspiracy or even a dozen, but hundreds – all competing for resources. And when they come into conflict – tragedy is the inevitable result."

"Like the dead rising, you mean?"

"A definite possibility. Regardless, I do not think this was anyone's intention. *Cui bono* – who benefits? No one. Therefore, it was a mistake, or maybe even random chance." He frowned. "Of course, that does not preclude a conspiracy forming to take advantage of the current state of affairs..."

Sayers kissed him. Ptolemy stood there frozen for a moment, images of germs swarming across his mind's eye. Then he relaxed. Sayers had always been the only one he didn't mind touching – or being touched by.

They stood pressed against one another for long moments. Then she broke the kiss and Ptolemy felt something press against his abdomen. He looked down and saw the thin barrel of a Mauser C96. His eyes widened slightly. "Is that your father's gun?"

"It is."

"I thought it was lost." Her father had collected antique weapons, mostly from the world wars. The Mauser had been one of his favorites. Sayers had once confided that her father's collection could have outfitted an army. They'd made plans a long time ago, to collect it from his home near Lake Champlain and put it to use. But when they'd arrived, they'd found it gone – or so she'd claimed.

"I know."

"You lied."

"I did," she said, somewhat sadly.

He began to step back, but she stopped him with a look. "Don't move."

"What are you doing?" he whispered.

"Don't say anything," Sayers murmured into his ear. "I will shoot you, Calvin. I don't want to, but I will. I want you to listen to me. We are going to leave. Now. Tonight. You and me. We're going to go back to my cabin, collect supplies, and vanish."

"Vanish?"

"Yes. There are places we can go. Places to hide."

Ptolemy stiffened. "Why?"

Sayers stared at him. "What do you mean why?" she asked, softly. "You know why."

Ptolemy read something in her gaze. Understanding cascaded over him. "You already knew."

Sayers hesitated. "Yes."

"Why did you never say anything?"

"Because you don't want to find that place, Calvin. Trust me."

"Strange words from a woman who has a gun pressed to my abdomen."

Sayers shook her head slightly. "God, I've missed you." She looked into his eyes. "I'll explain everything, I promise. Now, let's take this slow. Me and you. Turn around."

Ptolemy turned, searching for any avenue of escape. None presented itself. They started towards the steps that led down to the docks. But as they reached them, the door to the lodge opened and Hahm stepped out. "Hey, Ptolemy, there you are. I wanted to ask..." The woman's voice trailed off, and her eyes grew wide. Ptolemy realized that she'd noticed the gun in Sayers' hand. She opened her mouth.

Sayers gripped Ptolemy tight – and fired. Hahm fell with

a cry. Ptolemy turned, trying to tackle Sayers, but she deftly avoided his lunge. As he tried to recover, she cracked him on the side of the head with her pistol. He slumped against the rail, clutching his ringing head. Through pain-addled eyes he saw Sayers race down the steps. He heard shouts as the sentries hurried over. "Stop her," he croaked, waving a hand towards the steps as he staggered towards Hahm. The woman was alive, but badly hurt.

"She shot me," Hahm panted in disbelief, her hands pressed to the wound in her side. "Why did she shoot me?"

"I do not… I don't know," Ptolemy said, apologetically. He looked back towards the steps, and heard more shouting – no, cries of alarm. He turned his attentions back to Hahm. "I need help!" he called out. "Someone! Anyone!"

Ramirez burst out onto the deck. "What's – *shit*." She dropped to her knees beside the injured woman. "What the hell happened, Ptolemy?"

"Elizabeth… Sayers, she…" He trailed off, shaking his head, unable to complete the thought. Why had she done this? What had she meant?

Ramirez grabbed him, startling him. "Where did she go, Calvin? Where is she?"

Before he could reply, he heard the Mauser bark again, somewhere below them, and a sound like a chain snapping.

Then the wet slap of dead flesh against the wood of the dock.

CHAPTER TWELVE
Breach

Westlake couldn't sleep. He'd never been able to, before a job. So instead, he contented himself with making a list and checking it twice, with the help of Kahwihta after the meeting. The young woman didn't seem to need rest either. Westlake didn't mind. There were things they needed, and a second pair of hands was always useful.

"So, you were planning to take on an army by yourself, huh?" Kahwihta asked. They were in a room on the second floor of the lodge. Westlake thought it resembled the stock room of a sporting goods store.

"Something like that." He picked up a sleeping bag. "Some of this stuff still has price tags on it."

"We hit every type of store in the area as soon as we had the fences up," Kahwihta said, as she opened a box containing MREs. Attila snuffled at them, causing the foil to crinkle loudly. "Even managed to clean out the local National Guard armory, not that there was much there by then."

"People went for the guns first," Westlake said. "Much good it did them."

"Never cared for them myself," Kahwihta said. She patted her cattle-prod, laying atop a nearby box. "More comfortable with this."

Westlake glanced down at his sidearm. Ramirez had finally given him his Glock back, and even an extra magazine she'd salvaged from somewhere. It wasn't much, but it was something. And he had his knife, of course. "There are plenty of guns at the Villa. I'm more worried about getting there. What we need are essentials – backpacks, food, water, iodine tablets, sleeping bags, tents. That sort of thing."

"All of that's in here, somewhere." Kahwihta gestured around the room.

"So, we start getting it together. More we do tonight, less we have to do tomorrow. We'll put together a go-bag for everyone."

Kahwihta looked at him. "You sound like you've done this before."

"Any robbery worth the name involves logistics," he said. "That was always my end of it. We needed guns, I got the guns. We needed masks, or accelerant or explosives – I got it, or I talked to people who could get it for me." He hefted a camouflaged MOLLE-style backpack and set it aside. "See if you can find a few more of those."

"So what's this place like – really, I mean?" she asked, as she began to rummage through another box. "Hutch made it sound like a resort spa for mafia bosses."

"Sort of. And I don't know, not really. I only know what I've heard."

"So, what have you heard?"

He retrieved a case of bottled water and slit it open with his knife. He set aside eight bottles as he spoke. "Lots of things. I've heard it's the unofficial nerve center of the Bonaro operations on the East Coast – a criminal Pentagon, if you will."

"That doesn't sound good."

Westlake smiled. "I've also heard some stories about server farms and automated emails – cryptocurrency silk road bullshit."

"Boring," Kahwihta murmured, setting aside a pile of MREs.

Westlake snorted. "OK. How about a tiger? How's that grab you?"

"A tiger?"

Westlake nodded. "Guard tiger."

"No way."

"Hand to God," Westlake said, holding up his hand. "Though I don't put much stock in that one myself. Though I did know a guy who had one of those."

Kahwihta looked at him. "What, really?"

"He kept it in his penthouse. I ran into it when I was relieving him of some valuable paperwork. Damn thing nearly eviscerated me."

"I see," Kahwihta said, clearly bemused. "You have led an interesting life."

"I suppose I have at that." Westlake paused. "We all have, at this point."

"True." Kahwihta found another backpack and set it beside the first. "Do you really think this Bonaro guy is up there?"

"Maybe."

"And if he is?"

Westlake paused. "I don't know," he said. It might even have been the truth. "Though if they are up there, I'm beginning to get curious as to why they haven't made their presence known. Sal isn't the sort to hide his light under a bushel, if you get me."

"Maybe one or more of them was infected," Kahwihta said, idly. "Infection rates vary depending on the severity of the injury. All it would take is one bite and boom. Exponential spread, unless they acted quickly."

Westlake stared at her. She cleared her throat. "I've been paying attention. Bites are bad news, and the infection is almost always fatal. Some people can shake it off, but others can't. Like poor Morris."

Westlake frowned. "Morris?"

Kahwihta nodded. "The original owner of that van you came to the lodge in. He got bit on a supply run about three weeks after the dead rose. Two days later, he was down with an infection. On day three, he died." She paused. "A few hours later, he got back up." She reached down and stroked Attila. "If Attila here hadn't warned us, things might have gone very bad, very quickly."

Westlake eyed the animal. The dog thumped his tail placidly. "I see why you keep him around."

"I try to look on the bright side of things." She scratched Attila's head. "For instance, I've always wanted a dog. Now I've got one."

"Optimist, huh?"

"I guess so. What about you?"

Westlake didn't meet her gaze. "Realist."

Kahwihta stared at him for several moments. Long enough to make him uneasy. He met her gaze. "What?" he asked, sounding defensive.

"Just thinking that a realist wouldn't have come up here. A realist sure as heck wouldn't be planning to do something like this." She held up a backpack for emphasis. She tossed it to him, and he caught it.

"No?" he said, setting the backpack down carefully. "So what am I, then?"

"Tricky."

Westlake frowned. "What's that supposed to mean?"

"It means you're up to something." Kahwihta laughed at the expression on his face. "Don't worry. I won't tell."

"Nothing to tell," Westlake protested.

Kahwihta snorted. "Right. Lucky for you, I know tricksters teach lessons, even when they don't mean to. Especially when they don't mean to." She looked at him. "They show us how to live, and how not to live."

"Is that what you think I am? A trickster?"

Kahwihta shrugged and then peered at him. "What do you believe in?"

Westlake bared his teeth. It wasn't quite a smile. "In myself."

Her reply was interrupted by the door being thrown open. Labrand leaned in, looking even more disheveled than usual, his eyes wide. "We got trouble!"

Westlake looked at Kahwihta in alarm, and then they both hurried out of the room after Labrand. They found Ramirez, Dunnigan, Saoirse, Frieda, and Ptolemy out on the balcony that overlooked the front of the lodge. There was smoke coming from somewhere, and Westlake could hear the groan of a generator in its death throes. "The fence is down," Dunnigan said, pointing towards the smoke. "Someone put a bullet in it."

"Not someone," Ramirez said, grimly. "Sayers."

Westlake looked at her. "What the hell happened?"

"That's what I'm trying to figure out." She glanced at Ptolemy. Westlake followed her gaze. The other man stood silently near the door, his shirt stained with blood.

"Who…?" Westlake began.

"Hahm," Ramirez said. "Sayers shot her. She's still breathing. Barely."

"Hahm ain't the problem – that is!" Saoirse said. She pointed towards the front of the camp, where fences of chain-link and concrete barricades held the dead at bay. Spotlights played across their ranks, and Westlake saw a brute slowly plowing through its smaller compatriots. It was dressed in rags of tight purple spandex and the remnants of a yellow bodysuit. It was bigger than the one he'd seen in town and covered in enough blubber to soak up small arms fire. He could barely make out its features, hidden as they were beneath loose folds of swollen flesh – not that he particularly wanted to know what it looked like.

"That," he said, somewhat in awe, "is a very big zombie."

It hit the fence like a wrecking ball, uprooting the posts and tearing through the chain-link like it was tissue paper. Westlake watched in dull horror as the walkers poured through the gap with eager, hungry groans.

Olivia and the others on fence duty met them head on.

The young woman slid beneath a zombie's awkward grasp and punched her trident through its skull and throat. As the walker fell, she twisted her trident and wrenched its head off. She flicked her wrists, sending the decapitated cranium into the skull of another walker, staggering it long enough for one of her companions to finish it off. The brute staggered towards them, dragging a chunk of broken fencing in its wake.

Rather than risk getting near the hulking zombie, Olivia turned and whistled, signaling for the others to fall back. They weren't the only ones. Everyone who could get away was hurrying towards the lodge – and the zombies were following. They caught those who were too slow, or just inobservant.

Westlake saw a man stumble and turn, only to be tackled into a pile of crates by a runner. Nearby, a woman was backed against a car by several walkers, the length of rebar she held doing little to keep them at bay. There was no one near enough to help her, and as he watched, the dead fell on her with ravenous savagery. He could hear children crying, and someone screaming, a high, wild wail that spiraled up into inaudibility.

He knew what would happen. They'd be trapped, no way out, surrounded by zombies on all sides. "We have to get out of here," he said, hoarsely. His hand fell to his pistol. It was useless, though. There were more zombies than he had bullets.

"I'm not going anywhere," Ramirez said.

Dunnigan caught hold of Ramirez' jacket and spun her around to face him. "He's right. You need to go, *now!*"

"What about the camp?"

"Ain't going to be no camp come the morning," Saoirse said. "Too many of them coming in now from all sides. Sayers also busted open the gates on the docks." She stared daggers at Ptolemy. "Your girlfriend screwed us but good, Calvin."

Ptolemy shook his head. He looked like he'd been poleaxed. "I don't... She... I don't understand..." he murmured, half to himself. Westlake saw a look in the other man's eyes he didn't like, a sort of wounded confusion. He was no good to anyone right now.

Ramirez stepped between Ptolemy and Saoirse. "It doesn't matter. We'll deal with her later. For now, we need to get everyone inside."

"You need to go," Dunnigan said again. "Take what you can carry and get out of here. Find this Villa of yours. We're going to need it."

"What are you going to do?"

Dunnigan grimaced. "The only thing we can do. Get as many out as we can, head for North Elba and hope the bastards don't follow. We can always come back later to get what we need. If there is a later."

There was a crash from somewhere below – a window. Shouts and shots. The zombies were at the door. Westlake's hands clenched into fists. He didn't like the thought of being trapped in here. Dunnigan grabbed one of his hatchets and brandished it. "Time's a-wasting, folks," he said, heading for the door.

"Wait for me, Dunny," Saoirse called, wheeling herself after him. Frieda made to follow, but paused. She looked at Ramirez. Something passed between them; Westlake wasn't sure what. It was only when they kissed that it was confirmed.

It was a gentle thing, soft and passionate. Frieda caught Ramirez' face in her hands. "Be careful, Estela. I want you back in one piece."

Ramirez clutched the other woman's wrists and pulled Frieda's hands to her heart. "That goes double for you. And keep an eye on things for me. I'll be back."

Frieda nodded and stepped back. Their fingers lingered, touching, but only for an instant. Then Frieda was gone, and Ramirez' mask was back in place. She looked at Westlake. "You have something to say?"

"Not me."

"Good." She looked at Kahwihta, Labrand, and Ptolemy. "We need to get together whatever gear we can scrounge, and quick."

"Already done," Westlake said. Ramirez glanced at him, and he thought there was something like gratitude in her eyes.

"Then let's grab what we can carry and go." She paused and snapped her fingers in front of Ptolemy's eyes. He hadn't moved in all the time they'd been talking. "Calvin, focus up. I need you. We need you."

Ptolemy snapped to attention. "I apologize," he said, haltingly. "I am good."

"Good. Take point. We're going to grab our gear and head for the docks."

Westlake stared at her. "What? Saoirse just said–"

"It's the only way out of here. Unless you want to try and

wade through that mess out front. Which I most certainly do not."

"So we're going to swim instead?"

"Of course not." Ramirez drew her pistol. "We're going to sail."

CHAPTER THIRTEEN
Breakout

"Looks like tourist season is in full swing, boss," Hutch shouted, as Ramirez led the others out onto the deck. The former biker had been firing his Stoner over the rail when they arrived, alongside Muriel and the others on deck duty. "We got Hahm inside just in time." He lowered the smoking weapon and caught the backpack that Ramirez tossed to him. "We leaving?" he said, uncertainly.

"We are leaving," Ramirez said, hoping she was making the right decision. "How's it look?"

"Lots of floaters. Not as many as out front." Hutch turned to the others on the deck. "Muriel, do me a favor and pop a flare."

The old woman set her bow aside and lifted an orange flare gun. She let one pop off into the sky over the lake. The light of the flare turned the shore red. As it flickered and shone, Attila began to bark frantically.

Ramirez could see shapes wading – or crawling, in some

cases – onto the docks and pushing through the open gate to stumble towards the courtyard or beneath the deck. Others were pressed against the sagging chain-link, prying it loose from its posts through sheer, insistent weight. "Maybe more than I thought," Hutch said, as the number of floaters was revealed. "What's the plan?"

"Hutch, with us," Ramirez said. "Everyone else – inside, bar the door. Then head towards the evacuation point."

"Where we going?" Hutch asked, shrugging into his backpack.

"Boating, apparently," Westlake said. "Whatever that means."

Hutch grinned. "Under the deck. You'll see." His grin faded. "Of course, there'll be a bunch of them waiting for us down there."

"Which is why you and Calavera are going to clear us a path." She glanced at the masked man, who nodded brusquely. He'd said little since she'd woken him, but he was fairly vibrating with restrained energy.

"A pleasure," Calavera said.

"Took the words out of my mouth," Hutch said.

"And try not to draw any more attention than you have to," Ramirez added. "Labrand, Ptolemy – cover them. And conserve ammunition. What we're carrying is all we have." She paused and looked at Ptolemy. He was clutching the Benelli M4 semi-automatic shotgun he'd brought with him like a drowning man holding onto a life preserver, his gaze absent. "Ptolemy – you still good?"

He jerked, nodded. "Yes. Yes, I… Yes." He raised the shotgun and went to the rail. Labrand lifted the CDX camo-pattern hunting rifle he'd confiscated from the supply room and made to join him. Ramirez caught his arm.

"Watch him," she said, under her breath. Labrand nodded.

Calavera and Hutch had already reached the bottom of the steps. Floaters lurched towards them. Calavera caught the first with a big kick, knocking the dead man back against the fencing. As the zombie rocked back upright, Calavera punched it in its soggy features – knocking its skull clean out of the sloughing sack of skin that was its head.

As the decapitated zombie collapsed, Hutch uncoiled his whip and gave it a snap. A bullwhip was a nasty thing. It could split muscle from bone, if you knew what you were doing. Someone, probably Kahwihta, had told Ramirez that the Romans had used them as weapons. And some Inuit hunters used them to kill caribou.

Hutch cracked the whip and tore a rotting head from frayed neck. Another crack took the legs out from under a floater. A third sent two of them stumbling back into the water in a tangle. Hutch let the whip play out in a wide arc, splitting flesh and tearing loose meat from bone. The sting of the whip wouldn't necessarily put a zombie down for good, but it would make them less of a threat.

Those the whip missed had to deal with Calavera. He'd snatched up a broken oar from the pile of scrap wood near the bottom of the steps and almost casually thrust it through a floater's chest. He lifted the zombie with no apparent effort and swung it around, smashing another flat. He jerked the oar free, spun it, and then drove it through two more floaters, pinning them to a mooring post at the end of the dock.

Ramirez led Westlake and the others down the steps. Between them, Hutch and Calavera had cleaned out all the immediate threats, but there were more floaters at the fences, and walkers wandering around from the front. Crumpled bodies littered the shoreline, in heaps and drifts. Many of them had arrows sticking out of them.

"Under the deck, let's go," she said, as she quickly led them all to where the lodge's few boats were stored out of sight, hidden beneath tarps. They'd permanently stowed most of them when the floaters had gotten too numerous to bother with. But they kept a few of them gassed up and ready, just in case. "Labrand, find one that's ready to go. Calavera, you help him get one out. Hutch, get the fence. The rest of us will cover you."

Hutch hurried towards the fence, raising his Stoner, as Calavera and Labrand uncovered one of the boats. The fiberglass hull was painted camo, and the go-fast boat was big enough to hold four people – five, if one of them was small. Ramirez felt her heart sink.

"Bit small," Westlake noted.

Ramirez shot him a glare. "Really? Had no idea." She took a breath. "We'll just have to make do. Labrand?"

He gave her a thumbs up. "Gassed up and shipshape, boss."

"Good. Get it into the water – quick! Before any more of those bastards arrive." As if the thought had been an invitation, she heard a hiss to her left. A smell like a leaking septic tank hit her as a water-logged zombie, clad in the flopping remnants of a wet suit, lurched towards her. It gripped the struts of the deck, shoving itself along. Its eyes gleamed in the darkness as it flung itself full upon her, knocking her to the ground.

Ramirez heard the others cry out, but had no breath to respond. It was all she could do to keep the walker's teeth out of her throat. It was strong – stronger than most of them – and it dug pulpy fingers into her shoulders as it ducked its head towards her jugular. She fumbled for her collapsible baton, cursing under her breath. Anger was good – it kept the panic at bay.

She caught hold of the zombie's scalp and tried to pull its head back, but the rotten hank of hair and flesh tore away from the skull like wet paper, and she only just managed to interpose her forearm between its teeth. It gnawed at the thick leather of her sleeve, giving her time to snatch her baton out and crush its head.

She rolled it off her and looked towards the others, ready to chastise them for not helping, until she saw what had distracted them. Walkers clambered over the junk strewn beneath the deck, coming from the direction of the gate. Labrand, Ptolemy, and Kahwihta were handling them, while Calavera bodily hauled a boat towards the water as quickly as he could, with some help from Westlake.

Ramirez pushed herself to her feet just in time to meet a second walker – this one wearing a football helmet – and slammed her baton into its head, knocking it to its knees. It fumbled back to its feet almost immediately. She heard Hutch's Stoner roar, and the sound of a section of fencing tumbling into the water.

"Fall back to the water!" she shouted, hitting it again, as hard as she could. The worn plastic of the helmet cracked, exposing the maggot-infested scalp beneath. The zombie swayed, and her third blow with the baton knocked it down. It didn't get up again.

Panting from her effort, she checked to see if the others were falling back as she'd ordered. They had – all save Ptolemy. He swung his shotgun one way, then the next. Each shot was powerful enough to knock a zombie down, if not out. But Ptolemy wasn't going for headshots. They were hard to do under these conditions. Instead, he was clipping spines and necks, reducing walkers to crawlers and creating obstacles for those behind. But they were getting too close, too fast. And he wasn't retreating.

Ramirez heard a sound, turned, and sent a walker in priestly vestments to meet its maker with a swift thwack. She turned back and saw that Hutch and Calavera had gotten their boat to the edge of the shore. "Get going!" she bawled. "Don't wait! Ptolemy, fall back!"

He ignored her. It was almost as if he were in a trance. She hurried towards him and caught his shoulder, shaking him loose from his reverie. He seemed to come to his senses, and then together they fell back towards the boat. By that time, Hutch had managed to rip down a large enough section of fencing for the boat to pass through.

The runner came out of nowhere, sprinting over the bodies of its crippled fellows with a pantherish yowl. It was clad in the remnants of a sundress, though the bright colors had been dulled by weather and grime. It sprang for Ptolemy, and Ramirez shoved him aside.

Lacquered nails, sharp as razors, sank into Ramirez' coat, and she was borne backwards onto the ground, losing her baton in the process. She gave silent thanks for the thick leather gloves she'd thought to wear as she pummeled the dead woman. She hit it again and again, dislodging pearly white caps from cracked teeth, tearing apart what had once been expensive plastic surgery, forcing it off her. The runner didn't seem bothered, as it clambered to its feet. It just kept snapping at her like a rabid dog.

Ramirez crouched. It was between her and the boat, and from the sound of it more walkers were on the way. She dropped a hand to her pistol. The runner darted forward, smashing into her before she could draw the weapon.

As she fell, she heard an engine growl to life. The runner straddled her, snarling. She flung the zombie with a convulsive heave, rose to one knee, drew her pistol, and shot a walker dressed like an escapee from a John Waters film. She turned the weapon on the runner, took aim, and the gun made an unfortunate sound – jammed.

The runner's eyes were fixed on her hungrily. Ramirez saw its withered muscles tense. Time slowed. She saw Frieda's face in front of her eyes, felt the other woman's lips against hers. She wanted Frieda to live – she wanted all of them to live. If that meant she had to die, some part of her was content in that.

The runner hissed and leapt, but stopped short as Westlake caught a handful of its hair and yanked it back. It turned to snap at him, and he drove his knife through its eye. He gave the knife a twist, popped it loose, and let the runner fall face-first into the water at the edge of the shore. "Time to go," he said, indicating the idling go-fast boat with a nod of his head. "We're on a schedule, remember?"

"I thought I told you to go," Ramirez said. She snatched up her fallen baton and waded out towards the boat. Westlake followed.

"You did. We didn't listen. You're welcome."

"I didn't say thank you," she said, as she climbed onboard. It was a tight squeeze. Calavera took up a lot of room, despite his best efforts. Hutch wasn't much smaller. Kahwihta and Attila crouched in the stern, beside Ptolemy. There wasn't much room for either her or Westlake, but they made do.

He shrugged as he joined her. "Even so."

Ramirez nodded to Labrand, who was at the wheel. "Hit it." He grinned, and the go-fast boat ripped through the water, heading away from the lodge. Behind them, walkers waded into the water, following. Floaters turned, their hands grasping uselessly at the sides of the boat as it whipped through their ranks.

She looked at Westlake. After a moment, she said, "Thank you."

Westlake smiled like he'd won the lottery. "Anytime."

CHAPTER FOURTEEN
Floaters

Westlake hunched forward in the prow of the boat as they arrowed across the water, motor growling loudly. The shore was an indistinct stretch of trees to his left. The lake wasn't as big as some, but it seemed infinite in the dark. For a moment, Westlake fancied they were sailing into an abyss from which there was no return. He shook the thought aside.

Shit happened. Things went wrong. Plans failed. It was a common hazard of his profession. But in those earlier instances, he'd always had the option to cut his losses and retreat from the field, honor and person intact. But that wasn't a route open to him this time. If things went bad here, that was it. He was screwed, blued, and tattooed, as the saying went. And things were definitely on the cusp of going bad.

He looked at Ptolemy. "Why'd she do it?"

Ptolemy didn't look at him. "I do not know, but she wanted me to go with her."

"She must have said something else to you."

Ptolemy took a deep breath. "She did not."

Westlake was about to press the issue when he caught a warning look from Ramirez and settled back. It was clear Ptolemy was shaken. But was he worried because Sayers had pulled this stunt, or because he knew something they didn't?

He sat up. "Can't we go any faster?"

"Not without disturbing the floaters," Kahwihta said. She had her arm around her dog. Attila, for his part, sat silently, his blocky head on his mistress' knee.

"They looked pretty disturbed to me already."

"That's because the ones closest to shore wake up quickest," she said, simply. "Lots of zombies wander into the lake. Being submerged doesn't particularly bother them. And sound carries better underwater. But a lot of times, they'll just… stop."

"Stop?"

"I'd say they go to sleep, but being dead and all, they don't sleep. But it's definitely a sort of dormancy. Might be the cold that does it. They just… stand down there." She looked at the water, her expression pensive. "At least until they hear something."

Westlake swallowed. "Like the motor of a boat?"

She tapped her nose. "Bingo-bango, bud."

"Wonderful." He turned to Ramirez. "How long?"

"A few minutes, if we don't hit trouble." She squinted through the boat's windshield. "Problem is, I can hardly tell where we're going. Plus, we're carrying too much weight. The motor's already starting to strain." She indicated the bulky spotlight attached to the opposite side of the prow. "Would someone turn that thing on? Let's see what we can see."

"You sure that's a good idea?" Westlake asked.

"Can you navigate blind?"

"No," he said, grudgingly.

"Neither can I. Hutch, turn on the damn light."

Westlake sighed as Hutch fumbled for a moment before turning the light on. Almost immediately, Westlake noticed the gleam of what might have been bone. It bobbed in the water like a buoy and vanished as they growled past. Westlake was tempted to ask Hutch to swivel the light, to try and see what it was, but he had a feeling he already knew. From the look on Ramirez' face, she'd seen it as well.

"They're starting to surface," Kahwihta said, quietly.

"The dead do not rest easy here," Calavera said.

Hutch grunted. "Where do they, these days?"

Ramirez said something Westlake didn't catch over the motor, and Labrand hunched forward, pressing the throttle up as far as it could go. "We're not far from shore," the cowboy shouted. "Y'all just hold on." The boat swayed off course as something thumped against the bottom. Several somethings, by the sound of it. Attila started to growl.

"Bit late on the warning, pal," Westlake said. "Can zombies rip through fiberglass?"

The boat bobbed, as if lifted by a wave. "They don't have to rip through it, not when they can just capsize us," Ramirez said. "Hutch, keep that light on the water."

Westlake stiffened. He could make out the sound of scrabbling at the bottom of the hull. Like so many dead fingers, scraping at the boat as it went by. "I vote we speed up," he called out. "Like right now."

Ramirez shook her head. "This boat wasn't built to carry this much weight. We speed up, we risk burning the motor out. Or chopping up zombie bits to get stuck in the propeller. Then we'll have to swim for it."

"So then, we lighten the load," Westlake said. "Got to be something we can toss out." He eyed Attila speculatively.

Kahwihta frowned and looped an arm around the dog's neck. "Don't even think about it," she said.

"I will go," Calavera said, making as if to rise. "I am a strong swimmer."

"Nobody is going anywhere," Ramirez said, firmly. "Would everyone just sit down and try not to make any more noise than you have to, please? A few minutes more and we'll reach shore…"

Attila began to bark and twist furiously in Kahwihta's grip. Surprised, she let go. Attila scrambled onto the back of the boat and Kahwihta went after him, even as the aft section of the boat suddenly shuddered and rocked. Kahwihta yelped, and when the boat rocked again, she went over the side with a splash. Attila gave a frantic bark and followed, leaping in after her. Westlake lunged after both of them, grabbing at empty air. If he'd been thinking, he might not have done so, but instinct propelled him against the boat's side. And as he did, a dead face, flesh sloughing from the skull, broke the water like a torpedo. He fell back with a shout and clawed for his Glock.

Ramirez turned even as the zombie hauled itself over the side and went for him. "What's happening back there –

Jesus!" she shouted, going for her own gun. Calavera and the others reacted slowly, all equally surprised by the suddenness of the attack and trying to keep from going overboard themselves.

"Not quite," Westlake grunted. At the last second, his hands found a life preserver and he rammed it down over the zombie's head and shoulders, pinning it. It thrashed in the bottom of the boat like an ugly fish, snapping black teeth at his ankles as he hauled himself to his feet. "Kahwihta went over!" he shouted, stomping on the dead man's head until it stopped moving.

Ramirez stared at him blankly for a moment before scrambling to the boat's side, her face pinched in terror. "Anyone see her?" They could all hear the dog barking, but it was too dark to see much of anything.

"There – follow the barking!" Ptolemy shouted, pointing. Hutch swung their light around and found Kahwihta floundering in the water some distance from the boat, Attila doggy-paddling in circles around her, barking for all he was worth.

Ramirez turned towards the front of the boat to keep it balanced. "Labrand, turn this boat around, now!"

From Westlake's position, he watched as rotting heads mushroomed to the surface, one after the next. His hands tightened on the rail. The floaters were waking up. They weren't able to swim, not like a person at least. They flapped and floundered, grabbing at the boat and each other in their blind eagerness.

Several were rising near Kahwihta and splashing wildly in an effort to reach her as she tried to stay out of their reach as best as she could. Labrand drew near the young woman and eased up on the throttle. The boat slowed. "Kahwihta, swim," Ramirez cried. She snatched up Labrand's rifle and fired at one of the zombies, but succeeded only in causing it to bob awkwardly. Ptolemy, following her example, took out a floater that was closing in on the young woman, blowing its puffy head clean off with his shotgun.

"She's not going to make it," Hutch said. A floater grabbed onto the light, and he punched it in the head, forcing it to let go. Westlake saw that he was right. There was no way she'd make it back to the boat before one of the zombies pulled her under.

Westlake heard a scrabbling behind him and turned. A floater swayed on the rail, its skinny form covered in rotting plant matter. Labrand hitched the wheel of the boat, and the floater fell back into the water. But more of them were clawing at the sides and bottom with every passing moment. The growl of the motor was drawing them all to the surface.

"They're all over us," Labrand shouted. "I got to speed up or they'll capsize us!"

"Labrand is right," Westlake said. "If we stay out here, we're going to pull them all onto us. We need to get to shore." He calculated the odds of Kahwihta getting to the boat. They weren't good.

"I'm not leaving her out here," Ramirez snarled. "If I have to, I'll toss you in to distract them." She grabbed Westlake's jacket, yanking him close. Westlake read the truth of it in her eyes. She'd sooner put a bullet in him than leave the girl.

"No need. I'll do it myself." Thinking quickly, he snatched

up a coil of rope. "When I give you the word, hit the gas and don't stop." Ignoring her questions, he climbed onto the back of the boat, tied the rope to the aft cleat and dove into the water, still holding the other end of the rope. It was a dumb idea. Not the dumbest one he'd ever had, but definitely in the top five or thereabouts. But every so often, you just had to roll the dice.

The water was cold, and he immediately regretted his decision. He cracked a floater in the head with his elbow and tore the jaw off another before it could sink its teeth into him. Being in the water so long had reduced some of them to soggy, fragile messes.

He reached Kahwihta a moment later. "Nice night for a swim, huh?"

She goggled at him. "Are you insane?"

"Pragmatic. Ramirez was planning to toss me in anyway. Or dive in herself. Way I see it, I beat the rush. I – Jesus!" A floater surfaced suddenly between them, rising with a gurgling snort, like a diminutive hippo. Flabby arms enveloped him even as its stink washed over him. A flowery tropical shirt strained to hold in its water-swollen flesh, and most of the meat had slid off its face, leaving a sludge-brown skull staring out of a hood of rotten muscle. The waterlogged camera hanging from its neck slapped against his chest as it made to embrace him. Kahwihta splashed closer, an icepick in her hand.

She sank the thin pick into the side of its head, through the hole where its ear had once been. The floater spasmed and slid away from Westlake, bobbing in the water.

"How many corpses are in this goddamn lake?" he

spluttered, pushing away from it. Kahwihta didn't answer, seeing as she was busy trying to pull her icepick free of the floater's head. When she did so, she turned, desperate gaze searching.

"Where's Attila?"

Westlake realized the dog's barking had ceased. Worry filled him until he saw the dog already making for shore, paddling for all he was worth. He was no dummy, at least. "Doing what we should be doing." He felt icy fingers grope his legs and decided the time for caution was over. He grabbed Kahwihta and wrapped the rope around her. "You ever water-skied?"

She looked at him incredulously. "What?"

"It's really easy. Just don't let go. Ramirez! Punch it!" he screamed.

A moment later, the motor purred to life and the go-fast boat started towards shore, dragging them along in its wake. The first few seconds were dicey, as the floaters that had been pawing at the boat closed in on them. But as the boat pulled away, they left the floaters behind. The water hurt, but it was better than being eaten.

Kahwihta twisted in his arms. "Attila!" she cried out.

Westlake followed her gaze as much as he could with the water rushing around him and saw that the dog had reached the shallows – but not alone. A pair of floaters splashed after him, and the dog was clearly flagging. A wave rolled over them and by the grief on Kahwihta's face, Westlake sighed. "Oh, goddamn it."

He let go of the rope and found himself tumbling through the water. Fighting the vertigo that threatened to leave him floating, he focused on the dog and started swimming toward the mutt. He reached for his knife as he went. He snapped it open even as he paddled closer to the first floater. He rose up behind it and rammed his blade into the back of its head with all of his strength. The floater went face down, carrying him with it.

His feet briefly touched bottom as the second zombie swung around, muddy locks of hair whipping about. It lunged through the water, graceful as a trash barge, and slammed into him. He stabbed it again and again as they rolled in the water. Finally, he hit something it couldn't survive without, and it drifted away from him. He kicked loose from its grasp and surfaced, spitting water. He spotted Attila, not far away.

When Westlake reached the dog, the animal was almost pathetically grateful for the chance to let someone else do the swimming. He heard the growl of the go-fast boat and, buoying the dog as best he could, he dragged them both to shore.

A floater broke the surface just as his feet touched something solid. It rose with a guttural sound – not a roar, but a bellicose wheeze, like an angry asthmatic. Two fists, swollen and peeling, crashed against his collarbone, and he went down, the dog spilling out of his arms. The floater loomed over him, stinking of lake bottom and rotten meat.

He coughed and tried to get to his feet as the floater grappled with him, trying to haul him up and back. He kicked at it, but it just caught hold of his leg and yanked him back down. Water flowed over his head. Its jaw was missing, and he realized that it was the same one he'd mangled earlier. It was persistent, he had to give it that. A black tongue flopped from the cavern of its mouth and throat as it gurgled at him.

Another blow and he was scrambling on his hands and knees, head spinning. He could hear someone shouting, trying to get the floater's attention – Attila barking – and the roar of the go-fast boat as it drew close. He heard rocks crunch beneath the keel. But the zombie kept attacking him and wouldn't *that* be something, if Westlake died from drowning by zombie?

Boots splashing in the water and the sound of a Colt being cocked. The floater shoved him face-first into the water with a bemused gurgle. Then a gunshot, and it collapsed into the water beside him.

Hand on his knee, he shoved himself to his feet. He turned and saw Labrand standing in the water, twirling his pistol. "Are you OK?" he asked, offering his hand.

Westlake took the outstretched hand. He couldn't believe he was alive. "Better now. I owe you."

"I'll make a note of it." Labrand slid his pistol into its holster and turned as Hutch and the others clambered down out of the boat. None of them looked the worse for wear, despite the fact the craft had been crawling with floaters only a few moments before. He spat out a mouthful of lake water and looked at Ramirez. "How far are we from the trailhead?"

Ramirez looked down at him. "The Old Marcy Dam Trail is thataway." She gestured in a vaguely southerly direction. "But the thought of tramping through it in the dark isn't filling me with glee."

Westlake hesitated. He wanted to push forward, but she was right. It was too dark, and God only knew what was out there, and he was shivering and wet. He sighed and sat down on shore. Across the waters, he could make out the lights of the lodge and the snap-crackle of gunfire. He could also just make out the shapes of the floaters, bobbing in the water, watching them. He glanced at Ramirez. "Right, what now?"

She was staring across the water, her expression unreadable. Then she shook herself and said, in hard, clipped tones, "Let's get our gear and move back up into the trees. Away from the shore and out of sight. Get a fire going, dry out, and wait for dawn."

CHAPTER FIFTEEN
Campfire Stories

The forest was quiet. Westlake took a sip of camp coffee and watched the stars.

They'd made camp off the trail, back up in the trees but within sight of shore, after searching for any zombies that might pounce. It was safer that way. Kahwihta's research had showed that walkers largely congregated on the trail rather than in the woods, despite what Westlake had experienced. Zombies followed people, and people walked the trail. Of course, there were more zombies than people these days.

Ptolemy brewed camp coffee as Hutch broke out the jerky and trail mix. Westlake lit a fire. Kahwihta attempted to dry her hair. She was putting on a brave face, but Westlake could tell she was still freaked out. "You sure they're not going to follow us?" he asked, indicating the lake.

She shook her head. "No. I think that if they could, they would have by now." She paused as Ptolemy filled her mug with coffee. She gulped the scalding liquid down gratefully. Attila huddled next to her, panting slightly. "The ones closest to shore will, but the ones that are farther out – they'll just sink back down and go back to sleep, or whatever passes for it among zombies." She took out her notebook, gave it a mournful shake, and set it down beside the fire to dry.

"Until the next poor sucker tries to cross the lake, you mean," Westlake said.

"Until then, yeah."

"You did good, by the way," he continued. He tapped the side of his head. "With the icepick, I mean."

"Go for the brainstem," she said. "Surest way of putting one down. They're not much more than a brain and a stomach." She shivered slightly. "Even so, they almost had me. That's the closest I've come in, well, ever." She looked at Westlake. "Thank you. I mean it."

"We're a crew, and you look out for the members of your crew." He patted Attila. "Even those with tails."

"Still – thank you."

He waved her words aside. "De nada. We were both lucky."

"Luck had nothing to do with it, I think," Calavera said, startling Westlake. He'd been sitting so quietly he'd almost forgotten the big man was there. He'd rolled the bottom of his mask up, exposing his mouth, and he'd lit a cigarette. He held a tiny icon in his big hands. "Santa Muerte was watching out for you, as she watches out for me." As he spoke, he leaned forward and blew a thin plume of smoke from a lit cigarette onto the icon.

"Who?" Kahwihta asked. In the light of the fire, Westlake could just make out the image on the icon – a well-dressed skeleton, though whether that of a man or a woman, he could not tell. It was clearly religious, however.

Calavera looked at her. "Senora de la Noche – our Lady of the Night." The big man touched his chest. "I have her tattooed here as well, over my heart, though my grandmother would not approve, I think." He cradled the small icon gently and puffed on his cigarette. A moment later he blew another mouthful of smoke onto the icon. "She protects us against the darkness, and that which prowls the night… living or dead."

He brought the icon up to his forehead and then slipped it back into his coat. "It was she who called to me and made me what I am. I was lost, and then Santa Muerte found me and led me once more to the light. It is she who guides us all." He flicked his cigarette into the fire. "And it is she who will lead us safely through the forest of the night."

Ptolemy cleared his throat. "Forest of the night. An apt phrase given our surroundings." He chewed thoughtfully on a mouthful of trail mix, swallowed, and added, "The word Adirondacks was thought to be Mohawk in origin."

"*Haderondah*," Kahwihta said. "Eaters of trees. Not exactly an auspicious name. Thomas Pownhall, the British governor of Massachusetts Bay, wrote that the Oneyotdehaga peoples referred to it as the Dismal Wilderness or the Habitation of Winter." She looked around. "Makes you wonder why people ever wanted to vacation here."

"It is pretty, though," Labrand drawled. He leaned back, hat tipped over his eyes and his hands crossed behind his head. "That's why I came."

"Yeah, well, it'd be prettier without the zombies," Ramirez said. She prodded the fire, raising a scattering of sparks into the air. Privately, Westlake had thought a fire wasn't the best idea – they didn't need to attract any attention – but he hadn't argued about it. He needed to dry out. He inched closer, letting the heat wash over him.

Ramirez looked at Ptolemy and asked casually, "Where does she hole up?"

Ptolemy frowned. "What do you mean?"

"Sayers. She's got a place somewhere out here. Where is it?"

"She won't be there."

"I didn't ask whether she was there, Calvin. I asked where it was." Ramirez stared at him.

Ptolemy shifted uneasily. "Why?"

"Because I am a trained investigator, and I do not like mysteries. Ergo, I want to know why she decided to do what she did. More, I want to ask her myself."

"He's right, she won't be there," Westlake said. He could see the plan going even further off the rails, and he didn't like it.

"Doesn't matter," Ramirez said, not taking her eyes off Ptolemy. "Tell me," she said, her voice like iron.

Ptolemy looked away. "Marcy Dam. At least that's where she was a few weeks ago."

"If you haven't spoken to her, how do you know?"

Ptolemy looked suddenly uncomfortable. "I… might have come looking for her. Once. Or twice. To talk." He glanced at them. "I could not bring myself to intrude, in the end."

"Well, that's not creepy at all," Kahwihta murmured. Ptolemy hunched forward, visibly stung by the comment.

Ramirez silenced the young woman with a stern look. "Is that where she was planning to take you?"

Ptolemy rubbed the top of his head. "Possibly. I cannot say with any certainty. If she was planning to risk coming back, it would be because she does not know that I know."

"Then that's where we'll go."

Westlake gave her a sharp look. "What about Lake Cutter? What about the Villa?"

"It's on the way," Ramirez said.

"Is it?" Westlake looked at Labrand. The cowboy tipped his hat up and shook his head. Westlake turned back to Ramirez. "Apparently not."

"Relax, Westlake." She leaned forward and prodded the fire. "I haven't forgotten why we're out here. But I don't like loose ends. Or betrayers."

Conversation petered out after that. One by one, the others fell asleep, even the dog. Ramirez and Ptolemy were the only ones who stayed awake. Long nights on stakeout had prepared her for this sort of thing, Westlake figured. He pulled his jacket back on as the night chill gripped him. It was dry enough, but he was still too wired to sleep. He felt Ramirez' eyes on him. "What is it?" he asked, softly.

It took her a moment to answer. "Nothing."

"Something, otherwise you wouldn't be staring at me." Westlake straightened and met her gaze square on. "You have something to say, say it." He noticed Ptolemy watching them, but thankfully the other man had decided to mind his business.

"You didn't have to dive in after her."

He shrugged. "Somebody had to."

"Didn't have to be you."

"Is this your way of saying thank you?"

Ramirez snorted. "I already said it once. You're not getting another one."

"We'll see." Westlake hid his smile. He sat back, pulling his coat tighter about him. The wind brought the sound of distant moans. Attila perked up but didn't growl. After a moment, the dog laid his head back down and closed his eyes. Westlake peeked at Ramirez, and saw that she had her hand on her pistol. She caught his eye and relaxed.

"Not close enough to worry about," he said.

"Maybe." Ramirez looked away. He could see the worry eating at her. Not for them, necessarily, but for those they'd left behind.

"Surprised you didn't bring a radio," Westlake said. "We got everything else."

Ramirez ran a hand through her hair. "Couldn't spare one. It's hard to get a signal on the mountain. Not worth the hassle, frankly. Besides, there's one at Sayers' cabin if we need it that badly. She seemed to get signal just fine," Ramirez finished darkly.

"Seems like it might have been worth a little hassle."

Ramirez frowned. "If we don't come back, they'll know why."

"I suppose." He paused. "They'll be fine."

"You don't know that."

"I do. One thing I'm good at is evaluating risk. Every thief must be. You need to be able to look at a job and tell whether it's the next – or the last."

"And if it's the last?"

"You don't do it," he said, simply.

"So, what's this one?" she asked.

He fell silent. He didn't have an answer for her, or maybe he did and just didn't want to say. It wasn't nerves, exactly, so much as a certainty that something, somewhere, had gone irretrievably, inevitably wrong. He'd gotten that feeling the night Tommy had shoved him into the trunk of his rental and hadn't been able to shake it since.

When he didn't reply, she said, "I read your file, you know. Seven years in Folsom. Angola before that." She looked at him. "Angola as bad as they say?"

Westlake paused, and then pushed down the brief stirring of memory. "Worse, in the summer. What else did my file say?"

"The usual. We had those prissy jagoffs from the BCA put together a profile on you."

"Bullshit," Westlake said. "Why would you bother?"

"Not my idea, I assure you."

"Good, because it was a stupid one." Westlake leaned towards her. "I'm a simple guy, Ramirez. I'm a good thief because I was shit at everything else. I tried day trading, car repair – even acting. Bad at all of it." He held up a finger. "But I'm good at stealing shit."

"Yeah. Let's hope."

Westlake decided to change the subject. "Hutch said you saved him."

Ramirez glanced at Hutch's snoring form. "Yeah. He's not all bad. And I got a soft spot for motorcycle-types." She looked away from him. "My dad rode with some bullshit motorcycle club out in California's Central Valley. They used to run guns for real bad guys."

"Ah," Westlake said. "That explains a lot."

"Shut up. I shouldn't have said anything." She shifted uneasily, looking out into the night. Then, abruptly, she turned back to him. "What about you? Tell me something about yourself. Fair's fair, after all."

It was Westlake's turn to look away. "Nothing much to tell."

She leaned forward. "You said you hadn't always been a thief. Start with that."

"OK. I used to be an altar boy."

She laughed. Then, "What, really?"

"Hand to God." He smiled. "My first job was the donation box for the Children's Fund. I skimmed the cash, tucked it in my cummerbund, left the change. Bought a nice bicycle with it that summer."

"Jesus."

"Jesus had very little to do with it, I assure you." Westlake prodded the fire and fed it a few more twigs. "After that, well, my dad ran a carpet store, and I did some work for him. Used to case people's houses while I laid carpet."

"This reminds me of a damn Warren Zevon song."

"The one about the werewolves?"

"No."

Westlake sighed. "Shame. I dig that one."

Ramirez was silent for several moments. The fire crackled on the new twigs. "What are you planning, after all this is done?"

"You mean, assuming we survive?"

Ramirez snorted. "Yeah, assuming."

"Atlantic City."

She peered at him. "Atlantic City."

"That's what I said."

She shook her head. "You know it's probably full of zombies, right?"

"Everywhere is full of zombies."

"Why Atlantic City?"

"Why not?" Westlake stirred the fire. "I always liked it there. One of the few places I ever felt at home. Even had an apartment there. Under a different name, of course."

"Oh, of course," Ramirez said. "So you're just going to… kick back and enjoy the apocalypse?"

Westlake nodded. "Pretty much."

"Figures." She pulled her jacket shut and zipped it up. "Getting cold."

"It gets cold in the mountains."

"Thank you for that trenchant observation, Westlake."

"I try to be helpful." He went quiet and then asked, "What about you? Afterwards, I mean. What are you going to do?"

Ramirez frowned. "The same thing I've been doing." She paused, looking up. Westlake followed her gaze. The trees rose so high and thick that the stars were all but hidden from view. It reminded him of being in the city, somehow. Ramirez continued. "There's an airport near Saranac Lake. Small. Lot of charter flights. Or used to be. Figured I might be able to use it to get supplies. Find survivors. Something. Anything." She looked back into the fire, rubbing her hands together. "Something other than hiding up here. Waiting for the day it all goes wrong."

"Noble sentiments."

Ramirez looked at him. "That a joke?"

"Would you believe me if I said no?"

"No."

"Then yeah, it was a joke."

She studied him for a few moments. "I wish I knew why you were here, Westlake. It would make me feel a lot better about this whole thing."

"It wouldn't. Your problem, Ramirez, is you don't know how to trust people." He fixed her with a cool eye, knowing she'd never understand his reasons. "Most cops don't. Especially Feds."

"And you do?"

"Of course. If you're in a crew, you have to trust the other guys to do their jobs and not get funny when it comes to splitting the take. Otherwise, nothing would get done. When that trust gets broken, that's when things get nasty."

"That's what Sal did, huh? Broke your trust. Or did you break his?"

Westlake made to reply when a distant explosion rumbled through the night. Through the trees, the lake's surface was painted red by fire. Ramirez lurched to her feet, expressionless but for a slight widening of her eyes.

"Fuel dump," she said, softly.

"Why would they blow it up?" Westlake asked, getting to his feet.

"They wouldn't, not unless they didn't have a choice."

The others were stirring, their sleep disturbed by the explosion. Ramirez clapped her hands once, sharply. "That's our cue, everyone up. We need to move. That big a boom is going to attract every walker for a hundred miles to the lake. We need to put as much distance between us and it as possible. Labrand, think you can lead us in the dark?"

Labrand nodded. "I expect so. Might be slow going, though."

"Slow is fine, so long as we go." Her fingers tapped the sidearm holstered on her hip, and Westlake was suddenly glad that the cold fury in her eyes was directed elsewhere.

"I have a few things I want to say to Sayers."

CHAPTER SIXTEEN
Marcy Dam

"You're certain this is the place?" Ramirez asked. She crouched behind a decaying lean-to and surveyed the dam. She and the others had reached the western shore of Marcy Pond just after dawn. A soft, orange light rested on the tops of the trees, painting everything in ruddy hues.

"It looks like a construction site," Westlake murmured, from behind her. He wasn't wrong. The dam itself wasn't much more than a skeleton, with water rushing through and over it from the Marcy River. Piles of salvaged timber and scrap metal dotted the shore of the pond, and there were several porta-potties and weather-damaged trailers scattered around the demolition area.

Ptolemy, laying stretched out nearby, peered through Ramirez' binoculars and said, "The government scheduled the dam for demolition a few years ago, after Hurricane Irene damaged it. They had just started on it when the apocalypse preempted the schedule."

"How inconvenient for them," Westlake said. "Where's this cabin?"

"It's not a cabin as such," Ramirez said. "But it's just there, along the trail, back up near the treeline. See it?" She gestured, and Ptolemy handed Westlake the binoculars. He peered through them.

"That's a cabin," Westlake said, fixing on the building.

"They call it an interior outpost."

"It's a log cabin, Ramirez. It's a goddamn Abe Lincoln log cabin." Westlake handed her the binoculars back. "Don't see any signs of life, though. You sure she'd risk it?"

Ptolemy looked at him. "Like I said, she would because she does not know that I know. There is a good chance that we can catch her by surprise, but only if we act quickly."

"So, what are we waiting for?" Hutch asked, from behind a nearby tree. "An engraved invitation? Let's go knock on the door and say howdy."

"I would not advise it. Sayers' father was a collector of military memorabilia, before he passed away," Ptolemy said, his voice pitched low. "Most of it functional."

Westlake frowned. "Meaning?"

"Weapons," Ramirez said.

Ptolemy nodded. "Guns. Explosives. And the knowledge to use them to best effect."

"You make her sound like Rambo," Westlake groused.

"That would be an apt comparison."

Westlake shook his head but didn't reply. Instead, he looked at Ramirez. "What do you think? Forget it and move on?"

"No." Ramirez got to her feet, one hand on her weapon.

She thought of Frieda and Dunnigan and the others. The screams as people raced for the safety of the lodge. She let the anger fill her. Anger was good. It kept you moving when the world got tough. "Feel free to stay here, but I'm going in. I want to know what the hell is going on, and the quickest way to do that is to kick in her door and ask, like Hutch said."

"Now we're talking," Hutch growled. He heaved himself to his feet as well.

"What about the rest of us?" Westlake demanded.

Ramirez ignored him. "Ptolemy, Labrand, you two will stay here to keep an eye on things. You see anything, give us a signal. Kahwihta, you stay with them. No, don't argue." Ramirez gestured to Attila. "There're walkers all over the mountains. You and Attila are our early warning system." Finally, she looked at Westlake. "You and Calavera follow me and Hutch. Keep low, don't make any noise. Once we get to the cabin, see if you can circle around it. Use the trees for cover. Hutch and I will go in the front."

Ramirez kept her eyes on the cabin as she made her way past the lean-to. She paused and then darted for the trailer, Hutch following. No alarm was raised, so no one had seen her. Calavera and Westlake came next, keeping low.

Ramirez' heart was thumping as she moved around the trailer, keeping herself pressed flat to the corrugated metal of the wall. Tumbleweeds of scattered papers danced across the ground. There were hard hats and hi-vis vests scattered everywhere. She wondered what had happened – had the workers been attacked, or was the debris simply the result of no one being around to pick it up?

She dismissed the thought as the front of the cabin came into view. This close to the river, the pulse of the water was omnipresent, drowning out all other sound. She turned to Hutch and saw that he was about to step on a thin wire, stretched from a nearby log pile to the edge of the trailer. Attached to the wire were several tin cans – a crude alarm system.

She flung up a hand, and Hutch froze. She gestured to the wire, and Hutch gently pulled his foot back – and stepped on a broken plank. The rotten wood snapped beneath his weight, nearly pitching him off balance. He grinned helplessly as she rolled her eyes in consternation. Luckily, the noise from the river seemed to have hidden the sound.

Ramirez turned back to the cabin. There was still no sign of anyone. Sayers might have already been and gone. But they had to be sure. She took a breath and stepped out into the open. If anyone was in the cabin, they would be able to see her clearly.

"Sayers," she called out. She waited, listening to the river. Her hand dropped to her weapon. "Sayers, I just want to talk." She heard the lie in her voice even as she said it. She didn't know whether she was planning to shoot Sayers or not, and that scared her a little bit. She pushed the fear down and forced her hand away from her gun.

There was no reply from the cabin. No sign that anyone was home. Ramirez took a step forward. Hutch covered her from the edge of the trailer, his Stoner aimed at the cabin. She caught a hint of movement out of the corner of her eye – Westlake, or maybe Calavera, circling towards the trees.

"All right. I'm coming in." Ramirez started towards the

front steps of the cabin. As she drew close, she slowed. There was something off. The ground wasn't quite–

Ramirez leapt to the side even as the soil-covered boards beneath her feet gave way. The boards had been placed carefully, so as to give the impression of solid ground – they were anything but. Crouched on the side of the hole, she heard a strange sound emerging from within it. She risked a look and stiffened.

Crawlers. Walkers that had lost the use of their lower halves, either due to spinal damage or, well, just plain lacking legs. Four of them, at the bottom of the hole, five feet down. The mangled zombies moaned and scrabbled at the sides of the hole with ragged arm-stumps, but were unable to haul themselves up with no hands. So instead they gnawed the air mindlessly. Ramirez felt her stomach lurch as she considered what might have happened had she not noticed the ground shifting beneath her feet.

Angry now, she took the steps two at a time and made to kick the door in, but then stopped. First the alarm, then the deadfall, there was no telling what was on the other side of the door. She'd been a part of enough tactical entries to know a closed door was more dangerous than an open one. She rocked back on her heels, drew her sidearm, and sidled around to the opposite side of the door.

Ramirez caught Hutch's eye and signaled to the doorknob. Hutch nodded. He lifted the Stoner and fired. One shot, but a good one. It blew off the doorknob and the door sagged outwards. Ramirez tensed, waiting for whatever surprise was on the other side to go off. But nothing happened. Slightly disappointed, she leaned over and pulled the door the rest of the way open. Still nothing. Taking a deep breath, she stepped inside.

The wire was strung across the doorway, just above eye level. She caught sight of it at the last moment, and it gave her enough warning to duck beneath it. She followed it with her eyes and trailed it to the trigger of a sporting crossbow, mounted on a tripod arrangement to her left. "Jesus tap-dancing Christ," she muttered. Sayers wasn't playing around.

Ramirez looked around. Sayers' cabin was Spartan. No luxuries anywhere. Only a table, some chairs, a bed, an old-fashioned ice box, and a small shelf with a few books. Moving carefully, she drew the hunting knife strapped to her thigh and cut the wire, disarming the trap. Then she unloaded the crossbow and set it aside.

Briskly, she checked out the kitchen and the bathroom. Neither were boobytrapped. She went back to the front door and signaled Hutch. "It's clear," she called out. "Let the others know." That done, she started searching for something – anything – that might answer the questions she had. In the end, all she found was a folded map of the Adirondacks, with circles drawn on it around Mount Marcy and the lodge, and notes written in the margins. The notes were all numerical in nature. She was staring at them in puzzlement when Ptolemy cleared his throat behind her.

"It is a cipher," he said. Kahwihta and Westlake had come in as well. Calavera stood outside, looking down into the crawler pit with Hutch. Labrand had shimmied up onto the closest of the trailers and was keeping an eye out for the locals.

Ramirez glanced at Ptolemy. "I know. I'm trying to figure

out what type. I don't suppose you know?" She extended the map in his direction. Ptolemy took it, with some hesitation.

"I do. I made it for her."

"Can you read it?"

Ptolemy looked around. "Where did you find it?"

"On the shelf. By the books."

"Out in the open?"

Ptolemy frowned. Ramirez read his sudden unease on his face. "She left it out for someone to find. For you?"

"Perhaps."

Before he could say more, the air was split by a sudden loud noise – an airhorn. It took Ramirez a moment to recognize it. It had been so long since she'd heard one. The airhorn blared again, and again. She pushed past Ptolemy and stepped out onto the porch, scanning the treeline.

"Can't see nothing," Labrand called down. He had his rifle up and was peering through the scope. The airhorn sounded again. It was close by, but where?

Ramirez felt a sudden prickle of apprehension. There was only one reason to make so much noise out here. "Shit," she said. Inside the cabin, Attila began to growl.

Labrand swung his rifle around, back the way they'd come. "We got company!"

The airhorn had done its job. A walker stepped out of the trees, swaying slightly. Then another and another. In moments, almost a dozen of them had appeared. Attila began to bark. A twig snapped on the other side of the cabin. Ramirez turned.

The dead man hissed and took a tentative step forward. He was dressed in country club casual, but the clothes had seen better days. "Calavera," Ramirez called out, in warning. As if that were a signal, the zombie sprang for the big man like a chimpanzee full of methamphetamines.

Calavera spun and smashed the dead man from the air with a blow from his fist. The zombie hit the ground and flailed like a crippled crab, unable to right itself before Calavera stomped on its head. But there were more of them on the way, wearing tattered business suits and tennis outfits. They boiled out of the trees like angry insects, lurching towards the cabin.

Hutch swung his Stoner up and fired, dropping the closest of them. "We need to go, *now*," Ramirez said, drawing her pistol. "Labrand! Cover us!"

The gunshot took her by surprise. It plucked at the porch rail, sending splinters into the air. Ramirez flinched back in surprise. Another shot sent Labrand scrambling off the side of the trailer. "Sniper," he shouted, clutching his hat.

Two more shots tore divots from the ground, sending Hutch hopping back. He swung his Stoner around. A third shot smacked into the weapon, nearly tearing it from his hands. He almost fell into the crawler pit, but for Calavera's quick reaction. The masked man caught Hutch by his colors and swung him away from the pit. "We must get inside," Calavera shouted as he all but tossed Hutch bodily onto the porch.

Ramirez nodded. "Labrand, come on," she shouted. The cowboy hurried towards her as a rapid series of shots pursued him onto the porch. Ramirez was the last one in. She paused in the doorway. There were more than two dozen walkers plodding towards the cabin. She kicked the door shut and looked at Ptolemy. "Is there a back way out of this place?"

"The windows," he said. But as he moved to open one, the glass spiderwebbed from another bullet and he fell back onto the floor, eyes wide, glasses askew. "I am mistaken. Not the windows."

"A trap," Ramirez said. She slid down the door into a crouch, suddenly overwhelmed by the enormity of her mistake. "She suckered us."

Westlake peered out one of the front windows, and for a moment she thought he was going to say "I told you so." Instead, he gave a weary smile and said, "Yeah. So, what do we do about it?"

"*Nothing,*" Sayers said, her words leavened with static.

Ramirez looked up, spotted the walky-talky in its solar panel charging station, and lunged for it. She snatched it up. "Sayers. What are you–"

"Shut up, Ramirez. You're only going to get one chance – so you better listen."

CHAPTER SEVENTEEN
Under Siege

Kahwihta sat on the floor beside the door and scratched Attila's head as the others argued. She looked around the cabin and wondered how Sayers had stood living here. It was so lifeless. Barren. Not even any pictures on the walls.

Then, Sayers had always been something of a mystery to her. She'd been a park ranger stationed in the Adirondacks when the dead started rising. Rather than joining the rest of them, she'd retreated to the wilderness – a not inconceivable option, but one Kahwihta found somewhat lacking, what with no one around to talk to and all. Not that she was one to talk, of course. She'd roughed it for a time, after all. But not out of choice. Maybe Sayers just didn't like people very much. Given what had happened, that seemed the likeliest answer.

She flinched as a dead fist thumped against the door. It had been jammed shut and reinforced with the addition of a bookcase. Hands clawed at the windows. The glass was stormproof and reinforced. It would take the walkers hours, if not days, to bust through it. That didn't make her feel better about the situation, though.

She watched as Ramirez snatched up the walky-talky and spoke into it. Sayers replied, then a hiss of static. Followed by, "*Now, let me talk to Calvin.*"

Ptolemy held out his hand. Ramirez gave him the walky-talky. He pressed the button. "I am here, Elizabeth."

"You should have listened to me," Sayers said. Her voice sounded flat to Kahwihta. Unemotional. "You didn't. Now you're stuck. There'll be more of them on the way. There's canned food and venison jerky in the root cellar."

"This place does not have a root cellar."

"It does now. I spent a month digging one. For us." Another static-filled pause. "There's also a few days' worth of supplies – more if you ration. Water as well. There's a rain filtration system on the roof, near the chimney. I put in an access hatch in the kitchen ceiling. The ladder is beside the fridge."

Ptolemy glanced back in the direction of what Kahwihta guessed was the kitchen. "Elizabeth, why are you doing this?"

"You didn't give me much choice, Calvin. It's for your own good. Like I said, you should have listened to me. But as usual, you fell prey to bad influences." She paused. "Yes, Estela, I am referring to you, if you were wondering."

Ramirez frowned. But she said nothing. Kahwihta wasn't sure what that was all about. Sayers had already been gone by the time she arrived. There'd been some falling out, but she wasn't privy to the details and hadn't been curious enough to ask. Now she was wondering if she ought to have made the effort to find out.

"Elizabeth, we can discuss this…" Ptolemy began.

Sayers cut him off. *"It doesn't matter now. You're trapped. I count… two dozen walkers outside that cabin, and another dozen moving through the trees below me. If you try to break out now – or any time in the next twenty minutes, say – I'll put a bullet in the first one out the door. I have no doubt that you'll eventually come up with some clever plan for getting out, but it won't be today, if you're smart."*

"Then why bother?"

"Because while they chew on you, I get a head start."

Westlake snatched the walky-talky from Ptolemy's hand. "You're heading for the Villa, aren't you?"

"Hello, Mr Westlake. Yes, I am."

"All by yourself?"

A hesitation. *"I prefer it that way."*

Westlake licked his lips. "We can still deal, you know." Ramirez made to protest, but Westlake held up a hand. She fell silent, glowering at him. "There's no reason we can't approach this like professionals."

"I think Ramirez might have some choice words for you on that. But it doesn't matter. Without me, you won't find the place. And if you try – well. There's a lot that can happen out here. Especially if you don't know what you're doing." A moment of static. Then, "Last chance. Go back to the lodge. Go to North Elba. I don't care. Just get off my mountain."

Ptolemy grabbed the walky-talky back from Westlake. "Elizabeth. Elizabeth!" But there was no reply. He stood for a moment, looking down at the walky-talky. Then, very deliberately, he sat it back in its cradle. "She is gone."

Westlake ran his hands over his head. "Yeah, and we know where. Damn it."

"This makes no sense," Ptolemy said, looking around. "Why would she care?"

Hutch patted him consolingly on the shoulder. "I hate to say this, Ptolemy, but the Villa sounds exactly like the sort of place Sayers might like. Isolated, hidden, fully supplied. If I were her, I'd definitely be going for it."

Ptolemy flinched away from his touch and stared towards the window. He said nothing. Ramirez shook her head.

"It doesn't matter. We need to get out of here, and quick." As if to emphasize her point, there was renewed pounding on the door and windows. It would take the walkers some time to forget what they were after and wander off. Unless they were the persistent type. She looked at Labrand. "She mentioned the trees."

Labrand nodded. "I caught a glint just south of the lake before I had to roll off the trailer." He gestured towards the southern facing window – the one Sayers' shot had cracked. "She's probably up around one of the trailheads on that side. She'd have a good view of the cabin, and of us. She must have been waiting all damn day for us to show up."

"She was counting on it. Why? All this for a head start that she already had?"

"It seems obvious," Calavera said, as the moans outside grew. "She wished to draw us into a trap. To prevent us from reaching the Villa, not just reach it herself." He smacked his fist into his palm. "Clever."

"She must have counted on us escaping," Westlake said. "She knew we wouldn't let it go. So, she planned accordingly."

"You sound like you admire her," Kahwihta said.

Westlake nodded. "I do. Be a shame to put a bullet in her."

Kahwihta saw Ptolemy looking at him, a strange expression on his face, but he said nothing. If Westlake noticed, he gave no sign. Instead, he went on, "Either way, we're in the trap now. So how do we get out?"

"We go out the front door," Calavera said.

"And then she puts a bullet in you," Ptolemy said, harshly. "Or the zombies pull you down. Either way, you do not get far." He sat down heavily in a chair and set his shotgun across his knees. "Face it. We are boxed in."

That set off a new round of discussion that Kahwihta found somewhat tedious. So instead, she turned her attention to the window, and what lay outside. Some of the walkers were wandering now. They had been drawn by the noise, but seeing nothing to immediately assuage their hunger, had begun to drift away.

The rest, however, weren't going anywhere. Stubborn, or maybe too stupid to give up. She took out her notebook and pried apart the stiff, water-stained pages. Something about these walkers was different – not their behavior, but their appearance. But she couldn't say what exactly. Not without more study.

A hand on her shoulder made her jump. She looked up at Westlake. "What is it?" she asked.

"You seemed lost in thought."

She frowned. "Were you… checking on me?" Usually, Ramirez was the one who did that. It felt strange to have someone else interrupt her train of thought.

Westlake shrugged. "Crew, remember?" He tapped on the

glass, provoking a walker into hammering on the window frame. He twitched back. "Ugly bastard. Looks like a side of beef jerky."

Kahwihta smiled. "Some of them do. Initially, people figured that they'd starve over time. Walkers don't do well without a source of food. They start breaking down a lot faster, as if whatever is making them walk around starts to consume them. Mostly they get skinny and fragile. But some of them turn, well…"

"Into jerky?" Westlake ran a palm over his head. "Given how many of them are still around, I'm guessing they didn't starve."

Kahwihta shook her head. "No, they adapted." She was warming to her topic now. It was rare she got the chance to talk about it. "They're ridiculously adaptable, but that's not always due to obvious environmental factors."

"Meaning?"

"Take brutes. Why do some of them balloon up like that? What causes it?" She paused and studied the zombies outside with new insight. "*Oh.*"

Westlake blinked. "What?"

"None of them are dressed for a hike." She indicated the window, and the zombies prowling beyond it. "These weren't campers or hikers. Not dressed like that."

"So?"

"So where did they come from?"

Westlake paused. "Does it matter?" Behind them, Ramirez cleared her throat and he and Kahwihta turned.

"Any ideas?" Ramirez asked.

Westlake shrugged. "Other than trying to sneak out, not

really. We might just have to risk it. If we're fast enough…"
He trailed off and glanced at Kahwihta. "Maybe our
zombologist has an idea."

Kahwihta's gaze went back to the window. "Why don't
we wait for nightfall," she said, after a moment. The others
looked at her. She sighed. They never listened. "Zombies
hunt by sound. But their eyesight is no better than ours, and
in some cases, a good deal worse. At night, they won't be
able to spot us as easily, if we don't make any noise."

"And how do you suggest we do that?" Westlake asked,
encouragingly. She realized he'd been telling the truth
earlier; as far as he was concerned, she was part of the crew.
He was actually listening and trusting in her expertise.

She pointed up. "The access hatch. We get on the roof,
climb down on whatever side looks easiest, and book it for
the trees, post haste."

"You think we can do all that without being spotted?"
Hutch asked, doubtfully.

"No. But that's why we need a distraction, to get them all
going in the opposite direction." She looked down at Attila
and kissed the top of his head. He panted happily.

"Just like a supply run," Ramirez said, looking relieved.

"Just like a supply run," Kahwihta agreed.

Westlake laughed and shook his head. "Well, that's one
problem down. What about afterwards?" He looked at
Ramirez. "She was our guide, remember?"

"We know where we're going." Ramirez hiked a thumb at
Labrand. "Labrand can get us there. He used to hike these
mountains all the time."

Labrand blinked in surprise. "I… reckon?" He tipped up

his hat and rubbed his head. "Never saw Lake Cutter, but I was up on the southwest slope more than once."

"What about Sayers?" Kahwihta said. Again, everyone's attention came back to her. "She didn't sound like she was leaving."

"She is right," Ptolemy said. "Sayers is not likely to make it easy for us."

"More traps, you mean?" Ramirez asked.

"At the very least." Ptolemy frowned. "Something does not sit well with me about this. Why would she tell us where she is going?"

"Doesn't make much sense to me either," Ramirez said. "Let's ask her about it if and when we catch up to her." She went to a window and twitched aside the curtain. A zombie flattened itself against the glass, smearing bloody saliva across the panes. She let the curtain fall back into place. "But for now, try and rest. We'll sleep in shifts. Eat if you need to."

"Dibs on the bed," Hutch said. Kahwihta whistled and Attila bounded onto the bed before Hutch could reach it. The dog growled and Hutch backed off, hands raised. "No one respects dibs anymore," he complained.

"Civilization has collapsed and the old ways with it," Kahwihta said, taking her place on the bed. "Now only the law of the jungle matters."

"I hate that mutt, and I hate you," Hutch said, grumpily. He snatched up a chair and dragged it across the room. Kahwihta serenely huddled down next to Attila. She heard some of the others drift off, but despite her best efforts, sleep was hard to come by.

She kept thinking of the water and unseen hands clawing

at her, trying to drag her down. She'd had nightmares before and would again. The only thing to do was endure them and wait for the memories to fade. That was all anyone could do, these days.

She pulled out her by-now much wrinkled and stained notebook. If she couldn't sleep, she might as well record what she'd observed. You never knew when it might come in handy.

CHAPTER EIGHTEEN
Escape

Hutch watched the walkers wander across the porch. He counted almost thirty of the zombies in the dim light of the setting sun. Not many and too many, all at once. He checked his Stoner for the third time in as many minutes. Sayers' shot had dented the casing but not otherwise damaged the weapon, at least not that he could tell.

He looked back out the window. The sun was a slip of light on the horizon, but it was already night beneath the trees. And the zombies kept coming. The more of them there were in one place, the greater the likelihood of more of them showing up.

He stared at the trees, but there was nothing to see in the dark. Something told him they were out there, though. They were always out there. Always walking towards him. He dreamed about it sometimes. Running and running and running, and every time he looked back – there they were. And no matter how fast he ran, or how far he rode, they were always gaining on him.

A rotting fist thumped against the reinforced glass, startling him. He stepped back from the window, letting the curtain drop.

"The sun is just about down," Ptolemy said, from behind him. The other man stood in the doorway to the kitchen, eating out of a can of mixed fruit slices.

Hutch grimaced. "Great. So how we doing this?"

Ramirez, sitting in a chair near the door, looked at him. "The same way we always have. We let Attila run, and see how many he can pull away from us. Then we handle the rest – but quietly." She pointed to the Stoner. "No loud noises. Otherwise, we'll have all of them right back on us before we know it."

"Yeah, I got it." Hutch slung the Stoner across his broad back and reached for his bullwhip. He pulled the braided leather tight between his hands, giving it a snap. He looked at Calavera, crouched nearby. The masked man was studying his icon, as if it held some truth that the rest of them weren't privy to. "You ready, big man?" Hutch asked.

"Yes, very much so." Calavera placed his icon back into his coat and flexed his hands. His knuckles popped like muffled gunshots and Hutch winced. He wasn't any more superstitious than the next guy, but something about Calavera made him uneasy. It wasn't just the way the masked man fought; it was his whole "guided by saints" deal. But one thing he couldn't deny was that it worked. And if it worked, it was OK by Hutch.

Ramirez stood. "Hutch, you, Ptolemy, and Calavera are with me. We'll go up first and get ready. Kahwihta will stay down here with Westlake and Labrand. They'll boost Attila through one of the windows, then follow us up. We go down as a team. We stay together. Don't get separated." She glanced at Labrand.

He cleared his throat. "If you do get separated, head for the southeastern trailhead. Should be marked. That'll take us to Mount Marcy."

"We will not be separated," Calavera said.

Hutch glanced at Calavera and nodded. "Yeah, no worries there. I intend to stick to him like glue. Nothing short of a howitzer is going to take you down, big man. Or maybe a nuke." He frowned. "I wonder if we could find a nuke."

"Yes," Ptolemy said, without elaboration.

"And on that note," Ramirez said. She checked her sidearm. So did Westlake. They looked so similar in that moment – not in their appearance, but in their behavior – that Hutch almost laughed. Two professionals, going about their job.

"Everyone gone tinkle?" Kahwihta said. Hutch and the others looked at her. She grinned. "What? You don't want to be caught out in the woods, needing to pee, with zombies on your trail, do you?"

"She makes a fair point," Hutch said. Ramirez looked at him. Hutch shrugged. "Hey, I don't know about the rest of you, but I did my business."

Ramirez shoved him towards the kitchen. "Thank you for sharing. Roof. Now."

Calavera already had the ladder out and was sliding the access hatch aside. It wasn't locked or even barred – just a simple square of wood and tile, positioned over a single-piece plastic hatch, like the sort people installed in order to get under their houses. Calavera moved it aside as quietly as possible and then boosted himself up onto the roof. A moment of silence followed, then he stuck his head back down. "All clear," he said.

Ramirez went next, followed by Ptolemy. Hutch was last. As he climbed to the top of the ladder, he saw Labrand ease open a window around the back of the main room, facing away from the river. Attila went out a moment later. Hutch heard him begin to bark even as Calavera helped him through the hatch – which was a tighter fit than it looked – and onto the roof. Hutch nodded his thanks to the big man and crept carefully across the roof tiles to join the others over by the chimney.

The sun had slipped behind the trees, and the sky was painted in purples and blacks. The stars were out, gleaming pinpricks overhead. The moon wasn't quite full, but there were no clouds, and silver light fell across the river and the remnants of the dam. He could hear the water rushing past. From the roof, the ground around the cabin looked like a junkyard.

There seemed to be walkers everywhere. More than the thirty he'd counted before. "That's a lot of zombies," he murmured softly.

"It will only get worse if we stay here," Ptolemy said. His hand rested on his hunting knife. "By morning, their numbers may well have doubled."

Hutch wasn't sure about that. He couldn't imagine where they were all coming from. But he refrained from commenting. Instead, he watched as the mutt went to work. At first, it seemed as if the zombies were ignoring Attila's presence.

"She was right – they can't see him," Ramirez murmured.

Hutch realized what she was getting at. The zombies turned this way and that, following the sound of Attila's barking, but they couldn't pinpoint the dog. At least not until he went after one of the slower ones.

Hutch, crouched beside the chimney, could barely make out what was happening, even with the moonlight. He saw a brownish blur, and a walker fell over. He heard growling as Attila chewed at the zombie's leg with every ounce of ferocity he possessed. Then, just as quickly, he let go and bounded away, barking loudly.

Hutch almost laughed. The mutt didn't have much in the way of brains, but he was good at this game. Slowly but surely, the zombies started moving after the dog. Soon, the area below the chimney was all but empty. A few stragglers, slower than the rest, were all that remained. Kahwihta and the others climbed out through the hatch and joined them on the roof. "Time to go," Ramirez said. "Remember, boys. Keep it quiet."

Calavera was the first off the roof. He crept down the incline to the lowest point and dropped the six feet to the ground without issue. Hutch grimaced. He'd jumped off plenty of roofs as a kid, but it had never turned out well for him. He hoped this time was different. He waited for Ptolemy to get down and then followed, somewhat clumsily. He nearly lost his grip on the edge of the roof more than once.

When his feet finally touched solid ground, he sighed in relief – and froze, as a walker lurched around the side of the cabin. He had his whip in his hand, but the thing was too close for him to get a good wind-up. Instead, he snapped the end of the bullwhip around the zombie's head and dragged it towards him with a swift jerk. It was clad in a pantsuit and pearls; a businesswoman, never to make that last important meeting.

Off balance, the walker stumbled into him, and he snapped its neck. It fell, making gagging sounds as it tried to gnaw at his boot. Carefully, he set his heel on the center of its forehead and pressed down with all his weight. Bone popped and flesh tore. The walker spasmed and lay still. Hutch pried his foot loose and scraped it against the ground.

When he turned back to the others, he saw that his walker wasn't the only straggler. But they'd been handled quietly as well. Ramirez had baton-pounded one in the head, and Calavera stood over another, wiping his hands on his trousers. Hutch grinned and started towards them when something tugged at his boot. He froze again, expecting to see a crawler. Instead, he saw a thin wire extending across the ground and into the open door of a trailer. The stake the wire was attached to hadn't quite been dislodged. He'd stopped in time. A booby-trap. Of course Sayers would've left a few, just to make things difficult. God only knew what would have happened if he'd fully dislodged it.

Taking a deep breath, he crouched and gently – gingerly – pushed the stake back into the dirt. He almost called out to the others but stopped himself. They were already moving towards the trees, Labrand in the lead. He could hear Attila barking, then splashing. The dog was leading the zombies into the river.

Hutch started after them, moving as quickly as he dared.

He saw someone – Ramirez, he thought – look back, and he gestured frantically, pointing at the ground, hoping they'd understand. Too late. He saw Ramirez stumble, heard her curse, followed by a loud clatter. Cans, pans, metal striking metal and loudly.

From behind him came a guttural sound – not quite a growl, but close. Hutch turned slowly, suddenly aware of the moon overhead and how exposed he truly was. A zombie dressed as if for Wimbledon crouched atop a nearby stack of wood. It shrilled and dropped to the ground, swiftly scuttling on all fours towards him, tennis skirt flaring.

Hutch narrowly avoided its lunge, throwing himself to the side. His fall dislodged another stake, and a further clattering filled the night. "Hell with this," he snarled, dragging his Stoner up and around as the runner came for him again. He let rip, his shots punching the runner backwards. It fell, twitching, and he scrambled to his feet, not waiting to see whether it was down for good.

The next few moments were loud ones. Walkers staggered out of the trees or stumbled around the cabin. Realizing they'd been spotted, the others gave up on quiet. Ptolemy's shotgun boomed, and he heard the crackle of Kahwihta's cattle-prod. Hutch fired from the hip as a walker reached for him, and its head popped like a balloon. "We need to get out of here before they surround us," he shouted to the others.

"They will do no such thing," Calavera roared, charging towards the largest of the walkers that stood between the group and the trees. The big man caught the zombie up around its midsection, grabbed it by the back of the head, and tore its skull and spine free in a burst of gore.

Then, grasping the blood-slick spinal column, he began to whirl it over his head. He swung the still twitching head of the zombie down atop the cranium of another, flattening it. Using his improvised weapon, he battered the rest of them aside. "Come then," he bellowed. "Come to El Calavera Santo!"

The nearest walkers obliged, converging on the loudest target. Calavera was like a hurricane in human form, using every limb – including some that didn't belong to him – as a weapon. Wherever his fists or feet went, a walker fell and soon enough the way was clear. Hutch watched in sickened fascination as Calavera twisted one's head off and hurled the gory missile at another.

"Calavera is clearing us a path," Ramirez called out. "Hutch – covering fire!" Her pistol barked, and a walker fell. "Everyone else, into the trees!"

Hutch didn't argue. Big gun, big responsibilities – that was how he'd always seen it. He turned back to the cabin and sank to one knee. He took careful aim, suddenly, unavoidably, aware of how little ammunition he had left. But there was no choice. He fired a burst, and a pair of walkers stumbled and fell. One began to rise, and Hutch fired again. Two down, but too many to go. He rose, backing away.

"Hutch!"

At Kahwihta's cry, Hutch spun and saw a walker lurching towards him, too close to avoid. A brown blur took it off its feet and knocked it sprawling. Attila. The dog growled deep in his chest as he dragged the walker by its throat to Kahwihta's feet.

She gave the zombie a tap with her cattle-prod. Electricity

did the same thing to dead muscles that it did to living ones –
made them seize up. Smoke billowed from the zombie's jaws
as it thrashed and went still. "You OK?" she asked Hutch.

He nodded. "Thanks." He glanced back and saw the rest
of the walkers approaching.

"Time to get the hell out of here, I think," Kahwihta said,
hurrying into the trees after the others. Hutch followed,
after only a moment's hesitation. He considered letting off
another burst from the Stoner to take more down, then
decided against it. He might need the ammunition later.

"Past time," he muttered, as he slipped between the trees.

CHAPTER NINETEEN
Double Whammy

Labrand walked point as the group made its way southwest. Tall pines surrounded them, rising to blot out the brightening sky. The trail was uneven, a rough stretch of tumbled rock that wound up and around in serpentine fashion. It grew narrow at points, and they found themselves hemmed in by walls of birch and pine.

The undergrowth was thicker than Labrand recalled, but then, given that no one had been tending the trails, perhaps that wasn't a surprise. He ranged ahead of the group, checking the condition of the trail. He liked walking point. He hadn't been much for talking, even before the dead had risen. Even so, he listened to the quiet murmur of the others' voices and took some comfort in it. Though he wasn't by any means social-minded, he liked having other folks around.

That was part of the reason he'd sought shelter at the lodge in the first place. He'd tried to make it on his own for a month, give or take a few days. He'd been set up for a long weekend in the wilderness when things went bad, with plenty of camping gear and a burning desire to escape a recent divorce. She'd taken the house, the dog, and his record collection – all vinyl, lots of Nashville firsts.

He wasn't bitter; he'd gotten away cheap, all things considered. Sometimes, he wondered what had happened to her. Whether she was still in their house, or whether she'd had the sense to find someplace safer. He hoped so. But part of him was glad he didn't know either way. Ignorance was bliss, as the saying went.

Hell, he hadn't even known what had happened until he'd stumbled across a hiker with a hole where his stomach had been and a mad-on for fresh meat. It had taken him more time than he liked to admit to figure out how to put the poor fellow down for good.

The solar-powered radio he'd brought with him filled him in on the rest. Not that there was much in the way of news. It had happened so quickly that most major media outlets had gone black before they even noticed what was going on.

These days, life was simple. He knew what he needed to do, and anything else was just a distraction. Maybe that would change once they'd found this place of Westlake's. So long as it was bigger and easier to defend than the lodge, Labrand would count it a win. They needed one, especially after the last few months. Too many losses, too many close calls, too many scavenging trips coming back empty-handed.

He stopped suddenly and raised his hand, bringing the others to a halt. Branches cracked under the weight of something heavy. Labrand gestured to the others. "Back up a bit. Now. But don't run."

"Bear?" Ramirez asked, softly.

Labrand didn't look at her. "Yep." He lifted his rifle and sighted through the scope. "Big one." The bear was still keeping itself out of sight, back among the trees at the bend of the trail. But from the sound of its grunts, it had caught their scent and was decidedly curious.

"I thought black bears didn't get very big," Westlake said, as they retreated.

"Seven feet, if they're on their hind legs," Labrand said.

"That's bigger than I thought." Westlake clutched his shotgun more tightly. "Animals shouldn't be that big. It's not right."

"You sound scared, Westlake," Ramirez said, glancing at him. "Worried that the big bad bear is going to eat you?"

"No. But then, I'm faster than you are."

The black bear ambled into the open and pushed itself up onto its hind legs, surveying the trail with dark eyes. Labrand held his breath as the animal's gaze fell on them. It scented the air, then, when they showed no sign of approaching, it fell back onto all fours and gave a grunt. Two cubs bumbled out of the underbrush, and together all three went on their way. Hutch whistled softly. "Don't see that every day."

Labrand lowered his rifle. "We'll give her a few minutes to get clear, then keep going." He looked at the others. "There's a lot of bears up here, especially this time of year. And without people to bother them, they've been extending the range of their territories. There's plenty of deer now, fish… carrion."

"Extending the range back to their *natural* territories," Kahwihta corrected softly.

"They do eat zombies, then?" Westlake asked. "I don't know how I feel about that."

"Better than eating us," Ramirez said. "Now let's keep…"

The explosion rocked them on the trail, and a boil of smoke came rushing down towards them. Everyone took cover as best they could. Labrand scrambled behind a fallen tree, seeking safety in its flare of roots. The dust settled, and no more explosions followed. Labrand took off his hat and peered around the roots.

There was nothing up ahead but trees and dust, and something red and wet that had splattered all over the ground. He looked back at Ramirez and signaled silently that he'd go up ahead. She nodded, looking shaken. He rose to his feet, but kept low, rifle at the ready.

He wondered if it was another of Sayers' traps as he crept around the end of the tree, sweeping the trail ahead. There were bits and pieces of… something, everywhere. Several somethings, maybe. As the smoke cleared, he caught a flash of color in the dawn light – canary yellow. It was accompanied by a soft, animal grunt. Almost an exhalation, rather than a true sound. A walker.

Labrand turned and gestured, using two fingers to mime someone walking – their signal for a walker. Ramirez nodded and waved the others back into cover. Where there was one walker, there might be more. Labrand slung his rifle and drew his hunting knife. He crept through the trees towards the swaying figure. You didn't often find walkers alone, even out here. They tended to clump up when they could.

The first thing he noticed about the walker was that it wasn't dressed for a hike. Or for much of anything at all, save the remains of a flight attendant's uniform that flapped alarmingly as the walker swung its head about in a motion reminiscent of a snake tasting the air. He could see no patches of gnawed flesh, and wondered how the woman had died. Not that it mattered. She – it – was covered in splashes of blood.

Labrand paused to take stock. Sometimes runners used walkers as bait, though he wasn't sure that they knew that was what they were doing. Kahwihta would probably know. Hell, that girl probably had a whole damn thesis prepared on the subject.

He waited for any other zombies to show themselves. When none wandered into view, he took a low breath and crept forward. The walker was looking one way, and Labrand came from the other. He took the last few steps at a run and drove the knife up through the base of the zombie's skull before it had noticed he was there.

He gave the blade an expert twist, severing the spinal column and turning off the walker's lights. He lowered the body gently to the ground, and then saw there was a blackened crater in the trail, still smoldering. A large chunk of something that might once have been human lay nearby, twitching mindlessly.

Labrand wasn't a military man, as such. Peripherally, perhaps. But he'd been some places and seen some things, and one of those things was IEDs – improvised explosive devices – and what they left behind. The hole and the splatter looked awfully familiar, and he felt a chill sweep through him as he considered the trail.

The zombie – probably one of several – had been torn

apart by the blast. Unlike the others, it was still moving. Its arms and legs were gone, leaving only most of a torso and part of a head. The newly made crawler snapped its splintered teeth at him as he raised his knife to finish it off. When he'd done so, he cleaned his knife in the grass and sheathed it. He looked up as a twig cracked.

"Everything copacetic?" Hutch asked. He stopped. "What happened here?"

"Some zombies stepped on a mine and blew themselves up."

Hutch glanced at the one Labrand had knifed. "That one?"

"That one didn't," Labrand drawled. He was about to continue when he saw the mound of dirt a few inches behind Hutch's foot. "Don't move," he growled. Hutch, true to form, stepped back.

Click.

"Damn," Labrand said. "Now, definitely don't move."

Hutch froze. "Why?"

"Because you stepped on a goddamn mine."

"I did what now?" Hutch said, in a wheezy voice.

"A mine, Hutch. An explosive device, which is activated by a pressure plate. Like the one that blew these walkers up. You have stepped on it – like an idiot – and now it is activated. So shut up and don't move, or we're both going to die. You dig?"

"I dig."

"Right." Labrand peered past Hutch and gave a whistle. Ramirez led the others up the trail towards them, a look of concern on her face.

"What is it?" she asked, as she drew close.

"Hutch stepped on a mine," Labrand said, calmly.

"What?" Ramirez said, startled. She looked past him. "Is he…?"

"He's fine."

Hutch twisted his head around. "I am not fine. I am standing on a land mine!"

Labrand didn't look at him. "I thought I told you not to move."

Hutch muttered an obscenity and hunched his shoulders. Labrand paused and rubbed the back of his neck. "What do I do?" Hutch asked.

"Don't move."

"I'm already doing that. What are you going to do?"

"I'm thinking."

"Think faster," Hutch said.

"Not a time to rush me, Hutch."

"I beg to differ."

Westlake snorted.

Hutch looked at him. "You think this is funny?" he demanded.

"A bit, yeah."

Hutch looked appealingly at Ramirez. "Boss…"

Ramirez couldn't repress a chuckle. "Tell him, Labrand."

"Tell me what?"

Labrand grinned at Hutch. "Relax. It's a dud. If it wasn't, it'd have already gone boom. I just wanted you to stay still until the others got here. Teach you a lesson about listening."

"Asshole," Hutch growled, stepping gingerly off the mine. Labrand's grin widened and he stooped to brush the dirt from the device. It was shaped something like a small pancake, and made from what he thought might be aluminum. That meant it was an old one – World War 2, or thereabouts.

"Others?" Ramirez asked, crouching beside him so she could get a look at it as well.

"We're in a minefield," Westlake said. Labrand nodded and looked up at Ptolemy.

"Maybe. How many of these would you say she had?"

Ptolemy paused, then shook his head. "I would expect no more than a handful." He peered up at the trees and then at the trail ahead of them. "I cannot imagine that she has enough to mine the entire trail."

"She don't have to," Labrand said, scratching his chin. "One or two on the trail would be enough. She knew we'd come this way, probably figured the odds were good we'd step on it. We're just lucky it didn't go off."

"We?" Hutch said, looking pale. "Me. That thing would have taken my leg off."

"It would have taken more than that," Labrand said, poking Hutch.

"Quiet, both of you," Ramirez said, sharply. She looked up. "Anyone else hear that?"

"What?" Westlake asked, looking confused.

"Nothing," Labrand said, rising to his feet. The forest was silent, save for the creak of branches in the mid-morning breeze. The lack of birdsong, even at night, left him chilled to the bone. The woods were supposed to be noisy. But not here, not now. Something was wrong. "The birds have gone quiet."

"So? Maybe the blast scared them."

Labrand shook his head. "If it had, they'd have come back by now."

"Walkers," Kahwihta said, softly. "Birds always go quiet when a lot of zombies are in the area. They've learned to shut up and sit still." She reached for her cattle-prod. "The explosion must have drawn them."

"Let's keep moving," Labrand said, eyeing the way they'd come. The wind shifted, and Attila began to growl, deep in his throat.

"Yeah, about that," Westlake said. "If she's planted mines on the trail, is it a smart idea to follow it?" When Labrand and the others looked at him, he spread his hands. "I'm just saying, this might be what she wants us to do."

"You have a suggestion to go with that?" Ramirez asked. "Because if not, Labrand is right, and we need to move."

"We'll take it slow," Labrand said. "I'll stay on point, mark a safe path along the trail. Step on my shadow and keep tight. Don't veer off." He tipped his hat and smiled.

"We'll be right as rain."

CHAPTER TWENTY
Slow Going

Westlake was tired. Contrary to what his mother had always said, a hike hadn't done him any good. His calves were cramping, his ankles ached, and his ribs felt like they were being squeezed. He said nothing about any of it. They were all feeling the same, though some, like Calavera, showed it less.

They were taking it slow, as Labrand had said, and dawn had come and gone. Every so often on the trail, the lanky man would stop, prod any patch of ground that wasn't rock with his knife, and then move on. But it made for an interminable journey, especially up a steep incline.

The trail had devolved from a relatively open path to a jumble of glacial rock, all angled as if to twist ankles or break legs. As they climbed over the slippery rocks, Westlake noticed an abundance of white flowers that he didn't recognize.

No, the climb wasn't easy, but it was picturesque. They passed plunging waterfalls and babbling creeks. Slowly, he was coming to understand why someone might willingly spend time out here. Not that he was in the mood for it.

They had been walking most of the day when Ramirez finally called a halt. They'd come to a fast-moving stretch of water broken by innumerable round stones, that Labrand said was a flume in the Opalescent River. The trail went up at a steep angle ahead of them, and trees hung low over the water, some almost bent parallel to the ground.

"Used to camp out here a good bit," Labrand said. "Makes for a relaxing evening."

Westlake thought it anything but, yet he was too busy sucking wind to comment. From behind them, down the trail a distance, came the moan of the dead carried on the wind. He stared at the close-set trees, wondering when the walkers would catch up to them. He imagined it would be soon but knew that they were likely having more trouble with the trek than he and the others. On the other hand, they didn't have to stop to rest.

Kahwihta sat on a rock a little distance from the others, Attila laying beside her. She looked up from her notebook as he approached and pointed down in the direction they'd come. "Smell that? They're still on our trail." She paused to write something in her battered notebook. "And there's more of them than there were before."

"You can tell that by smell?" he asked, taking a gulp of water from his bottle.

"Yeah." She tapped the side of her nose. "The stronger the smell, the more of them there are. Stands to reason, right?"

Westlake shook his head. He put his water away. "If you say so."

Kahwihta chuckled. "You're not a very outdoorsy sort of guy, are you?"

"What makes you say that?"

"Because you look like you're about to keel over."

He glared at her. "It's been a stressful day." He turned to head back up the trail.

Kahwihta laughed, hopped from her perch, and fell into step with him. Attila trotted ahead of them. The dog made to head into the underbrush, but a quick whistle from Kahwihta brought him back, tail wagging sheepishly. "Did you notice what the one Labrand killed back there was wearing?" she asked, in a low voice.

Westlake nodded. "A flight attendant's uniform." He'd been thinking on that as well. It hadn't seemed odd at the time, but the more he thought about it, the more it puzzled him.

"Funny thing to find in the middle of the woods, right?" Kahwihta frowned and flipped through her notebook. "And she wasn't the first. I've been noting a discrepancy in their attire for a few weeks now. Lots of unusual outfits – all wrong for this area. It's almost like someone bused them in."

"Ramirez mentioned that there was an airfield over near Saranac Lake. Maybe the passengers and crew wandered into the mountains."

"Long way to come," she said.

"Yeah, but they don't know that, do they?"

She chuckled and put away her notebook. "True. They're probably an hour or two behind us, by the way. You don't need to keep checking."

"What about runners?"

Kahwihta shook her head. "They usually stay close to walkers."

"I noticed. Never could figure out why, though."

"Camouflage," she said.

Westlake scratched his chin and considered this. "You know, sometimes you make it sound like the zombies ain't got two braincells between them, and other times you make out like they're as smart as us."

"You don't have to be intelligent to be cunning," she said, after a few moments. "They don't think anymore – not in any sort of way that we'd understand. But there is something going on in there. Some spark of… something."

"Evil," he said.

She looked at him, and then back down the trail. "Maybe. I don't like that word. Makes it too easy to forget that they used to be people." She sighed. "Too many survivors want to pretend that the zombies were never people. That they're just a faceless horde, to be mowed down."

"You saying they're not?"

"I'm saying they didn't start that way, and we have to remember that." She looked at him. "We're going to forget so much, you know? In ten years, twenty… thirty… how much knowledge is going to be lost? The last handful of electrical grids in this country will start shutting down in the next few months. Any remaining server farms will go with them. That'll be it for the internet."

"No big loss."

She shook her head. "Bigger than you imagine. So much of our knowledge is stored on perishable media. Even the best kept books will eventually rot." She paused. "Everything rots. And I don't see anyone setting up a printing press anytime soon."

Westlake frowned. That sort of problem was beyond him. He'd never been one to waste his time worrying about things he couldn't change. But he didn't say that. Instead, all he said was, "Maybe. But who knows how it will all shake out in the end?"

She snorted. "Not great at pep talks, are you?"

"Never been my strength, no."

She patted his arm. "That's OK. You have other talents. Come on. Let's go see what the others are up to."

"Fine by me." He tossed a last glance back down the trail, thinking about what she'd said. Somehow, the thought of everything falling apart only made finishing this thing seem all the more important. If he was going out, he intended to do it on top. One way or another.

Up ahead, Labrand was in quiet conversation with Ramirez. When Westlake and Kahwihta joined them, Ramirez turned to address them.

"We're going to press on and make camp up ahead. Labrand says there's a lean-to around here. We can get a fire going, get some sleep."

"You sure that's wise, given what's dogging our trail?" Westlake asked.

Labrand scratched his cheek. "The lean-to is a bit off the trail. They shouldn't be able to spot us if we're quiet. I got some ideas on how to slow them down a bit, if some of y'all can give me a hand." He reached into his backpack and pulled out a roll of wire. "Found this in Sayers' place. Thought it might come in handy."

"You mean to make a tripwire," Ptolemy said. He was sitting nearby, his shotgun across his knees. Labrand looked at him.

"I mean to make several. There's enough wire here to make a handful, at least." He gestured. "We'll stretch most of 'em at ankle height, but a few at head or neck height. That should give them something to think about – not that they think, mind."

"So, you're hoping to cause a traffic pileup?" Westlake asked.

Labrand nodded. "Seems to me if we slow 'em down enough, they might just wander back down the mountain. Make them a problem for another day."

"Sounds like a plan to me," Hutch said. He heaved himself to his feet. "Let's string some wire, boys." As he, Ptolemy and Labrand got to work, Westlake looked at Kahwihta.

"What do you think?"

She frowned. "No reason it shouldn't work."

"But?"

She looked back down the trail, still frowning. Then she shook her head. "But there's no reason to think they won't just tear through it after a time. Zombies don't turn aside at resistance – they double down. The only way to stop this bunch will be to outpace them so thoroughly that they forget about us entirely."

"Not likely," Westlake said.

Kahwihta looked down at Attila and scratched his head. "No. Not likely at all."

It took the others almost an hour to string the wire. Westlake felt some relief when they were ready to move again. The zombies did not seem to be in any hurry, but they did not stop, either.

Westlake and the others climbed up the rocky sides of the flume – rough going, even for Calavera. The path they took ran parallel to the trail, but Labrand was hoping to avoid any more of Sayers' surprises. More than once, Westlake thought he might slip and fall, but he made it to the top in one piece, though not without some help.

They camped twenty minutes from the river. Twenty minutes closer to the summit. Twenty minutes further away from the pursuing zombies. Westlake would have preferred to camp somewhere he couldn't hear the distant moaning, but Labrand swore they were safe enough. As the shadows lengthened, Hutch started a fire. In its glow, conversation turned invariably to important matters.

"Meteors," Hutch said. He'd produced a bag of marshmallows from his backpack and was gleefully roasting them.

Westlake, who'd only been half listening, came to attention. "What?"

"Meteors are why the dead rose. Or maybe cell towers."

Westlake laughed. "I think you're confusing reality for a Stephen King novel."

"Then you give me a better explanation." Hutch chewed angrily on blackened sugar. Westlake thought they must have been stale by now, but Hutch seemed to have no issue with that. Curiosity won out over prudence.

"First, give me a marshmallow."

Hutch clutched the bag protectively to his chest and turned away. "Get your own. I had to fight a brute for these."

Ramirez looked at him, eyebrow raised. "It fell into a shelf after we killed it and knocked bags everywhere."

Hutch frowned. "Fine, I had to fight the mutt for it." Attila growled softly, eyes on the bag. Hutch growled back. Westlake kept his hand out. Hutch finally deposited one into his palm. Westlake chewed thoughtfully, then spat it into the fire. Definitely stale.

Taking a gulp of water to clear the taste out of his mouth, he said, "I see no point in speculating on something we'll never have the answer to."

"Amen," Labrand said, from where he lay near the fire, hands on his chest and his hat tipped over his eyes.

"You guys are no fun," Hutch said. He glanced at Calavera. "What do you think it was, big man?"

"The shadow of God's hand," Calavera said, dolefully. "Where it passes, birds fall from the sky and the dead rise. The world is unmade." He had his icon in his hands and turned it over and over as he spoke. "Only Santa Muerte can make a dead world live again."

"Makes as much sense as anything else," Westlake said. He looked at Ptolemy. "I bet you think it was aliens, right?"

Ptolemy looked up at the slip of sky visible beneath the nodding boughs of the close-set trees around them. "There's a quote by Charles Fort that I am fond of: the Earth is a farm. We are someone else's property."

Westlake studied him. "And the zombies are… mad cow disease?"

"Or an intentional culling," Ptolemy said, stirring the fire with a stick. "While resource scarcity and overpopulation were largely sociopolitical conspiracies designed to demonize the less affluent, it may be that our unseen owners have decided to start over. For when the dead have devoured the living, and stripped this world bare, they too will perish. As Calavera said, the world is unmade... and then made anew."

An uncomfortable silence fell, save Attila, who started to growl softly. Somewhere out past the reach of the fire, a branch cracked. Westlake stared into the dark, trying to spot whatever it was. But nothing revealed itself. Attila's growl increased in volume before fading to a discontented rumble. The dog laid his head down on his paws. Ramirez released a slow breath and laughed softly.

"And on that note, someone pass me a marshmallow."

CHAPTER TWENTY-ONE
Murk

Ramirez took a deep breath as birds chirped and the morning light dappled the mossy forest floor. "It really is pretty," she murmured to no one in particular. It was easy to forget how beautiful things could be, when you were always worried about something taking a bite out of you. She only wished Frieda was with her to share it. Pushing the thought aside, she adjusted the strap on her backpack and ducked beneath a low hanging branch as she and the others followed Labrand along the narrow path.

The trail had gotten so steep that sometimes they had to bend double, using exposed roots and rocks as handholds. In other spots, they had to risk free-climbing, which brought its own headaches – the rocks were flat and slick, damp with morning dew. The trees were getting shorter as well. There were no trail markers to be seen, either.

The night had passed without incident. She'd slept badly, but that was par for the course these days. Everything ached. She'd thought she was in good condition, but her feet and back were saying otherwise. She was looking forward to reaching the summit. From there on in, they'd be going down rather than climbing up. But, unfortunately, that relief was still several hours of hiking away.

She tried not to think about the lodge as she walked. About what might have happened after they'd left. More, she tried not to think about what might have happened if they'd stayed. Would it have mattered? Maybe they could have done something – saved the camp. She shook her head, trying to banish the thoughts. They had a job to do, and she intended to see it done. One way or another.

It was colder up here. She'd read somewhere that every thousand feet of elevation in the Adirondacks was the equivalent, temperature-wise, of driving five hundred miles north. The higher you went, the colder it got, with some exceptions.

They hit one of those exceptions a few minutes after the thought occurred to her. They entered a cut in the mountain – two steep walls of rock that rose along the slope of the mountain. The trail went along the top of the narrow scree that ran up through the cleft. It was full of fallen skinny pines and leafy, obscuring ferns.

The air was almost humid in this isolated pocket, and as Ramirez scanned the heights she felt a sudden prickle of unease. She stopped, gesturing for the others to do the same. Then she whistled for Labrand. He turned, one hand on a tree. "What is it?" he called back.

"Look around," she said. "What do you think?"

Labrand tipped back the brim of his hat and looked up. He frowned. "Ambush?" Even as he asked the question, the answer came in the form of a gunshot. His Stetson was sent flying, and Labrand ducked around the closest tree for cover.

Ramirez dropped low, hunkering in the lee of a fallen tree. As the echo of the shot faded, the others sought what cover they could find. Westlake, halfway down the scree, shouted, "Where is she?"

"Above us," Ramirez answered. She peered around the edge of her tree, but saw no telltale glint to mark the shooter's position. Sayers was smarter than that. "Somewhere, anyway," she muttered. Her fingers tapped at the holstered shape of her pistol. After a moment's hesitation, she drew it. She felt better with the weapon in her hand, even if she couldn't see her target.

"So what do we do about it?" Hutch bawled. He huddled down as a shot plucked at the branches above his head, showering him with pine needles. He covered his head with his hands and gave a muffled curse.

Ramirez had no answer for him – not a good one, at least. Sayers had the high ground, and if they hunkered down for too long, the walkers would catch up with them. If they made a run for it, they'd make themselves targets. "Can anyone see anything?" she called. "Calavera, Westlake, anybody?"

Westlake gave a sour laugh. "If I could see her, I'd have already shot her." He had his back against a rock, partway down the scree just above Hutch. Kahwihta and Attila crouched nearby. She was relieved to see that neither of them was hurt.

Ramirez turned back the way they'd come. Ptolemy had been bringing up the rear. "Ptolemy, what's the status on our tagalongs?" They hadn't seen or heard from the zombies since the night before. It was too much to hope they'd lost them, but maybe they were far enough away that they hadn't noticed that their quarry had stopped.

Ptolemy leaned against the side of the cleft, back at the last bend. He dropped into a crouch and craned his neck. "I do not see them! Perhaps they have wandered off."

"Or perhaps that is why she ambushed us," Calavera said. He lay flat against the scree, trying to make himself as small as possible with little success. A moment later, the blat of an airhorn proved his theory correct.

"She must be operating it by remote somehow, otherwise she'd just be drawing them towards herself," Kahwihta said.

"Does it matter? It puts our butts in a sling, however she's doing it." Ramirez turned back to the head of the trail, and Labrand. "Time's up. We need to move. What are our options?"

Labrand peered up ahead and held up two fingers. "Got two routes. One straightaway, and one to the southwest. Neither of them are marked that I can see." He looked back at her. "We take the straightaway, we might as well be inviting her to follow us and take potshots. Southwest might give us some cover."

"Good enough," Ramirez said. She turned to the others. "On my mark, we make a break for the southwest trail. Labrand, think you can cover us?"

"If she shoots again, I'll try and spot her," Labrand said. "No promises, though. She's dug in like a tick, if she's smart."

Ramirez nodded. "You don't need to hit her, just keep her head down." She looked at Kahwihta. "You and the dog take point. If there are any surprises waiting for us up there, maybe the mutt will spot them."

Kahwihta nodded, clutching her cattle-prod close. "Will do, boss." Guiding Attila by the collar, she and the dog squirmed along the scree, causing the ferns to rustle. No further shots came, thankfully. But she could hear moaning now. If the zombies had somehow lost their trail earlier, they'd certainly found it again.

Ramirez waited until Kahwihta had made it past Labrand, then waved Westlake and Ptolemy forward. "Stay low. Move fast." Neither man replied, but they did as she ordered. Hutch was next. He tapped his Stoner meaningfully as he scrambled past her.

"Sure you don't want me to…?"

"Don't waste the ammo," Ramirez said, waving him on impatiently. Calavera was last. The big man didn't so much creep as prowl, his eyes on the heights.

"I could scale it," he murmured, pausing near her.

"Quickly?" she asked.

"Fairly so," he said, after a moment's hesitation – or perhaps calculation.

Ramirez was tempted, imagining the look on Sayers' face. She shook her head. "No. Plenty of time to settle up later. Go. Join the others."

When only she and Labrand were left on the path, she started to inch forward, but froze as something shuffled into sight at the far end of the trail, from the direction they'd come. A zombie, wearing what was left of a park ranger's uniform, including a wide-brimmed hat perched on its withered head.

There was no telling how long it had been wandering the trails. She knew at once that the airhorn had drawn it, though she didn't think it was part of the horde that had been following them. She took aim, hesitated, wondering if it was worth wasting a bullet. A twig snapped as she shifted position, and the zombie's head jerked around.

It moved before she even had a chance to do more than register that it had been looking at her. A runner, and a fast one. It was on her before she could get a shot off, and she fell back, nearly rolling down the scree in her haste to avoid its grasp. She grabbed onto an exposed root and halted her fall. She fired, but the shot was bad, punching into its torso. The runner staggered, but didn't fall. Its hat hung from its neck by a cord as it lunged at her again – then stopped dead as a shot perforated its skull.

The runner toppled and slid limply down the slope. Ramirez turned and waved to Labrand. "Thanks."

Labrand stared at her in confusion. "I didn't… I couldn't get a shot off."

Ramirez blinked and then looked up. "Sayers?" she murmured. Had Sayers been aiming for her, and accidentally hit the zombie? Or had she shot the runner intentionally? Ramirez had a feeling that no answer would be forthcoming. Warily, she climbed to her feet. She could feel Sayers watching her, studying her through the sights of her rifle.

Ramirez extended her middle finger in the direction of the heights and then turned and hurried towards Labrand. He rose, retrieved his hat, and followed her as she passed him. "What was that about?" he muttered, casting suspicious glances back the way they'd come.

"No clue. Maybe Ptolemy can tell us."

When they reached the others, they found that the southwestern trail ran down into a muddy swamp before rising at the next bend. The undergrowth had become a mire of stagnant water, and the hum of mosquitoes was heavy on the air. The scattered trees were thin blades of birch. At some point, someone had built a ramshackle walkway of raised duckboards over the worst of it. But the undergrowth was rapidly reclaiming the path.

Kahwihta stood at the opposite end of the duckboards. She waved a hand. "Looks clear up ahead, as near as I can tell," she called out. The others were already crossing, Calavera in the lead. Ramirez was the last onto the duckboards. She paused, looking back. No sign of any more runners. The boards creaked beneath her weight.

At the midpoint, Calavera stopped suddenly. "Wait. Something is…" he began, but before he could finish, the boards beneath his feet splintered, and he plunged down into the murky water below. A moment later, Ramirez saw that he hadn't done so unassisted. A waterlogged walker had a death-grip on the masked man, and was attempting to bite and drown him. The water wasn't deep, but it didn't have to be if you couldn't raise your head. She started forward to aid Calavera but stopped as one of the boards beneath her feet cracked and fell away.

"Everyone off!" she shouted. "This thing is coming apart!" As she spoke, she felt something clutch at her ankle and looked down. A muddy hand gripped her trouser cuff. A wizened, almost mummified face broke the surface of the dark water beneath her a moment later as a dead woman, dressed in the filth-encrusted remnants of a park ranger's uniform like the runner earlier, tried to haul herself up onto the duckboards.

The zombie gave a gurgling hiss as it forced itself up through the gap. Ramirez didn't bother trying to pull her leg free of its grip. Instead, she drew her baton, snapped it out to its full length, and struck the walker's grimy wrist.

Bone snapped, and paper-thin flesh tore. A second blow was all that was needed to break the dead woman's hand off at the wrist. Ramirez stepped back and sent a third blow whistling down onto the zombie's mud-plastered skull. It slid off the duckboards and back into the water below. She looked up to see two more of the bog-walkers crawling stiffly out of the mire and onto the duckboards between the group and Kahwihta. Attila barked furiously, and Kahwihta fought to control him.

"Labrand, they're yours," Ramirez shouted. Labrand snatched his Colt from its holster and fired twice, quick as thought. Both walkers fell, but one still crawled towards the cowboy, ruined features twisting around the newly made hole in its nasal cavity. Kahwihta finished it off, stabbing her cattle-prod down on its head as Attila held it still. Labrand nodded his thanks.

Ramirez hurried towards Calavera. Hutch, Westlake and Ptolemy were already in the muddy water, trying to pull the walker off him. Like the others, it was dressed in the stained remnants of a park services uniform, but it had the matted tangle of a once bushy beard hiding its lower jaw. The three men managed to wrestle the walker up and off Calavera, with some effort.

Calavera rose from the water, spluttering. Before the others could react, he punched his attacker, sending its head bouncing across the boards to stop at Ramirez' feet. She used her baton to flick the bearded head into the water. Calavera wiped mud from his mask and growled his thanks. "It surprised me. That will not happen again."

Ramirez nodded, studying the headless corpse. She wondered if Sayers had known them, and whether they'd come out here looking to escape or for survivors when they'd run afoul of whatever had turned them. "These things were waiting on us in the mud." Ramirez looked at Kahwihta, who was crouched over the one she'd killed.

"Yeah," the young woman said. "That's why Attila didn't smell them when we crossed." She frowned. "Like I've said before, they're adaptable, both physically and behaviorally." She stood, her eyes narrowed in thought. "Of course, it's all speculation at this point. I don't even know if these are random permutations or distinct sub-species. How does a brute become a brute, or a runner a runner? What determines it?" She paused. "And what if there are more to come?"

Westlake grimaced. "You mean more permutations?"

"Well, you saw the floaters, although those are really just walkers who got stuck." Kahwihta hiked a thumb over her shoulder. "And those things were walkers too, but sneaky ones. There's no telling what other sort of variations could exist out here." She indicated the broken boards. "Either way, they had some help."

"Yes. The boards were sawed," Calavera spoke up. "That is what I was planning to say earlier. Someone was meant to fall in."

"Another trap," Labrand murmured. "That's why Sayers didn't shoot at us."

"But not an immediately lethal one," Ramirez said. "Dangerous, but this was mostly meant to delay us. This was all about slowing us down. The question is, why?"

"Because she wants to lay more traps, obviously," Hutch said.

Westlake shook his head. "Yeah, but what's the point? Why not just pick a spot and shoot us? Why waste the time setting traps that she knows we're likely to find, or the walkers are just as likely to trip?"

Ramirez put her hands on her hips. "She's trying to scare us. Make us turn back. I wasn't certain of it before, but I am now. She doesn't want us to get to the Villa, that much is obvious. But she's not willing to outright kill us to prevent it." She frowned and ran a hand through her hair. She looked at the rocks above and wondered whether Sayers was up there somewhere even now, watching them. If it looked like they'd been in danger, would she have pulled the same trick twice and shot the walkers?

"Maybe there's something we don't know," Kahwihta said.

"Yeah. Is there, Calvin?" Ramirez asked.

Ptolemy looked at her, eyebrow raised. "What are you implying?"

"I'm not implying anything. I'm outright saying it." Ramirez faced him. "Back at the lodge, she tried to kidnap you. She only started shooting when she got spooked, and even then, she could have easily put one right between Hahm's eyes, but instead aimed for her side. Then there was that stunt at the cabin, and now this – another warning."

"What about the mines?" Hutch asked.

Ramirez glanced at him. "Tell me, have we seen any more? No. Because two was all she needed to slow us down. And I'd put good odds on her herding those walkers onto the first one. Just to give us a hint of what was waiting for us." She looked back at Ptolemy. "She's got her kid gloves on… and I think it's because of you, Calvin."

Ramirez studied Ptolemy. He looked almost insulted, but also somewhat relieved. As if he'd found the answer to a question that had been bothering him. Finally, he said, "If so, it is to our advantage. We should press on. Use me as a shield." He took a breath. "From here on out, I will take point. Labrand can tell me where to go."

Ramirez hesitated. Part of her was suspicious – who wouldn't be? But they didn't have time to argue. Not really. She released a slow sigh and nodded.

"Fine. Keep your eyes peeled, though. No more surprises if we can help it."

CHAPTER TWENTY-TWO
Bear-Bait

At around 3,300 feet, the mud and mosquitos disappeared and the rocks started again, much to Ptolemy's relief. Many of the trail markers that had once signified the routes hikers should take had long ago fallen away, or been removed. Maybe Sayers had done it, maybe someone else. The trees were shorter here, and the fierce wind hummed along the rocks, making the branches creak oddly.

The domes of nearby peaks rose, marking the gaps in the trees. They were less than an hour from the summit, or so Labrand insisted. Ptolemy took a quiet comfort in the laconic man's calm directions. While Ptolemy was no stranger to the wilderness, even he wasn't sure where he was anymore. But Labrand seemed to have no such difficulties.

Ptolemy kept such thoughts to himself. Indeed, he'd said nothing to the others since he'd taken point. Not simply because he was paying attention to the way ahead, but also because he could feel them watching him, with suspicion or perhaps pity.

He didn't care for either. He'd had his fill of both in his lifetime. Sayers was – or had been – one of the only people to see him simply as he was, rather than what they imagined him to be. Not crazy or gullible; just skeptical. About everything and anything.

People had thought Charles Fort was crazy as well. Except for those, like Ptolemy, who understood what the great man had been getting at in his writings on the nature of science and belief. The proper authority saw to it that the proper belief should be induced, and the people believed properly. No truer words had ever been written. But even Fort might have had some difficulty accepting the presence of the walking dead.

Ptolemy had seen some survivors go mad even when safe from the dead outside, but imperiled by their own inability to accept the situation. It was too big; vast, black and brooding – a shadow moving across the sun, as Fort wrote. It took a certain fortitude to endure the new world order. A certain hardness of soul.

Sayers had it. Perhaps that was why she was doing what she was doing. Even so, it made little sense to him. She hadn't always been that way, he thought. If she had, he hadn't seen it.

So lost in these thoughts was he that he did not notice the trap until he'd sprung it. There was a sharp twang, a sudden pain about his ankle, and then he was yanked off his feet, turned upside down and dragged bodily into the air. He yelped, losing hold of his shotgun. A snare trap – Sayers, again. He felt like laughing and crying all at once, though that might have just been the blood rushing to his head. It seemed he wasn't much of a shield after all.

He smelled something pungent and saw a cloth sack of something laying on the ground below him – obviously the counterweight. "What is that stink?" he groaned as he spun in a slow circle. "Also, could someone get me down?"

Labrand approached, one hand over his mouth. "Bear bait," he said, coughing. "Homemade by the smell of it."

"Oh, well, so long as it's artisanal," Westlake groused. He looked at Ramirez. "We need to get him down, and quick."

"I concur," Ptolemy said, rotating slowly.

Labrand squinted at the tree. It was larger than some, nearly seven feet and with broad branches. "I can climb it. Calavera, can you support him?" The big man nodded and got up under Ptolemy, boosting him up so that the vertigo lessened somewhat. Ptolemy smiled gratefully.

"I guess I was wrong," Ramirez said, as Labrand handed her his rifle and started up the tree.

"She probably set this one thinking it would be Labrand," Westlake said, suddenly. He picked up Ptolemy's shotgun and cradled it in the crook of his arm. "He's been on point the whole time. Or she set it a while ago, before we even started this trip."

"Why would she do that?" Ptolemy asked, trying to crane his neck to look at the other man.

Calavera grunted. "Stop squirming."

"She's been trying to divert us from the beginning. Even at the lodge. If she already knew about the Villa, it stands to reason that she probably set traps on every path leading to it." He stepped closer to Ptolemy. "How well did you know Sayers?"

"What are you getting at?" Ptolemy asked.

Ramirez frowned. "He means that the Bonaro would have needed someone – several someones – in the local park service to help keep hikers from stumbling on the Villa. One camper with a camera phone and the Villa appears on the front page of ever newspaper in the country. We should–"

Whatever she'd been about to say was lost as an explosive grunt split the air. Everyone froze. Ptolemy looked up. "I would like to get down now."

Labrand was halfway up the tree, one hand on his Colt. "Hush," he said. Attila began to bark frantically, struggling to escape Kahwihta's grip. She tried to calm the dog, but to no avail. Another grunt issued from the trees somewhere to their left. Ptolemy heard heavy crashing through the brush. A moment later, whatever it was roared, a thunderous echoing cry that sent an atavistic chill through him. The animal shouldered its way through the trees, and his breath caught in his throat.

A bear, but not like the other one they'd seen. This bear was sick; that much was evident. Its hair was coming out in clumps, exposing cancerous flesh. Old, unhealed wounds marked the exposed skin. Its eyes were the color of a fish's belly, and its nose was raw and pink. Ragged lips peeled back from long teeth as it gave another whuffing grunt.

It heaved itself up onto its hind legs and roared again. Its belly was scraped raw and covered in oozing wounds. A smell, like the county dump at the height of summer, rolled over him and Ptolemy and the others gagged. "Jesus," Hutch coughed, pressing his arm to his mouth and nose.

The bear fell onto all fours and took a jolting leap towards the group, just enough to show them that it was unhappy with their presence in its territory. It groaned again, and Ptolemy could hear the pain in its voice. Something was churning inside its guts; maybe something it ate had disagreed with it.

Ptolemy, left hanging as Calavera moved to face the bear, scraped his mind for what he could remember from his wildlife survival classes. Making himself seem bigger wasn't a practical solution. Neither was playing dead.

The bear took another step, and another. Its head swayed from side to side, as if it was having a hard time focusing on him. Westlake raised Ptolemy's shotgun. "Might be able to bring it down if we can hit it in the head," he said, glancing at Ramirez.

"Or we might just make it mad," she said. "Either way, we need to keep it away from Ptolemy. Maybe we can draw it off…"

The bear abruptly bulled towards them with a roar, more quickly than Ptolemy thought possible. It was like a hairy express train, and they were standing on the tracks. He tensed, waiting for the impact. But before the others could fire, or flee, Calavera leapt into action, a long tree branch in his hands. Darting in from the side, he clubbed the bear across its muzzle hard enough to shatter the end of the branch and startle the animal. The bear shook its head and pawed at its snout. Its eyes fixed on Calavera, and it gave a bone-jangling roar.

The masked man lunged, using the branch like a spear. The blow seemed not to bother the animal at all. It reared up again, and again Calavera danced back. "Aid would not go amiss," he bellowed.

"One side, folks," Hutch said, shoving Westlake out of the way as he levelled his Stoner. "This is a job for the big gun. Calavera, get it to turn around!"

Responding to Hutch's cry, Calavera ducked the bear's swipe and slammed the branch against its ribs. The animal roared and turned, following him as he retreated. "Now!" Ramirez shouted. When it had turned its back on the group, Ramirez and the others began to fire, their shots tearing great gouges in the hairy form.

The bear wheeled about and took a faltering step towards them. Ropes of saliva hung from its open jaws, and it gave itself a massive shake that looked like a muscle spasm. Its eyes rolled in its sockets, and it uttered a low whine that set Ptolemy's teeth on edge.

The bear barely noticed the hits it took. It slowed some, but just kept attacking. It bled from a dozen wounds but didn't seem in the mood to stop. It was dragging a paw, its gait awkward and off-kilter. Ptolemy could see its stomach bulging oddly as it swayed and stumbled. "It is dying," he cried.

"Not fast enough," Ramirez snarled. "Keep shooting."

"I'm almost out," Westlake said.

Ramirez didn't look at him. "I said keep shooting!"

The bear was nearly on them – it rose onto its hind legs, towering over them, as if inviting them to do their worst. Ptolemy groped for his knife. It wasn't much, but if it got past the others, he would need something.

Westlake fired the shotgun, and the bear's stomach burst open like a wet paper bag. Something tumbled out, wrapped in a gory shroud of intestine and stomach lining. It fell to the ground and thrashed, flailing mauled limbs in a parody of birth.

"Jesus Christ," Ramirez yelped, as the crawler flopped onto its stomach and slithered towards them. At the same moment, the bear screamed and toppled like a newly cut tree, hitting the ground hard enough to make the rocks jump and Ptolemy swing into the tree and bounce off, painfully.

Another crawler, barely more than a head and a spinal column, slid out of the dying animal's guts and snapped at Ramirez' feet. Westlake drove the stock of the shotgun down, pulping the crawler's partially digested skull. Hutch did the same to the other and spat on the body for good measure.

The bear gave a final, pathetic wheeze and fell silent. Ptolemy stared down at it in pity. Westlake crouched beside it, one hand pressed to his nose and mouth. Kahwihta joined him, leaning over the body with little evident concern. "Fascinating," she said. "He must've eaten them before they were fully dead. I wonder how long he's been wandering around like that." Her expression was one of sadness, and she stroked the animal's head. "Poor old bear. You didn't deserve that."

A glint of metal caught Ptolemy's eye. He pointed. "What's that?"

At his direction, Calavera reached into the mess of the bear's guts and fished out a tiny pin, shaped like a pair of wings. It gleamed in the sunlight.

Ramirez looked at it. "What is it?"

"Pilot's pin," Westlake said, taking the pin from Calavera.

"Put it together with the flight attendant from earlier and what does that add up to?"

"Plane crash," Labrand said, from where he still crouched in the tree. "Over yonder, looks like. There's a sort of trail like a big scorch mark, up on the summit and down the southwestern slope. I see what might be debris as well." He looked down at Kahwihta. "I think I just figured out where all them zombies are coming from."

The wind shifted. Attila growled. Ptolemy could hear the distant groan of the dead; but not the ones who'd been pursuing them. These were closer – too close. Startled, Labrand turned back to his efforts with the snare. He drew his knife and started to cut at it... or tried, rather. Ptolemy forced down the panic that threatened to overwhelm him as Labrand hacked ineffectively at the rope. As it frayed, it revealed a gleam of wire.

"Taking too long," Ramirez said, watching the trail.

Kahwihta nodded, reluctantly. "They'll be on us in a few minutes, maybe less. The gunfire drew them, but they're not sure where we're at yet." She paused. "Sounds like a lot of them, as well. Probably from the plane."

"Wonderful," Ramirez said. "How's it coming, Labrand?"

"It's a damn wire," Labrand said, harshly. "Too strong to cut through." He sheathed his knife and reached for his Colt. "Going to have to risk a shot, boss."

"That'll bring them all down on us that much quicker," Hutch said. "Especially if there are runners. And we ain't got much time as it is." He hefted his Stoner. "I'm almost out. Got maybe five shots left."

"Three," Ramirez said, patting her sidearm.

"Two," Westlake added, checking the shotgun. "And a full magazine in the Glock."

"Six shots for the Colt, three for the rifle," Labrand said, as he climbed down and reclaimed the rifle from Ramirez. "Sounds like there's three times that coming this way."

"Not enough," Ramirez said, softly. "Not nearly enough."

"Go," Ptolemy said.

Ramirez looked at him. "What?"

"Go. I will be fine." It was patently a lie, but a necessary one. If they stayed, they would be overwhelmed. Perhaps not immediately, but eventually. Better they depart now, before the zombies had seen them. If they did so, they might still make it to the Villa unscathed, though how they would fare after that, low on ammunition, he could not guess.

"Are you insane? Wait, no, stupid question." She gestured sharply. "We're not leaving you. End of story."

Ptolemy grimaced. It was getting hard to focus, and his stomach was doing strange things. Being upside down for this long was not pleasant. "I do not wish to be left. But if you are right about Sayers, she will not let the walkers get to me. And it might well give you the chance to get past her."

"We can't be sure of that."

"I can. She is probably watching us even now. Leaving me behind forces her to cede her control of the field. She will come for me, Ramirez. I know it. She is probably waiting to see what you do, even now." He tried to smile. "Go. I will be fine."

Ramirez closed her eyes. Then, with a shuddering breath, she opened them and made to speak. But Westlake interrupted.

"No." He looked at Ptolemy. "You always look out for your crew." He tossed the shotgun to Ramirez. She caught it, frowned, and then smiled.

"Yeah," she agreed. "Calavera?"

"Ha, yes!" Calavera ducked under Ptolemy, catching him around the shoulders.

"What are you doing?" Ptolemy demanded.

"We're going to need to run," Hutch said, but he was grinning.

Ramirez fired. The wire parted. Ptolemy fell into Calavera's arms. She handed him the shotgun. Her smile was wide as she met Ptolemy's astonished gaze.

"So we run."

CHAPTER TWENTY-THREE
Wreckage

It was cold on the summit, and the air tasted brittle. It was bare of life save green moss and scrub growth. At around four Empire State Buildings high, Ramirez thought, Mount Marcy was a true skyscraper – not like those pikers of steel and glass that dominated the city. It was too bad that there was no time to enjoy the view.

She inhaled a lungful of frigid air and waved the others on. They'd left the treeline less than ten minutes ago, but already the first walker had appeared, head swinging this way and that. It spotted her within a few moments and stretched out a hand, as if seeking help. It released a gut-churning moan and began to clamber awkwardly up the slope. Another appeared, and another.

She didn't bother to count them after the tenth dragged itself out of the trees. No runners yet. Small mercies. She rejoined the others as quickly as possible. They were already starting down the southwestern slope – all save Hutch, who was waiting for her. "How many?" Hutch asked, as he fell into step with her.

"More than we got bullets."

"Good thing we got more than bullets, then." Hutch grinned, but there was no humor in it. "Hell, we throw Calavera at them, we might wipe them all out."

Ramirez returned his grin. "Not even him. What'd Labrand say?"

"Lake Cutter is about an hour's hike from here. There's apparently an old logging trail that leads right to it, or so he claims." He glanced back. "Hope there's more than that, though. Otherwise, we're delaying the inevitable."

"I'm not in a hurry to die, are you?"

Hutch snorted. "Now that you mention it – no."

The descent was easier than the climb, but not by much. As they navigated the rocky path, Ramirez kept her eyes out for the plane. It was bound to be full of walkers – or worse. She hoped they'd already wandered off somewhere, rather than sticking close to home. If not, things were going to rapidly go from bad to worse.

"Can't believe a plane crashed and we didn't know about it," Hutch grunted, kicking aside a stray shard of silver metal. They'd been stumbling over debris since before the summit. There were marks on the rockface – not to mention lots of broken or uprooted trees – that Ramirez thought were from the plane striking and skidding.

"Planes were practically falling out of the sky the first week of the apocalypse for many reasons, I assume, such as the disruption of navigation aids," Ptolemy said, hanging back so that they could catch up with him. He was limping slightly, Ramirez noticed. "And the Adirondacks are beneath several major air routes. Frankly, I am surprised it was only one."

"How's your leg?" she asked. He glanced at her and then away.

"It hurts. But that is better than the alternative." He paused. "Would you have…?" He trailed off, as if uncertain how to voice the question.

"No," Ramirez said, but the truth was she wasn't sure. In a way, she was grateful to Westlake for making the choice for her. In another way, she was pissed that she had yet another reason to thank him. She stared at his back, wondering what was going on in his head. She'd never figured Westlake for the idealistic type. It didn't fit his pattern. Or maybe it did, and she hadn't noticed.

"Is it true he never shot anybody?" Hutch asked, quietly. "Westlake. I heard he never shot anybody. Even when they came to arrest him."

"And where did you hear that?" Ramirez asked, startled.

"Around. Is it true?"

She frowned. "Yeah. Far as it goes." Westlake had carried guns – used them to intimidate or threaten – but never shot anyone, as far as she was aware. That he could shoot was obvious. The profilers had made a point of it in their workup, she remembered that. They'd waxed lyrical about John Dillinger and Robin Hood. But thief was a thief as far as she was concerned, whatever sort of hat he wore.

"Remind me to thank him," Ptolemy murmured.

Ramirez nodded. "If this thing pans out, we'll throw a damn parade in his honor." A flicker of shadow caught her eye and she looked back. The first walker had reached the summit. It stood on the peak, buffeted by the wind, looking down at them. Then it took a step after them. "Crap," she said. She gestured to Labrand. "Time to pick up the pace, people!"

The wilderness vastitude spread out below them as they slid, crab-crawled, and stumbled down the last few meters of rock to the treeline below. With the sun setting, they were preceded by long shadows that stretched into the gloom beneath the boughs. The shadows of the pursuing walkers accompanied them.

Labrand paused when they reached the trees. "We got a problem," he said.

"Another one?" Ramirez asked.

"The plane. Looks like it crashed right on the trail." He pointed towards a blackened clearing just below them. Now that she was looking at it, Ramirez could see that the plane had carved a ragged wound across the summit of the mountain, shattering trees and mangling the landscape for what seemed like miles in the fading light.

"Hell. Can we get around it?" she asked.

"Yeah, but it'll take time. Time we don't have, if those walkers keep coming the way they are." He gestured towards the largest concentration of wreckage. "Fastest route to the lake is right through that debris field."

Ramirez bit back a curse as she continued to study the wreck. The rear half of the plane stood at an awkward angle, like a leaning silver tower, supported by bent and broken trees. The front half had broken loose and skidded on some distance away, until it had finally come to a stop. The debris field stretched in all directions, as far as the eye could see, and grass was already growing in yellow patches from the puddles of spilled fuel.

"Looks like we don't have much choice." She looked at the others. "Here's the plan: we do this quick. Stay close, don't get separated whatever else. Kahwihta, keep the mutt on a short leash and keep him quiet. No guns, unless absolutely necessary. One shot and we'll have every walker in that wreck falling on us like a ton of bricks." She looked at Labrand. "Lead us in, cowboy."

Labrand tipped his hat. "See y'all on the other side."

A flock of black birds rose into the air as the group left the treeline and rose with a raucous din into the gloaming. A few minutes after they entered the debris field, Labrand held up his hand and stopped next to a jagged chunk of fuselage. Ramirez waved the others to a stop. "Welcoming committee," Labrand said, without turning around.

A walker lurched into view, a fragment of metal jutting from its chest and a pilot's cap sitting askew on its head. The walker took a clumsy step towards Labrand, who deftly clubbed it to the ground with his rifle and crushed its skull. They left the walker where it lay and moved on. Attila growled constantly, but softly. Kahwihta kept him quiet, but Ramirez had the feeling that he might start barking at any moment.

From behind them, Ramirez heard the guttural moaning of their pursuers growing louder. It was too much to hope that they might be able to lose the walkers in the debris, but it might slow them down some.

"I wonder what happened," Kahwihta murmured as they pressed on, looking around. "Malfunction?" She paused as they caught sight of another walker nearby. It had snagged its trailing intestines on a bit of fuselage and now walked in a stumbling circle, losing ever more of its innards with every interminable circuit. It was so preoccupied by its predicament that it didn't notice as Calavera crept up behind it and brained it with a chunk of metal.

"Or someone turned," Ramirez said, imagining what it might have been like. A plane was just a metal tube crammed with anxious people. Throw in a zombie or two and it would have been chaos. She shook her head. "Doesn't matter now. Too late to help them."

"We might be able to find identification for some of them," Ptolemy said. He kicked at a fallen chunk of landing gear, exposing burnt remains. Between the work of the fire and the animals, it was impossible to tell whether it had been a man or a woman. "In the event we reestablish a national communications network, we might be able to provide closure to certain families."

Ramirez looked at him. "You're really thinking ahead there, aren't you?"

Ptolemy shrugged. "Thinking ahead is why I am still alive. I see no reason to end the practice." He looked up. "Though in this case, it might well be wasted effort."

Westlake whistled softly as he took it all in. "Boeing 737," he said, looking at Ramirez. "Commercial capacity of about two hundred passengers or thereabouts."

"Why do you know that?" she asked.

He shrugged. "Some corporations used the same type for their company planes. I had to memorize the specs one time, for a thing."

"Did you rob a plane?"

He shrugged again. Ramirez stared at him. "It was on the ground, right?" she continued. "Westlake. It wasn't in the air, was it?"

He didn't reply. Instead, he turned to examine the shattered pieces of the fuselage. She looked at Ptolemy. "D B Cooper robbed a plane in flight," he said, helpfully.

"He's not D B Cooper."

"That you know of," Ptolemy said, studying Westlake speculatively. "He was never caught. How old is Westlake, anyway?"

"I'm not having this conversation," Ramirez said. She turned and spied a walker trapped in an improvised cage of wreckage and strode towards it. The walker was – or had been – a young man, dressed casually, a pair of old-fashioned hi-fi headphones over his head. He was still strapped into his seat, which was wedged in the split of a tree. The walker thrashed as she got close, but he was pinned tight. She winced as she saw that the birds had been at him.

"Not a good way to go," Westlake murmured, from behind her.

"The problem is, he's not gone yet."

Westlake drew his knife from his pocket, flipped it open and took a step towards the struggling walker. He avoided the grabbing hands, leaned in, and stabbed the zombie between its empty eye sockets. It stiffened and slumped. Westlake turned, wiping his knife on his trousers. "Now he's gone," he said.

Something hissed to their left. Ramirez turned, reaching for her baton even as she did so. "Yeah. Now how about the rest?" She jerked her chin towards a thin shape creeping towards them through a broken section of seating. It was a damaged, pathetic thing – fried by a long-ago fire, limbs askew. But still hungry, still moving, and it wasn't alone. "Everyone focus up," she said, louder than she intended.

"Just about to say the same myself," Labrand said. Ramirez followed his gaze and saw several walkers creeping towards them from the right. First class passengers, some still wearing their complimentary headsets, and directed by a burnt-out stick of a flight attendant. The latter had been nearly bisected by something, and only had one arm to stretch towards them, but at its flailing gesture the others staggered towards the group.

"These look a lot more alert than I like," Hutch said.

"They're hungry," Kahwihta said, absently. "We need to keep moving."

Ramirez nodded. They navigated towards the other side of the wreck, where the back of the plane balanced on what was left of the wings and several bent trees. The walkers followed. A handful, then a dozen spilled out of the wreck, creeping ever closer. She wondered what they'd all been doing in there. Had one wandered in and the others followed and gotten stuck in the process? Whatever the reason, they were pouring out now. From the sound of it, there were more to come.

Attila began to bark. "Keep moving," Ramirez said, shouting to be heard over the dog. "We've just got to–"

The crack of a bullet interrupted her and sent them all ducking for cover. "I told you not to come up here," a familiar voice shouted. "I warned you!"

Sayers.

Ramirez shook her head. "Goddamnit. We cannot catch a break."

CHAPTER TWENTY-FOUR
Ambush

"I warned you," Sayers called out again, her voice loud and clear. Calavera peered over the chunk of wing he'd taken cover behind, but saw nothing. "But you didn't listen. And now there's nothing I can do for you."

"You make it sound like you've been doing us a favor," Ramirez hollered back. She crouched nearby, one hand on her sidearm. Labrand and the others were scattered about the immediate area. They'd taken what cover they could, while still keeping an eye on the approaching walkers.

No answer. Calavera looked at Ramirez. "What now?" he asked.

"We can't go forward, can't go back," Westlake said. He sprawled nearby, trying to make himself a smaller target behind a pile of broken seats. "Need a new plan."

"I thought that was your thing," Ramirez said, acidly.

"I'm thinking," Westlake said. "All advice welcome."

Calavera leaned towards Ramirez. "I believe I can make it, if someone can cover me."

Ramirez looked at him. "Make it… what do you mean make it?"

"We are caught. We must rush her. A frontal attack." He glanced back at the walkers. "At the very least, I can draw her fire and give the rest of you a chance to make a break for the trees."

"We don't even know where she is," Ramirez protested.

Labrand low-crawled towards them. "I got an idea on that score, boss. I think she's up around the rear of the plane. Probably been perched up there since before we arrived. It's safe from walkers and she's got a good view of everything." He tipped up the brim of his hat and grinned weakly. "Might be we could smoke her out. Just need to get past the zombies."

"Easy enough," Kahwihta said. She caught Attila by the collar and dragged him close. She murmured something to him, then gave him a swat on the rear. The dog raced through the wreckage, barking. The closest zombies turned as Attila tore past them. He wove through their legs, avoiding their hands as they clutched for him. More and more zombies shambled after him, drawn by the sharp noise and sudden movement.

"I never get tired of watching that," Hutch said.

Ramirez looked at Calavera. "Now's your chance, big man. We'll head for the trees, keep her eyes on us." She paused. "Be quick."

"As lightning," Calavera said. He looked at Labrand. "Come. Cover me."

Together, they crept through the debris field towards the upright rear compartment of the plane as the others began to head for the trees. Between them, those with Ramirez, and Attila, Calavera was confident that Sayers wouldn't know where to look first. Labrand was wary, tense, twitching at every little thing. "You do not have to be frightened," Calavera said, softly. "I will protect you from the dead."

Labrand glanced at him. "And who's going to protect you?"

"Santa Muerte." Calavera flexed his hands, forcing back the ever-present ache that haunted him. Too many years of hard floors and physical abuse took their toll, even on the most magnificent physical specimen. He caught a flash of a reflection in a bit of broken glass. Santa Muerte looked at him from behind the glass, and smiled her wise, rictus smile. The aches and pains fled. "It is she who made me the hero I am."

Labrand glanced at him, then away. "You're crazy is what you are."

"Perhaps. Perhaps one must be crazy to survive such madness." Calavera smiled, knowing Labrand would never understand. "Either way, we are companions, and I will keep you safe." He paused as he caught the sudden boom of Hutch's Stoner. The wind shifted, carrying with it a low, agonized moaning – the hunting call of the dead. "Our pursuers have caught up with us, I fear."

"Yeah well, day ends as it began, don't it?" Labrand said. He hunkered down next to a chunk of crumpled hull, and Calavera followed suit. They'd circled the rear of the plane, away from the path the others were taking.

Up close, Calavera could see that it was not all in one piece as he'd first thought – rather, the rear of the plane had been broken into sections, forming a sort of ramshackle tower. At the top of the largest section was the tail assembly, and it was festooned with the remnants of broken trees.

Beneath it was another section, which leaned against the first, supported as it was on a web of broken trees. "She is up there somewhere, then?" he asked, quietly, gauging the climb ahead of him. Difficult, but not beyond his abilities.

"It's where I'd be, if I were a no-good backshooting park ranger." Labrand paused and studied him. "You sure about this?"

"I am." Calavera gestured to himself and smiled. "I am not built for sneaking, if you hadn't noticed."

Labrand looked him up and down. "No, I suppose not." He turned. "OK, here's the plan. I'll go up onto the wing there, try and get a bead on her from below. When I give the signal, you make your play. I'll cover you."

Calavera nodded. "I believe I can handle that." He tensed, ready for action, but then turned as metal creaked behind him. "We have an audience." The zombies had crept up behind them, moving silently through the debris that was their hunting ground. Five of them, by his count. All burnt to tatters and sticks, their remaining flesh pulled tight over blackened bones. They were still some distance away, but close enough to cause problems.

Labrand followed his gaze. "Oh, come on," he muttered. He raised his rifle, but Calavera pushed the barrel down.

"Save your ammunition and get into position. I will deal with them." Without waiting for a reply, he advanced on the zombies. As he did so, he snatched up a chunk of wing-flap and positioned it horizontally across his body. The metal slammed into the zombies like the edge of a saw blade, and those that weren't driven back by the masked man as he bulldozed forward were broken in half. Three fell in as many seconds.

The fourth walker lunged towards him, out from under the plane's bent wing. Calavera caught it in mid-leap and tore it in half with a flex of his shoulders. He cast the still-writhing pieces aside and turned to snag the fifth as it lurched past him. He drove it face-first into a spar of metal and left it to dangle, twitching.

A cry from the plane caught his attention. Labrand, perched on a piece of the wing just beneath the largest section, studied something inside the body of the plane. He turned towards Calavera, mouth open, as if to call out, and then – in the blink of an eye – was gone. Calavera blinked in surprise. "What...?"

Labrand screamed from somewhere inside the plane. Calavera charged to the rescue. He leapt onto the wing and, an instant later, he hauled himself up into the back of the plane, grabbing any handholds he could find.

He heard Labrand cry out again and looked up to see Labrand struggling with... an indistinct mass. It was only when the other man fired his Colt that Calavera at last saw his attacker clearly in the flash of the gunshot.

The zombie had been crushed and flattened by the impact of the landing – splattered all over the rear of the compartment. But not destroyed. Instead, it had adapted. Calavera thought that might be the wrong word, but it was the only way to explain the loops of intestine and strands of flensed muscle tissue, squirming like the tentacles of an octopus, stretching down from the broken mass of the brute's carcass. The tangle of guts hung from the rear of the compartment like a canopy of stinking jungle vines and had somehow ensnared the luckless Labrand.

Now, with a grunting gobbling sound, the brute reeled Labrand in. The Colt was empty now, and Labrand hacked at the tendrils of tissue with a knife – but not fast enough. Calavera hauled himself after the other man, using the backs of the seats like the steps on a ladder. But it was slow going, and the brute was strong and desperately hungry. He cursed himself for having paused, even for a moment.

"Labrand!" Calavera shouted. He stretched out a hand. Labrand reached for him – their fingers touched – then, with a final wrench, Labrand was yanked back into the cavernous maw of the brute. Its mouth had become a ruptured split stretching from its face to its gullet, and the wound pulsed wide as it shoved the struggling Labrand inside. He flailed, cursing, as teeth and ribs stabbed into him from all sides, and viscera choked him.

The brute gave a convulsive shudder, and there was a horrid squelching sound as Labrand was pulped and masticated within the zombie's body. Blood splattered down, momentarily blinding Calavera and nearly causing him to lose his footing. As he wiped blood from his eyes, he saw fronds of ligament and glistening intestine edging towards him. The brute was focused on him now, ruined gums flapping with mindless greed. Labrand's hat drifted past him, heading for the ground.

Calavera roared and caught hold of the flapping intestines, knotting them in his fists. "You like to eat men? Come eat me!" Bracing himself, he hauled back with all his strength. The brute rocked and roared, causing the wreckage to shift in its treetop perch. Calavera was thrown from one side of the compartment to the other, but he managed to keep his grip on its intestines. The brute thrashed as if trying to tear itself free. He decided to give it a helping hand and redoubled his efforts.

Its large intestine spilled loose, and Calavera found himself falling backwards. He held tight to his gory, makeshift rope and slid closer to the ground below. As he did so, he heard an awful, wet sound and saw that the brute was following him. Flabby fingers gripped at the sides of the compartment as the zombie squeezed itself along. Loops of intestine drooped, and a broken seat crashed down, nearly braining him. He took a chance and dropped the rest of the way to the ground.

He fell heavily, rolling down the wing and only barely landing on his feet. He looked up – and nearly lost his head to a crawler as it slithered out of a gap beneath the wing. He scrambled back as the broken zombie clutched at him, slamming his fist into its head repeatedly. The crawler went limp, and he slid out from beneath it, panting.

Above him, the body of the plane gave another loud creak. Leaves and broken branches rained down. Calavera tensed and leapt aside as his pursuer plummeted the rest of the way to the ground. The brute hit like a rock, splattering Calavera with foulness. He staggered back. The brute heaved itself upright and lumbered towards him even as he cleaned the slime from his mask.

The brute paused. Calavera saw that its intestines had

gotten tangled in some of the wreckage. It didn't notice and continued to strain towards him, grasping uselessly at the air. Then a shotgun roared, and the brute's head snapped back. More gunfire, and the mangled carcass staggered back a step. Then, slowly, it gave a wheezy grunt and toppled backwards. Calavera straightened and turned, expecting to see Ramirez and the others.

Instead, an unfamiliar face smiled crookedly at him. "Jesus Christ," the newcomer said, looking around. He was a heavyset man, clad in piecemeal tactical gear and carrying a shotgun. He lowered his sunglasses, peering at Calavera over the rims. "I thought Sayers was joking, but you really are a one-man wrecking crew, aren't you?"

Calavera flexed his hands. "Who...?"

The click of a weapon being readied made him pause. He turned his head slightly, and saw Sayers standing behind him, her Mauser pressed lightly to the back of his skull.

"It's over," she said, softly. "Put your hands up, Calavera. Or so help me, I'll send you to meet your saint in person."

CHAPTER TWENTY-FIVE
Lake Cutter

Westlake kept his hands interlaced behind his head as Sayers and her new friends walked Calavera out of the wreckage and into the trees to join them. Ramirez and the others knelt nearby, all of them divested of their gear and held at gunpoint by two of the quartet of men in tactical gear and hiking outfits who'd been waiting for them just past the treeline.

Truth to tell, Westlake wasn't that surprised to see them. He'd half-expected something like this, only... there weren't enough of them. Four? Sal wasn't the sort for half-measures. Something was going on. He didn't know what, but he expected to find out soon enough. All he had to do was be patient.

"Where's Labrand?" Ramirez, kneeling beside him, demanded as Calavera sank to his knees with the others. The big man looked like he'd been through hell.

Calavera shook his head, and Westlake felt – rather than

saw – Ramirez deflate slightly, though the expression on her face didn't change. Before he could say anything, however, the heavyset man who was in charge laughed and displayed a battered, bloody Stetson. As he approached, he put it on. "What do you think, Westlake? Is it me?"

"It looks like shit, so yeah – it's you, Carl," Westlake said.

Carl frowned, whipped the hat off his head and flung it against Westlake's chest. "You still haven't learned to watch your mouth, Westlake. That's going to get you in trouble one day. Hell, maybe today."

"I take it you know him?" Ramirez said, giving Westlake a sidelong glance.

Westlake gave a sour smile. "Agent Ramirez, may I introduce you to Carl Waingro, professional asshole on Sal Bonaro's payroll. Carl's little brother Tommy tried to kill me before the whole zombie thing kicked off."

Carl's smile faded. "Yeah. I've been looking forward to asking you about that, Westlake." His hand fell to the pistol on his hip as he took off his sunglasses and clipped them to his collar. "It's going to be a real intense conversation."

Sayers looked at him. "Spinoza wants him alive."

"Spinoza ain't here," Carl said, still staring at Westlake. He had the same sort of stare that Tommy had had, Westlake observed. The sort of intensity usually reserved for lunatics and children. Either would have been a good descriptor of Tommy. But while the stare was the same, Carl was a different sort of beast altogether. Tommy had been chiseled from too many afternoons at the gym; Carl was nothing but prison yard muscle. "Hell," he continued. "No reason we shouldn't shoot all of them here and now, you ask me."

Sayers swung her Mauser around until it was aimed at Carl. "No one asked you."

Carl glanced at her. "You shoot me, they shoot you," he said, indicating his men. He didn't sound frightened. Then, Westlake doubted there was much that could frighten Carl.

Sayers didn't so much as flinch. "You're still dead in that scenario."

Carl laughed. "That is true. I'd hate to be dead."

The standoff was interrupted by a sudden barking. Carl looked around. "Is that a dog?" he asked, in disbelief. "What is a dog doing out here?"

"No, that's trouble," Sayers said. "We need to move, now." She looked towards the wreckage, a frown on her face. "The walkers will be coming."

Carl gestured dismissively. "Yeah, yeah. Get them up."

"Where are you taking us?" Kahwihta asked, as one of Carl's men jerked her to her feet. She yanked herself free, and the man raised his fist. A loud growl caused him to turn. Westlake saw a blur of brown as Attila came out of nowhere and sank his teeth into the man's wrist. He yelped and fell backwards, the dog on top of him. Attila jerked his head, yanking his screaming victim around like a rag doll.

For a moment, no one moved. The attack had been so unexpected, so quick, that no one knew what to do. Then Carl went for his sidearm. "Shit, Fifer! Somebody get that mutt off him!" A moment later Ramirez slammed into Carl, knocking him on his ass and the gun out of his hand.

Westlake went for the gun instinctively. But even as he did so, he heard the bark of Sayers' Mauser. Attila gave a piteous yelp and Kahwihta cried out. Westlake froze as

Sayers said, "Don't," and swung her Mauser towards him. She wasn't the only one. Carl's men – except Fifer – still had Calavera and the others covered.

Carl shoved Ramirez back and got to his feet. He picked up his gun and kicked the still-crouched Westlake in the chest, knocking him onto his back. He took aim, and Westlake waited for the bullet. But it never came. Instead, Carl grunted and holstered the weapon. He looked at Ramirez. "Nice try. Try it again, and I'll shoot you." He glanced over at where his man had gone down under Attila. "Fifer? You still alive? Good. Taylor, Esposito, get him up." He glanced at Sayers. "Good shooting."

"Yes." Sayers holstered her Mauser. "Something for you to remember." But she was looking at Westlake as she said it. He gave a shallow nod and sat back down. Ramirez went to Kahwihta, who knelt beside Attila.

Amazingly, the dog wasn't dead. "She shot him," the young woman said, in a hoarse voice. Attila's tail thumped weakly at the sound. From what Westlake could see, the bullet had gone into the dog's flank. Not lethal, but painful – a shot designed to incapacitate, but not kill. He glanced at Sayers again, but she wasn't looking at him now.

Instead, she stared in the direction of the wreckage, a pensive look on her face. "Too many of them," she murmured.

Carl glanced at her. "What was that?"

Sayers shook her head. "Nothing. We need to go. Now." As if to add emphasis to her statement, the wind carried the sound of moaning into the trees. Carl's men looked at one another nervously. They didn't share their boss' lack of worry.

"Don't have to tell me twice," Carl said. "On your feet, folks. Unless you want us to leave you with the dog here. I'm sure the zombies will take good care of you." He laughed as if he'd made a joke.

Kahwihta looked up. "I'm not leaving him."

Carl shrugged and reached for his gun. "OK, have it your way."

Calavera rose to his feet. "That is not necessary. I will carry him." He stooped and gently scooped Attila up.

Carl stared at him for a moment, then nodded. "Fine. Your problem, not mine." He turned. "Enough of this bullshit, let's go." He reached down and hauled Westlake to his feet. "You stay close to me."

"You still haven't said where you're taking us," Ramirez said, as she was shoved into motion by Fifer. The man had a pained expression on his face, and his sleeve was dappled with blood. But his gun didn't waver as he pushed her forward.

"We're taking you where you wanted to go. The Villa." Carl pointed down through the trees, towards a silvery crescent of water just visible from where they were. "Ain't that nice of me?"

"Yeah, you're a real saint, Carl."

Carl laughed. "That I am." He shoved Westlake along. "Frankly, you're going to wish I'd shot you before this is all over. Or that you'd let Tommy do the job the first time."

"Yeah, well, what happened to Tommy wasn't my fault," Westlake said. Carl didn't stop, but his next shove was more forceful.

"Be quiet and keep moving."

"Zombies got him, if you were wondering."

"I said be quiet," Carl said. Westlake could hear the fury in his voice.

"And then he got back up again," Westlake continued. "I probably should have shot him, but… well. I was in a hurry."

Carl hissed and drove a punch into Westlake's side, dropping him to his knees. "Stop talking about my brother, Westlake, or I swear to God, I'll do you in here."

"Spinoza wouldn't like that," Westlake coughed. "Isn't that what Sayers said? And by Spinoza, she must have meant Vinnie Spinoza, right? Sal's right-hand guy?" Westlake looked up at Carl and grinned. "Why are *you* playing soldier for Spinoza?"

Carl's features tightened. "You'll see. Get moving." He dragged Westlake back to his feet. As he rose, Westlake caught Ramirez' eye. She looked at him as if he were crazy. But the truth was, guys like Carl told you more with reactions than with words. And Westlake's dig about Spinoza had struck a nerve. He just didn't know why, not yet.

It took them twenty minutes to reach the lake, and the sound of the walkers only grew louder with every passing moment. Not just the ones from the wreckage, he thought. The ones that had followed them up the summit. A veritable army now. Carl and his boys knew it, given the nervous looks some of them shot over their shoulders.

When they reached the lakeshore, Carl gestured expansively. "Lake Cutter. Not the most scenic of views, but it does have its charms." The lake was a flat expanse of water stretching beyond an uneven shore. On the other side, the mountain fell steeply towards the lowlands below. But on that slope, at the edge of the water and overlooking the descent, was perched a structure straight out of the better class of traveler's guide.

"Is that … ?" Ramirez began.

Westlake nodded. "It is. Welcome to the Villa."

It was a three-story building with a peaked, split-frame roof and more windows than he could count. High security fences with reinforced foundations girted it on three sides, stretching from the shore and up along the slope of the mountain, and creating a horseshoe courtyard in front of the entrance to the building. Marking the lakeside entrance was a quay made of quarried stone and an attached boatshed. The quay had an old-fashioned timber roof and heavy support beams connecting the two.

Hutch whistled. "Someone spent some money."

"Yeah, and his name was Salvatore Bonaro," Carl said. He indicated a wooden jetty jutting from the shore nearby. Two inflatable motorized rafts were bobbing gently in the water. "Come on. Our rides are waiting."

The rafts were big enough to hold half a dozen passengers apiece. Carl climbed on one and indicated for Ramirez, Westlake, Sayers, and Ptolemy to join him. Fifer sat by the motor, and another gunman sat in the back. Calavera and the others got onto the second. The two rafts started across the water just as the first walker broke from the trees and stumbled towards the shore. Carl watched them and shook his head. "You riled them up but good, Sayers, I got to say."

"I was doing my job," she said, flatly.

Carl scratched his chin. "Yeah. I thought you'd be better at it, though. We got enough problems. We don't need more of them crawling all over us, even with Spinoza's toys to even the odds. Makes me wonder if you're thinking of going back on our deal, Ranger Sayers."

"Deal?" Ptolemy said. He looked at Sayers. "You made a deal with them."

Sayers didn't look at him. "I did what I had to do."

Carl laughed. "That's one way of looking at it."

"What do you mean?" Ptolemy pressed. He reached for her hand. "Elizabeth, why would you make a deal with these people?"

Sayers jerked her hand away. After a moment's silence, she said, "Why? Why do you think, Calvin? If I'd said no – if I'd even attempted to warn you – they'd have blown your camps off the map. I was doing it to protect you, you idiot."

"Protect us?" Ramirez stared at the other woman. "From what?"

Westlake knew the answer. He looked at Carl. "So, Sal decided to play king of the mountain, huh?"

Carl frowned. "Something like that."

"How's that going for him?"

"Shut up."

Westlake looked at Ramirez. "Something's going on," he said. "Sal's never been the patient type. If he'd been planning to attack the camps, he'd have done it already."

Carl rounded on him but said nothing. Instead, he looked up and shaded his eyes against the fading gleam of the setting sun. "There's our escort. Right on time." Westlake followed his gaze and saw several squat black shapes rolling onto the quay.

"What the hell are those?" Ramirez said, half rising.

"Oh my," Ptolemy said. "I do believe those are Foster-Miller TALON SWORDS. Four of them, in fact." He leaned forward, adjusting his glasses. "Autonomous tracked military robots. They used them in Iraq, mostly for bomb disposal. These appear to be armed."

As the rafts drew near the quay, Westlake could see that the robots resembled squarish steel boxes with heavy caterpillar treads. Each of the four was topped by a different assemblage. One bore a SAW M249, while another an M240 machine gun. The other two he didn't recognize. He glanced at Ptolemy and indicated the one surmounted by a long, thin barrel. "Sniper rifle?"

Ptolemy squinted. "An M82 Barrett rifle. And that one, with the six barrels, is a 40 mm grenade launcher. Fantastic." Westlake realized the other man wasn't being sarcastic. He was genuinely entranced by the devices.

"Yeah, that's a word for it, certainly," Westlake murmured, as the rafts bumped against the quay and the four robots took up firing positions. Carl got off first, hands raised. "It's just us, Vinnie," he called out. "We got the package you ordered." He reached down and half-hauled Westlake onto the quay with him. "See? All in one piece, as requested."

The robot with the SAW backed towards the courtyard. Carl glanced at Fifer. "Get the others off, stow the rafts. Keep watch on the water just in case any of our neighbors decide to take a swim." He held tight to Westlake's arm. "Come on. Time to meet the boss."

"Sal and I have already met," Westlake said.

"Sal? Who said anything about Sal?" Carl said. "The Villa is under new management, Westlake. Just like this whole goddamn mountain will be, soon enough."

CHAPTER TWENTY-SIX
New Management

Carl pushed Westlake towards a concrete outbuilding across the courtyard from the quay. The robots followed them the entire way. Westlake's skin crawled. He was used to men with guns, but robots were something else. It was like a bad movie, and he couldn't even get up and leave. To distract himself, he took in his surroundings.

The courtyard was clean of life, but Westlake could see shapes shuffling behind the windows of the Villa, thanks to the spotlights mounted on the outbuildings. Something told him that they weren't paying guests. Add that to the bullet holes in the walls of some of the outbuildings and the dark smeared stains on the ground, and he felt an uncertain flicker in his stomach.

The flicker only got worse when he caught sight of what waited beyond the fences. Walkers – dozens of them. All pressed tight to the reinforced fencing, so that it creaked softly. The nearest zombies set up a bone-chilling wail as they caught sight of Westlake and Carl. Carl cursed softly. "Damn it. More of them every day."

"I thought this place was supposed to be well hidden," Westlake said.

"You found it, didn't you?" Carl said. He turned to the robots and gestured. "You going to handle that, Vinnie?" Westlake realized he was gesturing to a camera mounted on the hull of the robot. The four machines rolled past them, heading for the fences. Carl grinned. "Watch this. It's going to be good."

The robot with the M240 rolled forward until its hull struck the fence. The barrel of its weapon slid through a gap. There was a click, then – sharp thunder. The closest zombies managed to avoid the shallow scything fire pattern, but those further back in the press were chopped to pieces. After a few moments, the SAW kicked in from farther up the fence line. More zombies fell, ripped into quivering chunks by the storm of lead.

Westlake pressed his hands to his ears. It took two minutes to clear all but a few of the zombies from the front fences. The first two robots retreated, weapons smoking, ammunition hoppers rattling. The third, armed with the Barrett, picked off the survivors with a handful of precision shots. Between them, the three robots had eviscerated a horde in less time than it took Westlake to kill one walker.

But there were more where that came from. Always more. Westlake could see them now, through the haze of cordite, hauling themselves up the logging trail that led to the front gate, twenty or maybe thirty of them. A motley assemblage of the great majority – broken shells, driven by an insatiable hunger. Most were dressed like hikers or tourists. Some wore military uniforms. Westlake dimly recalled Ramirez mentioning something about a National Guard base. "They got enough ammunition for that bunch?" Westlake asked.

Carl scratched his nose. "Don't need it. Watch."

Westlake's eyes widened as the front gate began to clatter open. The fourth robot trundled out. There was a soft clunking sound as it launched the first grenade towards the approaching zombies. Then another, and another.

The explosions split the air. Birds hurtled skywards. Westlake saw that there were several old craters littering the slope. New ones joined them. As the dust settled, the other three robots rolled out to join their companion. They cranked up their weapons and started rolling down the slope, firing as they went.

Five minutes later, there wasn't a zombie to be seen. At least not in one piece. The four robots reversed course, climbing the slope as easily as they'd descended. A crawler was caught beneath the treads of one and was pulped even as it tried to pull itself away.

The robots rolled back into the courtyard as the gates slid shut behind them. Carl nodded in satisfaction. "One of Vinnie's better ideas, I got to admit."

"Jesus," Westlake breathed, staring out at the devastation the four machines had wrought. He imagined what even one of them might do to a camp like the lodge and felt a chill. "What was he planning to use those for?"

Carl shrugged. "Who knows? Vinnie had a lot of bright ideas before the world went to shit. This is one of the few that panned out." He signaled to a security camera mounted above the door of the concrete outbuilding.

The door buzzed, and Carl pulled it open. "Inside." He shoved Westlake through the door and closed it behind them. "He's here." The room beyond was set up like a server farm, save for a small office space off to one side. The office was nice enough, modern in its simplicity, with clear plexiglass walls and black furniture. A bottle of something expensive and dark sat on a sideboard, with two crystal tumblers beside it.

"I can see that," said the man sitting before the semicircle of display monitors that occupied the desk pressed to the wall. He spun his chair about and tipped it back. He smiled in welcome but didn't rise from his seat. "Westlake."

Westlake paused. "Vincent Spinoza."

"The one and only." Vinnie Spinoza sat in the chair like it was just another day at the office. His collar was undone, he wasn't wearing a tie, but he was still dressed for success, despite the apocalypse. He grinned at Westlake as he leaned forward. "Long time no see, Westlake. When Sayers radioed us and said who'd showed up, I didn't believe her. Couldn't be my old pal, Westlake. He's dead and in a shallow grave in the Barrens."

Westlake met his gaze steadily. "Sal should have sent someone more competent." He felt Carl tense behind him.

Vinnie's eyes flicked to Carl, and then back. He shrugged. "Not my call." He looked at Carl. "Wait outside."

Carl frowned. "What?"

"I want to talk to Westlake here in private. Go wait outside."

Carl opened his mouth to protest further. Vinnie's smile didn't waver as he reached over and pulled a revolver out of his desk. He set the weapon down but didn't take his hand off it. "I can handle him, Carl. Go see to the others. Make them comfortable. They're guests, after all. First ones we've had in a while."

Carl grunted. "Fine." He slammed the door behind him when he left.

"He seems tense," Westlake said.

"It's a stressful time for all of us." Vinnie shrugged, trying his best to look unconcerned. But Westlake could read the fear beneath the mask. "And, well, good help is hard to find. Carl's a bit… limited in his thinking."

"True. Tommy wasn't exactly a mastermind either now, was he?"

Vinnie peered at him. "You kill him?"

"Not me."

Vinnie made a dismissive gesture. "Ah, well. I never liked Tommy anyway. Punks like that give the Outfit a bad name." He paused. "Not that it matters much anymore, I guess. *C'est la vie*, ain't that what they say?"

"That is what they say." Westlake took one of the other chairs and sat without being invited. Vinnie smiled and offered him one of the tumblers.

"Hair of the dog?"

"Don't mind if I do." Westlake took the offered glass and Vinnie filled it.

"So," Vinnie said.

"So."

"I suppose you're wondering where Sal is, huh?"

"Not really." Westlake studied the liquid in his tumbler for a moment before taking a sip. "I'm guessing he's safe inside the Villa, right?"

"In a manner of speaking." Vinnie leaned back and idly tapped at the keyboard. The images on several of the screens changed. He indicated one of the screens – a security monitor, Westlake realized. The compound was full of walkers. Every room, every corridor, seemed to swarm with them. "I managed to lock things down from out here." He gestured to the servers. "Sal thought I was crazy for setting this place up."

"Let me guess – cryptocurrencies?"

Vinnie nodded. "Wave of the future." He frowned. "Or it was. Anyway, I set up all this shit. Rerouted everything to go right through here. Plenty of time on my hands, and I like to keep busy." He took a long drink. "So trust me when I say they can't get out – unless I let them out." He tapped one of the monitors. "Imagine that flood, sweeping down this mountain, right into those little camps."

"Is that what you threatened Sayers with?"

Vinnie shook his head. "That was Sal's big idea, before… you know. Sayers was one of ours from before. Helps to have a park ranger on the payroll, keep people from wandering too close. Sal figured she could keep doing the job, until we were… ready to introduce ourselves to our neighbors, you might say."

"And she agreed?"

Vinnie snorted. "Not really. But we made a new deal. She helps, we don't kill all her new friends. She agreed to that real quick."

"I bet." Westlake studied the other man. Vinnie was talking fast, his words coming in a rush – like he'd gone a bit stir crazy. He was enjoying the conversation, giving too much away in his haste to seem friendly. Given who he had to talk to, Westlake didn't blame him. "So, what happened?"

Vinnie looked back at the monitors, his smile almost a rictus. "We were so worried about the zombies outside, that we didn't think about one getting inside. My own goddamn boss – would you believe it?"

"Sal?" Westlake said, in disbelief.

Vinnie nodded, his eyes still on the screens. "Don't know how. But I guess it's not important anymore."

"My condolences."

"Save it." Vinnie tapped at the keyboard, and one of the cameras focused in. "There's the bastard." On the screen, a hulking shape that couldn't possibly have once been human moved. But it was out of sight before Westlake could make out any details. "Sal is why I'm out here, and not in there."

"Sal and the zombies, you mean. There must be a hundred of them in there."

"Not quite that many. We – and by we, I mean me and Carl – got out of there with thirty, maybe forty people. Sure, we lost the staff, but to hell with a bunch of waiters and cooks, right? So, I figured, hey, hazards of the new status quo, right? We'll send some people in, get what we need, pop a few, and in a few days the whole place will be clear. Only Sal had other ideas." Vinnie leaned close to the monitors, his eyes narrowed. "He was always a contrary bastard. Being dead didn't change that much."

"Did you try shooting him?" Westlake asked.

Vinnie snorted. "Who you talking to? Soon as I knew he was infected or whatever you call it, I put a round in his head myself."

"So much for loyalty."

Vinnie grunted. "Only he didn't stay down. Pauly unloaded a whole clip from an AR-15 into his head, didn't even slow him, once he got over being spooked by the blasts." He grimaced. "Pauly didn't last much past that. Soon enough, nobody was left to send. If Sal didn't get 'em, the walkers did. And then there were even more zombies inside."

"What about Carl?"

Vinnie frowned. "Carl… Carl is a problem."

Westlake leaned back, swirling what was left of his drink. "Ah. Let me guess, he's not happy with the situation."

"You could say that."

Westlake was silent for a moment, considering the angles. "If he doesn't like it, why hasn't he left?"

"Where would he go? Besides, this place is full of everything a man might want in this post-apocalyptic economy." Vinnie leaned back, hands clasped behind his head. The revolver was within easy reach of both of them, and Westlake considered going for it. Then he dismissed the idea.

"If only you could get to it," Westlake said.

Vinnie frowned. "Yeah. If only."

"Why not send your little friends in? Those robots can do damage."

"You like them? Got 'em wholesale. Sal thought it was

a waste of money, but they don't eat, they don't sleep, and they will absolutely mess up a zombie's day."

Westlake smiled. "Guess you got the last laugh, then."

"You could say that," Vinnie said. "Anyway, they've kept me safe and sound up here. I even had them converted for solar charging stations. Keeps them nice and functional all the live long day."

"And they stop Carl from getting any ideas, am I right?"

"That too." Vinnie tapped the rim of his glass. "Problem is, they eat ammunition like nobody's business. And once they run out, they're just really expensive paperweights." He paused. "They patrol the fences, keep the neighbors on their side of the line. They're the only reason the Villa hasn't fallen to the dead."

"So back to my original question: why not send them in after Sal?"

"Because they only got about eight hours of battery life, and if they get stuck or trapped, they ain't coming back out. I need them out here too much to risk them."

"And you can't send in Carl, obviously."

"Nope."

Westlake held his glass in both hands. "Carl wanted to kill me. But you wanted me alive… Why?" he asked, though he already knew the answer. "What's the deal?"

"Who said there was a deal?"

Westlake frowned. "Don't play stupid, Vinnie. You told Carl to bring me here. You want me to do something, so lay it out for me."

Vinnie pointed at him. "You're a smart guy. I always said that. That's why when I realized you were coming this way,

I said to myself, 'Vinnie? Here's an opportunity.' If anybody can get in there and solve my problem, it's Westlake."

"The deal, Vinnie."

Vinnie gestured to the monitors. "Simple. I want you to get me my Villa back."

CHAPTER TWENTY-SEVEN
The Deal

"Why?" Westlake said, after a moment. "Why should I take that deal?"

Vinnie glanced at the revolver. Westlake ignored it. Vinnie wasn't planning to shoot him. He wasn't the sort to get his hands dirty. Vinnie sniffed. "If you don't, maybe I open the shutters, and we all take our chances. I'm sure Sal is in the mood to stretch his legs. He always was a bit of a fitness nut." He leaned close, his chair squeaking across the tiles. "The walkers? Not much of an issue. But Sal… Sal is a whole different kettle of nasty Hudson River fish. Imagine what he'd do to one of those camps down there."

Westlake shrugged. "What do I care about that?"

Vinnie peered at him. Then he laughed. "Yeah, I didn't think that'd bother you. Not like Sayers. Tell me this, why were you coming up here, Westlake?"

Westlake was silent for a time, considering. "Sal owed me. I wanted to collect."

Vinnie nodded. "You came to kill him."

"No. I wanted my money."

Vinnie froze, shocked. "What?"

"Money, Vinnie. Sal owed me my cut for the Milwaukee job, remember? The one you set up? Sal decided not to pay us, even after we delivered. He dimed us out to the cops instead. Or maybe you did."

Vinnie sagged. "You're crazy." He shook his head. "What does that matter now?"

"It matters to me." Westlake held out his glass. Vinnie stared at him for a moment, and then refilled it.

"So you're saying you climbed a goddamn mountain in a goddamn zombie apocalypse *to get some money*?" Vinnie asked, incredulously.

"My money," Westlake corrected. "It's the principle of the thing."

Vinnie gave a hollow laugh. "Crazy. You've gone crazy. But that's why I like you, Westlake. You think outside the box and yet you're tunnel-visioned at the same time. No one who's gone in to kill Sal is as determined as you. I remember that job you did with the plane." He ran both hands through his hair. "I didn't dime you out. First I knew of it, Sal was breathing fire about you talking to the Feds." He gave Westlake a sly glance. "Which didn't sound like you at all."

"Soft pressure," Westlake said.

"What?"

"I was letting Sal know what I was capable of. Then he sent Tommy." Westlake flexed his hands. "Do you have my money or not?"

Vinnie shook his head and looked back at the monitors.

"If it's anywhere, it's in Sal's safe, in the office. In there." He waved at the monitors. "Go ask Sal to cut you a check, see what he says."

"Yeah, but I'm asking you." Westlake leaned forward, and Vinnie made a convulsive twitch towards the revolver. Westlake smiled. "I want my money, Vinnie."

Vinnie met his gaze. "And I want my Villa, Westlake."

Westlake smiled thinly. "So let's make a deal. A different deal."

"What sort?"

"One that benefits us both. What other kind is there?"

Vinnie sat back, one hand on the revolver. "Alright, talk. But if I don't like what I hear, I might just use your friends for target practice."

"No, you won't. You need us. All of us. We go in, we take care of your problem, and clean house. I get my money, and you get the benefit of being the man whose generosity saved a bunch of people. How's that sound?"

Vinnie tapped his lips with the revolver. "What do I get out of it?"

"The warm glow of helping your fellow man?"

Vinnie laughed. "Try again."

"What was Sal's plan, Vinnie? Sweep down like a bunch of medieval Sicilian bandits and take over? Make this place a castle, and the camps below your peasant villages?"

Vinnie was silent for a moment. "Something like that," he said, ruefully. "I told him it was a stupid plan, but he wasn't in the mood to listen. Guys like him and Carl – they think like old world *banditti*. Guns solve all problems."

"But we're different, aren't we, Vinnie?" Westlake said,

softly. "We see the angles." He took a sip from his drink. "You want me to go in there and take care of your Sal problem. I'm game. I'll even talk Ramirez and the others into helping. But what about after?"

Vinnie frowned. "After?"

"There's a whole bunch of people down at the foot of this mountain, waiting for someone to save them – to give them a safe place to live, supplies, ammunition. Why shouldn't it be you?" Westlake looked around. "What else are you going to do with this place? Hide up here with Carl and his idiots?"

"Carl… might not go for that," Vinnie said, slowly. "He's not big on sharing."

"There are ways to deal with that." Westlake watched Vinnie's expression. He had a good poker face, but not perfect. His eyes went vague when he was calculating his odds. Vinnie was smart enough to know that he wouldn't survive much longer on his own – or with Carl. Even with his toys to even the odds, he wasn't built for it. Westlake took another sip and waited.

Finally, Vinnie smiled and said, "I've been up here mostly alone for the better part of two months, and this is the most fun I've had in a while. OK. You do me a solid, I'll do you one. I'll open my kingdom up to your friends… as long as they acknowledge who's in charge here." He tapped his chest. "Me."

"I'm sure they'll have no problem with that, once they realize what you're offering them." Westlake finished his drink. "Specifics, please."

"Onto business now, huh?"

"No sense wasting time."

Vinnie laughed and turned back to the monitors. "You can get in through the service entrance. I can unlock it manually from here. I'll do the same for the fire doors inside."

"And then lock them all back behind us, huh?" Westlake said.

Vinnie didn't look at him. "You want me to leave it open? That might go poorly for your friends down the hill. No, I'll lock it back up, just in case."

"Weapons?"

"Plenty of guns laying around in there. Take your pick."

"Helpful," Westlake said.

Vinnie turned away from the monitors and grinned at him. "You're a smart guy, Westlake. I'm sure you'll think of something."

Westlake scratched his chin and studied the monitors. "And when we send Sal to his eternal reward, you'll just let us out?"

"I'll just let you out."

"What about the rest of the zombies?"

Vinnie flapped a hand. "I'll let my toys earn their keep. They can handle cleanup. You concentrate on Sal. I'm not letting you out of there until he's dead." He paused. "And just to make sure you're on your best behavior, I'm going to need a hostage." He tapped at the keyboard and brought up a view of the courtyard. The camera focused in on Ramirez and the others, standing under guard near the quay. "The girl."

"Kahwihta," Westlake said.

"Whatever. She stays here with me. You try and play me, I'll put a bullet in her head. You feel me, Westlake?"

"I feel you," Westlake said. He doubted Kahwihta would have left Attila, and it was probably safer out here – for a given value of "safe." He pushed himself to his feet. Vinnie rose with him, gun in hand.

"Yeah, I can see that you do." He gestured with the revolver. "Let's go let your people know who they're working for, huh?"

Outside, Carl paced impatiently in front of the boatshed. Ramirez and the others were sitting nearby, under the watchful eye of Fifer and the other gunmen. Kahwihta was bent over Attila, preoccupied with his injury. Sayers stood nearby, her attention on seemingly anything and everything – except Ptolemy.

Carl turned as the door opened. "So?" he demanded, as he stomped over. "Do I get to shoot him now?" Behind him, Ramirez got slowly to her feet and followed.

"No," Vinnie said, mildly. "I still got a use for him."

"What use?"

Vinnie smiled widely. "He's going to get us our building back. Him and his friends. You know Westlake will stop at nothing to get a job done. Ain't that neighborly of them?"

"We're doing what now?" Ramirez said, looking startled as she joined them.

"Bullshit," Carl said, glaring pugnaciously at Westlake. "Bullshit!"

"Carl, calm yourself," Vinnie said, in a mild tone. He paused. "I mean, unless you want to take a run at Sal yourself?"

Carl blanched. He shook his head. "I keep telling you, send the robots in. That's what they're for!"

Vinnie's smile could have cut glass. "They're for what I say they're for. As I recall, you weren't much of a fan until they saved your ass."

Carl grunted. "I don't think we should do this." His hand hovered over his sidearm. Westlake could read the tension in Fifer and the others. At the end of the day, there wasn't any way to predict which way they'd jump. He wondered if any of them were made men. He doubted it. None of them had the look. They probably weren't thinking about anything except how to get through the next day and they'd follow whoever promised to keep them alive – Carl or Vinnie, it didn't matter.

"Then it's a good thing we're not a democracy," Vinnie said, glibly. He was pushing Carl's buttons intentionally – trying to make him mad enough to do something stupid. "This place belongs to me, Carl. I say what we do with it."

Carl frowned. "It belonged to Sal, Vinnie. Only Sal's... dead."

Vinnie leaned close. "Yeah, and I was his consigliere. You, on the other hand, are a soldier. So do what a soldier does and follow orders."

Carl flushed. "I'm getting real tired of your attitude, Vinnie," he said, in a rough, low voice. "I put up with it, because you're the one who knows how to open all the doors and run the robots, but I'm about ready to move on and leave you to rot up here by yourself."

"Yeah? And what about all those supplies in there?" Vinnie gestured. "Food, guns, medicine – you just going to leave all that behind?"

Carl glanced at Fifer. The other man looked away. Carl's

frown deepened. He looked at Vinnie. "And what if they fail? Just like Pauly and all the rest?"

"Then you've lost nothing," Westlake said, simply. "And I'm dead. Or worse."

Carl nodded slowly. "That does sweeten the deal a bit, I admit." He shook his head. "Still a bad idea. Is this why you didn't want me to kill him?"

"Among other reasons," Vinnie said. He looked at Ramirez. "Sayers tells me you were a Fed. Ordinarily, I'm not what you'd call a fan of Federal agents, but in this instance, I'm willing to let bygones be bygones. What about you?"

"Is that supposed to be a joke?" Ramirez asked.

Vinnie looked offended. He placed his hand over his heart. "I'd never joke about that. This is the start of a new era. We're going to do great things together, Agent Ramirez. You, me, and Westlake here. Once we take care of our mutual problem."

"And what problem might that be?" Ramirez asked.

"Yeah, Vinnie, what problem might that be?" Carl said, eyes narrowed in suspicion. "Illuminate us, please."

"I want you to kill a zombie," Vinnie said, with forced cheerfulness.

"Just one?"

"A big one," Westlake said. "Surrounded by a bunch of little ones."

Vinnie laughed. "Very big. Bigger than any you've ever seen. Immune to small arms fire, fast and mean. You kill it for me, and I'll let your people come in. We'll make this place a paradise."

Ramirez frowned. So did Carl. "We need to talk about this," he said.

"Later," Vinnie said, not looking at him.

"*Now*," Carl snapped. Vinnie looked at him. Westlake tensed. Was this how it was going to go down? He hoped not. He didn't even have his knife. Carl had taken it, as well as his Glock. He met Ramirez' eyes and read the question there. He gave a slight shake of his head – whatever happened, it was best to let it play out.

Vinnie smiled broadly. "Of course, Carl. Let's step over here and do it in private, huh?" He gestured to the boatshed, and Carl's eyes tracked the revolver in his hand. Vinnie glanced at the weapon, as if noticing it for the first time. He laughed lightly and slid it into the back of his waistband, under his jacket.

Westlake watched them go. Ramirez followed his gaze. "And what do you think that's about?" she murmured.

Westlake looked up at the night sky overhead. The stars were out in force. "The usual. Vinnie's probably explaining to Carl that he intends to screw us after we solve their problem for them."

"Speaking of which – what have you gotten us into, Westlake?" she hissed. He turned, and she grabbed his collar, driving him back against a support beam of the boatshed. "What sort of deal did you make with him?"

"The only one that kept us alive," he said, hands held up in surrender.

"By sending us into a walker-infested house of death?"

"Better than a bullet in the back of the head." He met her angry gaze without flinching. "Look, we're here, aren't we?

This place is real, just like I promised. Now all we have to do is take it."

"From a giant zombie," she said, dubiously. "Not to mention your pals over there."

"One problem at a time," he said, smiling crookedly.

CHAPTER TWENTY-EIGHT
Entry

Ramirez let Westlake go. "There's something you're not telling me," she said, flatly. "Some angle you're playing. What is it?"

Westlake straightened his shirt. "No angle. I saved our lives. You're welcome."

"I didn't say thank you."

"I noticed." Westlake smiled. "I'll add it to your tab."

Ramirez' hand knotted into a fist, but she restrained herself – not without difficulty. Her eyes strayed to Vinnie and Carl. "You know that if whatever is in there doesn't kill us, they probably will, right?" she said, in a low voice.

"I know," Westlake said.

"You don't seem concerned."

"I'm not."

She glared at him. "Care to let me in on the plan?"

"No plan. Not yet." Westlake nudged her gently. "What do you think of the place so far?"

Ramirez frowned and looked around. "Big." The courtyard

was twice the size of the lodge parking lot, even taking the outbuildings into account. "The Villa itself is likely three times the size of the lodge. And better defended with those reinforced fences." She paused. "Those robots..." she began.

"Would come in handy," Westlake finished. Ramirez nodded grudgingly. She scanned the outbuildings. Each was multilevel, made from wood or concrete. Most were storage, she thought. One looked to have been converted into living quarters, probably by Carl and his men. Another was larger than the rest, and sat directly opposite the front gates. It had hinged garage doors on the front.

"What's in there, do you think?" she muttered. "Fleet of sports cars?"

"Probably something more practical than that." Westlake scratched his chin. "But there's a fuel pump over on the side there and another over in the boatshed. That means there's probably a full reservoir under the courtyard. That might come in handy, huh?"

"If we survive." She looked at the Villa again, and the indistinct shapes pressed against the windows and the glass doors at the front. "I don't suppose you know anything about the layout of this place?"

Westlake shook his head. "Not really. From what my guy told me, I know that it's got four levels – three above the ground, one below. Other than that, nothing."

Ramirez looked at him. There'd been something, a hesitation, in his voice. But his expression gave away nothing. "Maybe we should ask your pal, Vinnie. I bet he might even give us blueprints."

"That's a good idea. You're starting to think like a thief."

Ramirez snorted and continued her examination of the Villa. Westlake was right about the place, whatever else. There was so much space and safety for those left behind at the lodge. But thinking of the lodge made her wonder how many had made it out. How many had made it to North Elba. Her hands clenched and her eyes found Sayers, over near the quay.

Ptolemy was talking to her, quietly – or trying to, rather. She clearly wasn't having any of it, however. She glanced at Fifer. Carl's goons didn't seem all that concerned that he'd wandered away. Fifer and the others lounged about lazily, but their eyes were hard and they held their weapons close. They were overconfident, but more than likely just burnt out. They'd been up here too long, under siege. But that was a problem for later.

She started towards Sayers and Ptolemy, keeping one eye on Fifer and the others. Westlake called after her, but she ignored him. She had something she wanted to say to the other woman, and she might not get another chance. By the time she got there, Ptolemy was furiously cleaning his glasses on his shirt and saying, "I still do not understand any of this. What were you thinking?"

"I told you," Sayers said, not looking at him. "If I'd said no, they'd have killed you. All of you. Why do you think I argued against staying at the lodge?"

"I thought you simply liked your privacy."

Sayers laughed, though it was more a croak to Ramirez' ears. She cleared her throat as she approached, letting them know she was there. Sayers turned, eyes narrowed. "You. You wouldn't listen, would you?"

"Maybe if you'd explained, I might've."

"If I'd explained, you'd have come up here guns blazing and then you'd be dead." They were almost nose-to-nose now, snarling at one another. Ramirez didn't flinch. Part of her had been wanting to have it out with Sayers for a long time, even before she'd tried to kill them. Now was as good a time as any.

"So instead, you shot Hahm. You let zombies into our perimeter. How many people died because you did that, do you think?" Ramirez growled, trying not to imagine it. But it was hard. Her stomach twisted as she recalled the explosion they'd seen – and what it might mean for Dunnigan and the others. For Frieda.

She'd tried hard not to think about Frieda all this time. She'd convinced herself that they'd gotten away. But now, doubt crept in again, adding to her anger. It filled her like a lightning-heavy cloud, and all she wanted to do was hit Sayers.

Sayers grimaced. "I was doing what I thought best."

"You got Labrand killed. You know that, right?"

Sayers looked away. "That wasn't my fault. I didn't... He shouldn't have come after me." Her voice softened. "None of you should've. Why didn't you listen?"

"You know why," Ptolemy said. Sayers glanced at him, then away.

She was silent for a moment. Then, "I didn't know it was like this. The last time I spoke to them Sal was still alive. If I'd known..." She trailed off.

"What? You'd have told us?" Ramirez asked.

Sayers looked at her, her gaze hot and fierce. "No. I'd have handled it myself. I spent years – *years* – at Bonaro's beck and call. My father was sick; I needed money. They paid well. Then he died, the apocalypse happened, and I thought it was over. But no. Sal showed up one day, with Carl and Vinnie and half a dozen others and said I'd better keep up my end or they'd wipe out the camps. And they could've, too. Then, at least."

"But not now," Ramirez said, quietly.

Sayers paused. "No. Not now."

Ramirez fell silent. Suddenly, she wasn't angry anymore. From the look on her face, neither was Sayers. They studied each other in a newly reached mutual understanding. They both wanted the same thing, Ramirez thought.

"If we don't come out of there," she began, in a whisper.

"You will," Sayers said, her eyes on Ptolemy. She gave a crooked smile. "You managed to get this far."

"But if we don't…"

Sayers' smile faded and her gaze flicked to Carl and Vinnie, still talking in low voices over near the boatshed. "Then I'll make sure the others are safe. One way or another."

Ramirez nodded. She turned as Vinnie laughed and clapped Carl on the shoulder. They'd finished their conversation. She looked at Ptolemy. "You ready?"

"Would it matter if I said no?"

"No."

"Then yes. I am ready." He held out his hand to Sayers. After a moment's hesitation, she took it and gave it a brief squeeze. Then she released him and looked away, her arms crossed over her chest. Ramirez and Ptolemy walked across the courtyard to rejoin the others. Vinnie was already expounding at length on his plan.

"Now, to make sure you keep up your end, this enchanting young woman here is going to keep me company." He indicated Kahwihta, who sat nearby, Attila's head in her lap.

Ramirez' eyes narrowed as she heard this, and she hurried over. "No way. That's not happening."

"I'm afraid you haven't got much choice," Vinnie said. He gestured, and Carl drew his sidearm. "Keep in mind, every one of you Carl has to shoot, lowers the odds for the rest. Besides, Westlake already agreed."

Ramirez shot a look at Westlake, who met her glare with a bland gaze. She forced herself to calm down. To think it through. She glanced down at Kahwihta.

"I'll be fine," Kahwihta said, looking up from Attila. "Attila is hurt. I wasn't planning on leaving him anyway." She laid her hand on the dog's bloody flank. Attila's tail thumped the ground once and then he lay still, panting. She pulled out her notebook. "Besides, if he's got cameras, I've got a ringside seat."

Vinnie smirked. "See? She's fine. Everybody's fine. Right?" He looked around. "Anyone else have something to say? No? Great." He turned to Westlake. "I think this is the start of a beautiful working relationship, don't you?"

"Depends on whether I make it out in one piece."

Vinnie laughed. "I suppose so. You just make sure you get the job done." He poked Carl in the shoulder. "You and your people hang back. Make sure none of them slip past my toys, huh?"

Carl nodded – somewhat grudgingly, Ramirez noted – and started organizing his people. He clearly wasn't happy with the situation. But he was going along with it for now.

She wondered what Vinnie had promised him. She caught Westlake's eye, and he gave a slight shrug. He either didn't care or wasn't worried.

"So, how are we doing this?" Hutch asked. "You going to give us guns or what?"

Vinnie laughed. "Hell, no. Like I told Westlake, there's plenty of guns in there. Not that they'll do you any good against Sal."

"They'll do plenty of good against the walkers in there," Ramirez said. "But that's our lookout, isn't it?" She rubbed her wrists and nodded. "Fine. Like Hutch said – how are we doing this?"

"Service entrance," Westlake said, studying the building. "That's close to the kitchens, isn't it?"

Vinnie nodded. "Hall to your left, elevator at the end. Don't see why that matters, though."

"Just getting the lay of the land. To the right?"

Vinnie smiled. "Hospitality. The lobby, main dining room. Ballroom."

"Ballroom?" Hutch said.

"What can I say? We liked to party."

"Fascinating," Ramirez said, drily. "Anything else we should know?"

"Once you go through the door, there'll be a stairway dead ahead. You go up, it'll take you to the second level."

"And what will be waiting for us up there?" Ptolemy asked.

"Guest bedrooms. Third floor has the master bedrooms." Vinnie paused. "Sal's office is on the third floor, by the way."

"Good to know," Westlake said. "After you open the door, what then?"

Vinnie patted the top of one of the robots. "My pals here will cover the entrance. Soon as that door opens, the zombies will come out. No point in having you torn apart three seconds after you get inside. So just stand back and let my toys do their job. After the way is clear, in you go. Door goes click behind you, and after that... it's in the hands of God." Vinnie put his hands together piously. "I will say Sal comes running pretty quick when he hears gunfire, so... you know."

"Yeah," Ramirez said. "We know." She took a breath and looked around at the others. "We ready, folks?"

"Let's get this done," Westlake said. He stared at the service door, hands in his pockets. She wondered if it was bravado, or just that he was that confident. She hoped it was the latter.

"That's the spirit," Vinnie said, ambling back to the server room. "You got about five minutes to get ready, then the door is opening." He gestured to Kahwihta. "Come on, kid."

Kahwihta looked at him. "I'm not leaving my dog."

Vinnie frowned. "Well, I'm not carrying him."

Without a word, Calavera stooped and picked Attila up. He carried the animal into the outbuilding, Kahwihta following after. A few moments later, the masked man returned. Vinnie, watching him, grinned. "Got to get me one of them," he said. He gave Westlake a lazy salute. "Anyway, have a good time."

"I'm starting to hate him," Ramirez murmured. She looked at him. "Why did you care about Bonaro's office?"

"That's my business."

Ramirez shook her head. "No, it isn't. We're all going in

there together. I need to know I can count on you, Westlake."

Westlake said nothing. There was a look in his eye she didn't like. She'd seen similar in the eyes of fellow agents, ones too close to a bust they'd been chasing for years. A sort of tunnel-vision, like pilots got. All they saw was the target. Westlake had his target in sight, whatever it was, whatever had drawn him up here, and he wasn't going to let anything get in his way now.

She leaned close to him, holding his gaze. "I need to know I can count on you, Westlake," she repeated flatly. "Can I?"

"Yes," he said, finally. She didn't believe him, but there was no time to argue, no time to do anything but roll up their sleeves and get the job done. Afterwards, they'd talk – if there was an afterwards.

She cracked her neck and rolled her shoulders. "Good. Now let's go kill some zombies." Even as she spoke, the robots started towards the service entrance. Ramirez, Westlake, and the others followed the machines at a trot. Ramirez' hand fell to her side, where her pistol normally was. She felt off-balance without its weight. And no baton either. Both of them had been her constant companions since the dead had risen. Longer, even.

The door was an innocuous rectangle of gray in the side of the building. An electronic lock sat just above the handle, and its red light turned green as they drew near. Ramirez gestured to Calavera and he went to the door. He opened it and a walker lurched out, its clothing stiff with dried gore. Nor was it alone; two more followed it.

She heard Carl curse softly, but a moment later the robot with the SAW opened up, punching the zombies from their feet. The robot trundled forward, still firing through the open doorway. The other three machines stood by, as if waiting for their turn. But there was no need. Finally, the SAW fell silent, and the robot reversed course, backing out of the way. She forced herself to relax. "Let's go." She started for the door, but Westlake stepped past her.

"I'll take point," he said.

"You're volunteering?" she asked, surprised.

Westlake grinned at her. "It only makes sense. After all, it was my idea, right? Follow me." He ducked through the doorway without waiting for a reply.

Ramirez looked at the others. "You heard the man. Follow him."

CHAPTER TWENTY-NINE
Inside

The door closed with a hiss of its pneumatic hinges. Westlake heard the electronic lock beep softly, the tiny lights on the handle going from green back to red. The access corridor was composed of white tile, now largely marked by bloody handprints and smears of offal. Flies buzzed thickly on the recycled air. Westlake swallowed a sudden surge of bile.

For all intents and purposes, it appeared a massacre had taken place in the narrow corridor. Not just the walkers the robot had gunned down. Heaps of mutilated meat stretched the length of the passage, as if a crowd had been trying to escape and failed. Westlake tried not to imagine what it must have been like. He glanced up and saw the glass eye of a camera tracking them. He hoped Vinnie enjoyed the show.

"God," Ptolemy choked. He pressed his hand to his mouth, and Westlake wondered if he was going to throw up. He turned away from the carnage, and Ramirez patted his back in sympathy.

Westlake shook his head. "They must have tried to get

out, but Vinnie must've locked the building down. He always was a weasel. Soon as he popped a cap in Sal, he probably booked it for the outside with whoever he could get. Everyone else… he left."

Calavera sank to his haunches beside a red mass that might once have been a person. "Whatever did this, did so quickly and brutally." He pointed out a series of deep grooves cut into the tile. "And see there? Blades of some sort."

"Claws," Westlake said. "The thing on the camera – Sal – it had claws."

"What sort of zombie has claws?" Hutch muttered, as he accidentally trod on something that uttered a sickening squelch. He grimaced and leaned against the wall in order to check the sole of his boot. "I mean, the mess I get – zombies ain't exactly neat eaters. But this is something else." He looked at Westlake. "What the hell have you gotten us into?"

Westlake ignored him and picked his way through the debris, moving slowly towards the end of the hall. "See if they got any guns on them. If there are any more walkers nearby, they'll be on the way."

He stopped at the end of the hall. A set of stairs rose ahead of him, bending up and around, leading to the next floor, as Vinnie had said. A set of glass-topped double doors were to either side of him. Left was the kitchens, right was–

Westlake jerked back. A walker stared through the glass at him. Ragged fingers scratched at the pane as the dead man beat his head against the door frame. Bushy white mustache, nice hair – or it had been – and a pinky ring that scratched divots in the glass. Westlake didn't recognize him, but wondered if he'd been somebody important. He looked down and saw that someone had shoved a broken broom through the handles, securing the door, at least temporarily.

The walker grew more agitated the longer Westlake stared at it. The sound of its thumping filled the corridor. The noise would bring more of them. Westlake wished he had his knife, but Carl had taken it. His big hands flexed uselessly as he watched the thing flail at the door. "Ugly sonnuvagun," Hutch said, startling him.

Westlake glanced at him. "Yeah. Find anything?"

Hutch held up a revolver. He popped the cylinder. "Three shots left." He slapped it back into place. Westlake took it from him.

"That'll do."

"Hey!" Hutch protested. Westlake ignored him and thrust the gun into his coat pocket. He started for the stairs. He had a job to do, one that was solely his.

"Where are you going?" Ramirez called.

"Upstairs, obviously."

Ramirez caught up with him. "Why?"

Westlake paused on the bottom step. "I have a feeling that thing will find us. In the meantime, I'm going to do what I came here to do. Now, you can come with me, or you can wander around aimlessly. Your choice."

Ramirez stared at him. "You know, just when I was starting to think you weren't an asshole, you pull this shit. You're not going anywhere." She made a clutching motion at her side, reaching for a gun that wasn't there.

Westlake couldn't help but smile. "Sort of a tradition for us, wouldn't you say?"

Ramirez threw up her hands. "Jesus Christ. Whatever happened to having your crew's back, Westlake?"

"This Sal is not here," Calavera said, joining them. "But Santa Muerte walks these halls. I can feel her presence. She will watch over us." He studied the walker through the glass, then craned his neck to peer past it. "I count five more in the hall beyond. There will be more soon, and these doors will not hold." He tapped the broom with a thick finger. The walker gave a groaning snarl that they all ignored.

Ptolemy offered Ramirez a battered Glock. "I found it in a shoulder holster. Full magazine. No spares."

She took it gratefully and checked the magazine for herself. As Ptolemy said, a full clip. Whoever its owner had been, they hadn't had time to get a shot off. "Anything else?"

Hutch shook his head. "Nothing useful."

"Might be more upstairs," Westlake said, in a gently wheedling tone. "Sal was a big fan of gun safes. Had one in every room of his house. I don't see why here would be any different." He gestured. "Shall we?"

Ramirez stared at him, and for a moment he thought he'd pushed it too far. Then her pragmatism kicked in and she gave a grudging nod. "Fine. But remember what we talked about."

Westlake nodded and started up the stairs. They took it slow. The stairs and the walls were stained with blood. No bodies – a bad thing. That meant they were walking around somewhere. Their footsteps and breathing sounded loud in the cramped space. Westlake rested his hand on the revolver in his pocket.

At the first landing, he paused. "Right. The rooms are

laid out in American hotel standard. Tight corridors, bad carpeting, all extending out from a central space. If you need them, there are access stairs like these on the opposite side of the building."

Ramirez nodded slowly. "Fine. Everyone take a room. We'll meet back here in five."

They took the rooms as slowly as they'd climbed the stairs. Westlake took the first one, and then, when the others were checking theirs, he slipped out, closed the door gently so that it made no noise. He trotted down the hall, heading back for the access stairs they'd come up before anyone spotted him. Ramirez would figure out where he was once she noticed he was gone, but if his luck held, he would be done by then. If she wanted to yell at him, she could. He didn't care.

He was too close to care. He went up to the next floor, his hand on the revolver in his pocket. It was quiet upstairs. He'd known it would be. People would have been going down to get out, and the zombies would have followed. There were always a few stragglers, but he figured he could handle them.

There was blood on the carpet and bullet holes in the plaster. And more than in the plaster – big holes in the ceiling and the floor, like a bomb had gone off at some point. Only there was no scorching, only a black, tarry residue staining the edges of each hole.

He didn't stop to wonder about it, and instead made for the largest office, at the end of the hall. His man inside had told him where Sal's office was, and Vinnie had confirmed. Apparently, Sal had had an en suite toilet installed.

He stopped upon hearing a shuffling in one of the rooms. A thumping. He decided to leave it be. So long as it didn't get in his way, there was no reason to waste the bullet. He pushed through to the office.

The office was big and tacky; just like Sal. Wooden bookshelves held false front books – glued together covers with gilt spines and nothing else. The pictures on the walls were pool hall chic, and the desk was too clean. The far wall was nothing but glass, overlooking the courtyard below. The bathroom door was closed. Blood covered the knob. Westlake studied it for a moment, then turned his attention to the safe.

Sitting against the wall, between the bookshelves, the big, old-fashioned, black safe seemed straight out of a Poverty Row gangster film. It had probably been in the Bonaro family for decades. It was funny; Sal had never struck him as the sentimental type.

Westlake checked the drawers of the desk, looking for a code to open it. Sal wasn't the sort to have memorized that kind of thing – he had people for that. He found it taped to the underside of the uppermost drawer and felt a rush of discovery.

He went to work. He'd never been much of a jugger – a safe-cracker. It was always better to have the code, when you could get it, by guile or force. Whatever did the job. As the tumblers clunked, he kept an eye on the door. But when the safe popped open, he had eyes for nothing else.

The money was there. Not his money, necessarily – but somebody's money that was owed to Westlake. He reached out, traced the first brick of cool green currency with a finger. He'd been dreaming about this moment for months, and now it was here. He felt vindicated.

A hand fell on his shoulder, startling him. He spun with a muffled cry. The walker behind him groaned and clutched a handful of his jacket. Judging by the toilet paper on the bottom of its wingtips, it had come out of the bathroom. He'd been so preoccupied by the money, he hadn't even heard the door open. He cursed himself for ignoring the thumping.

It hauled him up and flung him onto the desk. The zombie was big and had been big in life. A goon in a three-piece suit, with a hole where his throat should have been, and a face like raw meat. His large fists came down as Westlake rolled aside and groped for something – anything – he could use. He found a letter-opener, nice and sharp.

The zombie scrabbled towards him, reaching to get him. Westlake slammed the letter-opener down, pinning the dead man's hand to the desk. Then, for good measure, he slugged it in the face. The zombie tried to free itself, but to no avail. Westlake circled the trapped walker and made for the safe. "Now, where was I?" he murmured, ignoring the zombie. He began to stuff bricks of cash into his jacket. Not all of it. Just what he was owed.

A guttural sound filled the room. Westlake froze. "Shit," he muttered. A wave of primal fear passed through him as he turned to take in the thing that now stared at him with red, dead eyes.

Sal Bonaro grinned at him from the doorway. Or, rather, the thing that had been Sal. It was a hulking nightmare now, a mass of swollen muscle and contorted limbs. Shards of bone jutted from its ravaged flesh, and it flexed clawed hands as it studied him.

Westlake looked up into the thing's eyes and read his death in them. Unlike the walkers, there was a lot going on in Sal's head. None of it was good. The thing's jaws split open like a flower, revealing a maw of interlocking teeth. Tarry drool dripped from a slick gullet, plopping onto the carpet.

"Hey Sal, how's it hanging?" he said, in a cracked voice. It was better than screaming, but not by much.

Sal screeched in reply and Westlake threw himself aside as a talon slammed down, smashing through the desk and the pinned walker. Westlake scrambled to his feet and bolted for the door as Sal surged after him with a deafening roar.

Westlake ran for all he was worth, heading back towards the stairs, the monstrous zombie loping after him. The calcified extrusions that emerged from its swollen flesh tore gouges in the walls to either side of the corridor as it ran, filling the air with dust and plaster chips. Sal bellowed again, and answering groans echoed from up ahead – walkers, alerted to the prospect of a meal. Westlake didn't stop. Instead, he dropped and slid beneath the feet of the first of the zombies to appear out of a room.

He stayed low as Sal hit the walkers like an express train, slamming them against walls or stomping them flat. He saw the stairwell door and went for it, Sal's howls pursuing him. A thud behind him alerted him to a new player – a runner, clad in a red tracksuit and with sunglasses firmly fixed to its cadaverous face.

It came skidding out of a room to his right and bounded after him. Westlake reached the stairs just ahead of it and, thinking quick, hit the door and grabbed the rail, swinging himself over even as the runner pounced. The world seemed to slow as he held on tight.

As a blur of meat and muscle, Sal crashed into the runner in midair and both zombies tumbled down the steps, growling and moaning. Westlake waited until they hit the next landing before making to swing himself back onto the stairs. Only the walkers beat him to it. They crowded forward onto the landing, groping for him.

He hesitated, but only for an instant. Then he leapt. The landing below was a mass of broken inlay and torn carpeting. The runner had been flattened, but still had a bit of twitch left to it. Sal, on the other hand, seemed in fine fettle. The creature heaved itself up with a grunt, piggy eyes fixed on Westlake. It lifted what was left of the runner and casually popped the zombie's head off with a flick of one clawed thumb.

"Well, that's one way to handle it," Westlake muttered, as he pushed himself to his feet, fumbling for the door to the next floor behind him. He hoped the others had found something useful. Sal followed, drool hanging in glistening webs from his jaws. There was a glint of something that might have been amusement in its eyes as it took a step towards him.

"Down!" someone screamed.

CHAPTER THIRTY
Game-Plan

Westlake hit the floor. A shotgun roared, and Sal jerked back – more in shock than pain, he suspected. The monster reeled, squalling like a startled cat. It spun and smashed through the doors leading to the next corridor over, leaving a trail of ichor in its wake. He heard its screams of frustration even as it vanished from sight.

Panting, he looked up at Ramirez, who stood over him protectively. "Took you long enough. Another second, he'd have been chewing on my femur."

Ramirez stared in the direction Sal had gone, her eyes wide. She looked at the weapon in her hand as if it had betrayed her. "The gun didn't even slow it down."

"Yeah, noticed that, did you?" Westlake stood and glanced up the stairs. The walkers at the top hadn't yet figured out how to make their way down, but from the sound of it, others were on their way, drawn by the gunfire. "Where's everyone else?"

"Over here," Ptolemy called, from one of the rooms.

Westlake and Ramirez went inside, and Ptolemy slammed the door after them. Calavera shoved a chair beneath the handle. It was a guest room, with a bed, a television, and an en suite.

"Did you injure it?" Calavera asked.

"I don't think so," Ramirez said. "Startled it, though. Your pal Vinnie was right. That damn thing's bulletproof."

Westlake shook his head and sat down on the bed. "It's not bulletproof, it's just too tough to be bothered by getting shot." He ran his hands over his head. He was wrung out from the run, adrenaline fading. He needed to think.

"Maybe you shouldn't have gone off alone," Ramirez said, looking down at him. Her voice was calmer than he'd expected. She didn't look angry so much as disappointed. She used the barrel of the shotgun to open his jacket. She reached inside and took out a wad of cash. "Was this what you were after?"

He reached for it. She stepped back and swung the shotgun up. He sank back. "That's mine," he said. "I earned it."

"Milwaukee job," she said. It wasn't a question.

He nodded anyway. "Sal owed me. I came to collect."

She looked down at him, her expression unreadable. "Really." That wasn't a question either. He decided to answer it.

"It was the principle of the thing. Sal owed me. He tried to kill me rather than paying, so I came to get it."

Hutch stared at him. He was sitting by the window, another shotgun across his lap. "You … came all this way for some cash? What are you going to spend it on?" He looked around. "Does this sound insane to anyone else?"

"No," Calavera said.

Westlake looked at the big man. Calavera adjusted his mask. "A man must stand by his principles, even unto the end of the world. I understand this." He nodded to Westlake, and Westlake could not help but return the gesture. It was good to know that someone understood – even if it was the lunatic in the mask.

Ramirez wasn't so easy or so ready to forgive. She lifted the shotgun and set it across her shoulder, but her eyes hadn't left him. "All of this was about the money. From the beginning." She waved the cash brick for emphasis.

"What else would it have been about?"

"Were you planning on telling us?" she asked, still speaking in that same low tone.

"Why would I?" He looked around. "What does it matter? I held up my end of the deal – I'm still holding it up." He pointed at the money in her hand. "But that? That's mine. That's all that's kept me moving since I saw a dead woman take a bite out of Tommy Waingro. It's all I have left." His voice cracked again, as it had when he saw Sal.

The horrors of that night suddenly flooded back and hit him like a fist. He swallowed a rush of bile and looked down at his hands. They were steady. "I just wanted my money. I don't care about this place. You can have it. I'll help you take it. *But I want my money.*" He rose to his feet, and she stepped back, a frown on her face.

Then, with a sigh, she slid the brick of cash into her jacket. "You can have it. When we're done." She looked at him again with such disappointment. "Afterwards, you can take it and go wherever the hell you want. Just so long as I don't have to see you again."

He was silent for a moment, but now that he'd completed one task, he had to focus on the next: surviving. He forced a smile. "I was right. You are learning to think like a thief." He pointed to the weapon in her hand. "Find anything other than the shotgun?"

"Slim pickings," Hutch said. "Found another Glock. Two shotguns, and what was left of an AR-15. Everything else is either out of ammo, or broken."

"It's a start," Westlake said, but it didn't feel like it. He looked up as something thumped against the door. It wasn't Sal. If it had been, he would have burst through the door. "How many on this floor?"

"We weren't exactly keeping count," Hutch said, his eyes on the door. More thumping sounded, and the big man clutched his shotgun more tightly. "Ten, maybe fifteen. Not good odds. Worse odds with that big one running around."

Westlake looked at Ramirez. "Speaking of which, did you see his eyes? There's something going on in there."

"You're saying he's intelligent?" Ramirez asked, incredulously.

Westlake shook his head. "Think about what Kahwihta said. Walkers aren't dumb, they're just ... focused. They don't have a lot going on, but there's something there, otherwise they wouldn't be trying to eat us. Sal is like that – he's not stupid. He's just ..."

"An animal," Ptolemy finished for him. "He is an animal."

"Right." Westlake snapped his fingers. "A big animal. Which means this ain't going to be like taking down walkers, or even runners. We have to hunt him. Since I don't feel like creeping through this death-trap looking for him with a couple of shotguns between us, we need another way."

"Bait," Ptolemy said. Westlake looked up at him. "We need bait." He gestured. "Something to draw it out. One of us."

"And then what?" Hutch asked. "Because we only got a pretty pathetic handful of guns, or have you forgotten?" Another thump against the door. Hutch wasn't the only one to flinch this time. "And there's a lot more of them than us."

Calavera grunted. "We do not need guns. We need something more potent. An explosive of some variety. Something we can shove down the beast's gullet."

Ramirez shook her head, her eyes straying to the door. The chair blocking it shifted as something pressed against the other side, but at least it seemed some of the zombies were losing interest as the thumping decreased. "Whatever we do, it'll pull in the walkers as well. We can't handle both. Not without more firepower."

Ptolemy looked at Hutch. "The kitchens."

Hutch frowned. "What about them?"

"Alcohol."

Westlake smiled as he got what Ptolemy was driving at. "Molotov cocktails. We might not be able to shoot him, but we can certainly burn him."

Hutch nodded, a grin spreading across his face. "Yeah, I can do that."

"Good. You and Ptolemy head down to the kitchens. Get what you need. The rest of us will make some noise and get all the guests moving in the right direction."

Ramirez looked at him. "Got any ideas as to which direction that might be?"

Westlake scratched his chin. "According to the plans Vinnie mentioned, there's got to be a sound system in the ballroom. You know, for birthday parties and weddings and such."

"So?"

Ptolemy nodded. "Sound. Sound draws them. If we can turn on the sound system – if it's working – it might draw most of them in. Even Sal."

"Means somebody has to go in there and turn the shit on," Hutch said, dubiously.

"I can do it," Westlake said.

"I will go with him," Calavera said.

Ramirez nodded. "Good enough." She looked at Hutch. "Whatever you do, don't screw this up. We're going to need that stuff, and we're going to need it quick."

"When have I ever screwed anything up?"

"I point you to your entire life up to this moment," Ramirez said.

Hutch paused. "Fair enough. I won't screw up." He looked at Ptolemy. "Me and you."

Ptolemy frowned and adjusted his glasses. "After you," he said, and Hutch stared at him.

Calavera pulled the chair aside and opened the door. A walker lurched through. Before it could so much as groan, Calavera caught it and rammed its head into the doorknob. Its skull crumpled and the zombie slumped. "Time to go, I think."

"Lead the way," Westlake said.

Calavera stepped into the hall, taking out three more zombies with his bare hands, and motioned for the rest of them to follow. Westlake was next, his revolver out and ready. No sign of Sal, but he knew the monster was close. He glanced up at the camera watching the hall. He wondered what Vinnie was thinking right now. He flipped the camera the bird and fell back towards the wall. Ptolemy and Ramirez came next. Hutch was the last one out.

None of them saw the walker. It came out of a blind corner, moving quicker than any of them would have expected. It had been a woman, once – old, withered. Dressed to the nines, with hands chewed to the bone, missing lips exposing its teeth, yet its elegant hairdo was still in place. It sprang onto Hutch's back, riding him to the floor. He bellowed in shock and tried to hurl it off, but it held tight, fingers digging into his chest as it tried to gnaw at his neck. Westlake dove to help him, but was immediately distracted by the walker's companions. They came down the hall in a crowd seven or eight strong. He used one of the revolver's three shots and took down one in a custodial uniform.

Ptolemy got behind the one clawing at Hutch, grabbed a handful of its hair, and drove the butt of his Glock down between its eyes. Bone crunched, and the thing released Hutch, but not before taking a bite out of his neck. The zombie fell back, making a thin, squealing sound. The other walkers closed in.

Something – a noise, a smell, he wasn't sure what – made Westlake look up. He saw one of the holes he'd noticed before in the ceiling – and then a long, muscled limb shot down towards him. He leapt back at the last second, accidently crashing into Ramirez, knocking them both to the floor. Sal glared down at him from above and began to squeeze its abnormal bulk through the hole, like some deranged lizard. Westlake stared up at it in shock, unable to believe what he was seeing. "Shoot it!" he bawled.

Ramirez rolled onto her back, raised the shotgun, and fired. Sal vanished with a screech. "Trap," he breathed, as Ramirez hauled him to his feet. "He set a damn trap for us."

"Worry about it later – move!" She turned. "Ptolemy…!"

Ptolemy, Hutch's shotgun in hand, had the bloodied, groaning Hutch on his feet, and half-carried the biker towards the doors, as the walkers approached down the hall. "I have him! Go, go!"

Calavera was already at the doors, holding them open. He tensed, and Westlake thought he was planning to go after Sal. "Calavera," he said, snapping the big man out of it. "Later," he added, when he caught Calavera's attention.

Calavera nodded tersely. "Later," he said.

They managed to get Hutch out onto the landing where he collapsed, and Westlake slammed the doors. "We need something to keep this closed," he said, as dead fists began to pound on the other side. Calavera stripped off his coat, twirled it tight and looped it through the handles. Together, they managed to tie it into a sufficiently robust knot.

"It won't hold for long," Calavera said.

"Long enough for us to get downstairs, at least." Westlake stepped to the edge of the landing and looked up. There were still walkers milling about above. Eventually, one of them would figure out how the steps worked, and the rest would follow or fall down. But until then they were no threat. They weren't like the zombies outside, who seemed experienced at climbing anything to get to their prey. He wondered what

Kahwihta would make of it. He'd have to be sure to ask her, if they survived. The thought made him glance at Hutch. "How are you?"

"How you think I am?" Hutch croaked, one hand pressed to his neck. "She took a chunk out of me." He leaned against the rail, breathing heavily. "Gonna start craving finger sandwiches made out of real fingers any minute now."

Ramirez crouched beside him. "Can you stand?"

"Yeah." Hutch winced and flailed at Ptolemy. "Help me up."

"Not yet. Sit still." Ptolemy had pulled a small first aid kit out of his tactical belt. While Carl's people had taken all his weapons, they'd left him everything else. "It is a good thing you are overweight. Otherwise it might have torn out your jugular." He started to apply a bandage to the side of Hutch's neck. Hutch hissed in pain.

"Wish it had." He looked at Ramirez. "I need you to shoot me." He grabbed the barrel of her shotgun and brought it to his head. "Do me a solid and put me out of my misery before I do something I'll regret."

Ramirez pulled the weapon out of his grip and stepped back. "You're not out of the game yet," she said, flatly. "And you might not be, if your luck holds. Not everyone turns." Despite her words, Westlake could hear the pain in her voice. First Labrand, now Hutch. He felt a stir of regret himself. He liked Hutch. "Get on your feet," she commanded.

Hutch groaned as Ptolemy helped him up.

"I'll come with you to the kitchens," Ramirez said to Ptolemy, even as she glanced at Westlake. "Think you two can handle the rest?"

"Give me one of those shotguns and we'll see," Westlake said, holding out his hand. She hesitated, then slapped the weapon into his waiting palm. She pulled a handful of shells out of her pocket and offered them over as well.

"Make them count," she said.

"Do my best. Let's go." Westlake started down, shotgun ready. Calavera brought up the rear, as Ramirez and Ptolemy helped Hutch make the descent.

Down at the bottom of the steps, they found that the walker at the glass-paneled door had been joined by three others. Calavera stretched slowly, rotating his shoulders, readying himself. Westlake hefted his shotgun and looked at Ramirez. "We'll give you a few minutes to get to the elevator before we open these doors and head for the ballroom. After that, it's up to you."

"Yeah." Ramirez shook her head. "I hope Kahwihta is having more fun."

CHAPTER THIRTY-ONE
Friendly Chat

Kahwihta sat on the floor of the server building and tried not to worry about the others as she watched the monitor feed. A building full of zombies was normally something they tried their best to avoid. Especially when one of the zombies was the size of a truck. "Amazing," she said, despite herself, leaning forward. "Can you pause that?"

"What?" Vinnie asked, startled. She wondered if he'd forgotten she was there, despite her status as hostage. He was so used to being alone that he jumped reflexively every time she spoke. It would have been funny, if he hadn't been armed.

"The big one – can you play it back?"

"Why?" He studied her with suspicion.

She indicated the notebook sitting beside her. "I want to make some notes. I've never seen one like that. I thought at first he was a brute–"

"A what?"

Kahwihta mimed being bloated. "A brute. The big ones."

He frowned. "Oh. Yeah, there's one of those in there too. Caesar Campanella." He gestured to her notebook. "You writing a book or something?"

"I study zombies."

"Why?"

She shrugged. "Why not?" There was a sudden flash of silent gunshots on the screen. She saw someone fall, and felt her heart seize in her chest. Careful not to show any concern, she asked, "How are they doing?"

"They're still alive," Vinnie said, watching the screens.

"You're surprised?" Kahwihta asked. She stroked Attila's head. He was a tough dog, but a bullet in the side was enough to slow anyone down. She probed the edges of the wound, feeling for the bullet. Attila whimpered, and she paused to soothe him. Sayers could have killed him, she knew, but hadn't. Maybe she wasn't all bad.

"A bit. Most died about now. Want me to put him out of his misery?"

She looked up. Vinnie had the revolver aimed loosely at Attila. "No," she said, with as much calm as she could muster. "Thank you for the offer, but once I get the bullet out, he'll be fine."

Vinnie leaned back in his chair, watching her. "You a vet or something?"

"Or something."

Vinnie grinned. "I like animals myself. Sal, though… Sal hated 'em."

"Then I'm glad he's dead."

"Oof. Cold one, ain't you?" Vinnie looked back at the screens. "Not that anybody will miss him. He was a pain in my posterior before all of this happened, and he only got worse."

"Then why work for him?" Kahwihta probed the wound. The bullet was close to the surface – it had only been a glancing hit, thankfully. "Is there a first aid kit in here anywhere?"

"You going to waste a first aid kit on a dog?"

"Do you waste time cleaning your pistol?"

Vinnie frowned. "What's that got to do with anything?"

She sighed in frustration. "He's my pistol. You don't throw away a perfectly good gun just because it's dinged up."

Vinnie shook his head and reached into the desk drawer. "Here," he said, tossing her a green plastic box with a red cross stamped on it. "With my compliments."

She caught the box and set it down. "Thank you." She could feel him watching her as she set to work. "You didn't answer my question. Why work with someone like Bonaro?"

Vinnie laughed. "Making conversation now?"

"Call it curiosity."

He scratched his neck. "Sal and my dad, they were peas in a pod. Old school gangsters. Me, I'm new school all the way. I got me a business degree, I'm a registered CPA, hell, I can even officiate weddings."

She peered up at him. "Weddings?"

Vinnie nodded, clearly amused by her befuddlement. "I'm a one-stop shop. Had to be. Those old school guys, they didn't miss a trick, but they weren't what you call modern thinkers. They put their money into guns, into drugs. Me, I wanted to invest in emerging markets. Cutting edge pharmaceuticals, cryptocurrencies, that sort of thing. I needed the university sheepskin and the four-dollar words to convince them I knew what I was talking about. Not that it always worked, mind."

"I can see where that might have been frustrating," she said, her tone neutral. He wanted to talk. She'd been the same way, after her time in the wilderness.

Vinnie nodded. "Truth is, I was planning to put a bullet in Sal the same week this all went down. He was getting a bit... loose, if you understand me. But then – zombies. Figured loose was fine, so long as he was alive and useful."

"And after you decided to come down from the mountain?"

"Oh, he'd have been first against the wall, once everything was under control. Guys like Sal, they're always looking for an edge, for opportunity. Never happy with what they have. Like our pal Westlake." He glanced back at the monitors. "Not that I ever trusted Westlake, mind. Never trust a thief – my father taught me that."

"Good advice," Kahwihta said, more to keep him talking than because she agreed. It was clear Vinnie was starved for conversation, or more likely, an audience. He was the sort of guy who needed to show off how smart he was, how dangerous. Hiding up here alone must have been like slow death, with no one but Carl and his men to perform for.

"Smart man, my father." He paused and looked around. "He's the one who had most of this installed, you know. Foresight – that's how the Bonaro have survived all these years. The foresight of others. That's why they're still in the game, when the rest of the families cashed out. He knew, my old man – he knew there'd come a day when this would be our refuge. And theirs, though they never would have admitted it."

"And now you're going to share it with us." She finished cleaning Attila's wound, and began to probe it with a pair of tweezers. Attila whimpered and tried to move, but she held him still with one hand. "He'd be proud of you."

Vinnie laughed. "My old man would shoot me if he thought that's what I was doing. Luckily, I ain't that stupid."

Kahwihta, who'd been expecting something like that, nodded. "I figured."

"Yeah?"

"I'm not an idiot, Mr Spinoza. And my people know better than to trust the promises of white men in fancy suits." She raised an eyebrow at him. "In the end, you're always looking to screw over the other party. It's just how you are."

Vinnie blinked, as if trying to figure out whether that was an insult or a compliment. He settled on the latter and nodded. "Yeah. Fish got to swim, tiger got to eat – and gangsters got to get their share. Dog's bleeding again, by the way."

"I know." She gave the tweezers a twist, and the bullet popped loose with a wet sound. Attila shuddered and thumped his tail. She studied the bullet for a moment and then dropped it into the kit. "I'll deal with it momentarily."

"You don't flinch, do you?" Vinnie said, in mild admiration. "Tough broad like you, I might have a use for. If you were looking for employment." He paused. "Tell me about zombies."

"What do you want to know?"

He grinned. "Depends. How much do you know?"

"I know a lot."

He made a florid gesture. "Impress me."

She began to clean out Attila's wound. "I can calculate the time between a bite and possible turning, to within a few minutes."

"Oh yeah?" He indicated the screen. "How about your pal there? Looks like he got bit. How long has he got?"

She turned to the screens; her eyes widened. "Hutch?"

"I don't learn names," Vinnie said. "How long?" He was teasing her. Testing her. Wanting to hurt her, she thought. He had a sadistic streak to go with everything else. "I figure he's got – what? – a few minutes?"

"It depends."

"On what?"

"Whether he turns at all. Some people don't."

"Maybe he's one of the lucky ones, huh?"

"Maybe." She kept her head down so that he couldn't see her face. She wanted to cry but didn't. It wasn't going to do anyone any good. "Hutch is in good health. He's got no pre-existing conditions, and the wound is superficial. It'll take a few hours before he starts to feel ill. After that, it's up to his immune system and luck. He might fight it off. I did, after all."

"You what?"

Kahwihta pulled down the collar of her jacket, revealing the old bite mark on her shoulder. Vinnie stared at it for a moment, then shook his head. "OK. Care to make a wager on it?" he asked.

Now she did look at him. "No." She pulled her jacket back up.

He sat back, a cruel smile on his face. "No need to give me that look. I was joking."

Carl chose that moment to interrupt. He came in without asking permission, and from the look on his face, Vinnie wasn't pleased. "What do you want?"

"To talk," Carl said. He glanced at Kahwihta, but otherwise ignored her. "About this deal you made with Westlake. I think you should have spoken to me first."

"We already talked about this," Vinnie said. He set his revolver on the desk. Carl glanced at it, but didn't seem bothered. Maybe he figured Vinnie wouldn't shoot him.

"Yeah, but I got new concerns." Carl grabbed a chair and sat down. "I wanted to double-check on a few things, make sure we were still on the same page."

Vinnie looked nervous, though he was trying hard not to show it. Carl, on the other hand, looked cool and collected. Kahwihta tried to shrink into herself and escape the notice of both men. "Why wouldn't we be?" Vinnie said.

Carl sat back, causing the chair to creak. "See, I know you, Vinnie. I know how your crooked little mind works. We could get a good thing going here, if you're smart. That's the only reason the others and I are still here. But now you're doling out shares to people we don't even know – not to mention Westlake."

"I told you, I just needed to keep him sweet," Vinnie began. Carl gestured sharply.

"I don't care what you needed. I care that he killed my brother."

Kahwihta looked up at that. Carl caught her glance and mimed shooting her. He chuckled as she looked away. "I don't care what you promised him – he's dead. Minute he steps out of there, whatever his condition, I'm putting a round through his head."

"And I agreed," Vinnie said, forcefully. "None of them are coming out of there alive." He sat back. "So long as they kill Sal first, there won't be any problems."

"You're assuming they can."

"They can," Kahwihta said.

Carl sneered at her. "I don't recall asking you."

She met his gaze squarely. "They can and will."

Carl made to speak, but Vinnie interrupted him. "You heard her. Besides, the minute I open those doors, my toys will be there to greet them – and whatever else tries to get out. That includes Westlake."

"What about her?"

Vinnie glanced sidelong at Kahwihta. "I haven't decided yet."

Carl grunted. He fingered his gun. "She's one of Westlake's friends."

Vinnie laughed. "You know Westlake doesn't have friends." He scratched his cheek and peered at her. "But she does. Lots of them. The sort of people we might be able to use once we've got access to the Villa again."

"What do you mean?" Carl asked.

Vinnie smiled. "The future, Carl. Sal wanted to be king. But me, I'm more a president sort of guy. How would you feel about being vice-president?"

Carl nodded slowly, clearly thinking it over. "Yeah. I can get behind that."

"Good. First order of business – figure out who's essential.

I'm not having a bunch of mouths to feed up here, not unless they can be useful. You're in charge of that. Think you can handle it?"

Carl smiled. "I think so." He paused. "What about Sayers?"

Vinnie paused. "I leave that up to you." He turned back to the screens. Carl hesitated, then left. Kahwihta cleared her throat.

"You can't trust him."

Vinnie glanced at her. "Hey, tell me something I don't know. But a guy has to work with what he's got, you know?"

"You have better tools available." Kahwihta finished cleaning Attila's wound and reached for her coat. Vinnie stiffened, and she said, "Just getting a needle and thread. The medical tape won't be enough for this."

"Go on. But slow."

She reached into the pocket of her coat and found her sewing kit. She also found her icepick. But no need to let him see that, not yet. She pulled out the sewing kit, showed it to Vinnie, and went to work. Attila whimpered again, but not much. It wasn't the first time she'd sewed him back up. The first time had been when a black bear had used him as a chew toy. This was nowhere near as bad as that had been. As she worked, she said, "You mentioned something about employment?"

Vinnie was watching her work with a glazed expression on his face. "Yeah, yeah. Figure when all this is cleared up, I'm going to need people who can help me keep things running smooth, you know. Your useful types – doctors, that sort of thing."

"I'm a college student."

He waved her answer aside. "But you clearly know your shit. And that's what I'm talking about. Takes all types to make a community work, you know?"

All in a flash, it came to her. Vinnie wasn't just lonely – he was scared. For all his bravado, he was simply another survivor, trying to make the best of a bad situation. Only he didn't have any friends to help him, only restless underlings. She almost felt sorry for him.

She sat back on her heels and slid her sewing kit back into her coat. Her fingers lingered on the hilt of the icepick. She was only going to get one chance at it – best to make it a good one. "No, we can't have that, can we?" She paused, watching the monitors.

She could see Sayers, standing on the quay alongside Carl. And something else. Something in the water. Many somethings. She smiled. "Though you may not have to worry about it. It seems you have uninvited guests."

Vinnie turned to the monitors, a question on his lips.

She snatched the icepick free and lunged.

CHAPTER THIRTY-TWO
Uninvited Guests

Sayers stood on the quay, trying not to think about Calvin, or what had become of her life. Across the lake, the dead gathered, more than she'd ever seen in one place, or had ever wanted to see. They'd emerged from the trees and now milled about on shore, as if uncertain of where to go. With nothing to hold their attention, they would begin to disperse in a few hours, a day at most.

When they did, she would be free to leave. She doubted Spinoza would care. Unlike Carl, she had no interest in playing soldier for a self-proclaimed king on the mountain. She would go back to her cabin. Or maybe she'd find a new place to live. Somewhere no one could find her. Not Spinoza. Not Carl. Not Ramirez.

She would be alone. Finally, and completely.

That urge for solitude was why she'd taken a job as a park ranger. It meant days spent clearing brush and checking trails, away from people. She'd never been one for crowds or small talk. She'd enjoyed her job, for the all-too brief time it had lasted. Then the world had ended, and she'd been forced to deal with people, and not just living ones. The dead ones were somehow even more annoying.

Her hand dropped to the Mauser on her hip. Her father's last gift to her. Her father's favorite. There was no denying it had come in handy. She thanked whatever god might be listening that her father had insisted on teaching her how to shoot the thing.

Of course, she'd soon be out of ammunition for it. Then it would be one more useless thing in a world full of them. But there were other weapons – she had dozens of caches hidden in the mountains. There were other places to live.

She could vanish. But she wouldn't. Couldn't. She owed Calvin and the others that much at least. So, she would stay and do something incredibly stupid. She just wasn't sure what yet. Sayers had tried deadly methods to protect others and now she realized her morality was on the line. It was just as decayed as the undead.

She frowned. Across the water, something had the dead stirred up, though she couldn't see what. Maybe they'd spotted a deer. Zombies would chase a deer for hours, if they caught sight of one. But they weren't leaving, so it probably wasn't that.

Thinking of deer, of animals, made her think of the dog, and she felt a twinge of guilt. She liked animals – not in a soppy sort of way, but with a general sympathy for their daily tribulations. Like her, most animals wanted to be left alone. She'd only shot Attila in order to keep Carl or one of his idiots from doing the same, but with more lethal results. She hoped Kahwihta would forgive her.

Thinking of Kahwihta made her glance back at the server room. She wondered how she was going to get the other woman out in one piece. Vinnie hadn't shot her yet, which was a good sign. But there was no telling how long that would last. He wasn't planning on honoring any agreement he might have made with Westlake, she was sure of that.

On the far shore, more zombies had joined the throng. Ramirez had somehow managed to pull every walking corpse on Mount Marcy to this one spot. Sayers felt a twinge of annoyance. Maybe it wasn't solely Ramirez' fault.

"Planning to leave us?" Carl asked, from behind her.

Sayers didn't turn as he joined her at the edge of the quay. She kept her eyes on the water. "You don't want me here. I don't want to be here."

Carl chuckled. "Did I say that?"

"You didn't have to." She looked at him. Carl had never liked her. The feeling was mutual. Carl thought she was a complication, a loose end in need of snipping. He'd been the one with a gun in her face when Sal had paid his visit to her. She'd pressed a knife to his crotch in return. She wondered if he ever thought of how close he'd come to singing in a higher register. She indicated the water with a twitch of her chin. "I'll leave when they've cleared out some. Probably tomorrow morning."

"Why not the front gate?"

"Wrong side of the mountain."

Carl smirked. "You wouldn't be planning to go down the mountain and warn those nice folks there, would you?"

Sayers smiled thinly. "There's no one down at the foot of the mountain anymore."

Carl's smirk faded. His face took on a neutral expression. "That's probably for the best for everyone concerned."

"Is that what you think?"

He lit a cigarette. "Sure. Could be worse. We could be in there."

She cut her eyes at him. "And what happens if they die?"

Carl shrugged. "Damn shame." Something about the way he'd said it made her think he wasn't too concerned. Her eyes flicked down to his hand and saw that it was resting on the butt of his sidearm. She didn't wonder why he'd come to talk to her. She knew that he'd come to kill her. Carl had decided to snip the loose end.

Her hand was still on her Mauser. She could feel Carl's eyes on her hand. She smiled again. "I'm surprised you're still taking orders from him."

"Who should I be taking them from? You?"

"Yourself, maybe."

Carl laughed softly. Smoke plumed out his nostrils. "Yeah. But I want what's in here before I tender my resignation." A muscle in his cheek twitched. She tensed, ready to try and beat him to the draw. She wasn't sure what would happen afterwards. There was still Fifer and the others to worry about. Not to mention–

Sayers looked back towards the water at the sound of a splash. "Did you hear that," she said. "No, don't answer. Just shut up."

Carl's frown deepened. "You don't tell me to shut up, you–"

Sayers gestured sharply. "Shut. Up. I'm listening."

"To what?"

A rotting hand erupted from the water and clawed at

the edge of the quay. Carl fell back, cursing a blue streak. Sayers pivoted away from the zombie and peered towards the far shore. The zombies were no longer milling about, but trudging into the water. She'd been so lost in her own misery she hadn't noticed.

She stepped further back as the zombie hauled itself dripping onto the quay, filmy eyes focusing on her. Without breaking eye contact, she retrieved an oar and walloped the dead man hard enough to send him flailing back into the water. Carl scrambled to his feet.

"*Shit*. We got to tell Spinoza. We got to–"

"No. We don't." Sayers drew her Mauser, turned, and shot Carl. He pitched backwards with a cry. Sayers looked up, towards the entrance to the quay, where two of Carl's people stood staring at her in open-mouthed shock. She dove for cover behind one of the boats even as they opened fire. As she huddled behind the boat, another zombie hauled itself out of the water. Then another. And another. They paid her no mind, intent on the patter of gunfire coming from Carl's people, who'd switched targets from the living to the dead.

Sayers clambered across the boat, staying low and waiting for an opportune moment. Then she crept for the server room, using the butt end of her Mauser to take out any hungry zombies. It was the most secure spot in this place at the moment. She passed one of the robots and saw that it wasn't doing anything despite the attack. Just… sitting. So much for Spinoza's toys. She heard shouts as Fifer and one of the others hurried towards the quay.

They wouldn't last long. If they were smart, they'd run. The main gate was on the other side of the courtyard.

Though, knowing Spinoza, it was probably locked. She reached the server room at a run and hammered on the door. The camera stared at her.

She felt something brush her arm. Without a second thought, she turned and fired. The walker staggered back, fancy clothes dripping – another one from the plane. She fired again, finishing the job. She looked up at the camera. "Let me in, damn you!"

The door lock pinged green, and she shouldered it open as more walkers closed in. Panting, she slammed it behind her. Fists thumped against the door as she holstered her weapon and started towards the cubicle in the corner. "Spinoza…?"

The dog growled, and she stopped. "Mr Spinoza is indisposed," Kahwihta said. Sayers turned, saw the young woman sitting against the wall beside her dog.

Sayers looked at Spinoza, who still sat in his chair. The man was dead, an icepick jutting from his throat and a surprised look on his face. "You should have gone for the head." She looked at the monitor screens. "Are the others alive?" she asked, searching for any sign of Calvin.

"Do you care?" Kahwihta asked. Sayers heard the click of a revolver's hammer being pulled back and froze. "You shot my dog."

"But I didn't kill him." Sayers turned from the screens slowly, keeping her hands away from her weapon. "If I hadn't shot him, Carl or one of the others would have killed him."

"That thought had crossed my mind. That's why I haven't already shot you." Kahwihta held the revolver in both hands.

"Are you planning on it?"

"Still deciding."

Sayers grinned mirthlessly. "There are zombies outside."

"I know."

"Not worried?"

"No." Kahwihta indicated a laminated instruction manual on the floor beside her. "I've been keeping myself busy reading up on Spinoza's toys."

Sayers stiffened. "Can you use them?"

"Don't know yet." Kahwihta shrugged and patted Attila. "But I figured we might as well get some use out of them."

The door banged again under a rain of dead fists. Sayers ignored it, turning her attention back to the screens. She spied Calvin – and Ramirez, worse luck – helping Hutch down a hallway. "Where are they going?" she murmured.

"Kitchens, I think," Kahwihta said, joining her. "Don't know why, though."

Sayers tapped at the keyboard. "Where are the others? Calavera and the thief?"

Kahwihta pointed. "There. Looks like they're planning to hit the lobby."

There were walkers on every screen, stumbling through the halls and milling in the lobby. Fifty of them at least. Too many, as far as Sayers was concerned. They'd never make it. Her fingers traced Calvin's form on the screen. "Calvin…"

"Don't worry, you'll be joining him soon enough," Carl said, from behind them. Sayers turned, going for her pistol. The Glock in Carl's hand barked, and she felt a trail of fire burn across her ribs as she was knocked sprawling over the desk. Attila began to bark – too little, too late. Kahwihta was too startled to do more than raise the revolver.

"Put it down," Carl snarled as he staggered into the

cubicle, one hand pressed to his neck. Sayers cursed herself for not double-checking. "You should always remember to lock the door behind you," he added. He swung the gun towards Kahwihta. "And you – shut that damn dog up or I'll finish what Sayers here started."

Sayers dragged herself into a sitting position. Carl's shot had only grazed her, but it still hurt. She couldn't catch her breath. He swung the pistol towards her. "You're fired," he said. She tensed, waiting for the shot.

Spinoza jerked to his feet with a guttural wail. He crashed into Carl, and they fell to the floor. Carl screamed and fired, putting holes in Spinoza's nice shirt. The walker had grappled him, pinning the weapon between them. Spinoza's teeth sank into Carl's forearm, and he bellowed. Sayers fumbled for her Mauser, but Kahwihta beat her to it.

The revolver spoke, and Spinoza slumped – a smoking hole in his head. Carl gasped and looked up at Kahwihta. He made to speak, and Sayers fired. Then she fired again. She looked at Kahwihta. "Just double-checking this time." She nudged Spinoza. "How…?"

"Do you know how many zombies I've stabbed with that icepick?" Kahwihta asked, as she retrieved the robots' instruction manual and set it on the desk. "It's basically a bio-hazard at this point. Now help me figure out how to get these robots working or I'll stick you too." She looked up at the monitors. "I think we're going to need them sooner rather than later."

CHAPTER THIRTY-THREE
Lobby

The doors to the lobby juddered in their frame as walkers pounded on them. The broom holding them shut had snapped. Calavera kept his back to the doors, holding them closed through what could only be sheer force of will. He looked at Westlake, who stood nearby, shotgun in hand. "Are they safe yet?"

Westlake stepped back, glancing down the left-hand corridor. He could see Ramirez and the others heading for the service elevator. They weren't there yet. Hutch was slowing them down. Something fell down the stairs, drawing his eye.

The walker landed in a heap at the bottom of the stairs, and almost immediately tried to haul itself to its feet. Westlake lunged in, slamming the stock of the shotgun down on its head before it could recover. He leapt back as another walker plummeted down to land atop the quivering remains of the first. He took aim and fired, turning the newly arrived zombie's head to red mince. But he felt no sense of satisfaction. From the sound of it, more were on the way. He looked at Calavera. "Time to go, big man. You ready?"

"Santa Muerte guide our steps," Calavera said, pushing himself away from the doors. He crouched, readying himself. "Cover me."

Westlake levelled the shotgun. "Consider yourself covered."

Calavera launched himself at the doors like a battering ram. The heavy doors bent backwards, hinges popping from the wall as Calavera's full weight burst them open. He rolled across the floor as walkers fell back or were smashed against the wall by the doors. Westlake followed quickly, firing at any zombie that managed to stay upright. Three went down, including the mustachioed walker he'd noticed earlier.

A fourth scrambled towards him, its sweatsuit caked with old gore. Calavera caught it in mid leap and used its own momentum to drive it face-first into the wall. He dropped the twitching body and turned. "Is that all of them?"

"Nope." Westlake spun and fired as a broken-necked walker stumbled out of the stairwell towards them. "Let's move!"

Calavera took the lead, moving at a sprint. Westlake wondered how the other man could stay in motion for so long, at such a pace. Maybe he really did have a saint looking after him. Walkers came at them from all sides, some dressed in New York best, others clad only in bathrobes or underwear.

The lobby was a wide, semi-circular space, full of potted plants, couches and a front desk. He'd wondered a bit about that. What was the point of making it look so much like a hotel? Was it just for the Feds' benefit, or had the Bonaro been intent on making an authentic experience?

Four walkers stumbled towards them, three men and a woman, dressed in tracksuits and enough jewelry to choke a python. They came in a lurching rush, groaning savagely. He shot one, knocking it backwards over a potted plant. Calavera caught two as they stumbled past, and swung them into each other, hard enough to crack their skulls. Westlake drove his shotgun into the face of the fourth, dropping her and stamping on her head.

Dust sifted down from above, startling him. He looked up. The ceiling tiles shifted and bulged, and he had a sudden premonition. "Calavera, look out!"

The masked man glanced back, and then hurled himself aside as a heavy shape dropped through the ceiling to crash down in front of him. The floor buckled beneath Sal's weight, boards splintering. The monster roared, spreading its overly muscled arms in a parody of greeting – or perhaps challenge. Evidently taking it as the latter, Calavera shouted something that Westlake didn't catch, and leapt.

Sal backhanded the big man, sending him crashing into the front desk. Wood splintered, and Calavera didn't get back up. Walkers closed in, heading for easier prey. Sal shouldered through them as it made its way towards Westlake, mangling any walkers that didn't get out of its way fast enough. There was a gleam in its eyes he didn't like.

"I'm starting to feel like this is personal," Westlake said, biting back a flicker of panic. He questioned how much Sal remembered – was the gangster still in there somewhere? He hoped so. Otherwise killing Sal wasn't going to be as satisfying as he'd hoped. "Well, that makes two of us."

He fired the shotgun, and Sal twitched aside with a roar.

He didn't stick around to see if he'd hurt the thing. Instead, he juked past it, elbowing a walker in the chest as he went. Sal tore up the floor tiles as it bounded in pursuit. He didn't like leaving Calavera behind, but he knew Sal would follow him – the monster wanted him dead, and that might give the big man a chance to recover, if he was still alive after crunching into the desk the way he had. He headed for the doors at the far end of the lobby at a run.

He hit them a few seconds before Sal caught up with him. The zombie slammed into the doors like a cannonball, tearing them off their hinges. The force of its arrival sent him rolling down the hall. He scrambled to his feet and fired the shotgun twice into the cloud of plaster dust. Then he turned and ran, reloading as he went.

Sal followed, erupting from the destruction and bounding after Westlake. Spotting a restroom, Westlake darted to the side and through the door as his pursuer charged past. He hit the floor and rolled onto his back, shotgun levelled. He waited, but Sal didn't return. Breathing heavily, Westlake stood. There was blood everywhere, and one of the stalls had been torn apart. He wasn't the first to seek sanctuary in the restroom. He crouched for a moment, checking the other stalls. No feet to be seen, however.

He opened the door a crack and peered down the hall. No sign of Sal, but he could hear the groan of walkers nearby. He checked the shotgun. He had a few shells remaining, plus the two rounds in his revolver. Enough to get him to the ballroom, if he was careful. But not enough to get to Calavera and back again.

Behind him, a stall creaked.

He froze and then cursed his idiocy. Not all zombies had legs. The stall flew open even as he turned. The crawler had been perched on top of the toilet bowl, probably balanced on its hands. Now it rocketed towards him with a wet grunt.

As it crashed into him, he saw that it was dressed in the remains of a custodian's jumpsuit, the bottom shredded as if by dozens of greedy, clawing hands. Something had torn its legs and pelvis away, leaving only the wriggling splinter of a spinal column. It hit him hard, and he fell against the door and out into the hall.

Thin fingers tore at his shirt and coat as the broken thing bit at him in a frenzy. It was all he could do to interpose his shotgun and keep it at bay. As he wrestled with the crawler, he saw two walkers stumbling down the hall, drawn by the noise. Unable to bring the shotgun to bear, he fumbled for the revolver.

He managed to get the weapon out as they closed in. He emptied the cylinder, and both walkers fell. It was more due to luck than skill. Before he could congratulate himself too much, however, the crawler lunged for his arm. Its teeth sank into his forearm, and he shouted, dropped the shotgun, and dug the fingers of his free hand into its rotting head, trying to pry it loose. It released its grip on his arm reluctantly, his blood staining its ruined mouth. Westlake slammed its head into the floor, again and again until what was inside its skull slopped onto the floor.

His arm burned like fire as he rolled the thing off him. The bite wasn't deep, but that didn't matter. It had torn right through his jacket and into the flesh beneath. He stared at it for a moment, trying to understand what had happened.

He'd never expected to make it out of the apocalypse alive, but he hadn't expected to be taken down by a toilet zombie, either.

Swiftly, he choked back an obscenity and panic. If he started, he might not stop. Kahwihta had said not everyone turned. But everyone got sick. Sick, he could deal with. Propping himself against the wall, he tore off his jacket, ripped a strip from his shirt and wound it around the wound. More walkers stumbled towards him from the lobby. He forced himself to his feet and snatched up the shotgun.

When he reached the dining room, Sal was waiting for him. The big zombie was crouched on a table, watching the doors with catlike interest. A few walkers stumbled about the room, groaning to one another. Some had clearly been staff, going by their uniforms. Others had been Outfit guys, in tattered suits and chinos. Some of them were even still armed, but Westlake made no attempt to get to a weapon. Not with Sal watching him.

Their eyes met and for several moments they stared at one another, the living and the dead. Sal's grotesque features twisted into what might have been a smile. Westlake wondered whether it had been waiting for this as much as he had.

The ballroom was on the other side of the dining room. He took a step towards it and Sal leapt, springing to a nearby table. Westlake swung his shotgun up. But the monster didn't come for him. Instead, it settled down to study him.

The bastard was playing with him, he realized. Taunting him. "You always were a real sweetheart, Sal," he said. He raised the shotgun, but Sal didn't run this time. Westlake decided not to waste the shot. The ballroom was just ahead. Two big double doors, right where Vinnie had said. He took another step. Sal's growling changed timbre – like it knew what he was planning, and it was warning him off.

Westlake paused, as if considering the matter. "Nah," he said, and took off at a run for the doors. Sal howled and bounded in pursuit. Westlake hit the doors and kept going. There were walkers everywhere, wandering among a killing field of improvised barricades made from tables and chairs. From the looks of the room, someone had tried to make a stand here as well. He didn't have much time to enjoy the décor, though, as a blow from Sal sent him crashing into a crowd of walkers.

The zombies were all over him as he tried to get to his feet, and Sal was all over them a few seconds later. Clawed hands tore through the walkers, casting aside twitching hunks of rotting flesh. Westlake hauled himself away from the carnage, desperately scanning for something – anything – he could use as a weapon.

Despite his back being on fire where Sal's claws had torn him open, he wanted to laugh. The floor was covered in spent bullet casings, but he couldn't find a single gun. He kept crawling. Waiting for the claws, the teeth.

The rest of the walkers kept their distance. He wondered if they were actually smart enough to be afraid of Sal. Kahwihta would probably know. Too bad he couldn't ask her. He picked up a handful of casings and the decapitated walker head and twisted to throw all of them in Sal's face. Sal screeched; the head bounced, drawing his attention, and Westlake dragged himself behind an overturned table and paused to catch his breath. He could hear the scrape-click of Sal's talons on the dance floor. It picked up a chair and flung it aside with a grunt of frustration.

Westlake could see the sound booth at the far end of the room. The layout was familiar – he'd worked as a DJ for a brief period while casing a radio station. One of his earliest heists. A dozen rare records, the sale of which had paid his rent for a year. "Better times," he murmured.

If he could get to the booth, he could get the beat pumping. Granted, he probably wasn't going to last much past the first chord. The room was going soft and fuzzy at the edges, and things didn't hurt as bad anymore. That probably wasn't a good sign. Neither was the blood in his mouth.

He heaved himself to his feet and made a run for the sound booth. Sal didn't notice. He would in a minute, however. He got inside, and found the booth already occupied. A zombie sat in the DJ's seat, wearing a loud shirt and a shoulder holster. When it tried to rise, the headphones it still wore yanked it back. It pawed uselessly at the air, gurgling.

Westlake stuffed the shotgun in its mouth and fired. He dragged the door shut. It wouldn't keep the monster out, but it would buy him a few moments. The booth wasn't all that big – large enough for two people, maybe three. Shelves of CDs and even a selection of vinyl records occupied the back wall.

He scoured the control panel and hit the button, slumping against the console as he did so. Every breath hurt, and he couldn't feel his legs. The music started. Marvin Gaye's "Trouble Man" punched out of the loudspeakers, and every walker was suddenly looking up. So was Sal.

The monster bounded towards the sound booth, charging on all fours. Westlake shoved the chair over, wedging it against the door. Sal hit the booth and the wood cracked. The whole thing shook as Sal hit it again and again.

Westlake crawled back into a corner as Sal began to dismantle the booth. When part of the door came away, and one milky, bulging eye stared in, Westlake emptied the shotgun into it. Sal reared back with a wail, pawing at its face.

Westlake sagged back, dropping the now-useless shotgun onto the floor beside him. "Guess you can feel something after all, huh?"

CHAPTER THIRTY-FOUR
Kitchens

Ramirez heard the doors thump shut behind them. She tied them shut with her jacket, as she'd seen Calavera do upstairs. Ahead, the service elevator waited. "I hope to God this damn thing is working, otherwise this is going to be very embarrassing." She stepped back from the door as she heard Westlake's shotgun boom.

Ptolemy, supporting Hutch with one hand, pointed with his other. "Lights are on." He pointed to a security camera nestled above their heads. A green light blinked on its curved surface. "The cameras are working. This whole thing is wired up to a bank of generators. Long as they are running, so does everything else." He looked at Ramirez. "Keep us covered in the event something comes out."

The elevator only had two main button sets – up and down, open and close. They wanted to go down. Ptolemy thumped the button with his fist and heard the distant groan of the elevator car rising from the depths. He waved Hutch to the side, away from the door. Ramirez took a step back.

"Stay sharp, if this thing is full of zombies, they'll come popping out of there as soon as the door opens," she said.

As the shaft doors slid open, she saw the elevator was empty. It was an old-fashioned lift and hoist, with a fleximetal cage for a door, like you saw in old movies. You had to haul it aside if you wanted to get on or get out once the shaft doors had opened. The cage resisted Ptolemy's best efforts to pull it open, however.

"What's wrong?" she demanded. "It is locked?"

"No, just stuck." He looked at Hutch, who swayed side to side. "Give me a hand here." Together, the two of them began to work the cage back and forth. The metal squealed and creaked, and the sound echoed down the hall.

The doors behind them bent inwards as something struck them. Ramirez turned in time to see her jacket rip apart as the doors burst open. Two walkers stumbled in, falling over themselves. Both were dressed like housemaids. Both went down as Ramirez fired. She reached into her pocket, looking for more shells. A heavy shadow fell over the doorway, and a flabby hand gripped the edge of the wall.

"Ah, hell," Ramirez breathed, as she reloaded. "Ptolemy, hurry up!"

The brute stood for a moment, blinking at them owlishly, as if surprised by their presence. The zombie had been dressed in a suit and tie, before its body had swelled and torn through the expensive material. The brute gave a grunt as it realized what it was looking at. The cage chose that moment to pop loose, and Ptolemy wrenched it open.

The brute started to pick up speed, the weight of its footfalls sending cracks through the plaster on the walls. It groaned eagerly as it stretched out its bulging arms. Ramirez fired, but the brute shrugged off the shots. Ptolemy shoved Hutch into the elevator and yanked Ramirez in after him. He slammed the cage and hit the button.

The shaft doors started to close, but too slowly. The brute struck them like an artillery round, pudgy fingers gripping either door. It bellowed, filling the air with reeking spittle. Ramirez thrust the barrel of the shotgun through the bars of the cage and fired. The brute reeled back with a gurgling howl as the blast snatched away a section of its skull. The doors slid shut and the elevator began to move.

Soft cha-cha music began to play as they descended. Ramirez, still shuddering with adrenaline, looked at Ptolemy. "Let's hope the kitchens aren't too crowded." Ptolemy nodded and they both looked at Hutch, whose appearance was terrible. "Hutch…?"

The biker gave her a weak grin. "Still breathing, boss." The bandage on his neck was stained red and leaking. "Not feeling great, but I'm not dead yet." He straightened with visible effort.

Ramirez nodded. "Glad to hear it, Hutch."

The service elevator clanked to a halt. The shaft doors slid open, but they didn't open the cage just yet. There were a dozen walkers wandering through the wide, tiled corridor, their kitchen whites stained red. "Guess we know what happened to the kitchen staff," Ramirez said.

Several of the walkers stumbled towards the elevator and began to paw uselessly at the flexi-metal of the cage. Ramirez raised her shotgun, but Ptolemy stopped her. "No. The noise will just draw the others. Leave it." Instead, he hit a button, and the shaft door closed, blocking their view of the walkers.

"We need a distraction," Ramirez said. She stared at the shaft door, as if trying to visualize something other than walkers on the other side. "A way to draw them off, away from the kitchens." There'd been a corridor heading to the left – likely leading to stock rooms and the like. If they could get the walkers going that way...

"I got an idea," Hutch said.

"Yeah, what is it?"

"There's too many to fight. Somebody has to draw their attention so we can get into the kitchen. Might as well be me." Hutch winced and touched his wound.

Ramirez shook her head. "Absolutely not."

"He is right," Ptolemy said, softly. "A distraction is necessary."

"Fine. I'll do it," Ramirez said. She reached for the cage, but Hutch caught her arm.

"Don't be stupid. I'm probably on borrowed time as it is. Let me do this, boss."

She jerked her arm free. "Don't call me boss." She thought of Labrand. She hadn't had time to mourn him yet, and here was Hutch planning to join him. She looked away. They were right. She knew it, though she wished she didn't. She reached out and straightened Hutch's cut, her voice wobbly. "You're an asshole, you know that?"

Hutch grinned. "Just take care of my bike, huh? Don't let Muriel have it – that old bat has been drooling over it since the beginning. God knows what she'd do with it." He extended his hand to Ptolemy. "Gimme your gun."

Ptolemy handed the Glock over without comment. Hutch weighed it in his hand and looked to the closed doors. "You ready?" Ramirez asked. Hutch took a breath and nodded. Ptolemy hit the button to open the doors. Ramirez tossed the shotgun to Ptolemy, grabbed the cage, and hauled it open. The gathered walkers stumbled in – and Ptolemy took care of them. The shotgun boomed twice, and the first two walkers fell back into the hall.

"I am out," Ptolemy said, raising the shotgun like a club. But Hutch handled the rest, bulling into them and knocking them back. They clutched at him, but he was already moving down the hall, away from the kitchens, making a godawful racket. He hammered the butt of the Glock against the wall as he ran and yelled at the top of his lungs. Ptolemy stabbed the button with his elbow, and the elevator closed.

Ramirez closed her eyes, trying not to think about what was happening. What she was letting happen. Ptolemy coughed. "It is not your fault. This. Labrand. Hutch. Not your fault."

She looked at him. "Sure feels like it." She took a shuddering breath and said, "Shut up about it and hit the button."

Ptolemy punched the button and the door slid open. No walkers in sight, save the ones Ptolemy had dealt with. Ramirez hauled the cage open, and they stepped out. She flinched as she heard the boom of the Glock echoing down the hallway. She turned, but Ptolemy plucked at her shirt.

"The longer we delay, the likelier we are to get caught down here."

Ramirez nodded reluctantly and followed him into the

kitchens. The corridor was as much a mess as the others. When the Villa had fallen, it had done so quickly. People hadn't so much made stands as died without realizing what was happening.

She closed the double doors behind them, and thrust a nearby mop through the handles. No sense in risking interruption. The kitchens were massive; rows of stations and high shelving. Racks of stock, walk-in freezers and chillers. Only the best for the Bonaro. "Let's be quick about this," she said.

"Agreed. We need alcohol, baking soda or dish soap, and rags for wicks." Ptolemy scoured the shelves, grabbing what was needed. Ramirez nodded and went for the rags. It was a kitchen, so there were plenty at hand. She pulled a knife out of a block and quickly cut up several lengths of wick, grabbed a bottle of cleaning alcohol, and began to soak them. She found several lighters in the cutlery drawers, as well as a supply of cigarettes.

While she was doing that, Ptolemy had found three bottles of something appropriately flammable and he proceeded to empty a box of baking soda into them, as well as an entire bottle of dish soap. He shook them up, mixing the contents as best he could, and then handed them off to Ramirez. As she inserted the wicks, she listened to the sound of Hutch's last stand. The Glock had gone silent, but she could hear the clang of metal. When that too went silent, the only sound was the shifting of feet on the tile outside the doors.

"How many do you think he got?" she asked.

"Only one way to find out." Ptolemy grabbed a meat tenderizer and a cleaver, thrusting both through his belt, then made a sling out of an apron, stowing the Molotov cocktails. Ramirez pulled the mop out from the door handles, snapped the head off with a quick kick, and raised the sharpened end like a spear. They opened the door.

Outside, a lone walker swayed. Its head had been smashed in, but not enough to put it down. It took a step towards them, and Ramirez thrust her makeshift spear through its remaining eye and into its brain. She twisted the mop handle and yanked it free. The walker fell. She glanced at Ptolemy, knowing what she had to do. "Get to the elevator."

He made to speak, then thought better of it and nodded. Ramirez instead followed the corridor down, stepping over the walkers Hutch had downed with the Glock. He'd left a trail a blind woman could follow. Every few feet, another crumpled walker.

When she found him, he was sitting against the wall in what had been a stock room, drinking a bottle of something expensive and bleeding from too many wounds – bites, mostly. The Glock sat on his lap, and a gore-stained fire extinguisher sat beside him. He grinned redly at her and said, "Told you I could do it." He patted the fire extinguisher.

"You let one get away," she said, crouching in front of him.

"Yeah, well, I figured you could handle it. I don't know about you, but I am pooped." He peered at the bottle in his hand. "This stuff is terrible, by the way. Why people paid good money for this crap when you could get cheap beer I will never understand…" He broke off as a coughing fit racked him. "Oh Christ, that hurts." He caught his breath and shoved the Glock towards her. "One bullet left, boss. You know what to do."

She put her hand on the weapon, but didn't pick it up. "Thoughtful of you," she said, fighting to keep her voice even. She wanted to ask his forgiveness. To tell him it would be all right. Instead, she said nothing.

"I thought you might appreciate it." He slumped, eyes almost closed. "Got anything you want me to tell Labrand when I see him?"

She forced a smile. "You assume you're going to the same place?"

He gave a pain-filled laugh. "I figure I earned my wings by now." He leaned back, eyes fluttering as his pulse slowed. He was bleeding out on the floor, and there was nothing she could do about it. "I ever tell you about my dreams?" he asked, eyes closed.

"No." She swallowed a sudden rush of emotion. Tears stung her eyes. "Tell me."

But he didn't reply. "Hutch? Hutch." Ramirez reached out and felt for his pulse. She took a deep breath and picked up the Glock, and took aim. The sound of the shot was loud – too loud – and it made her ache.

She left the room and pulled the door shut behind her before the echo of the shot faded. She wanted to be out and away. Anywhere else.

Ptolemy was waiting for her by the elevator. Ramirez didn't look at him. Instead, she took one of the bottles from his apron and hefted it.

"Time to end this."

CHAPTER THIRTY-FIVE
Last Stand

Westlake listened to Sal rage outside the booth. He couldn't do much else but hunker down. Moving hurt, and he didn't want to attract any more attention to his presence. The music blared over the loudspeakers, and he could hear the doors banging as walkers flooded in.

Sal, being the territorial sort, expressed his displeasure at their presence – or maybe he was just venting his frustration. Either way, every so often, what was left of an unlucky walker would splat against the window of the booth. Westlake knew that eventually Sal's distractions would end, and he would remember where Westlake was and come sniffing around.

The shotgun was useless except as a club. He needed something better. He dragged himself towards the DJ zombie. There was a revolver in the dead man's shoulder holster. Better than nothing. He extracted it and popped the cylinder, checking the ammunition. Two shots. Still better than nothing. Especially if he could get Sal in the other eye–

His musing was interrupted by the sound of a thump against the glass window of the booth. He looked up. Sal grinned down at him, shotgun-scorched features pressed tight to the window – like a dog staring at a steak. Sal scraped the glass with its claws. The thing looked amused, despite the steaming hole where its left eye had been.

"Like to play with your food, huh?" Westlake said, rolling onto his back and raising the pistol. "You always were an asshole."

Sal reared back, fists raised to smash the glass. Westlake darted a glance towards the door. He didn't want to die in a DJ booth. It was undignified. But Sal's blow never came. Westlake looked back at the glass and saw the towering zombie had turned. Something had caught its attention. Westlake, never one to ignore an opportunity, dove for the door.

It took more effort than he liked to get to his feet, and when he did, he thought he might fall over again. But he made it to the door without collapsing and out. What he saw made him pause. It was the bear all over again.

Calavera, looking bruised and battered, stood on the other side of the room, staring at the monster like a climber seeing Everest for the first time. He cracked his neck and shoulders. "You are very big – that is good," he called out. "That means you will take some killing." Sal snarled and started towards the masked man. Calavera laughed. "Good, good! Come to me, monster – come to El Calavera Santo!"

With that, he flexed his hands, tensed, and sprang. Onto a table, across the heads and shoulders of the cluster of walkers gathered about the towering monster. Moving so quickly that the zombies barely noticed his weight before he was past and gone and they crumbled. Westlake watched in amazement as the luchador raced across a bridge of the dead towards his foe.

The masked man leapt – and drove both feet into Sal's midsection, sending the monster staggering. It turned, trying to fend off this new opponent. Calavera hauled himself up its form, using the spiky protrusions as handholds. Sal spun, trying to catch hold of him with bloody claws, but Calavera was moving too quickly.

"You are a stain on the world, and Santa Muerte bids me send you on your way," Calavera roared, as he hooked Sal's neck and dug stiffened fingers into the zombie's remaining eye as the sound system started up an Isaac Hayes song. The ceiling lights flashed in scintillating patterns as some keyed-up discotheque program began. For a moment, it looked as if man and monster were engaged in a dance.

Then Sal managed to catch hold of Calavera's shirt and drag him from his perch. The zombie slammed its opponent down onto one of the few tables still standing, breaking it. Calavera lay groaning in the wreckage as Sal loomed above him, blindly flailing.

Westlake shoved past a distracted walker and fired the revolver. Sal's head snapped around, following the sound of the shot. It shrieked and started in Westlake's direction. Calavera, still on his back, grabbed a chair and slung it under the monster's legs, causing it to stumble. Sal fell heavily, crushing a pair of walkers beneath its bulk. It screeched in frustration and shoved itself upright, casting aside the still-twitching remnants of the smaller zombies. Westlake circled the room, avoiding the rest of the walkers as best he could as he tried to line up a clear shot on Sal.

Calavera was on his feet as well. "You still live, Mr Westlake – truly Santa Muerte watches over you," he called out, as he snapped a walker's neck and tossed its body aside.

"Yeah, well, wouldn't want you to have all the fun," Westlake said. Sal's head turned, following the sound of his voice. It bared its teeth and stalked towards him on all fours. The walkers parted around it. Westlake backed towards the doors. "Any ideas, big man?"

"I could hit it again," Calavera said, helpfully. He paused and laughed. "Then, maybe I will not have to."

Westlake was about to ask him what he meant when the doors slammed open, admitting Ramirez and Ptolemy. She held a broken mop out before her, like a spear. Ptolemy had a meat tenderizer in one hand. Both makeshift weapons were dark with blood and other substances. Ramirez saw him and grinned. "Still in one piece?"

Westlake ignored a twinge of pain from his back – not to mention the one in his arm – and nodded. "So far. Hutch?"

Ramirez shook her head and turned her attention to Sal. "Looks like you two have been hard at work," she said.

Sal snarled and swung its head towards her. Westlake shot him. Sal whipped back around with a roar and advanced on him. Westlake tossed the empty pistol aside. "I hope you two found what you were looking for!"

Ramirez thrust her spear into a walker as it got too close, then held out her hand. Ptolemy shoved a bottle into it. She lit the rag wick and hefted the bottle. "Hey, ugly," she shouted. "Over here!"

The monstrosity turned with a loud snarl. She hurled the Molotov full into Sal's distorted features, eliciting a shriek of mingled pain and fury from the creature. Ramirez retrieved her spear as Ptolemy readied a new Molotov. Westlake hurried towards them. A walker, dressed in a dark suit and broken sunglasses, lunged for Ptolemy. The zombie knocked him sprawling, even as he brained it with his tenderizer.

The lit bottle rolled from his hand, and Westlake stooped to scoop it up. Sal, blinded by the fire, swiped blindly, smashed tables and knocked walkers from their feet. Westlake stepped forward and hurled the second Molotov, which smashed against one of Sal's flailing arms. Fiery droplets sprayed across the nearby zombies, setting them alight.

Alarms were going off now, drowning out Sal's howls. The sprinkler system kicked off, spraying down the room. The big zombie staggered away from them, retreating towards the back of the room where another set of double doors sat – the ones that led to the stairwell on the opposite side of the building. It was trying to get away, Westlake thought. Whatever was left of Sal's mind was urging it to retreat. He stooped and helped Ptolemy to his feet. "Get that last one lit and get ready to throw it. Ramirez, toss me that stick!"

She wrenched the mop handle out of a kneeling walker's mouth and used the blunt end to batter it to the floor before tossing it to him. "What are you thinking?"

"I'm thinking I owe Sal, and I always pay my debts." Westlake started towards the staggering monster. It was a bad idea – a terrible one, even. But there was no time for anything else. If Sal got away, that was it. Something told him it wouldn't fall for this trick twice. "Calavera, make me a path!"

Calavera flipped a table, crushing several walkers beneath it. Westlake ran across the table, trying to ignore the searing pain in his back and the tingling in his arm. He had to get between Sal and the far doors, and that meant catching the monster's attention. He snatched up a chair and threw it – bouncing it off Sal's back.

The zombie spun, hissing. "Over here, you dumb bastard," he shouted. "I'm right here! Come and get me!" As he'd hoped, Sal followed the sound of his voice, charging towards him with single-minded ferocity, all thoughts of flight forgotten in its rush to smash the life from him. He could hear Ramirez shouting, but had no time to listen. It was all he could do to get Sal in position.

Ptolemy came through. "Westlake!" he cried, as he sent the last Molotov arcing up over the heads of the walkers to smash down against Sal's spiky back. The flames spurted up, resisting the dampening effect of the sprinklers. Sal screamed. He could still feel pain, whatever else. Westlake was glad. If anyone, dead or alive, deserved to feel the full effect of three Molotov cocktails, it was Salvatore Bonaro.

Sal fell onto all fours as the flames consumed him, and lunged towards Westlake. There was no time – and nowhere to go. Westlake lifted the mop in both hands and readied himself, teeth bared. Blinded, burning, dying – Sal couldn't avoid his thrust.

His momentum carried both of them through the sound booth in an explosion of plaster, wood, and sound equipment. Sal shrilled like a faltering steam engine as

Westlake thrust his spear up through its jaw and into his head, twisting it even as he drove it deeper. "Be seeing you, Sal," he rasped, eyes stinging from the heat.

Finally, Westlake's improvised weapon struck something that made Sal spasm and slump with a disgruntled groan. The burning bulk of the zombie pressed Westlake down against the floor, and he wondered if this was how it was going to end. Not exactly a blaze of glory, though fire was involved. He coughed, inhaling the stink of burnt meat.

Then, with a roar, Calavera heaved Sal off and Westlake could breathe again. He lay for a moment, sucking air into his abused lungs and wondering if his ribcage was intact. "Jesus," Ramirez said, tossing aside bits of broken equipment. "Are you still alive?"

"I'll let you know," Westlake coughed. He reached up a hand, and Ramirez hauled him to his feet. "Sorry about your mop."

"I wasn't that attached to it." Ramirez stared at the smoldering bulk of what had once been Salvatore Bonaro. "Jesus," she said again, covering her mouth and nose. "I hope we never see one like this again."

"A good fight. A worthy foe." Calavera wiped his char-stained hands on his trousers. "Santa Muerte is pleased."

"I should damn well hope so," Westlake said, coughing again. His arm was throbbing now, and not just from the impact. The world spun about him, and Calavera reached out a hand to steady him.

"Are you injured?"

"I got knocked through a wall. What do you think?" He decided not to mention the bite, or the fact his arm was going numb. There'd be plenty of time to tell them later – or deal with it himself, if it came to that.

Calavera glanced about. "It was only a little wall."

Westlake stared at him for a moment and then gave a wheezing laugh and slapped the big man on the shoulder. Ptolemy cleared his throat. "As relieved as I am, we should think of retreating. This creature was not the only danger here." As if to emphasize his point, the sprinklers cut off. The remaining walkers were making their way across the room, eyes fixed on Westlake and the others.

"He's right, everybody out," Ramirez said. "Head back to the lobby. Don't stop for anything!"

CHAPTER THIRTY-SIX
Escape Plan

Calavera led the way, racing through the dining hall. There weren't as many walkers prowling there as there had been – between them, Calavera, Ramirez, and Ptolemy had cut a swathe. But there were still a few, and they joined the pursuit. Westlake was the last through the doors and into the lobby.

Calavera slammed the doors in the faces of the closest walkers. He wedged a table against them. "It won't hold them long," he said. "Perhaps we can find some more weapons?"

"I thought you liked it hand-to-hand," Westlake said, leaning against the wall. Everything ached, and he wanted to sleep. But not yet.

Calavera grunted. "There comes a time that one must bow to practicality. Even a man such as myself." He looked at Ramirez. "Maybe we can convince Spinoza – or Carl – to give us our weapons. We have earned some goodwill, I think."

"Goodwill is not a word Vinnie is familiar with," Westlake said. He straightened and halted. "And he might have other things on his mind about now. Jesus." The others followed his gaze. Ramirez cursed.

"That … is a lot of walkers," Ptolemy said, staring out at the courtyard through the glass that fronted the lobby. "Those were not there before. They must have followed us across the lake." He turned to Ramirez, but she had no answers. Westlake could see the relief – the hope – draining from her.

"Kahwihta," she said, softly.

He got as close to the doors as he thought wise and craned his neck. "The server room is closed. I don't think they've gotten in there yet." He looked up at one of the cameras mounted in a corner of the lobby ceiling and waved a hand. "Still alive, Vinnie?"

The phone on the front desk began to ring.

Ramirez turned, staring at it as if it were a snake. "The phone is ringing. Westlake – answer the phone."

"Maybe someone wants to make a reservation," Westlake said, as he limped to the desk and snagged the receiver. "Hello?"

"*Finally*," Kahwihta said. She sounded tired, and a bit put out.

Westlake blinked and looked at Ramirez. "It's the kid."

Ramirez sat down on a chair, a look of relief on her face. "Is she OK?"

"Are you OK?" Westlake asked.

"*I'm OK. Sayers is with me.*" Kahwihta paused. Then, before he could ask, she added, "*Mr Spinoza is… not.*"

Westlake grunted. "Good for you. How's the mutt?" A

stab of pain went through him, radiating from his arm, or maybe somewhere else, and he leaned against the desk. "Never mind. If Vinnie's out of the picture, does that mean you've got control of his little pals? And the front doors for this place?"

He could hear the uncertainty in her voice, as she replied. "*I… think so. But there's too many walkers. The courtyard is packed. You won't make it more than a few feet before they swamp you. Even with the robots.*"

Westlake bent his head, trying to think. He looked at Ramirez and the others. Then, clearing his throat, he said, "Can you open the garage?"

"Yes, I believe so."

"How about the front gate?"

"Yeah. Why?"

He closed his eyes. "Just get them open. Open everything. We'll handle the rest. But be ready to set Vinnie's mechanical pals to work as soon as you get my signal and have them herd the zombies towards the gates."

"What signal?"

"You'll know it when you see it." He dropped the phone back into its cradle. "We need to move. Get anything you can find to use as a weapon."

"What? Why?" Ramirez asked.

"We're going to finish what we started. But for that I need to get to the garage." He pushed away from the desk and straightened, despite the pain in his back and arm. He flexed his injured forearm and looked towards the doors. "And I need you three to get me there."

"That we can do," Calavera said. He picked up a chair and

broke it against a pillar. He joined Westlake and handed him one of the chair legs. Ptolemy and Ramirez did the same. Ptolemy hefted his meat tenderizer and handed Ramirez the cleaver.

"I will make for the boats," Ptolemy said. "They left our weapons there. If I can get to them..." He shook his head. "I might be able to draw some of them off."

The lock on the front doors beeped. Ramirez looked at Westlake. He nodded. She grimaced and pushed the doors open. The closest walkers reacted immediately, lurching towards them with loud groans. Ramirez and Ptolemy went first, followed by Calavera and, lastly, Westlake. He swatted a walker in the head with his chair leg and saw Ptolemy dart through the press towards the quay.

Calavera hefted a walker and hurled it into its fellows, momentarily clearing the press. Ramirez sank her cleaver into one's skull with a dull thwack, pulled the blade loose, and spun, slicing off the hand of another. Westlake swung his chair leg like a club, not bothering to aim – just lashing out at anything that got close. The walkers crowded in, impossible to miss.

Then the SAW started up. Then the M240. Zombies spun and danced into the fusillade. The two robots converged on Westlake and the others. "Guess she got them working after all," Westlake said, watching the immediate horde thin under the withering fire of the two lead combat robots. But more were stumbling out of the Villa, still smoldering, and staggering out of the boathouse. More than he could count. A tide of death, threatening to roll over them.

"Snap out of it, Westlake," Ramirez said, grabbing him

by the collar. He stumbled after her as she half-hauled him towards the garage, Calavera loping in their wake. "What's the plan here?"

He laughed. "I'm going to find the vehicle with the best sound system, pump the volume to full, and take myself to ride." With the four robots escorting them, they reached the garage in no time, and in one piece. The robots fanned out, covering the approach to the garage, their weapons growling.

Ramirez glared at him. "And what are the rest of us supposed to do while you ride off into the sunset?"

"Ideally, pick off the ones too stubborn to follow me. And close the gates behind them, of course. You should be able to mop up after that."

Calavera hauled the garage doors open, revealing a small fleet of around a dozen vehicles, including what looked to be several military surplus trucks. "Inside, quick," Westlake said. "Calavera, watch the door."

Calavera nodded. "Nothing will get past me."

Westlake patted him on the back. "I'm counting on it, big man."

"These might come in handy," Ramirez said, as she followed him down the rows of vehicles. "We can ferry people up in groups – start setting things up while we evacuate the rest. It'll take time, but we should be able to manage it, if we're careful."

Westlake stooped and peered in the window of an off-road truck. "Yeah, well, I'll leave the details to you." He checked the door, found it unlocked and climbed in. No keys, but that was no problem, given the age of the vehicle. It was old enough that he could hotwire it. He took out his knife and popped the panel on the steering column, revealing a mess of wiring. He searched for the red ones.

"What do you mean?"

He looked up. Ramirez stood in front of the truck, staring at him. He leaned out. "What do you think I mean?"

"You sound like you're not planning to come back."

"I doubt I'll have the option, to be honest." He ducked back into the cab of the truck and cut the wires.

Ramirez circled the truck. "This doesn't have to be a suicide run."

Westlake paused and leaned back. He held up his arm, showing her the bite. "Anything I do from here on out is a suicide run."

Ramirez stared at his arm, and then at him. "Jesus, were you going to say something?" she demanded. "We could have–"

"Could have what?" Westlake smiled mirthlessly. "Chopped my arm off? How often has that worked for you?"

"Westlake, do you know how many times I've been bitten?"

He paused. "I have a feeling it's more than once."

She dragged up the sleeve of her jacket, showing off a scar on her arm. "Two days after it started. I thought I was a goner. I recovered. You might too."

The wires sparked as he touched them together, and the engine turned over with a deep growl. He looked at her. "Maybe. But it's not the sort of thing I feel like leaving to chance. Besides, think of it this way... I'm performing a service for the community." He looked towards the front of the garage. "You do owe me a favor, though, right?"

Ramirez let her sleeve fall. "Yeah, so?"

"I want you to make sure I don't wind up like Sal. It's not dignified." He tapped his head. "Two in the noggin ought to do it. You know... afterwards."

"You want me to hunt you down after... all this?"

"If you'd be so kind."

Ramirez snorted sourly. "If I said it'd be a pleasure, would you think less of me?"

Westlake laughed again. "Depends on whether you said it where I could hear it." He peered up at the dawn, just visible past the edge of the garage roof. "Going to be a hell of a day, ain't it?"

"Yeah." Ramirez paused, then reached into her jacket. She pulled out the wad of cash she'd taken from him earlier and tossed it to him. "Here. Guess you've earned it."

He held the money and gave it a flick, hearing the delightful ruffle. Then he slid it into his jacket with the rest. "I always do." He put the truck into gear. "Take care of yourself, Ramirez."

She didn't look at him. "See you around, Westlake."

Westlake threw off the parking brake and rolled past Calavera into the courtyard. Vinnie's little pets had cleared the path to the front gates, but only temporarily. As the truck edged towards the front, the hydraulics controlling the gates started to grumble. Past the gates, he could see a packed dirt trail coiling down into the trees.

He flinched as a walker slammed a bloody hand into the passenger side window. The zombie made to strike the window again, and its head suddenly popped like a grape, splattering the glass. As it fell, he saw Ptolemy, standing near the quay, his rifle in his hand. He gave Westlake a brisk salute and started towards the server room.

Westlake turned back to the gates. They were open by the time he tapped the gas and the truck lurched through. As he'd hoped, the zombies followed the rumbling engine. They momentarily enveloped the truck, and then he was bumping along, crushing the dead beneath its wheels. Nothing on the radio, no CD or tape in the deck, which was a shame, so he gave the horn a few blasts. A runner caromed off the side of the truck and went under the wheels. Then another appeared, and another. The walkers followed, as they always did. He kept the truck at a steady speed. "Just like old times," he whispered.

A runner raced towards him. Just when he thought it would go under like the rest, it jumped onto the hood of the truck and started battering at the reinforced glass. Westlake gave it some more gas and picked up speed. In the side mirrors he could see that he'd pulled away most, if not all of them. Gunshots behind him made him certain the others were taking out the last stragglers. He gave the wheel a spin and headed for what looked like an old logging path. He didn't know where it would take him. He didn't much care.

The runner on the hood had decided to try the side. Glass spattered over Westlake as the zombie reached inside, clawing at him. He punched it and it fell away, but the others were catching up. He hit the brakes, heard a few thumps, and reversed up the path. The truck rocked on its chassis.

He stopped counting the thumps and crunches after thirty, and threw it back into first gear. The dead swarmed around him, clawing at the sides of the truck, holding on as he started forward again.

Hands reached through the broken window. He ignored them. This time, he wasn't scared and tapped the money bricks in his jacket for luck. It was impossible to see where he was going, but that didn't matter so much. He didn't have a destination in mind. The pain in his back was worse, but his arm was numb. The world was spinning around him, and black was creeping in at the edges. Exhaustion and pain pressed down on him. He shook his head, trying to clear it. Just a bit further. He had to give the others time. He glanced in the rearview mirror as an explosion rocked the trail.

As he'd hoped, most of the zombies had followed him. The robot with the grenade launcher sat in the gateway, firing at the rear of the horde. The other three robots rolled to join it, their weapons hammering at any zombie that turned from the pursuit.

He felt no fear. No anger. Some regret, maybe. But not much. He'd done what he'd come to do. He'd been hoping to do a bit more, after, but it hadn't been in the cards. Everyone's luck had to run out some time. He'd lasted longer than most.

He heard the rear windshield go, felt dead fingers grip the back of his neck. He threw an elbow back, and bone crunched – painfully. But the walker let go. His stomach lurched. The truck skidded on the muddy trail. Pines flashed across the arc of his vision as he started to spin out.

He couldn't control it anymore – the numbness had spread through him, and it was all he could do to remain sitting upright.

He let go of the wheel.

And smiled.

EPILOGUE
Wreckage

"This is it," Ramirez said, tossing a rock down the scree. It clattered to the bottom, scaring off the birds that had been perched in the branches below. The smell was awful – dozens of burnt briquette bodies littered the slope, in various states of decomposition and deconstruction. The wildlife had already been at them, but that wasn't surprising. This would be a buffet, as far as the coyotes and bears were concerned.

It took almost a week for them to get around to finding out where Westlake had crashed. Ramirez didn't beat herself up too much. They'd been busy, after all. And it wasn't like Westlake was in any position to mind. Besides which, she had others to mourn. People she'd known longer, and liked better. Hutch, Labrand – the ones who'd died at the lodge.

Even so, she frowned, annoyed by the wash of emotion that Westlake brought. She hadn't liked him, but she might have learned to tolerate him, in time. Or maybe she was kidding herself. Then, stranger things happened – she'd learned to tolerate Sayers, after all.

The former park ranger stood some distance away, watching the trees. The other woman caught Ramirez watching her and gave a brusque nod. Ramirez returned it and looked back at the wreckage below.

Sayers hadn't been welcomed back with open arms – not really. Not after what she'd done, even if the reasons had been good ones. People had died in the attack on the lodge. People Ramirez and the others had known and liked. Then, Sayers didn't seem all that concerned about being liked. But even so, she wanted to help, if only for Ptolemy's sake – and they'd let her, if only for Ptolemy's sake.

"What is it?" Kahwihta asked, from behind her. Ramirez glanced at the younger woman. Attila sat by her leg, his expression placid. The dog was still limping, but he was getting stronger every day. More importantly, he wasn't barking.

"Thinking," Ramirez said.

"About Westlake?"

"About everything." Ramirez looked back down at the burnt-out husk of the vehicle, and the broken, charred bodies that surrounded it.

Ptolemy cleared his throat. "I do not think there is merit in going down there. Whatever is left – it is clear it would be in no shape to get up again." He stood a ways back from the slope, a shotgun in his hands. He had insisted on coming. So had Calavera, who crouched at the edge of the scree, cracking his knuckles absently.

"I made a promise," Ramirez said. She looked at him. "You can go back, if you like. I'm sure Dunnigan and the others could use your help with the move."

The exodus had started with North Elba. With the vehicles they'd found at the Villa, they'd begun to trek people and supplies up over the course of a few, somewhat nerve-racking days. Nonessentials could wait until things had settled down.

She remembered her rush of relief upon reaching North Elba and finding Frieda waiting on her. Finding Dunnigan and Saoirse and Hahm. Muriel. All of them. She remembered their voices on the radio, the cheers. The tears of relief as the first survivors saw what awaited them. There were still the usual worries, of course. There were more zombies in the mountains than they'd ever imagined. And all of them knew where the Villa was. But they had the means to fight back now. The means to survive.

She took a deep breath, coughing slightly on the stink of burnt meat, still present after all this time. "Me, I intend to see it through. I owe him that much."

Ptolemy shook his head. "I owe him as much as you." He straightened and met her gaze squarely. "We all owe him," he said.

"Well said, my friend." Calavera picked up a charred skull and studied it. "Whatever his reasons, Westlake helped us a great deal. For that, he deserves a hero's burial."

Ramirez nodded. So far, the Villa had proved to be everything they'd hoped, once they'd finished off the last of the walkers that lurked in the buildings. The walls were high and thick, the buildings sturdy. Most importantly, it was well stocked. Hahm had practically wept at the sight of the kitchens.

Not that it was perfect, of course. It had never been meant to house so many people for an extended period of time. They'd have to send out scavenging parties sooner rather than later, and they'd have farther to travel. But, for the moment, that was someone else's problem. Ramirez was more concerned about finding the site of Westlake's last stand. She'd made him a promise, after all – one she damn well intended to keep. Maybe even take her irritation out on him: the only man who would survive an apocalypse for cash.

Suddenly aware of how quiet it was, Ramirez looked around uneasily, her hand resting on her weapon. But nothing showed itself. She glanced down at Attila and the dog thumped his tail genially. She smiled and rubbed his head.

Sayers cleared her throat. "If you're going down there, just go. And be quick."

Ramirez nodded to herself. "Right, enough lollygagging."

"My thoughts exactly." Calavera stood and stretched. "Shall we go down?"

Ramirez gestured. "After you, big man."

Calavera laughed and bounded heedlessly down the slope. She and the others followed more cautiously. "The animals have fed well – and continue to do so, judging by some of these marks," he called back to them. "We should tread lightly. Just in case something wanders by, in search of a quick meal."

Ramirez swallowed. "Well then, by all means, let's see

who's home." She gestured to the truck. "Calavera, do the honors, if you would."

"A pleasure," he said. When he reached the truck, he easily wrenched the mangled door off the frame in a litany of popping metal and cast it aside. A rush of charred bills fluttered into the air like startled birds.

Something groaned and half-fell out of the vehicle, cooked flesh tearing as it thrashed its way free of the cab. Blackened hands clutched at Calavera's throat as the big man stepped back. Ramirez stopped as the walker collapsed onto the ground. "Is it … ?" she called out hoarsely, her hand on her weapon.

Calavera shook his head. "I do not know – it is badly burned." He retreated a few steps, giving the walker room to haul itself to its feet. Its joints made an ugly popping sound as it rose, swaying. It staggered towards Calavera, ash flaking from its burnt form and drifting on the breeze. He looked towards Ramirez. "Should I … ?" he mimed breaking a neck.

Ramirez hesitated, but only for a moment. "Do it."

Calavera nodded and slipped behind the walker, digging his fingers into the blackened flesh as he did so. There was a sharp crack, and the zombie collapsed in a smoldering heap. Calavera absently wiped his fingers on his shirt as he looked down at the body. "It seems smaller, somehow."

"Fire does that," Ptolemy said, as he approached.

"Fire doesn't cut off a foot of height," Kahwihta countered, as she joined them. She crouched beside the body and carefully rolled it over. Using her icepick, she prodded the body. "Was Westlake wearing a tie?"

"No," Ramirez said.

"Then unless he decided to change outfits before he died, this isn't him." Kahwihta tapped the charred knot around the walker's neck. "Whoever this guy was, he wasn't Westlake." She looked up at Ramirez.

Ptolemy circled the truck. "The vehicle was covered in them when he hit the treeline. Some of them probably managed to squirm inside." He tried one of the rear doors and flung it open. A broiled carcass flopped out, its skull punctured by a bullet wound. Ptolemy ducked his head inside. When he stepped back, his expression was pensive. "I might be mistaken, but I do not see his body."

"Did he get thrown from the truck when it crashed?" Sayers asked, prodding one of the corpses with her foot.

"No, the windshield is cracked, but intact." Ramirez hurried to the truck and looked inside. Ptolemy was right. There was no sign of Westlake. She turned, scanning the broken zombified remnants that littered the ground. Even a cursory glance told her that he wasn't among them. She looked at the others and knew that her expression mirrored theirs. "He has to be here," she said, in disbelief.

"In point of fact, he does not," Ptolemy said. "There is every chance that he might have walked away from this."

"He couldn't have survived."

Ptolemy adjusted his glasses. "I didn't say survive."

A sudden growl from Attila interrupted Ramirez' retort. She saw a flash of a low, four-legged shape in the trees followed by another. Attila barked, his hackles stiff. The coyotes responded with shrill yelps.

Ptolemy raised his rifle and fired. He cursed and lowered it. "Too fast," he said.

Ramirez reached for her pistol. "How many do you make out?" she asked, trying to keep an eye on every direction at once. There was no telling whether these were zombified coyotes or the regular variety. Either way, they were dangerous.

"Not many. But there'll be more. We should go."

"He's right. Time's up," Sayers said. She was already heading back the way they'd come. "Best to leave them to it, unless we want to be part of the menu."

"She's right," Kahwihta called, as she wrestled a snarling Attila towards the slope. "If Westlake – or whatever is left of him – is out here, we'll find him. Or he'll find us. But not right now. Not today."

Ramirez hesitated a moment longer. She knew they were right, but she didn't want to leave – not without knowing for sure. Finally, she allowed Calavera to lead her towards the slope. Ptolemy fired off a few more shots to keep the coyotes at bay. But even as the quartet climbed the scree, the first lean, canine shapes prowled into view – eager to sate their hunger on the bounty before them.

Ramirez was the last up the slope, and when she reached the top, she paused. Searching, hoping to see something – anything – that might mark her debt as paid. Some sign as to whether Westlake was alive, dead, or otherwise. But nothing presented itself.

"Ramirez, we should go," Ptolemy said. "Dunnigan and the others will want to know about this. We should be back at the Villa before dark."

"I know," she said, but she didn't move. She watched the coyotes eat and waited. Finally, when she could stand it no more, she turned to follow the others back up the trail, followed by the sounds of coyotes squabbling over carrion.

And more distant still – but growing louder every day – the moaning of the dead, carried on the breeze.

ABOUT THE AUTHOR

JOSH REYNOLDS is the author of over thirty novels and numerous short stories, including the wildly popular *Warhammer: Age of Sigmar, Warhammer 40,000, Arkham Horror* and *Legend of the Five Rings*. He grew up in South Carolina and now lives in Sheffield, UK.

joshuamreynolds.co.uk
twitter.com/jmreynolds

WORLD EXPANDING FICTION
Do you have them all?

ARKHAM HORROR
- ☐ *Wrath of N'kai* by Josh Reynolds
- ☐ *The Last Ritual* by S A Sidor
- ☐ *Mask of Silver* by Rosemary Jones
- ☐ *Litany of Dreams* by Ari Marmell
- ☐ *The Devourer Below* edited by Charlotte Llewelyn-Wells
- ☐ *Dark Origins, The Collected Novellas Vol 1*
- ☐ *Cult of the Spider Queen* by S A Sidor (coming soon)

DESCENT
- ☐ *The Doom of Fallowhearth* by Robbie MacNiven
- ☐ *The Shield of Daqan* by David Guymer
- ☐ *The Gates of Thelgrim* by Robbie MacNiven

KEYFORGE
- ☐ *Tales from the Crucible* edited by Charlotte Llewelyn-Wells
- ☐ *The Qubit Zirconium* by M Darusha Wehm

LEGEND OF THE FIVE RINGS
- ☐ *Curse of Honor* by David Annandale
- ☐ *Poison River* by Josh Reynolds
- ☐ *The Night Parade of 100 Demons* by Marie Brennan
- ☐ *Death's Kiss* by Josh Reynolds
- ☐ *The Great Clans of Rokugan, The Collected Novellas Vol 1 (coming soon)*

PANDEMIC
- ☐ *Patient Zero* by Amanda Bridgeman

TWILIGHT IMPERIUM
- ☐ *The Fractured Void* by Tim Pratt
- ☐ *The Necropolis Empire* by Tim Pratt

ZOMBICIDE
- ☑ *Last Resort* by Josh Reynolds
- ☐ *Planet Havoc* by Tim Waggoner *(coming soon)*